AUSTIN ELLIOT

HENRY KINGSLEY'S NOVELS.

Uniform edition. 16mo, price per volume, $1.00.

RAVENSHOE. Two volumes.

AUSTIN ELLIOT. One volume.

THE RECOLLECTIONS OF GEOFFRY HAMLYN.
Two volumes.

LEIGHTON COURT. One volume.

AUSTIN ELLIOT

BY

HENRY KINGSLEY

NEW YORK

CHARLES SCRIBNER'S SONS

1895

TO

THE REVEREND

JOHN MILL CHANTER,

AND

CHARLOTTE CHANTER,

THIS BOOK

IS AFFECTIONATELY DEDICATED BY

THEIR BROTHER,

THE AUTHOR.

AUSTIN ELLIOT

Chapter I

It so happened that, in the early spring of the year 1789, three young men, each equally full of health, hope, honour, courage, and curiosity, separated at the gates of Christ Church College, Oxford, to pursue divergent paths across that world, which at that time seemed, to those three, only a sunny fairyland lying betwixt them and the grave — only some enchanted land full of glorious adventures, and they three young knights ready to achieve them.

To one of the three — the youngest and the most famous, by name Jenkinson — we shall only allude incidentally. With regard to the other two, George Hilton and James Elliot, we shall have to be a little more explicit.

George Hilton, the handsomer and cleverer of the two, went abroad, and, having met his friend Jenkinson at the storming of the Bastile, came home again in September, bringing with him a lovely, fragile, little being of a French wife, a daughter of the Duc de Mazagan, who had been pleased that his daughter should marry this fine young English merchant, and be out of the way of those troubles, which he saw gathering so darkly, and so swiftly, over the head of his devoted order.

He could not foresee that she would be dead before Christmas; still less, that in the Conciergerie and on the guillotine, he should rejoice that there was one loving heart the less to mourn for him. But so it was: the poor, gentle, happy, loving little creature died in her husband's arms, almost before that husband knew how well he loved her. The grand old Duke made his last bow, when he took precedence of his old friend the Marquis de Varly, on the scaffold, looked at the sovereign people through an eye-glass, shrugged his shoulders with infinite contempt, and died. The gallant young Vicomte Tourbillon, who should have been duke — George's dear friend — yielded to circumstances, and entered the Republican army; and George Hilton, disgusted with the world, from sheer want of anything to do or care about, plunged headlong into commerce.

Bringing apparently a keen, clear head, a reckless courage, and a vigilance which slept not by day or by night, to the assistance of his father's house, he tided that house successfully through those terrible revolutionary years, and raised it at last to be one of the great commercial houses in England. From very shortly after he assumed his place as an active unit in the firm, his father and his father's old partner submitted to him; and from that time these two terrified old men found themselves dragged (if one may use such an expression) by the heels through a seething whirlpool of audacious speculation, powerless and hopeless, only to emerge again, with wealth and credit such as they had never dreamt of, before this valiant, gloomy young man had joined them. There might be terror on 'Change, or panic in Lombard Street; but though these two might sit cowering in their chairs, fluttering papers which they scarcely understood, in their trembling fingers, yet there was always one figure before them, in which they felt forced to trust, the figure of George Hilton — the figure of a tall, handsome man in dark clothes, with a set austere face, who rarely spoke, into whose eyes they gazed with a look of awe, and a look of supplication painful to witness. Always kind, he was always undemonstrative, and they looked up to him as some god who held their fate in his hands.

Once he broke out. When an old clerk came into the

room where they sat, and, with a face only more ashy pale than their own, told them the terrible disaster of Austerlitz, the two old men fell to feebly wailing; but the younger, leaping from his chair, gave a wild hurrah, which made the respectable old ledgers on the shelves shake the dust off their leaves against him.

People began to talk. They said, " This man married a Frenchwoman. His favourite brother-in-law has notoriously deserted the traditions of his family, and become a rabid Buonapartist. He is a colonel in the Guards. This man, Hilton, is making money in some underhand way by means of his brother-in-law." It was partly true. George Hilton, with a keen and well-judged confidence in French arms, had advanced an immense sum shortly before this to his brother-in-law, with which to speculate in the French Funds. Austerlitz had been won, the coalition broken, and the Hiltons had pocketed forty thousand pounds. Since Lord Loughborough and Sir John Scott passed their Treason Act in 1792, no man had driven his coach and four through it to greater profit than George Hilton.

Some sharp and traitorous trading went on in those times; and we are sorry to say that the house of Hilton and Co. were always looked upon as being deeply engaged in transactions which, even by the commercial world in those days, were considered dangerous and odd. Even at that time, when certain trades were paralysed, and there were so many needy merchants ready to sacrifice almost any principle to keep themselves afloat, the house of Hilton and Co., with their enormously increasing wealth, were looked on askance. They always seemed to have such wonderfully correct information from abroad. The Jews might follow George Hilton about the Exchange with bent body and sliding foot, to listen and see whether some priceless hint might not fall from him; but the Christians were only distantly polite to him, although, when he had once been known to take a commercial step, there were hundreds eagerly ready to follow his example.

We have hardly to do with the ways by which his enormous fortune was made : our business is more with what ultimately became of it. There are plenty of houses, eminently respectable now, whose books, from 1790 to 1815, would hardly stand a closer examination than those of Hilton and Co.

And also the history of the accumulation of this fortune must be told ; because, in the mad and successful pursuit of his wealth, George Hilton had reached the age of fifty years before he bethought him that there was no one to inherit it.

The gold that he had wallowed in for thirty years had left its dross upon him; and the George Hilton of 1819 was a sadly different man from the George Hilton of 1789. The sarcastic young dandy had developed into a cold, calculating man of fifty; a man who seldom spoke in the House, but always shortly and to the purpose ; a man who had refused office, some said ; an odd man ; a man no one liked very much, but a man so careful in his facts, that when he spoke he put every one else, save four or five, in a flutter ; a man who would contradict the King on his throne, and had never had a genial smile or a joke for any man in the House, save for one, Lord Hawkesbury. After 1806 he laughed and joked no more in Parliament. Lord Hawkesbury never forgave him the Austerlitz affair before mentioned. He kept on speaking terms with him for a time, but after his removal into the House of Lords, in 1808, George Hilton found himself without a friend in the House, and only one friend in the world — that is to say, James Elliot, the third of those we saw at Christ Church Gate in 1789.

In 1819, then, he married. The wife he selected was a Frenchwoman. She was a cousin of his first wife's, and a daughter of an émigré count, Commilfaut, very little, very pretty, and an intensely devout Huguenot in religion. This marriage was a happier one than his first. She was soon the mother of two children, Eleanor and Robert.

Chapter II

WITH, perhaps, less energy and talent than his friend George Hilton, James Elliot, the second of the two men mentioned in the first page of this book, contrived, in after life, to land himself in a higher position in the world than did his friend. His taste would have led him into political life—for who could have been at Christ Church with Canning and Jenkinson, and not have been ambitious?—but his fortune was far too meagre to allow him think of it. He remained at his college, living on his studentship and his small fortune very happily indeed; keeping up a constant correspondence with the richer and better-born men who had gone out into the world to fight in the great battle which was then raging.

So his politics were confined to the common-room. But sometimes he appeared before the world and had his say with the rest. He wrote a pamphlet once which made a sensation; he found this very charming. Here was a way to make himself heard. He wrote another pamphlet and then another. They were all good. His assumed signature began to be looked for, and people began to ask who he was. These pamphlets of his were very humorous and full of stinging allusions, which, we daresay, made men laugh then, but which now fall dead on the ear of any but a very old man indeed. Some of them have absurd titles, such as one (1801), " Choking the Black Dog with Butter; " and again, same date, " Shall we have the Doctor's Boy or the Constable? " By which last delicate allusion to Lord Sidmouth, it appears, not that it is of any great consequence, that he was in favour of a vigorous prosecution of the war, and that his enthusiasm was slightly too strong for his manners.

The art of pamphleteering becomes, like most others, more easy by practice. James Elliot got to a great perfection in the art. He had considerable humour, and so his half-truths were put forward under a cloud of ridicule, and before people had done laughing, the question had gone by. He never spared but one man, Mr. Jenkinson. Once this gentleman (developed into Lord Hawkesbury since 1796) was accused of having written one of these pamphlets himself, but the very next one which appeared under the same signature entirely dissipated that notion. Lord Hawkesbury came in for his share of good-humoured railing abuse with the rest. It was evident that this man, this "Beta," as he chose to sign himself, was a man of great ability. Nobody was safe with him. His principles wanted fixing : he had no principles at present. They must really be fixed. Such a man was lost to the public business of the country.

In 1808, then, his old friend, Lord Liverpool, with the full consent of all his colleagues, offered place to his old friend and correspondent James Elliot ; the place of Inspector of Shoals and Quicksands, worth £1,500 a year. And of all the appointments made by the good Lord Liverpool during his long tenure of office, this was perhaps the best. It was made in quieter and less anxious times than those which followed—in the merry old war times, when a man's friend was his friend still, and one knew one's friend from one's enemy—when one's heart could warm up at thinking of dear old Jim Elliot's delight at getting this place, and one still had wit or folly enough left in one to put a few lines of doggrel into the postscript of the letter giving him the offer of it—in the times which came before the Peace, and before those weary fifteen years when one sat and drove, or tried to drive, four such terrible horses as Peel, Wellington, Huskisson, and Canning, four-in-hand, only to drop down dead from sheer anxiety and over-work at the end of it all. Peace be with Lord Liverpool's ashes ! We very strongly suspect him of having been a good and noble man.

The last Lord High Inspector of the Shoals and Quicksands was Admiral Sir Foreland North, who died in 1707. He accumulated a fortune in that office, and was made Lord Sands of Godwin. It was found that he had scandalously neglected his duties, and the peculiar revenues of the office being found remunerative, it was put in commission, my Lords of the Shoals and Quicksands being required to pay an Inspector so much a year, and to pocket the rest of the revenues themselves. This was found to work very well; it created patronage; and the Inspector being liable to forfeiture of his office for neglect, the work was better done than in the old times.

The revenues of the office of Lord High Commissioner of the Shoals and Quicksands were derived from several sources. Heavy tonnage dues were demanded from all ships which passed through the Needles, came within three miles of Eddystone Rock, passed St. Michael's Mount without letting fly topsail-halliards, threw empty bottles or garbage into the sea within three miles of any one of the Cinque Ports (counting from Old Hythe, and including eight miles east of Deal), passed through the Steat of Skye, and did many other things too tedious to mention. These revenues, though they doubtless cost a great deal to collect, paid in a great deal of money. The office might sometimes once a year have a grand battalion day in the Arches, and might have to spend several thousand pounds in proving " that John Smith, of the Hope schooner, master mariner, was within three miles of the port of Sandwich when, on the day aforesaid, he did then and there, not having the fear of God before his eyes, wilfully, maliciously, and devilishly, cast into the sea, sundry, that is to say, five hundred glass bottles, against the peace of our Lord the King, &c., &c.; " yet, in spite of all this, the revenues of the office were, for many years, a very pretty provision for five lords, and an inspector to do their work. There were good years and bad years. Sometimes John Smith would prove his case—prove " that he was a good five miles off Sandwich; that, being disguised in liquor, he had only thrown his empty brandy-bottle at his apprentice's head, and that it had gone accidentally overboard, and had floated within the prescribed limits;" in which case, my lords would take it up to Chancery, and have to pay. But the Inspector always got his salary; and my lords made a pretty good thing of it on the whole.

But after sixty years or so, master mariners began to have the fear of God before their eyes, to go round the Isle of Wight, to let fly topsail-halliards in the right place, to keep clear of the Eddystone, to kick the apprentice into the lee-scuppers before they threw the brandy-bottle at him—to conform, in fact, more or less, to all laws, human and divine; which proceedings had this result: that the Lords of the Shoals and Quicksands were left without money to pay their Inspector. It became necessary to supplement their revenues by a parliamentary grant, which was done. But the parliamentary grant was so small, that, since 1795, the position of a Lord of the Shoals and Quicksands had been merely an honorary one. Parliament paid their Inspector. Sometimes they got twenty pounds apiece; sometimes they did not. But Government allowed them a yacht, and the Inspector had the use of it.

When Mr. Elliot took the place, in 1808, he found everything in confusion. There were fifty squabbles on hand with the Lords of the Admiralty on the one hand, and with the Trinity Board on the other. He set to work like a young giant, although he was now forty years of age, and brought everything into order.

He had no special knowledge of his subject, but he soon knew more about it than any one. When a man has learnt how to learn, he can soon learn anything. The "experts" connected with his office, coasting skippers, pilots, lighthouse-keepers, and such people, came to him with their facts, put them before him, and looked at him, as much as to say, "Here are our facts, can you generalize from them?" They very soon found that he could. They were perfectly contented. It was a very good appointment.

My Lords of the Admiralty were high, and the Trinity brothers were mighty with him. There had been "heats" between these two great bodies on the one side, and the Commissioners of Shoals and Quicksands on the other, in which my Lords of the Shoals had left their Inspector to bear the brunt. The story of my Lords of the Admiralty having threatened to fire into the yacht of the Shoals and Quicksands, on the Motherbank, must be untrue, for the Admiralty yacht *had no gun on board*. Therefore, how could they have threatened to fire?

Mr. Elliot composed all these difficulties, and got his office into noble order. His beloved Lord Liverpool used to point to him with pride: "*My* man, gentlemen."

But what with soothing my Lords of the Admiralty, and doing battle with the Trinity House, for leave to do their work, it was five years before he thought of marrying. When he did think of it, there was no doubt about the lady whatever. He married a certain Miss Beverley, a lady of thirty-one, gentle and good, like himself; and on his forty-ninth birthday she bore him a noble boy.

Chapter III

It is with the fortunes of this boy, Austin Elliot, and with the fortunes of George Hilton's little girl, Eleanor, that we have principally to concern ourselves.

Mr. Elliot had lived in an atmosphere of politics ever since he was nineteen, and had known, and known well, some, nay most, of the leading men of his time. He had his grievance, his crotchet, like most other men, good or bad; and his grievance was this: That he, James Elliot, might have succeeded in public life, if he had not been so unfortunately poor. He was very likely right. No one will ever know whether he was right or not; the thought was a little, carefully unexpressed, grievance to him. He never got sour over it, he never expressed it in words; but the thought that he had been only prevented from holding a very high place in the world by his poverty, was at times a source of vexation to him, more particularly whenever he saw a beggar on horseback, or a fool in a high place.

He was poor no longer : he had a good place, his wife succeeded to a very good fortune, and his boy, Austin, was growing to be one of the handsomest, cleverest, bravest lads ever seen — a boy who at ten years old showed, as his father thought, most singular and precocious talent.

At this time, when Austin was ten years old, and when there was no doubt of his being a very clever boy of his age, Mr. Elliot took the great resolution of his life. That boy should be educated as a statesman. " That boy should be prime — Hush — don't let us talk nonsense," said Mr. Elliot to himself, with a radiant smile, as he sat one night over the fire, and saw various things in the hot coals.

The idea was rather a grand one. Mr. Elliot's creed was, that statesmanship was a trade, and that a man must serve his apprenticeship to that trade as to any other. A man should be trained to politics early, if he was going to succeed. Look at Pitt the younger. (He could not have read Lord Macaulay's " Life of Pitt ; " it would have killed him. Lord Macaulay's atrocious suggestion, that Pitt was not the most sublimely wise of the human race, would have cut the ground from under his feet.) Yes, a states-man must be trained ; of that there was not the least doubt in the world.

And he, James Elliot, would train and educate one. His own boy. If he, with his intricate knowledge of every political twist and turn for forty years, could not do that, who could ? And see the material he had to work on ; was there ever such a boy ? " Never," said Mr. Elliot :

" Seldom," say we. He certainly was a boy of the very highest promise, and the man who doubted that Mr. Elliot would succeed in making a leading statesman of him must have been a foolish person. It is no use for that man to say that Mr. Elliot did not succeed. By all rules he should have succeeded, therefore the charge of folly stands.

So Mr. Elliot was going to educate his son for a statesman. But how ?

This was the most delightful problem. The thought of it made Mr. Elliot's good face glow with happiness. Here was a beautiful soul, a noble intellect, ready to receive any impression whatever. Mr. Elliot worked at his task with a will, but he perhaps began it a little too early. The young ambition must be excited by the recital of noble deeds, and so little Austin heard many a long story of great debates, grand political tricks, and so on, which were far from interesting. At the same time, Mr. Elliot was very furious with the conduct of a certain great statesman on the Catholic question, and found it rather pleasant to denounce him to the wondering Austin, who, at ten years old, had acquired a distinct idea that Parliament was a place something like school : and that Sir Robert Peel was a traitor many degrees worse than Guy Fawkes ; had a distinct belief, indeed, that, when every one had their due, the Right Honourable gentleman would be carried about on a chair, with his boots on hindside before, and all the straw coming out at his knees.

When Austin was ten years old, his mother died, and he was left more exclusively to his father's care. And then these two contracted a strong personal affection for one another, which lasted to the very end, and which was never clouded for one instant. It was well for Austin to remember that hereafter ; well to remember that he had never cast one shadow on his father's kind, gentle face.

This boy Austin grew so rapidly in both moral and physical beauty, that the absurd chimerical plans of his father seemed to become, year by year, more probable of fulfilment, and his old friends began to leave off laughing at him and to confine themselves to shaking their heads.

There can be no doubt that the boy was not perfect, but really he was one of the finest and noblest boys ever seen. He made a great success everywhere. Possibly it would be better, instead of cataloguing his various perfections, to ask you to think of the handsomest and most amiable boy you ever knew, and call him Austin Elliot. You will know him as a man; let us skip his pædeìa.

One of Austin's earliest recollections was that of going to play with Eleanor and Robert Hilton; for, after Lord Liverpool's death, James Elliot resumed his intimacy with his old friend George Hilton once more. He had always kept up his acquaintance with him, but it had not been very close for many years. Lord Liverpool had never forgotten the affair of the French funds. It was the sort of thing that he could not forget; and, indeed, it is not a pleasant subject to dwell on. James Elliot never mentioned George Hilton's name before him, but he would not throw his old friend entirely overboard. And after Liverpool and Canning died, with the harness on their backs, the world was very lonely to him, and he once more grew intimate with his old friend, whom he had always tried to defend, even against his own conscience.

Eleanor Hilton was not, as a child, beautiful, or even pretty. At first, her features were too square and *prononcé;* but, from the very first, she was as gentle, good, and sensible as a child might be. Robert, on the other hand, was peevish and somewhat violent. He had, also, a strange wayward mendacity — at times refusing to tell a lie to save himself from punishment, at another lying without an object. A still more fatal vice had not hitherto shown itself, but was developed afterwards.

When Eleanor was twelve and Robert ten, their mother died; and, nearly at the same time, Austin Elliot went to Eton, and Robert was left with Eleanor to the care of a governess. Had old Hilton known as much about the boy, as the governess and Eleanor, he would never have, in all probability, sent the boy to Eton; but so it was. He followed Austin to Eton after two years; and we need hardly say, after the character we have before given to Austin, that he was affectionately kind to his old play-fellow, and did all for him he could. But Robert soon began to go wrong: he was always in trouble. Nothing serious, however, took place till after several months.

There came to Eton the very same half, and to the very same house as Austin, a certain Lord Charles Barty, of the same age as Austin, and by no means unlike him in person and manners. In a very short time, a great boy-friendship sprang up between the two. In the very first letter he wrote to Eleanor his new friend was mentioned, in most enthusiastic terms; and his intimacy with this friend seemed to increase as it went on. It is useless to describe Lord Charles Barty as a boy, for we shall see him hereafter in manhood, in far more terrible places than the old playing-fields, or the Brocas or Surly, or any of those places one hears Eton men talking about; nevertheless, it is necessary to tell you that, like Austin, he was a noble and manly fellow, and that he was as worthy of Austin's honest love as Austin was of his.

When Robert Hilton appeared, after two years of friendship between these two, whether it was through jealousy, or through mistrust, or what, it is impossible to say, but Lord Charles Barty took a violent dislike to him. To obviate this, and to interest his friend in poor Robert Hilton, Austin told him what he had not very long known for himself, that he was in love with Eleanor Hilton, and that this was her brother.

All the chivalry in Charles Barty's heart fired up at this. One sharp pang of jealousy shot through him when Austin told him that there was one in the world preferred to himself, but it was instantly smothered and killed. He would have liked a few more years of his friend's undivided love, but it was not to be, Austin was in love, *fiancé*. Mrs.

Austin's brother must be taken up, whatever might be his faults.

It is no use trying to laugh at all this, by saying that Lord Charles Barty and Austin were neither of them fifteen. They were quite as much in earnest, if not more so, than if they had been five-and-twenty. Lord Charles took up Robert Hilton and patronized him and was affectionate to him and fought his battles for him to the death, but all in a high and mighty manner, and under protest.

But the catastrophe came. One day, while Austin and Charles Barty were out at cricket, or what not, a boy, at home in disgrace, came into Lord Charles' room and found Robert Hilton at his desk. He seized him and raised an alarm. The master was fetched, and the wretched boy's boxes were searched. Everything which had been missed in the house for a long time was found there. The habit which the governess and Eleanor had noticed in him, and which they dared not mention to his father, was confirmed with a vengeance. The lad was a thief! When Austin and Lord Charles came innocently home, laughing, they found the whole mine sprung under their feet. Either one of them would have given their right hands to save the lad, whom neither liked, but it was too late.

He was so very, very young, they pleaded for him. Austin and Lord Charles went personally round to the other boys whose things had been stolen and begged their forbearance. He was so very, very young. I need not say what English boys did under those circumstances. There was no scandal : he was sent home.

So it came about, that George Hilton's inordinate, and somewhat unprincipled love of gain began to be revenged on him in the person of his only son. He knew it and felt it as keenly as any one, but he hardened his heart. He refused to see the boy for some time, and he saw him but very seldom until he died.

It becomes necessary that we should follow Robert Hilton to the end, before we return to Austin and Eleanor, and it is very shortly done.

This case was the one on which the Rev. Letmedown Easy gained his present enormous and justly-earned reputation for keeping young bears from growling, by feeding them with the toast from under the asparagus, with the ends of the twists, the eggs out of the pigeon-pies, and other soothing dainties, until the whole thing was blown over and everybody had forgotten all about it. He well earned the thousand pounds which George Hilton paid him for keeping his son five years without scandal, and for sending his father a good character of him each half-year. The Rev. Letmedown was not such a very great rogue ; he undertook to whitewash the boy, and he whitewashed him. He kept him at his parsonage in Essex safe out of temptation for five years, until the whole thing was forgotten. He was paid for doing it and he did it.

Our already old friend James Elliot begged his son not to renew his acquaintance with Robert Hilton, and Austin acquiesced. Old Hilton never allowed his son to come into the house, and so Austin never saw Robert after his unfortunate departure from Eton. It was no fault, however, of Austin's ; if Robert had ever been allowed to come home by his stern old father, they would have seen enough of one another. For Austin's love for Eleanor grew stronger year by year, and he was always with her.

More of this immediately. Just before Austin went to Oxford, Eleanor wrote to him that Robert and her father were reconciled at last, and that Robert had got his commission. At this point Mr. Easy's fictitious respectability suddenly and lamentably broke down. Before Robert had been three months in the army, people began to talk. Gossip was followed by open accusations, accusations by court-martial. The end was swift, sudden and sure : Robert Hilton was disgracefully expelled from the army.

Chapter IV

THE private residence of the Inspector-General of Shoals and Quicksands was at Mortlake, his official yacht generally lay at Gravesend, and his office was on the terrace of Somerset House.

The duties of the Inspector of Shoals and Quicksands are, to inspect them, and to report on the state of them to my Lords. This is done firstly by examination of local witnesses, and secondly by personal experience. The former of these two methods is, of course, in some measure performed at the office, and the second mainly by means of the yacht.

The office is one of the freshest and breeziest in London. On a summer's day it is a very cheerful spot; the steamers dashing ceaselessly up and down, and the river running in a great gleaming band eastward towards St. Paul's. When the wind is blowing strongly from the east or south-east, bringing with it, in spite of miles of brickwork and smoke, a fresh whiff of the wild glorious sea, and lashing the river into waves, it is a pleasanter and fresher place still. But the best time to be about that office is in a gale of wind from the southward, or southwestward; when the glass rattles in the windows and the driving rain comes spinning into the lobby, when the door is opened; and when the most prosaic clerk, wearily copying the " statement of William Grumble, master of the light-ship on the St. Margaret Sands, concerning the shifting of the N. E. Channel," cannot help staying for an instant to wonder how it fares with William Grumble in his light-ship just now; when the chimney-pots are flying, the water barometer varying four or five inches every quarter of an hour, and the gulls up the river in dozens.

Ever since he was a boy, and a very small one, Austin had been very fond of the office: it had always been a great treat to him to be allowed to come to the office, and plague his father, at his great square leather-covered table. When his father wouldn't stand him any longer he used to go out and " skylark " with the clerks, who, you may depend, did not object to that sort of thing. But presently, he being a very noisy boy, his father would come in, and turn him out of the clerks' rooms into the lobby, to disport himself there.

And an uncommonly merry, gentlemanly set of fellows were those aforesaid clerks as one could wish to meet with. No chief of any Department had his clerks better in hand than James Elliot, and no one scolded less — but we will say no more of this. Though the clerks were merry young gentlemen, yet when turned out of their rooms, Austin found in the lobby men he liked still better than the clerks.

Men with calm clear eyes, and deliberate thoughtful speech. Most of them men with brown horny hands and grizzled hair. A few of them dressed in rough pilot coats ; more, in old-fashioned long-tailed coats, with brass buttons ; more of them still, soberly dressed in unobtrusive black, but all with the same calm clear eye. These were the lighthouse-keepers, or such as they — men of the storm, of the lee shore, of the reef, of the quicksand — men from the lonely station standing far seaward on the thunder-smitten cliff, or from the solitary lighthouse, on the surf-washed ledge, miles out in the raging sea.

It was well for this golden-haired lad, with his beautiful face, to stand at the knees of such men as these, and listen to them ; to hear from one, how on a night, when sea and air were all mixed together in deadly turmoil, the light-ship he commanded broke loose without their knowing it, and was carried over dangerous sands, and thrown high and dry and safe on the beach ; and from another one, how he and his mate sat up one such night in the lonely lighthouse, five miles from land, watching the corpse of the third and oldest of them, who had died that morning — and how, while they sat there, they heard, but could not see, an unmanageable and dismasted ship strike the rock and go to pieces, a hundred feet below them ; and that, creeping down and opening the lower door, and looking out into the black horror of darkness, they could hear in the night, close to them, the crashing and cracking of timbers, and the sound of men, women, and children calling on God Almighty for help ! There was nothing there in the morning, said this one, in answer to an unexpressed inquiry from Austin's blue eyes. She had struck at low tide.

Yes ; the office was a pleasant place enough, but there was something better than the office — the yacht. Once a year, in the beginning of recess, there would come a long blue letter from my Lords of the Admiralty (not our Lords), the gist of which was that the Inspector of Shoals and Quicksands was to hold himself in readiness to accompany their Lordships in their annual inspection of buoys. Austin, of course, went with his father on these occasions, and enjoyed it mightily ; for, as he says in his reckless disrespectful way, my Lords are a deuced jolly set of fellows. When they were accompanying the Admiralty yacht they used to see a great deal of very pleasant society, and Austin had quickly won the hearts, not only of the Quicksand Lords (who held him being their own property), but also the hearts of all the Admiralty Lords, excepting one dreadful old sea Lord, with a cork leg and a grievance about his wife's nephew, whom nobody could manage.

Golden, glorious days were these. Sometimes the two yachts would come steaming swiftly and suddenly into the harbour of some great arsenal, by the ugly hulks, and under the rolling downs, flattened on the summit by dismantled fortifications, and so through her Majesty's fleet. But however swiftly and suddenly they came, they could never take them by surprise. Always, as the Admiralty yacht passed the first ship, the great guns began booming out their salute, and ship after ship took up with the glorious music, until the vessels of the ear began to throb with the concussion of the air, and in calm weather the harbour would be filled with drifting smoke ; for the time when these things happened was long ago, before gunpowder was so much needed for other purposes as now, and before we saved £30,000 a-year by stopping unnecessary salutes.

And once it came about that there was a discussion, as to whether or no a red buoy should be put at the outer edge of the Swing, to mark the entrance to the Mary Anne Channel. Mr. Elliot went to the chief Admiralty Lord, and represented that he thought it necessary. As a general rule, Mr. Elliot's suggestions were promptly attended to ; but on occasion, My Lords hum'd and hah'd a great deal. One said that there had been a good deal said about Naval expenditure lately, and that if it were necessary to have a buoy at all (which, mind you, he did not for one instant admit), he was for having a blue buoy instead of a red, because every one, who knew the least about their duty, were well aware that blue paint could be got a farthing a pound cheaper than red. Another denied this *in toto*, and said that red paint was cheapest. A third denied the existence of the Mary Anne Channel altogether. A fourth contradicted him flatly ; but said that if the wreck of the Mary Anne was moved, the sand would silt in again, and then what was the use of your buoy ? Mr. Elliot, like a man of the world, contradicted their Lordships, individually and collectively, and insisted on a buoy, and a red one, too ; the red paint was just as cheap as the blue. As Mr. Elliot had foreseen, their Lordships had a squabble among themselves, which ended in their turning on him, and ordering him to proceed at once on board his yacht, the Pelican, and proceed to Portsmouth to await their Lordships' orders. At the same time, a curt, short message was sent quickly down by the telegraph — which at that time was a thing like a windmill gone mad — to the commander of the Admiralty yacht Falcon, to hold himself in readiness to proceed to sea with their Lordships at once ; and then their Lordships departed to Belgrave and Grosvenor Squares, and where not, to pack up their things, and told their ladyships that it was getting intolerable, that they could not and would not stand being dictated to by a subordinate any longer, and that they were going to see into the matter for themselves.

The cause of all this dire anger, and all this Spartan self-denial, was as follows : — The Commons were adjourned, leaving Daniel O'Connell to the mercy of the Lords, but Parliament was not prorogued. The August sun was shedding a mellow sleepy light over cape and island, a gentle west wind was blowing up channel, scarce strong enough to whiten the purple waves. And well ! If their lordships in such case, having the power to go to sea, had stayed on shore, they would have deserved impeachment, or a contempt worse than impeachment. However this may be, however angry their lordships may have been with Mr. Elliot, there was no cloud, not the faintest speck of one, on any of their faces, when he boarded the Falcon at Spithead and reported himself. Three days afterwards, Austin, expressing himself in that low, slangy way which the young men of the present day seem so anxious to adopt, said that my lords were " uncommonly larky." This, however, is certain, that Austin and his father dined on board with their lordships ; and before the soup was off the table the great paddles got to work, and the Falcon, with the Pelican close in her wake, went thundering down the Solent, and so out into the leaping summer waves of the channel ; and that as the summer sun went down, Portland was hanging to the north — a vast purple wall overrun by threads and bands of green ; and that Austin and his father were put on board their own yacht at eight bells, speed being slackened for the purpose. And when they got on board, Austin remarked to his father that they seemed to be in for rather a jolly spree.

Then followed the short summer night, and soon after dawn Austin was on deck looking at the Start towering up to the north, blue, purple, with gleams of golden green. And while Austin is looking at the Start, let us look at him once for all, because his personal appearance will not greatly change before this story gets wellnigh told.

A very short description will suffice. We only wish to give you such an idea of his personality as to make him real to you. From a beautiful boy, he had grown to be a very handsome young man — as *some* said, one of the handsomest ever seen. He was light-haired, with a rather delicate brilliant complexion, and blue eyes. His figure was very good, his air graceful, his manner winning and gentle, his dress always perfect, his conversation easy, clever, and inexhaustible, all of which things caused every woman, high or low, whom he met to get uncommonly fond of him. But besides, he not only had the women on his side, which many a handsome young dandy has had before, but also the men.

The reason that he had the men on his side was, that he was a good fellow, and that means a good deal; so much so, that it is impossible to describe, with any exhaustive accuracy, what it means. Although we all of us know a good fellow, it is hard to be made to define one. Austin was one, certainly. He laughed with those who were merry, he condoled with those who were sad, nursed those who were sick, lent money to those who were poor, was a good companion to those who were rich, and carried comfort to those who were in love. Many others do all these things, and yet are not good fellows. Austin was a good fellow, for he was in earnest, and any one who took the trouble might see it. He was now at Oxford, and although his diligence might have been greater, yet his tutors had great hopes of a very high degree for him. Rarely does one find a young man of prospects more brilliant than those of Austin, as he stands this morning on the deck of the yacht, looking northward at the Start.

So the two yachts went tearing down channel, as though their errand were to arrive at the Swing before the channel was silted up, and before the second sunset they were passing St. Michael's Mount; the third they were gazing in amazement at the Worm's Head, rising like a serpent out of the sea; the next they were at the Swing.

Here there was an accident.* Austin was on board of the Falcon, and, as they approached the shoal, their lordships all began wrangling once more on the buoy question, which had been shelved just now, in the pleasure of the voyage. There was no need for them to have troubled themselves about it, Mr. Elliot would have explained, but no, they were not coming five hundred miles for nothing, and so they began to wrangle.

The commander asked, should he steer by the Admiralty chart, or by Mr. Elliot's directions? Mr. Elliot must be made to know that their lordships were not going to be hoodwinked by a subordinate. By the Admiralty chart, if you please.

Thump, bump! up goes her nose two feet in the air, and down she goes on the port side. The senior lord goes into the lee scuppers, and Austin indecently bursts out laughing. The Falcon was aground hard and fast. This is Austin's account of the matter. It seems somewhat apocryphal.

She was off again at high tide, with the loss of some copper. But the effect of the accident was, that they rounded the Lleyn and made for Liverpool.

It was a very important voyage this for Austin, and the conclusion of it more important still. Austin had been by

* If Austin is correct about this accident, there must have been two accidents to the Admiralty yacht, very similar; for it is a matter of history that My Lords bumped themselves ashore in the Bristol Channel in 1846. They should be more careful. What should we do if anything were to happen to them?

this voyage thrown into such close and intimate familiarity with some one or two leading men, as commonly happens on board ship ; where intimacies are so rapidly made, as to astonish those who are not in the habit of going to sea. Austin had used his time well. He was as irresistible as usual. He had never been presented to their own senior Lord before he went on board, and considered such an event rather a great one for a lad at the University, without any pretensions to birth. But after four days at sea, he had laughed when he picked that Lord out of the lee scuppers, and that Lord had somewhat eagerly appealed to his opinion, against another Lord, as to whether or no he had prophesied the accident. Which was getting on very well indeed.

But better than this happened to him. They turned into the Strait, and dropped anchor at Caernarvon, the Senior Lord of the Quicksands was going to disembark there, and post to his estate in Merionethshire. Austin's ears actually tingled with delight when the senior lord asked him to come with him, and spend a fortnight with him and his family among the mountains.

Austin was ambitious, and he knew that one of the roads to political greatness was the being well thought of in certain quarters. But he was no tuft hunter, and he knew besides that the only way to gain a footing in a house was, to come in at the front door and not at the back. From his first acquaintance with Lord Charles Barty at Eton, he had had the full run of Cheshire House, but, since he had been at the University, his sense had told him that he had better not go there till he was asked. In spite of Lord Charles Barty's friendship for him, which developed as they both grew older, Austin had, for the last three years, managed to avoid entering the house, until the time should come when he might be asked to do so by much more important people than his old school-mate.

But here was a real triumph. The Senior Lord was a very great man indeed. There were very few greater.

Austin had only been presented to him four days before, and had laughed at him but yesterday, when he picked him up out of the lee-scuppers, and yet here was his Lordship insisting on his coming home with him. It was a very great stroke of business to a young man so anxious to push himself in the world as Austin.

Even at Caernarvon Austin's wonder was excited, not merely at the reverence which was paid to his Lordship, but also at the, if possible, greater reverence paid to himself. He was very much amused by, and puzzled at it. The Landlord at Caernarvon bowed to him, and called him, "My Lord." "Simple people these Welsh," thought Austin.

But he did not think so very much of it, for this day was an era in his life. For the first time he saw mountain scenery — and I think that the reader will agree with the author that, of all the introductions to mountain scenery, that of the road from Caernarvon to Llanberis is one of the most sudden, most startling, and most beautiful.

My Lord, whom we will now call Mr. Cecil, sat opposite to him, and was very much pleased with his boyish enthusiasm ; and, indeed, the enthusiasm of a young person, when they first find their visible horizon tilted up some ninety-five degrees, is very pleasing. Mr. Cecil sat and smiled at him, with an air of calm pride on his face, as if he had made it all himself, and was pleased to find that his trouble was appreciated. But as we all do this, when we introduce a friend to some new scenery, we must not be hard on Mr. Cecil.

In the very middle of the finest part of the Pass, there came riding towards them a very tall, important-looking gentleman, with very black whiskers. He stopped and saluted Mr. Cecil, and looked with such lively interest at Austin, that the poor young gentleman felt inclined to laugh. The gentleman with the black whiskers asked, with a sweet smile, to be introduced. When Austin was introduced as Mr. Elliot, the gentleman looked very much disappointed and aggrieved, and was many degrees shorter in his speech towards Austin than the latter had supposed, from previous symptoms, he would have been.

It was a memorable and delightful day. A lucky rogue was Austin, to be shut up *tête-à-tête* in an open carriage with one of the most agreeable and famous men in England, and driven through a continual succession of such beautiful scenery. Mr. Cecil, on his part, was delighted with Austin's charming manners and ingenuousness. He listened kindly and with interest to his confidences, to his anticipations of a career in the world; and made Austin blush with delight, by saying, that from all he had seen of him, there was nothing whatever to prevent the realization of a very great portion of his hopes.

But the most beautiful among all the beautiful objects seen that day was the one seen last. More beautiful than a million silver threads of water, streaming from ten thousand crystalline peaks. More beautiful than all the soaring ranges of feathering birch, which hung purple over the winter snow, or shone golden over the summer fern, in all glorious Caernarvonshire.

And it was this. As the summer sun was still blazing on the topmost crag of Snowdon, and as each of the fourteen little lakes of that most exquisite of mountains was sending up its tribute of mist to wreathe all night around the brows of the sleeping cliffs — at such time Mr. Cecil and Austin came to a wall, inside of what was a dark band of plantation, and Mr. Cecil stopped the carriage, and said, — "This is the beginning of my park. Let us get out and walk; we shall be at the house as soon as the carriage, if we go by the short cut."

So they got out, and the carriage drove on. Mr. Cecil opened a gate in the wall, and said, "Come on."

And Austin, standing in the road, and looking at Snowdon, answered, — "One minute more, only one minute more, with the mountain! Remember, this is the first time I have ever seen this sort of thing. See! the black, purple shadow is creeping up, and gaining every instant on the golden glory lingering around the summit. And look, Mr. Cecil, every wreath of mist from every wrinkle and hollow among the great slate buttresses, is turning from fleecy white to a pale, ghostly blue. I beg pardon, I am keeping you waiting. People generally make asses of themselves when they are first introduced to mountain scenery."

"Generally, yes," said Mr. Cecil; "but you are slightly poetical for a young gentleman who proposes to succeed in politics. Come on, I have something to show you finer than that mountain before you get any dinner."

He was right. The path grew steep and rocky as it wound down through the dark wood, and to the right Austin began to distinguish a dim abyss, and to hear a sound as of a mighty wind coming through the trees ; and then suddenly they stood upon a slight bridge, and were looking up at a broad cascade which streamed and spouted a hundred feet over head.

He gave a cry of honest delight at the glorious spectacle. He was standing, still absorbed in it a few minutes afterwards, when he was touched on the shoulder.

He turned, expecting to see only his host, but beside him was standing the most beautiful girl he had ever seen, with her arm round her father's waist.

"My daughter!" But was it really his daughter, or was it some beautiful fairy of the stream, some being born of the amber-coloured water, of the white foam, and of the last rosy tints that hung on the cliffs over head? Such, for one instant, was his silly fancy, as he looked on this sudden apparition, at her light-brown hair, her pure red cheek, and her white gown. Was it fated that every one who met him this day should look disappointed? Miss Cecil, the most amiable as well as the most beautiful of women, even she seemed to have some slight shade of disappointment on her face. It was inexplicable, but very annoying.

26

If her beauty showed to advantage amidst the seething mist of the waterfall, it did not show to less advantage under the shadows of the woodland, as she, her father and Austin walked home together. Not to less advantage, at all events, to Austin, but to greater. And in his eyes her beauty seemed to increase as he looked at her, and grew even more and more divine at each turn of the head and at each fresh expression of the face. Austin had never seen such beauty before, Mr. Cecil had. The beautiful girl's dead mother was even more beautiful than she.

From the windows of Tyn y Rhraiadr (the farm of the waterfall), you can see, on a fine summer's night, Snowdon hanging aloft like a purple crystal, and the arch of twilight creeping along behind it from west to east, through the short summer night, until it begins to flash and blaze into a dawn more glorious than the scarce-forgotten sunset.

And all through that night, until the arch of sunrise had grown from dull orange to primrose, and even after, when the sun himself had looked over the distant Glyder, and the long shadows of tree and rock were cast along the dewy sward, and the mowers began brushing through the grass, and the murmurs of many waters, which had waxed and waned dully on the ear through the night, had died before the jubilant matins of a thousand birds; until such time did Austin sit at the open windows of his bedroom, and look out on the glorious prospect and all the wonderful changes of colour which take place between dawn and sunrise, but as one who saw them not.

For the arrow had gone home this time up to the very feather.

Chapter V

AUSTIN sat and thought what he could recollect to have heard about her. He had not been much into society where he would have been likely to have heard much about her. Many of the clerks in his father's office would be likely to know more.

He remembered one thing, however. He had heard, that she was an only daughter and an immense heiress, and that all the estates in four counties would go to this young beauty. And he was desperately in love with her.

He saw nothing absurd in this ; he did not get up in the dead of night and stealthily fly the house, without looking back for terror. No ! he waited impatiently for day that he might see her again, and get more madly, hopelessly entangled with her than ever.

If she had shown a trifling disappointment when he came the night before, she seemed to be very much pleased with him next day. She met him with ease, and almost with familiarity — with so much familiarity, indeed, that he, not knowing the cause of it, was very much delighted indeed.

She had gone into her father's dressing-room that morning, and said —

" Father dear, who is this Mr. Elliot whom you have brought home ? "

" He is a young Oxford man. He promises uncommon well. They say his degree will be very good indeed, and he is very ambitious. He may end by being a man of some mark. Who knows."

" Is he nice ? "

" Can't say, I am sure. That is your business. He is to marry that old scoundrel Hilton's daughter, and go into Parliament with her money, I believe. I have brought him down here for a few days to make his acquaintance, and introduce him to Mewstone. He will be useful to him. He must pack off soon, for he takes his degree in the October term."

" When is Mewstone coming ? " said she, with a sigh.

" When he chooses," said Mr. Cecil laughing, " you will find *that* out."

Miss Cecil laughed — the most charming merry laugh

you ever heard — and then sailed away downstairs, to entertain that poor fool, Austin Elliot.

Before she had been five minutes in the room with him, he saw that his first estimate of her extraordinary beauty was by no means too great. Not only was her face as nearly perfect as possible ; not only were her brilliant, yet quiet, hazel eyes, the most beautiful eyes he had ever seen ; not only was her golden brown hair, looped so carelessly and so gracefully around the perfect shaped head, beyond comparison in the world, as he thought — all these things he had seen approached — but her grace of manner — a grace he had read of as being achieved by some great actresses — was something which he had never seen approached — a grace seen only in repose, and her repose was continual. She moved, of course ; but there was no point of time about any of her movements : you could not say that at such a time she did so-and-so. She only slid from one posture of infinite grace into another. Austin thought that there was as much difference between her motions and those of another woman, as between those of a doe in the wild woodlands, and those of a soldier doing his exercise.

"I am so glad my father brought you home with him," she said. "I was rather dull here, all alone with the waterfall and the dogs. Will you please tell me about the yacht running ashore. Please make me laugh about it. I am sure you can if you choose. I can always like people who can make me laugh."

Austin certainly could do that. He described their Lordships' squabble — the heartless obstinacy of the commander, his sardonic grin when he had made their Lordships run the yacht ashore, and the extraordinary infuriated heap of administrative talent of the highest order, which lay kicking on the deck, at the first bump on the sand. He would have given five pounds, he said, to have been on board his father's yacht at the time, and seen his father's face. The expression of fun, he said, tempered with propriety, which would have been seen in that face, would have been better worth seeing than the whole of their seven Lordships, fighting together in the lee-scuppers.

She laughed very heartily, and she said, " I think I shall like you very much indeed. Will you come and walk with me this morning ; my father will be busy on the farm ? My father tells me you are going into politics. Will you tell me, for I have not seen a newspaper, what are people saying about this O'Connell business ? "

" Well," said Austin, " they are saying all kinds of things. Mr. Cecil hopes that the Lords will reverse the judgment of the lower courts. I entirely disagree with your father. There is something very charming in that. I, Austin Elliot, distinctly tell you, Miss Cecil, that I disagree with a privy counsellor and first Lord of Shoals and Quicksands. It makes one feel taller to say it. I have a good mind to tell him so himself."

" Better not," she said, laughing ; " such presumption might ruin your prospects. And now let us leave politics and come and see the dogs."

There was, in and about the kennel, almost every variety of dog conceivable. There were deep-jowled dogs, with sunken eyes and wrinkled foreheads, at the first distant note of whose bell-like voice, the hunted slave in the Cuban jungle lies down and prays for death ; yet who here is a stupid, blundering, affectionate brute, who will let you do as you like with him, and casts himself on his back at Miss Cecil's feet. English bloodhounds, too, stupid, sleepy, good-natured, slobbering. St. Bernards, too — dogs of the snowstorm and the avalanche, wise-looking dogs, self-contained, appearing to know more than they chose to say, but idiots withal notwithstanding, and very great idiots, as are many self-contained and wise-looking animals beside they. A great rough Newfoundland dog, chained up. Marry, why ? Because he had been the pet of the house, until one day he had become *Must*, *Berserk*, or what you choose to call it, until the devil, or the seven devils, which lurk in *all* Newfoundland dogs, gentle and docile as they are, had broken loose, and Mr. Cecil had had to fight with him for his life in his own dressing-room. There were two French poodles, which, as Mr. Sala says somewhere, so truly, "you can teach to do everything but love you." There was a British bull-dog, white, with small eyes; so short-sighted as to be obliged to examine everything with his nose (which gave Austin a creeping up his back), and with a wicked, lowering, face; yet which bull-dog turned out, like most other British bull-dogs, to be a good-natured, kind-hearted fellow, and a firm friend, as soon as he had (by smelling the calves of their legs, a nervous proceeding) found out his friends from his enemies.

And Austin, finding that the bull-dog, instead of biting his legs, wagged his tail at him, and proposed to accompany him further, broke out into raptures.

"Miss Cecil, I have never seen such a collection of dogs as this! And I am a great fancier of dogs."

"You have not seen them nearly all yet," she said. "This is, I believe, the best collection of dogs in England; or rather, I should say, better than any in England, for we are in Wales. You know how they came here?"

"No."

"My poor brother chose to have the best dogs in England; it was a passion with him; and since his death, my father has chosen to pursue his hobby. You know about my brother's death?"

"Oh, yes," said Austin, who knew nothing at all about it, but who did what was possibly the best thing he could do, utter a *façon de parler* (for it was nothing more), and try to turn the subject. At the same time he reflected, that it would be well for young men like himself, not in society, before they went into a house, to inform themselves somewhat about the history of that house, to prevent mistakes.

"Do you really know about my brother, Mr. Elliot?" said Miss Cecil.

" Well, no," said Austin, " I do not, since you ask me twice. Remember, I am only an undergraduate at Oxford, and that I knew nothing, even of Mr. Cecil, except that he was one of the first men in England, and had given such and such votes, until he asked me here."

" I like you very much," said she ; " you are so well-bred, and have so little pretension. I only wanted to mention my poor brother, whom I hardly remember, to warn you what not to talk about with my father. He was drowned boating at Eton. And you will find that it is as well to know all this sort of thing in the world."

Miss Cecil, the oracle, was much younger than Austin ; but she had been out two seasons, and knew a great deal of the world ; and he was at the University and knew absolutely and entirely nothing. If he had, he would have known what a consummate fool he was to fall in love with her, recklessly to go on feeding his passion ; and above all, what an utter fool he was to hope that it would have any other than one conclusion.

" I know nothing of the world, or about people, yet," he said, " I suppose the knowledge of people and their belongings will come to one in time. It seems tiresome to get it up. Do you know that none of the best fellows who I know are up in that sort of thing. Now, there is Lord Charles Barty, he is coming on very well indeed ; but, mind you, I believe if you were to put him into a corner he would not be able to tell you who his grandmother's father was."

Miss Cecil laughed. " I daresay not," said she. " *I* know. His grandmother was a Leyton, daughter of Sir . Robert Leyton, of Broadash. Leave the pedigrees to the women. One of the great uses of a woman in society is, I take it, to tell her husband who people are."

So she talked to him, as one would talk to an intelligent boy sent to one for a holiday ; and yet the fool loved on more madly than ever.

" Come on," she said, " and let us see the rest of the

dogs ; " for this conversation took place at the fountain in the centre of the kennels, and they had only come up one avenue, and only seen one fourth of the dogs as yet.

And as they turned to go she said :

" I like you very much, as I told you before. And to prove to you how much I like you, I will give you, out of all these hundreds of beautiful dogs, the dog you choose — the dog you think that you will love best ; and I only annex one condition — that whenever your heart warms towards that dog, that you will think of me, and think how much I like you. I have heard a very great deal of you. I rather believe that you did not know of my existence before you came here. But I have been in love with you for a long time."

Miss Cecil and Eleanor had been friends and correspondents ; Austin did not know this. He was not coxcomb enough to take her cool free-and-easy expressions as advances to himself, and yet he was foolish enough to think that they formed a basis of operations. He had hopes.

He was a great fool ; but I would not have cared to write his history if he had not been. Let us be Jacobin, democratic, and revolutionary for a season, until our reason returns. If a man is thrown into intricate relations with a woman, however much his superior in rank, that man is justified, if he so please, in falling in love with that woman. A man may fly from a hopeless passion, and be miserable. Granted. A man may yield to a hopeless passion, and may behave like a gentleman, and keep it all in his own breast, and tell no one but the friend of his heart, and be miserable. Also granted. But if a man comes to me and says, that although he was with such and such a woman, but didn't allow himself to fall in love with her because she was above him in rank, I choose to tell that man that he is no man at all, and no more knows what love means than a horse or a dog.

Now they began looking at the terriers. There was one

snow-white English terrier of such amazing beauty, that Austin very nearly chose it, but fortunately did not. Then there were some black and tans, equal in beauty to the white. Dandy Dinmont terriers, as long and as lithe as otters; and pert, merry, sharp little Skyes; rough long-legged English fox terriers, which ran on three legs, like Scotch terriers, and held their heads on one side knowing-ly. Austin was more and more delighted every step. He knew all about every dog; but at the last he was stopped. He came across four little dogs, the like of which he had never seen before.

Little long-bodied, short-legged dogs, a dull blue-grey colour, with clouded black spots; sharp, merry little fel-lows.

"What dogs can these be, Miss Cecil?" he said. "I am quite at fault."

"Cannot you guess? Why, they are turnspits, and all with the turnspit peculiarity. The right eye is not of the same colour as the left. I suppose you will hardly see such dogs as these in England. Will you choose one?"

Although one of the queer merry little rogues begged at him, he said no. "They are a sight," he said, "a sight worth seeing, but I will not choose one. In an artistic point of view, they are ugly, and they suggest to one the blue dogs which the Chinese fatten for table. No. I hardly dare to say so, but of all the dogs here I would soonest have that incomparable white terrier. I have dreamed of such a dog as that, but I never saw such a one."

"It is hardly possible that you can have. He is yours, with a thousand welcomes. I hope he may live long to remind you of me."

"I need no dog to do that," said Austin; "but I can-not take such a princely present."

She laughed. "It is done," she said; "the election is made for good or evil. Come and take possession."

The election, so terribly important as it turned out, was

nearly made. Who could guess, on that happy summer's day, how much was to depend on the choosing of a dog?

> " For the want of a nail the shoe was lost ;
> For the want of a shoe the horse was lost ;
> For the want of a horse the rider was lost ;
> For the want of a rider a kingdom was lost. "

If it were not that we knew that a tender, loving Father watches over us with all-seeing providence, each action of a prudent man's life would be accompanied with such a feeling of terror of ultimate consequences, that life would become a burden, and the grave rest; or we should run, like the Turks, and some of the West country sects, into the opposite extreme of saying that it was all " Kismet," that it mattered not what we did.

The white terrier was so nearly chosen, in spite of Austin's strong repugnance to accept such a valuable present, that they had turned, and Austin's hands were eager to seize the beautiful little animal, and call him his own, when, in the wood behind them, there was a wild jubilant bark; in another instant there was a rush past them, as of an eagle coming through a forest; in the next, a dog, different to any they had seen before, was madly, joyously careering round and round them in ever-narrowing circles; and in another he was leaping on both of them, and covering them with caresses.

But he saw that Austin was a stranger, and paused to look at him, and after a moment he reared up against him, and said with his beautiful soft hazel eyes, as Austin thought, " Choose me, choose me, and I will follow you through it all, even to the very end."

It was a most beautiful Scotch sheep dog, black and tan and white, with a delicate smooth head, the hair of which began to wave about the ears, until it developed into a deep mane upon the shoulders. The author has described such a dog before. The Scotch sheep dog is the highest development of the brute creation, in beauty, in sagacity, and in other qualities, which one dares, by leave of Messieurs of the Holy Office, to call moral. This was the most beautiful dog of that variety ever seen. If the reader wishes to realize the dog to himself he can do so thus. In Landseer's picture of "The Shepherd's Bible," the dog which is standing up is very like him; though the dog I am describing is drawn from the life, and from a handsomer dog than he.

"This is the dog for me," cried Austin. "Why, you beauty! Miss Cecil, I would give anything for this dog. Just look at his eyes, will you. Can I have him? Does he belong to any one?"

"Yes," she said, laughing. "He belongs to you. He is worth all the white terriers that ever were born. I like you the better for your choice of Robin."

At this moment a harsh voice behind them said:

"How d'ye do, Miss Cecil? By Jove! that dog is a deuced clever dog. He began by pitching into me, but when your father said, 'Go find, Robin,' he became docile, and brought me on your track like an Indian. Is he yours?"

"He is Mr. Elliot's. How do you do, Captain Hertford?" said Miss Cecil, very coldly.

Chapter VI

CAPTAIN HERTFORD, the man who had just found the group, was a man whose personal appearance requires some slight notice, and but very slight. He was a very big, thick-set man. He had a broad red face, the principal features of which were lowering bushy eyebrows, beneath which were cruel, deep-sunk, light blue eyes; and a thick, coarse mouth, too big to be entirely hidden by the moustache which met his deep red whiskers. The expression of his face was, towards men, scowling and insolent;

what it was towards women I know not, but should fancy that, if it was intended to express admiration, it was more repulsive than his ordinary look of defiance and ill temper.

He looked with intense eager curiosity at Austin—Austin did not look with much curiosity at him, or he would have seen him bite his lip impatiently. He might have been flattered had he heard the Captain say to himself, "Consume the young beggar, he *is* infernally handsome."

"You are unexpected, Captain Hertford," said Miss Cecil; "but not the less welcome. Whence have you come?"

"I have been at Brussels with Mewstone. I stayed a day or two there after him. He got hold of the old Countess Dentelles, and carried her off to Malines with him. They seem to have been pretty busy those two days. The bill has come to me in the course of business."

"Is it very large?" said Miss Cecil, laughing.

"A little over thirty thousand francs."

"That is very extravagant."

"I don't know," said Captain Hertford. "I don't think it is so very bad. Remember what it must have cost to get the old countess to leave her box at the St. Hubert, with Levasseur starring from Paris, and pack off to Malines with him, with her rheumatism and her monkey. When I looked at the bill, I pointed to an item of five thousand francs, and I said to him, 'That's the old woman's share;' and he laughed and said, 'Yes.' He got her uncommon cheap, I think, at that. She is the best judge in Europe. They would have cheated him horribly if she hadn't gone with him."

Austin had no more notion what they were talking about than the man in the moon. He looked at them both with wonder. Miss Cecil began again:

"Well, on the whole, he could not have done better. I suppose the poor old devotee will put it on the shoulders of some Bambino or another. Poor old lady!"

"What a delightful rummage she must have had.

There must have been a great excitement at Malines at her appearance."

" What detained you in Brussels, Captain Hertford ? "

" Well, a very unpleasant affair.   An affair touching my personal honour."

" Have you been out again ? " she asked, turning sharply upon him.

" No," said Captain Hertford.   " A young fellow, an Englishman, had forged Mewstone's name to a large amount.   I followed him to Namur, to see whether I could recover anything.   But when I got to Namur he had escaped me.   My honour was concerned in catching him, for he was my acquaintance, not Mewstone's."

" Did you follow him no farther ? " she asked.

" There was no need.   By the bye, Mewstone is in London, and will here the day after to-morrow."

" Is any one there to act for him, as the Countess Dentelles did at Malines ? "

" No," said Captain Hertford.   " I turned him into Rundell and Bridges, as I would turn a young colt into a clover-field.   They won't cheat him.   It is all convertible property.   Will you introduce me to Mr. Elliot ? "

She did so.   Captain Hertford did not scowl on him, but smiled.   Austin thought possibly that his smile was not a pleasant one, but he did not care for that.   This man had been talking for ten minutes to this woman, and Austin had not the least idea of what they had been talking about.   This man could talk to her and amuse her, when he sat mumchance.   He would make himself a pupil of this man.   This must be one of the men of the world his father talked of.   But had all the men of the world scowling eyebrows, and great coarse mouths, like this one?

Austin laughed as he asked himself this question.   He had seen other men of the world.   His father, and Mr. Cecil, and the seven other Lords of the Shoals and Quicksands, quite different in appearance to Captain Hertford.

He did not like the look of this gentleman, but he would be his pupil. He was as eager for Captain Hertford's acquaintance, as Captain Hertford was for his.

They walked back, all three towards the house, and Miss Cecil went in. Captain Hertford proposed that they should extend their walk, and smoke a cigar.

Austin was delighted. As they turned on the broad gravel walk, Austin noticed for the first time that the dog Robin was at his heels. His tail was down, and his ears were down. He was waiting for orders from his new master. The dog had *taken to him*. What that means I cannot tell you. I don't know, and you don't know, any more than this, that sometimes dogs take to men, and sometimes they don't. And we shall none of us know any more about the matter until the kye come hame.

Apparently, also, Captain Hertford had taken to Austin. His sudden affection for Austin is not nearly so mysterious a business as that of the dog's. We shall find out the reason of *that* before the kye come hame.

" Where shall we go ? " said Captain Hertford.

" Anywhere you like," said Austin, with the frankness of a boy. " I want to talk to you. I want to make your acquaintance. And any one place is as good as another for that."

Captain Hertford turned and looked at him as he said this. There was almost a smile on his face, as he heard Austin say this ; but when he looked at him, and saw how handsome he was, he scowled again. It is just possible that this was an important point in Captain Hertford's life. Austin, with his fresh innocence, might have won him back to better things possibly. Who knows ? But Austin stood between him and the light.

Hertford walked in, puffing his cigar. He began the conversation.

" By the bye, Elliot, you know the Hiltons, don't you ? "

" Infinitely well."

" Then I am afraid that the beginning of our acquaintance won't be very pleasant. I was detained in town on their account."

" Indeed."

" Yes. You heard me speaking about an affair concerning a young Englishman, which detained me at Brussels."

" Yes."

" Did you ever know Robert Hilton ? "

" Yes ; at Eton, poor lad. But I have never seen him since."

" You will never see him any more."

" Oh ! Captain Hertford, don't say that. Do you mean to say he is dead ? "

" If you are going into the world, you must learn to bear these things with composure, Elliot. Now, lean against that rock, and look me in the face. Robert Hilton committed suicide the week before last, at Namur."

" Suicide ! "

" Yes, suicide."

" God forgive me. I was going to say, that he would not have been so bold ; so — Poor lad. Yet, I don't know. Was there anything new against him ? "

" Yes. I will tell you what there was against him. He forged Mewstone's name."

" Good God ! "

" Yes. And when he thought it must be discovered, fled to Namur. I sent a man after him. A letter from Hilton, to me, crossed him on the road. It announced his intention of making away with himself. I was furious. I thought it was a miserable ruse to escape. I followed my friend to Namur. And there I found the whole business unfortunately true."

" Does Mr. Hilton know of this ? " said Austin, eagerly.

" Yes, I broke it to him."

" How did he take it ? "

" Very quietly. You know the whole thing is very sad, and very lamentable ; but Hilton is a man of the world. And with regard to this boy, the bitterness of death was passed. You must know that. He was a *mauvais sujet*. I don't mean to say that the old man was not deucedly cut up, and all that sort of thing, but he took it very quietly."

" Poor Eleanor," said Austin.

" You mean Miss Hilton," said Captain Hertford. " Well, she was very much cut up. But she will be consoled. You see this leaves her in undisputed possession of nine thousand a year at her father's death."

" She ! she weigh nine thousand, or nine millions against her brother's life ! You don't know Eleanor Hilton, Captain Hertford."

" Nor you either, I fancy," said Captain Hertford, laughing. " Did I say she weighed money against her brother's life ? Don't I know that she would pitch it all to the dogs to have him back again ? All I said was, that she would console herself ; and you will find that inexorably true. So she will."

" Indeed," said Austin. " I suppose she will. After all, the poor fellow was a sad source of anxiety to them. It is perhaps better she should forget him."

" What a child you are, Elliot," said Captain Hertford. " Five minutes or less ago you were ready to fight me — I saw it in your eyes — for saying she would console herself. Now you endorse it, repeat it, and say, it were better she should do so."

This is what some gentleman in " Martin Chuzzlewit " calls " Dreadful true." Austin had the good taste to acknowledge it.

" I ought," he said, " to go home, I think."

" Why ? "

" I don't know. I should like to be near poor Eleanor in her trouble."

" Are you caught there then ? " said Captain Hertford, turning the other way, and adding, " I wonder if he has any head of grouse here."

" I," said Austin, " Oh dear, no."

" I thought you had been."

" No," said Austin, blushing and hesitating, " Eleanor Hilton and I have been brought up like brother and sister, you know."

" Oh, indeed. I had heard that you and she were very good friends. What a beautiful girl this Miss Cecil is."

" Is she not ? "

" I suppose you are not caught there ? "

" After twenty-four hours," Austin had voice enough to say ; " No, I don't think I am."

" Then you must be a great fool, Elliot," said Captain Hertford.

Chapter VII

ONE cannot help doubting whether or no Austin would have written to Eleanor about his new passion, even had she not been in trouble about her brother's death. At all events, he did not. He merely wrote her a kind affectionate letter, full of condolence ; but said no word of Miss Cecil.

This was an exception to his general rule. For he usually fell in love with a fresh young lady, more or less ineligible, every three months ; and invariably told Eleanor all about it. So that poor Eleanor used to get into a state of confusion ; and was in the habit of confounding the last young lady, and the last but one, to Austin's great vexation.

But he wrote to Lord Charles Barty. He told him about Miss Cecil, her beauty, her wit, her grace, and how he was madly in love with her ; and he directed the letter to Turin. For in this year the Duke and Duchess of Cheshire invaded Italy, with an overwhelming force, exacting tribute from the various people over whose necks their chariot wheels passed, taking with them also scholars and experts, to show them the best things in the way of art, on which to lay their hands, as did Buonaparte, but, un-like Napoleon, paying for them, in hard cash, about twenty per cent. above their actual value.

Lord Charles Barty had a long letter written to Austin, and ready to send, when he got Austin's. Lord Charles's letter was full of flippant good-humoured nonsense. He had tried to whet his wits upon everything he had seen, and it is quite possible that he had made an indifferent success. We shall never know about this, however, for when he got Austin's letter he burnt his own, wrote a new one to Austin, an eager hasty one, of only six or seven lines, put it in the post-office himself, walked up and down until he saw the Diligence depart for Chambery, and then bit his nails and stamped when he considered that his letter would be too late to do any good.

Lord Charles Barty was not very clever : in fact, the Bartys are not a clever family. But they have higher qualities than cleverness. " In the house of Waverley the qualities of honour and generosity are hereditary." So it may be said about the Bartys. Lord Charles Barty would have telegraphed to his friend Austin ; but, alas ! in 1844, the only piece of telegraph working was from London to Slough, and from Vauxhall to Woking ; consequently there was none to Turin. He would have given up his holiday, and posted home, but he knew he would be too late. He could only fret and fume, until he told his father, who looked very grave, and said, that either Mr. Cecil, or Austin, or Miss Cecil, must be very much to blame.

And meanwhile poor Austin continued making a fool of himself with Miss Cecil. Her manner was very affection-ate towards him. She had known Eleanor Hilton, having stayed with her at a country house, and she had done what every one else did who saw Eleanor, got very deep-ly attached to her. This she told to Austin the very first morning of their acquaintance ; but she had, of course, not told him something else. To wit, that some one had told her of Eleanor's having been engaged to marry a young gentleman, by name Elliot, ever since she could talk. She was very anxious to see the man on whom so much of Eleanor's happiness depended. And she was delighted and charmed to find him so worthy of her. That was all.

And so he walked and rode and drove and read with her day after day, getting more hopelessly entangled. Captain Hertford was very busy, or seemed to be, with her father, and left Austin to cavalier Miss Cecil. Mr. Cecil and Captain Hertford did really seem busy ; but if they had not been, the latter would have contrived to leave them alone together. He had his reasons.

Once in the week or ten days, he went out with the Captain to walk idly across some farms to see some improvements. The bailiff was with them. A farmer, catching sight of them at a long distance, made towards them, and then, hat in hand, and addressing Austin every tenth word as " my lord," began with Welsh volubility to lay a case about draining improvements before him, and pray his assistance. He had gone on ever so far before the steward had time to stop him in a few hurried words of Welsh. The man scowled on Austin, turned on his heel, and departed.

When he was alone with Captain Hertford, Austin said to him, " It is a very curious thing, do you know ; but in the few days I have been here, that same thing has happened in different ways — not once, but a dozen times. I met a man in the pass of Llanberis, when I was coming here with Mr. Cecil, who first of all asked, with the greatest *empressement*, to be introduced to me ; and then when he heard my name, looked very much inclined to kick me. I hope no one will do that. Has any man called Elliot done anything very bad in these parts ? "

" Not that I know of. But I will tell you what I think. I fancy, mind, that seeing a handsome young dandy like you, brought down here by Mr. Cecil—mind, I only fancy — that the people think that you are going to marry Miss Cecil."

" Then why," said poor Austin, " the moment they hear my name, do they find out that I am not the man ? "

This was awkward. Captain Hertford laughed, and said, " I am sure I don't know." In another moment, Austin would, according to all laws of probability, have asked him whether Miss Cecil was engaged to any one. Possibly Captain Hertford knew that, for he said, before Austin had time to say anything, " Miss Cecil tells me that she gave you the choice of all the dogs in the kennel. Rather a compliment, eh ? What the deuce made you choose that infernal sheep-dog ? "

Austin was on his own dunghill immediately. Captain Hertford knew he would be. " Why did I choose him ? " he said. " Because he is the best specimen in the kennel."

" The most perfect specimen ! " said the artful Captain, scornfully.

" Yes."

" What ! a finer specimen than that glorious white ter-rier ? You must be a fool, Elliot. Why, there is not such another dog in the world as that white terrier. Snow-white as he seems, you can see, in certain lights, the mark-ings of a perfect black and tan under his white hair. There is no dog like him in England."

" He is only an Albino black and tan," said Elliot, scorn-fully. " He is a beautiful beast, and he is worth thirty guineas, I allow ; but do you know the points of a Scotch colley ? eh ! "

" Can't say I do," said Captain Hertford. " Can't say, either, that I know the points of a coster-monger's don-key."

" Ah ! " said Austin, " then you see I do. I know the points of any dog under the sun. This dog Robin is per-fect in all points. Here, sir ! here ! Look at him."

Captain Hertford looked at Robin, but Robin did not look at Captain Hertford. He caught his eye for a moment, and then laid his leaf-like ears back, drooped his tail, went behind Austin, and loped, or lurked, in his walk, which means, that he moved the two legs which were on the same side of him together.

Captain Hertford laughed, and changed the subject. He had done what he wanted. He had prevented Austin from asking an awkward question. There were three or four days to spare, by his calculations. He saw that Austin had fallen deeply in love, poor fool, with Miss Cecil; he wanted him to get deeper and deeper in that hopeless passion. Eleanor Hilton was heiress to nine thousand a year. He had an introduction to Eleanor through her brother's unfortunate death. Austin must be entangled with some one else for a time.

Captain Hertford, however, was playing a very dangerous game. He was "necessary man" to Lord Mewstone. He had been sent to Tyn y Rhaiadr as his avant-courrier. He had found Austin there, in the very act of falling in love with Miss Cecil.

He had come to England from Brussels, with the idea that Eleanor and her nine thousand a year were worth getting at. He had heard that Austin was supposed to be engaged to her. He had come to Tyn y Rhaiadr, and found him, of all men in the world, there, and he had acted as above. His plans were not well developed, and might be changed; but he had no doubt of this — that if he let him commit himself deeply to Miss Cecil, it must be better for his plans in the long run.

Chapter VIII

BUT, on the eighth day, Austin's eyes were opened to the true state of the case in this manner : —

It was Sunday morning ; Mr. Cecil and Captain Hertford had not gone to church, pleading that the service was in Welsh. Miss Cecil had gone, however, and Austin had gone with her.

They returned by the path which led past the waterfall,

where he had first seen her, and there, upon the giddy bridge, in the presence of the great sheet of rushing foam, he knew his fate. On the rocky path above them stood a tall and handsome man. Miss Cecil gave a little cry when she caught sight of him; and when Austin saw her two little gloved hands trembling out from under her shawl towards him, he knew everything. The eager movement of those little hands was as stern a death-blow to his hope, as though the man who stood above her, and held out his arms to her, had taken her in them, and cast her into the seething cataract a hundred feet below.

Alas, poor Austin! He was a gentleman, and looked earnestly at the waterfall, lest he should see the meeting. When he looked round again, they were standing side by side, radiant, handsome, and joyous; and he could see that she was talking about him.

So he went up to them, and was presented by Miss Cecil to Lord Mewstone.

Every one had known of the engagement between Miss Cecil and Lord Mewstone for months — every one except, apparently, poor ignorant Austin. All Mr. Cecil's enormous estates went to his daughter. These estates bordered, in two counties, on those of Lord Mewstone. His marriage with Miss Cecil would well-nigh double his already great wealth. Mr. Cecil had refused a peerage, because he saw that it would take place, and it was not worth while leaving the House of Commons — having no male issue, and being in full work — at least not at present. There was as much land as goes to make some independent states. There were deep political considerations at stake in this great match. It was an affair of enormous importance, and here was poor ignorant self-confident little Austin, flying his kite in the middle of it all with a calm unconsciousness of the fact that the only human being *there* who guessed his secret, Captain Hertford, was at one time laughing at, at another time admiring his amazing impudence.

" By Gad ! " said Captain Hertford to himself, " what the deuce is it ? Is it innocence, or is it mere vanity ? If I had had that amount of unconscious impudence early in life, I might have done better."

People said that this marriage of Lord Mewstone with Fanny Cecil was a family and political arrangement. If so, it was an uncommonly fortunate one, for each of them loved the ground which the other walked on. Let us wish them good-bye for ever. Our way lies in a very different direction. We must quit this happy house among the Welsh hills; but I am sorry to say we must take away Captain Hertford with us, and keep him with us altogether, or nearly so.

Austin's adieux were easily made. The poor miserable lad had only to say that he would take the opportunity of travelling as far as Chester with Captain Hertford (there was no railway farther than Chester in 1844), for that he must join his reading party. He received a hearty farewell from every one, and jumped into the carriage beside Captain Hertford, to go to Bangor.

And when Captain Hertford looked at him, he saw that his face was changed since yesterday. Yesterday it was the face of a remarkably handsome young man, with merry blue eyes. To-day it was the same ; the features as regular as those of Buonaparte or Castlereagh ; the firm cut mouth, with the lower lip slightly pouting ; the short curling brown hair, the pure complexion, were all there ; and yet there was a difference since yesterday. Austin, as he sat in the carriage, was as handsome as Buonaparte or Castlereagh, but had now, though his face was at rest, a look which Lord Whitworth must have seen on the face of the one, and Mr. Raikes on the face of the other—a look of angry, furious defiance. It was expressed in only one feature—in the eyes. Austin's great blue eyes, always set a trifle too near his eyebrows, were now prominent, surrounded with a black ring ; and whenever Captain Hertford spoke to him, he turned them on him angrily, though his speech was gentle. Those eyes seemed to say, " How dare you disturb me ? " And as Captain Hertford looked on them, that veteran warrior and bully said to himself, " The fellow will do. He has power."

And he remembered the look of those eyes, when Austin was in that humour. The old calm look soon came back again, and Captain Hertford never saw that look in them any more until the 16th of May, 1846. The night on which the Corn Law Bill was read the third time in the Commons.

But after a very few miles, scarcely more than one, a change took place. Austin was disappointed and humiliated beyond what one can well conceive, and he also fancied, and most properly, that he had been deceived by Captain Hertford. But the great good heart, which, in spite of all weakness and conceit, dictated all his actions, told him that he must speak to some one. There was no one but this red-faced, red-haired soldier, with his sly little eyes, his coarse moustache, and his great gluttonous mouth; and so he must talk to him. He had the strongest repugnance to him personally. Yes. He had deceived him and played with him, and hurt his pride. But — Well — the man was a man. The fellow could ride, for all his little deep-set eyes. Not only could ride, but would ride; not only would ride, but had ridden, so deep into a regiment of infuriated Affghans, that the squadron, which hated him while they followed him, could see nothing of him but the sword which flickered about his head.

So he was a man at all events, though he might be only a led Captain of Lord Mewstone's. And Austin must speak to some one. And so the expression of the eyes changed altogether when he next spoke to Captain Hertford. He had the dog Robin's head between his knees, and was smoothing his round forehead, when he looked up suddenly, and said to Captain Hertford, in a low voice—

" I was in love with that woman."

Captain Hertford looked uneasily at the coachman, but Austin had calculated on that, and spoken very low. Captain Hertford said—

" Well ! well ! and are in a rage with me, are you not ? "

Austin was easily disarmed ; he said quietly, " No ; I am in a rage with no one but myself. What right has a poor ignorant boy, like me, to be in a rage with a man of the world like you ? "

Captain Hertford turned suddenly upon him, and then turned suddenly away again. " I thought," he said, " that you might be angry because I did not tell you that she was engaged to Lord M."

" No. You were not called on to do so. What a fool I must have been on the other hand, eh ? "

" Well, I don't know there : you are singularly handsome, and very ambitious. That sort of thing happens very often. There was Charley Bates and Miss Dawkins, for instance. Charley had led a deuce of a life with her uncle, old Fagin, and Jack Dawkins, her brother, a fellow that every one knew, but who had gone to the devil lately. Old Fagin got hung, no one ever found out what for, and Charley hadn't got a rap. So what does he do. Makes up to Miss Dawkins, who had come into the old man's money (her mother was a Moss — one of the Monmouth-street Mosses — who had married Fagin's brother, about which there was a story, sir, and a devilish queer one, if you come to that) and married her, and made her cut the shop, and went into a quiet farm in the grass shires," &c. &c.

Mutatis nominibus, this was about the value of the consolation which Captain Hertford administered to Austin, as they drove to Bangor. It was possibly as good as any other ; for the way of consoling a gentleman in Austin's circumstances has got to be discovered, as far as the author is aware.

When Austin got to town, he found a letter from his father. Mr. Elliot had not returned from Liverpool. Certain Brethren, feeling that they had quite as good a right to a holiday as My Lords of the Shoals and Quick-sands, had made the discovery that the man Elliot had taken all the Shoals' Lords up in their yacht, and that they were (no doubt) tampering with the buoys on the Sarn Padrig, which buoys were their business. It was intoler-able. They started in *their* yacht in hot pursuit, overtook the miscreants in Beaumauris bay, had a wrangle, and then steamed off to the island of Mull, the two yachts racing till the boilers primed, to see whether the new light-house had been painted red, according to Mr. Elliot's sug-gestion, or white, according to their (the Trinity Brothers') orders. But they had a pleasant time of it, and dined mutually with infinite good fellowship, in spite of all this divine wrath.

Austin was still smiling over this letter, when he took up another. It was in Eleanor's handwriting, and ran thus —

" If you do come home unexpectedly, dear Austin, pray come and see me at once. Father is very ill.

E. H."

Austin rang for his servant, and asked when the note had come.

" Not half an hour ago," the man said. Austin started at once.

The Hiltons lived in Wilton Crescent. He hurried there as quick as he could.

He was shown into the dining-room. Of course his first question was, " How is Mr. Hilton ? "

He was worse. Miss Hilton would come down at once however.

There was a footstep in the passage he knew full well, and he looked out of the window. He felt disinclined to see Eleanor for some reason ; he would have to tell her of this foolish business about Miss Cecil, and was disinclined to begin. He heard the door quietly opened and the gentle rustle of a woman's dress, and he knew that Eleanor Hilton was in the room, so he turned and confronted this terrible lady, and felt his heart beat the quicker as he did so.

There stood before him a tiny delicate dark woman, dressed very neatly, in very quiet colours. She was like a little fragile brown moth, a thing you may crush with your finger ; and the wee little elfin thing stood before him with her hands crossed for an instant, without speaking. If Austin had looked at the eager twitching of those hands he would have known something even then. He knew what that motion of the hands meant a day or two before, when he saw Miss Cecil raise her hands towards Lord Mewstone ; but he did not notice it now, for he was looking into her face.

Was it a handsome face ? — ah, no ! Was it a beautiful face ? — ah, dear, yes ! Her hair was banded closely down on each side of her great forehead, and her eyes, her clear large hazel eyes, said as plainly as words could have said to him, " I am a poor little body and very ugly, but I will love you if you will let me." All her features were very regular but very small, and though her upper lip was sharp and her chin was short, the mouth was the best feature in her face, though it might be set too near her nose, and too near her chin, yet it was an exceeding tender mouth ; although it was as sharp cut as Sarah Siddons', it helped almost as much as the gentle eyes and the open forehead to make you say to yourself, " What a dear fragile loveable little body it is."

The Author wonders whether or no it would not have been better if he had said at first that she was like a gentle bright-eyed little brown mouse. It is possible that it may be so.

" I knew," she said, coming up and taking his hands, " that you would come to me."

" Dear sister," he said, looking into her face, "of course I came to you. How is he ? "

" Worse."

" Who is here ? "

" No one but Aunt Maria."

" Isn't she too much for him ? You know *I* have a profound respect for Aunt Maria, but at the same time you know —— "

At this moment Aunt Maria, always profoundly penetrated with the idea that young people should not be left too long alone together, came into the room.

She was a big, red-faced woman, with a Roman nose and a protruding chin. A woman of presence — of such powerful presence that when she entered the room at one end and you were at the other, with your back towards her, you knew it. Was it merely by the vibration of the air, one wonders, or is there, after all, such a thing as animal magnetism ?

She was a stern woman, with bangles and brooches and a shawl. She revolved in her orbit, surrounded by an atmosphere of Patchouli, calculated, by people curious in astronomy, as being from eleven to twelve times greater than her own diameter.

The moment that Austin found himself within the atmosphere, he spoke, and asked her how she did ? She kept her nose in the air, and motioned Eleanor out of the room.

" My poor brother is dying," she said ; " and, my dear Austin, he wants to see your father. What is to be done ? "

" Why, we can do nothing, dear Miss Hilton ; my father is in the Hebrides. Let me see him."

" It might be unwise ; I really don't know what to say. Whether or no a strange face — "

" Mine is not a strange face, Miss Hilton."

" No, no ! but I am in terror ; it is your father he wants. When did you come ? "

" Just now ; Eleanor wrote for me."

" She did, did she ! It was giving you a great deal of trouble," she said, looking very angry.

Now Aunt Maria did not want Austin to see old Hilton,

if she could decently help it, for these simple reasons. He had been raving to see Mr. Elliot; and one of his great anxieties was, as they gathered from his talk, that Austin should marry Eleanor. Aunt Maria was very strongly opposed to this. She was selfish. She had great power with Eleanor, and Eleanor would be an heiress. Eleanor *might* never marry at all, which would be for her benefit, and if she did marry she might marry a better man than Austin. She was a silly woman as well as a selfish one. She was taken by surprise at Austin's appearance, and not knowing very well what to do, did what silly women generally do when they don't see their way — that is to say, *did* nothing, but opposed everything. So she tried to prevent Austin from seeing Mr. Hilton. She failed, as we shall see ; and though the interview was not very important at first sight, yet it had some slight effect on the course of the story. Aunt Maria's intrigue against Austin (in which she was, according to her light, conscientious) grew to be much more important afterwards. She was a foolish woman, but her obstinacy, and her want of sensibility, gave her a terrible power. Greater and stronger people than dear Eleanor have submitted to an Aunt Maria for very peace sake.

Austin would never have seen Mr. Hilton, I believe, if it had not happened that Sir Rufus James, the doctor, had happened to be upstairs, and had come into the dining-room on his way to his carriage. Austin looked in his kind gentle face, and ignoring Aunt Maria, said —

" Sir Rufus, look here. Mr. Hilton wants to see my father, and he is in the Hebrides. Don't you think I might go up and see him ? "

The doctor looked kindly on him, and said, " Certainly. It may please him. It will do no man any harm to look at you, my boy. You have got your mother's eyes. Yes, go and see him."

And so Aunt Maria was vanquished, and Austin went upstairs.

It was hours before Mr. Hilton was sensible again. He was lying in an uneasy slumber. Austin came into the room, went out again, and waited.

At last the message came. He went in and found the old man sitting up in bed. At first he thought he was sensible, but the first words of Mr. Hilton showed him that he was wrong. They showed him that Mr. Hilton mistook him for his father.

" Ah, Elliot," he said, " I thought you would not miss coming to see me at the last — you who stuck to me through it all. And so you have gone before, eh ? "

Austin muttered something or another.

" Yes, you are like the others, you speak inarticulately. I can hardly catch what you say. I shall be able to hear you better soon. I could not hear them very well. Why were you not here with them ? "

Austin again said something. He was beginning to get awe-struck.

" It was such a pleasant meeting," continued the old man. " It was in the middle of the night. My daughter Eleanor heard me laughing with them, and she came and sat on the bed, just where she is sitting now, and listened to us three. Did you not, my darling ? "

Eleanor said, Yes, that she had sat on the bed at half-past twelve for some time, and she grew pale.

" Yes," he said, " she sat there ; and who do you think sat in those two chairs on each side of the bed ? "

" I can't tell," faltered Austin, who began to feel his hair creep. For the old man before him was talking as clearly as ever, and yet he was delirious and did not know him.

" Can't tell, foolish man ! Why, Jenkinson sat in that chair, and Canning in that, and my daughter heard us laughing, all three of us, and came to listen. Is it not so, little one ? "

" I heard you laughing, dear father, and came and sat on the bed to listen."

" See. She confirms me. Jenkinson had on his brown coat, and Canning was laughing at it. But the strange thing was, the alteration in them. They did not look haggard, and anxious, and worn old men, as they looked when we saw them last, but they had round merry beardless faces, just as you have now, and as we all four of us had at Christchurch fifty-five weary years agone.

" I mentioned that unhappy Austerlitz affair to them, but they said that was forgiven years ago ; that where they were everything was forgiven, and that the tears were wiped from all eyes. I will try to sleep a little before I wake and die."

After this he leant against his pillow for a minute, and then, with an anxious look, turned towards Austin, and said —

" Elliot ! Elliot ! are you there still ? "

Austin answered promptly, " yes." It was no use undeceiving him now.

" I was nearly," said Mr. Hilton, " forgetting the most important part of it. Elliot, do you think your son will marry my daughter, Eleanor ? "

Austin dared say nothing.

" I can't hear you. I wish he would. She is ugly, but she is amazingly gentle and good. She will have an immense deal of money. He is good, clever, and ambitious. With her money, he will be Prime Minister if he sticks to work. I wish it could be managed. I can't hear you."

" I put the case to Jenkinson last night. He said she was pretty ; but he is a fool, she is not. He said that he might do anything in the world with her money. Speak louder."

" Without her money he will be an office-hunter. He may have the world at his feet with my daughter's money. The doctor told me that that old rat, Cecil, had got him home, to throw him against that handsome daughter of his, and use him as a foil to bring Mewstone to the point. You must know, Elliot, that he is only fooling the poor

boy; but if he marries my girl he may have his revenge
on fifty prigs like Mewstone. See to it. See to it. Good
night."

We have slightly sketched Mr. Hilton's career, and this
was the end of it. He fell asleep, and awoke to die.

Let the cunning, avaricious, yet generous and high-
minded old man sleep in peace. He made one terrible
mistake in life — his treasonable investment in the French
Funds. He said on his death-bed that " Jenkinson " had
forgiven him. I dare say it is true.

Chapter IX

So after Austin went home, when poor Mr. Hilton was
dead, he found these two sentences ringing in his ears—
" He might be Prime Minister with Eleanor's money," and
" That old rat, Cecil, had him there as a foil to bring Mewstone to the point."

About the first of these sentences I have nothing to
say; about the second I have this to say—that whoever
put that into the dying man's head told, unwittingly, perhaps, a very great falsehood. You know that from what
has gone before. If ever there was a love-match between
two folks, that match was between Lord and Lady Mewstone.

We have very little more to do with them, or with people in their rank of life. Austin was getting out of his
depth, and we must follow him. But Austin was bred to
ambition from his cradle, and that visit to Mr. Cecil's
house, combined with one sentence which Mr. Hilton let
fall on his death-bed, influenced that ambition, whatever
there may have been of it at that time, tenfold, although
after the one great effort of his life that ambition went to
sleep again.

For he began to think, " Who was this Lord Mewstone,

to come cranking in that style ? and who was he, Austin Elliot, that a cunning old man of the world should use such a stinging, coarse sentence about him as that . . ." *

He was both handsomer and cleverer than Lord Mewstone ; he knew *that* very well, as did every one else. He had some private fortune. What was there in a young fellow in his position which made these men of the world treat with contempt, the idea that he should marry her ? She came of an old county family, hitherto not ennobled, so did he. Her family had certainly laid house to house and field to field. His family had done rather the contrary.

There was no earthly reason for it save this, that the world — that world in the dread of whose opinion his father had brought him up — wouldn't hear of such a thing. And then he began to say, " What right had the world ? " and so on. He had been a submissive young whelp hitherto, but the world had (as he thought) tried to take his bone from him, and he growled. But, like a good dog, he soon went to kennel, and behaved himself.

Another speech of the old man's still lingered pleasantly in his ears, " He might be Prime Minister." That was very pleasant to think of. He might be a greater man than that prig Mewstone still. His degree would be a high one, there was no doubt of that. The world was before him, and all that sort of thing ; but the old man had annexed one condition to his being Prime Minister, and that was, that he should have Eleanor's money.

And so he took a resolution, not, I hope, unworthy of him. A fortnight after Mr. Hilton's funeral, he ordered his horse to be saddled ; he mounted it, whistled to Robin, and rode off through the pleasant lanes and commons of Surrey towards Esher, where Eleanor was staying, accompanied by her Aunt Maria.

Sometimes, under very happy influences, men who have

* I have abstained from printing that sentence : it is as well to avoid unnecessary coarseness.

just had a terrible disappointment in love, will so far forget it as to whistle, and, to outward eyes, appear for a short time as if they had forgotten it. Such was the case now, as Austin rode along the deep, over-arching lanes, and past the pleasant village greens, with his dog bounding before him, and looking back to see if he were coming.

He had not ridden very far before he came to a deep, dark lane, with a silver ford at the lower end, and a clacking mill, with a pretty flower garden, and bees. It was a very beautiful place, and as he stopped to look at it, he heard a horseman riding quickly down the lane towards him.

He turned, and saw approaching him, on a noble horse, a young man in white trousers, gallantly dressed, who waved his hand to him. Austin took off his hat and waved it in return. The next moment, the new comer was beside him, and their hands were locked together.

" Dear Austin ! " said the one.

" My dear old fellow ! " said Austin.

Perhaps the miller's daughter, looking out slyly from behind the sunny flower-beds, faint with wallflowers, at these two noble young men, who rode,

"A bow-shot from her bower eaves,"

in the summer sunshine, said to herself, that they were the handsomest and noblest pair of brothers she had ever seen. Perhaps she talked too much about them walking home from church next Sunday with her sweetheart, and made him sulky about them, until he and she kissed and made it up again on the Sabbath eventide, between the tangled hedges of dogrose and honeysuckle, under the whispering elm-trees. Who knows ? But whether this happened or not, she might have walked all England through, and not found a handsomer pair of young men than they.

The young man who had overtaken Austin was Lord Charles Barty, the friend of his heart, as like Austin in mind as he was in features. Their friendship had begun at school, and had never waned, had never had a shadow cast over it as yet, and it lasted on to the very end, just the same, without let or hindrance, till the whole business was done and finished, and people began to take their partners for the next dance.

After describing Austin, there is hardly much need to describe his friend, for they were not unlike in face at this time. They were both blonde, handsome boys, really nothing more. Not a hair on either of their chins which they dared (not being in the cavalry) to let grow. If both faces had ever developed, we should, I think, have found that Lord Charles's face was the most aquiline of the two, and that his eyebrows were more lofty. But there was not much character in either of their faces just now. It would require, as any one might see, a great deal of the padding to come off those faces, before you began to see the death's head underneath.

" I know where you are going to, old fellow," said Lord Charles, as they rode together. " The butler told me, and I came on after you. I am glad you are going there."

" I am only going, Charles, to prevent my ever going again, perhaps."

" Do you mean to say that you are going to give up Eleanor Hilton ? " said the other, looking serious.

Charles told him what had passed at Mr. Hilton's death-bed.

Lord Charles rode in silence a little way, and at last said :

" You can't be wrong, Austin, because you are acting honourably. But is there nothing else you have not told me of ? "

" Of course there is. Your letter came too late, and all the mischief was done. All the whole business was inextricably entangled (he used four or five participles, which would not read well, and so we put it like that) before your letter arrived. And besides, before your letter came, Mewstone was there, and I saw it all."

" I am so sorry, by Gad ! What a nuisance it was you didn't know," said Lord Charles.

" Old Hilton said, on his death-bed, that Mr. Cecil had taken me there to make Mewstone jealous."

" *Who* said that, Austin ? " said Lord Charles.

" Old Mr. Hilton, on his death-bed ! "

" Well, ' *de mortuis*,' &c. But he was utterly mistaken, my boy. In his sober senses he never coupled such a vulgar intrigue as that with the name of such a man as Mr. Cecil, much as he might hate him. There were never two fools more in love with one another since the world began. Will you let me burn your wound out, my boy ? It will hurt, but the wound will heal. I know from fifty fellows that these two fell in love with one another at first sight. That marriage happens to be a splendid family arrangement, but it is only a parcel of cackling idiots who say that it was made up from family motives only. Let us be just."

" But why — now I know the truth, I still ask why was I to be considered so far below her ? " And poor Austin repeated a coarse expression of the old man's, alluded to before.

" Who said that about you ? "

" Old Hilton."

" God forgive him, Austin; he was a fool. Austin, that man lost every friend in the world but your father through short-sighted cunning. Even Lord Liverpool never forgave him some dreadful business about the French funds in 1806. You must not think of the words of a soured, ill-tempered man like that. Mr. Cecil is as incapable of saying or thinking such a thing as my own mother. And as for Fanny Cecil, she would have married a Welsh curate if she had chosen. But now, old fellow, to be perfectly just, we must remember this, that in the world the marriage of Lord Mewstone and Miss Cecil was as well-known a fact, as that Graham opens the letters. Old Cecil never contemplated the possibility of your being ignorant of it. You are not in the world or of the world yet. Neither am I, but I sit and listen even now. I hear all these things : you do not as yet."

So did Lord Charles Barty comfort his friend. His friend had more brains than he, but knew less on some points. When people begin to swim on the edge of that pool which is called society, they should take care not to get out of their depths as did Austin.

" How glorious it is," said he, " to have your dear old voice in my ears again, to give me comfort. I am a different man again. Tell me, old Mentor, who is Captain Hertford ? "

" Have you met him there ? "

Austin told him how.

" He is Mewstone's henchman. I believe Mewstone has been fast, very fast. Captain Hertford is cruel, brutal, false, gluttonous, and treacherous."

" Then why has Lord Mewstone anything to do with him ? "

" Because such men are useful. Let bygones be bygones. I really know nothing more than this. I heard that character of Hertford from my blind brother Edward, who is always right."

" But does ' the world ' know this of Captain Hertford ? "

" I don't know. I don't know the world yet ; but I know that much about Captain Hertford."

" The world seems to be fond of easy-going, Charles."

" Let you and I go into it hand-in-hand together, my boy, and see what it is like. And, Austin, I begin to see that there is another great world down below us, of which you and I know nothing — the world of commerce and labour."

" You are beginning to find that out, are you ? " said Austin.

" I think I am. It is there ; and it is beginning to mutter and growl under our feet even now. Did you ever read Humboldt's Travels ? "

" No."

" Nor I ; but I have looked into them. He says, in the Andes, that the earthquakes are preceded by the most terrible underground thunder ; it begins muttering and growling, and then it swells up into a horrible roar. After this the earth gapes, and those fools who have not moved their property and their persons are swallowed up. Have you heard this underground thunder yet ? "

" Yes, but very few else," said Austin.

" You are mistaken. Many have heard it, and are preparing to move their goods. All we want is a leader, to show us what move to make."

" Is there such a one ? " said Austin.

" There is."

" And the gentleman's name ? " said Austin.

" Robert Peel."

" And you have found *that* out, too," said Austin. " By Jove, Charles, I believe we have only one heart between the pair of us."

" Hurrah ! " cried Lord Charles Barty, breaking into a mad gallop across a common, and waving his white hat over his head. " Come on, friend of my soul, and let us follow him through it all — through misrepresentation, through obloquy, down to political death itself, which will only end in a more glorious political resurrection. An adventure, Sir Knight, an adventure. A Peel ! a Peel ! to the rescue ! Who is the laggard that won't win his spurs in such a cause ? Peel to the rescue. Hurrah ! "

Now it so befel that there were a great many geese on this common, over which Lord Charles Barty rode so madly, crying out the name of a certain right honourable baronet ; and he had the misfortune to ride over one of these geese, and on his return had to pay five shillings to a vociferous old woman who saw him do it. But of all the geese on that common, were there, do you think, two greater geese than Austin Elliot and Lord Charles Barty ? But that is exactly the sort of stuff that some young fellows talked in '44. We are all much wiser now, are we not ?

Chapter X

THEIR gallop brought them across the common and to the house where Eleanor was staying with Aunt Maria. Here Austin's friend left him, and went to an inn, and put up his horse to wait for him ; and Austin rang at the bell.

The house was a great red-brick house, with narrow windows, standing a long way back, with a wall and two carriage-gates beside the road. There were also two cedars, a big bell in a little pent-house just inside the gate, and a big dog, who barked when you rang it. That house will be taken by a doctor, and made a private madhouse of some day, as the march of intellect goes on, and London expands. If it were ten miles nearer town, it would be snapped up at once for that purpose. If you ask, " Why for a madhouse, not for a school ? " the answer is, that the grounds are too large for a schoolmaster, and until they began to build it in, and take the land off his hands, it wouldn't pay him. The house before which Austin stood will become either a madhouse or an institution of some sort or another.

A great deal might be said about these old suburban houses. The author would like nothing better than to dwell on their peculiarities, but this is not the place for doing so. He begs the reader's patience for only a very few words about them. They were built, most of them, in the beginning of last century, and have been degraded and degraded from one purpose to another, each one lower than the last, until they are pulled down because they interfere with a new terrace or square. The general fate which awaits all of them is degradation and death, but sometimes they are preserved even in the midst of the great flood of bricks, and then they fetch high rents.

Did any reasonable man ever go to walk through the western part of Chelsea on to Walham Green and Fulham, if he could manage to walk anywhere else? Most likely not. And yet there are some houses standing about there which will make a man think of if he choose to think. Take one of those suburban houses, built about 1700, and think about it, and people it over again with three generations. Take a long, low, back-lying house in the King's Road, Chelsea, in front of which they have built shops. That was once a quiet gentleman's house, with elm-trees round it, where several generations of children tumbled downstairs, and fell out of window, and lost their tops and balls in the water-butt, and laughed and cried and quarrelled and made it up, until they grew to handsome young men and women. How many pairs of happy lovers went a-courting in that summer-house at the end of the garden; before Mr. Mullins took it and made a madhouse of it, and the woman who thought she was queen took possession of the summer-house, and hunted us boys out of it when we dared go in; and before they put Miss H—, a strong, red-faced woman, with a big throat and thick lips, into the old nursery, where she screamed and yelled and tore night and day for above a year, till it pleased God to put an end to her misery.

And when the madhouse was removed to Putney, Waterer took the house and grounds, and exhibited his rhododendrons and azaleas there. And all society came down to look at them, and the line of carriages extended far up and down the King's Road. Then the dreary old garden, in which the madwoman used to walk so wearily up and down, was filled with a blaze of flowering American plants. And on the very same ground where the author, a frightened boy, looking over the palings, has seen poor Miss H—, in her strait-waistcoat, cast herself screaming down among the cabbage-plants, and bite the earth with her teeth; on that very same ground all the dandies and beauties of London were walking and talking. The last I know of that piece of ground is, that the man who lets flys had laid it down in oats. *Sic transit*, &c. That is the history of one suburban house, carefully told, and there are very many with far stranger histories than that.

The study of these old red-brick suburban houses has given the author so much pleasure in his time that he has tried to give the reader some interest in them, and make him partake of the same pleasure. This is the only time he means to offend in this way in this story, and so he casts himself on his reader's mercy.

Austin, who had dismounted, rang the bell again, and again the big dog barked; this time, also, a door was opened, and Austin heard a man, apparently a footman, say, " Four ounces is four, and two quarters is a tizzy, and a bob lost tossing makes two half-bulls and a bender, don't it, you aggravating minx ? " And then, instead of coming to Austin's assistance, Austin heard him shut the door again.

So he had to ring once more. This time he heard the door opened again, and footsteps approaching. Immediately the wicket in the carriage-gate was thrown back, and in the aperture stood a little lean old footman, with a cross face and very grey hair, who cried out, " Now then, young fellow ! "

" Now then, young fellow," said Austin, " how about the two half-bulls and the bender ? "

The old man laughed : — " It's them gals, Mr. Austin, got a shilling of mine among un somewhere, and wants to bounce me out of it. Told me you was the baker's boy too. Come in afore she sees you, else she'll not be at home. She is gallivanting in the paddock with Captain Hertford."

" The deuce ! " thought Austin ; " who is Captain Hertford ? " he said.

" The gentleman as you met in Wales the week afore last, when you fell in love with Miss Cecil ; and as you travelled with and told all about it ; and as come and told *we* all about it. That's about who Captain Hertford is, Master Austin."

"But what is he doing here?" asked Austin, only half aloud.

"Making love to the old woman," said the old man, speaking very loud and plain.

"Confound you, James, don't be a ridiculous fellow," said Austin, laughing. "Making love to Aunt Maria?"

"That's about the size on it," said James. "Now come quick into the stable-yard afore she sees you. You wouldn't see much of Miss Eleanor if she caught sight on you."

"How is Aunt Maria?" said Austin, in the stable-yard, after a groom had gone off with his horse.

"Owdacious," said James. "Drat her, she always were owdacious, worn't she?" he continued, scratching his head. When he saw Austin frown and shake his head: "I mean she always were a owdacious fine woman of her age."

"Where did you say she was?" said Austin.

"Where is she?" said James, getting desperate and rebellious. "Why, she's upstairs, and she's downstairs, and she's in my lady's chamber; all three at once sometimes. She always were a deuce of a woman to come round a corner on you sharp; but since the will was read, she shall come round a corner again any woman in England for a new hat, or a tripe supper for eight. The gals is losing flesh over her. They was giggling upstairs the day before yesterday, and I see her come slipping out of the drawing-room like a old pussy-cat, and so I hits myself down the back-stairs with a tray-full of glasses, and brings her *that* way, and now the ungrateful minxes wants to do me out of a shilling."

"I hope you caught it, sir?" said Austin.

"Catch it? There, let's talk about something else, Master Austin. However, I can always stop her when I have had enough. Come on."

"I hope you didn't answer her."

"I only told her not to regard my feelings, for that I

was used to the ways of old people, and that when people came to her time of life, they naturally got brittle in the temper, the same as they lost their teeth."

"How could you say such a thing, James? You know if you go on like that she will be obliged to ask Miss Eleanor to discharge you. And I warn you that, deeply attached as I and she are to you, I could not say a word in your favour."

"She'll never ask Miss Eleanor to do that. I know too much." And so saying, he opened the drawing-room door, and announced

"Master Austin."

Eleanor rose up and came towards him; she held out her hands towards him, but that was not enough; she took both his hands in hers, but that was not enough either; so the poor innocent, silly little body burst out a-crying so piteously that Austin took her in his arms and kissed her.

"I am so miserable, dear brother," she said. "How kind of you to come to me."

"And I, dear sister, am so unhappy too," said Austin, who, ten minutes before, had been galloping and shouting with Lord Charles Barty across the common. He did not mean to be hypocritical or untrue. He did really think he was unhappy, and so he was.

"What is the matter, dear Austin?" she said. "I ask for a very selfish reason. If you will tell me your sorrows, I shall certainly forget mine. So you have been staying at the Cecils?"

"Yes."

"And what did you think of —— Ah, Austin, you wrote me no merry letters from there. You would not confide in me about that. I expected a long letter, filled, as usual, with wild admiration for the last ineligible young lady; but when none came, I, knowing Fanny Cecil, knew what had happened at once."

"What do you mean?"

" Knew that you had fallen in love for the first time in your life."

" By Jove, Eleanor, you are right. How you guessed that I cannot tell."

If these two — this handsome, noble young lad, and this quiet, dark-haired girl — had at that moment been in the Palace of Truth, Eleanor would have answered :

" Because I have loved you and none other ever since I could love any one, and because I shall never love any other man as I do you to the day of my death."

But they were in an old red-brick house on a common in Surrey, and Aunt Maria was plainly to be seen in the paddock walking with Captain Hertford. They were in a palace which was not of truth, and so she only said :

" No one could doubt it who knew Fanny Cecil. I could have told you that she was to marry Lord Mewstone. I would gladly have saved you this, brother, but I never dreamt that you were to be thrown against her in that way. When I heard you were there I dreaded that it would happen. Why did not Charles Barty warn you ? "

" He did ; but his warning came too late."

" Ah ! he was at Turin. Austin," she said, very quietly, " I want to speak to you."

Austin looked up at her. Her hands were quietly folded before her, her eyes were more brilliant and prominent than usual, and she was very pale. Her mouth was tightly set, and there was not a twitch in the muscles of it. The upper lip and the chin, both too short at ordinary times, seemed shorter than ever now. Austin began to see what she would be like when she was an old woman.

Eleanor loved Austin so deeply, as never man was loved before, she thought. Better than herself by far ; for by the very slightest management she might marry him, advise him, feed his ambition, give him wealth and ambition, triumph with him in success, console him in disappointment, get him taught the ways of the world, bring him into society by her wealth — nay, more than all, teach him to worship at the same altar with her, to love the same God, to trust to the same hope of salvation — she would do none of these things ; she was going to give him his dismissal for ever — with a slight reservation.

And why ? Because Austin could never love her. Because if he did not love her he would merely marry her for her money. And then the consciousness that he was untrue to himself would prey on him, and render him miserable, lower his moral tone, and make him feel that his whole career was a false one.

That is the way she reasoned — that was the way she accounted for her conduct. She was one of the best and noblest little women that ever lived (as the reader will confess when he has read the book to the end) ; she reasoned in this way — it was satisfactory reasoning enough ; but, nevertheless, her own soul said something else, and would make itself heard, it said : — " He shall love me, and woo me, before he win me ! " But she said —

" Austin, do you remember my father's death-bed ? "

He said, " Yes ! " He could hardly believe that she could anticipate the very matter on which he was ready to speak. But she did so.

" I can speak to you quite openly, now your heart is so deeply engaged. You must forget everything that passed, everything he said, every hint he gave, or we must part here, once and for all."

" I know it," said Austin. " Things might have been which can never be now. My heart is gone ; I came to tell you so. I came to tell you that I would be your brother, your servant ; would go through the world at your side ; that your husband should be the friend of my heart ; but that your wealth alone would render it impossible for me to be more. Therefore, having said this to one another, we can now go through the world hand in hand, on just the same terms as we have hitherto done."

" We will, Austin. I will be aunt Eleanor to your children, and sister Eleanor to you ; but don't leave me all alone. You are the only friend I have. I dare talk to you now, brother, you see."

So they talked confidentially, till there was an alarm of Aunt Maria, and then Austin went away; this highly platonic arrangement being brought to a satisfactory termination.

A very satisfactory one, indeed. Eleanor, two minutes afterwards, had locked herself into her bed-room, and thrown herself on her bed, in a wild passion of tears, wishing that she never had been born; wishing that Austin had never seen Miss Cecil; wishing that she might die in her grief; doing everything, in short, but blaming Austin. And there she lay, till the tempest of her grief began to get less strong, and its gusts less frequent and violent, and at last raised her weary-worn little face up, and prepared to go downstairs, and be furiously scolded by her cruel old aunt. Yes, this half of the arrangement was very satisfactory; now for the other.

When Austin got back to Lord Charles Barty, he looked as black as thunder. He quarrelled with his horse, he quarrelled with his dog, and was very much inclined to quarrel with Lord Charles; but that was not an easy matter at any time, or by any person. So he contented himself with sulking all the way home, and giving short answers. Lord Charles was surprised at this. He had never seen Austin cross so long before. He did what every good fellow ought to do, when his friend is angry: he appeared concerned and anxious, but spoke of indifferent matters, leaving Austin to open his grief to him.

When they came to Mortlake, Austin said, "Let us ride on to London, Charles."

"Yes, suppose we do. I should like it. Will you take Robin?"

"Yes, I think so. You can trust him anywhere."

"Yes, he is a wise fellow, that Robin," said Lord Charles. "'Way forrid, Min!' that's what the Scotch shepherds say to their dog. See, he is gone away like

a thunderbolt after imaginary sheep. He is a fine fellow."

" I say, Charles."

" Ay, ay !"

" I have made such a cursed fool of myself."

So the second half of the grand platonic arrangement
seemed far from satisfactory also.

Chapter XI

LATE as it was, Austin and his friend posted off to join
their reading party at Bangor, and with them went the
dog Robin, of course.

There were nine of them in that reading party, and they
spent that summer — one of those happy golden periods
which surely comes at least once in a man's life, unless he
be an exceptionally unfortunate one. Very unlucky must
be the man be who has no golden age to look back at fondly
in after years. Dull must be the life of a child who cannot say, " Once, in spring-time, I went into a meadow,
and gathered cowslips."

Lucky, again — fortunate beyond most men — must
these nine have been, if any other period ever came, in
any of their lives, sufficiently happy to make them forget
this summer of theirs at Bangor, in 1844 ; a time of youth,
health, hope, ambition, and friendship. Snowdon was behind them, the sea before, Anglesey sleeping in the sunshine, the Ormshead floating like a blue mist in the horizon, and Penmaenmawr towering black and awful above
the little white farm in the wood at Aber. Golden sands,
blue sea, and slow-sailing summer-clouds aloft.

Were they idle ? Oh, dear, yes. Seven of them, God
bless them, were horribly idle. The good Professor
scolded, predicted that they would all be either " gulfed "
or " ploughed ; " said he sincerely hoped that they would

be ; said that the foundations of justice would be sapped at the root if they weren't : but it was no use ; they all loved him too well to mind him. They were very good for a few days after one of these terrible jobations ; but then two of them would be missing at their hour, the Professor would go to their lodgings, and find from their landlady, that some idle villain of a university man, who was not going to be in the October term, had arrived promiscuously, in the town, and had induced them to go off to Llyn Ogwen, or some of those places, the names of which the good Professor will hate to his dying day.

Hayton and Dayton went and lodged at Garth, because it was out of the way, inconvenient, and dirty, and a mile from the scene of tuition. Hayton, who was fat, fished for four months from the end of the pier, and caught nothing, but smoked 8 lb. 9 oz. of tobacco. He also, during this time, made love to Maria Williams, the pilot's daughter, and proposed to her on Michaelmas-day, after the goose dinner, on which occasion she refused him in favour of Owen Owens, a young ship-carpenter. Dayton, meanwhile, bought the yacht *Arhydanos*, of 1 cwt. register ; length between perpendiculars, 6 feet 4 inches ; extreme breadth, 18 inches ; depth of hold, 2 feet 6 inches ; and essayed to drown himself therein ; and did not succeed merely because, whenever he put forth into the deep, three or four small fishing-boats used to follow him, and when he was capsized — which happened every time but one when he went out — used to pick him up, and fight for him, at the rate of half a crown a-head per man, and a shilling for boys ; being at the rate of thirty shillings a voyage.

Horton and Morton did not live in Bangor, but stayed at Aber, five miles off, because it was out of the way and more expensive ; and they got so attached to the good people there, and the good people there so attached to them, that they refused to move into the town, though the Professor fulminated about it. They were the most tiresome fellows of all; for, not content with idling about, shooting seagulls and stints themselves, they would think nothing of getting half the party to dine with them, and, after dinner, of seducing the whole lot of them up the glen by the waterfall, and over the summit of Carnedd Llewellyn to Capel Curig, a trifling distance of fifteen miles or so, and sending them home to Bangor, after a couple of days, by Nant Frangon.

The other seven lived in Bangor, and were not so intolerably idle as these two. Only two of the whole party read really steadily and well, and those two were Austin Elliot and Lord Charles Barty.

Was Austin happy? I am afraid so; although he would have been very angry if any one had accused him of it. He was by way of being miserable. He thought he was, but he was quite mistaken. In the first place, he was getting over the disappointment about Miss Cecil; and in the next, there is pretty nearly as much pleasure as pain in an affair of that sort. For is that strange wild yearning jealousy, pain? Catch me a man, a penniless, friendless man, with all his hopes broken, and all his friends gone, and ask *him*. Ask him what he would give to feel his bitterest disappointment of this kind over again.

No, he was not unhappy. A nine days' affair of the kind does not, in this barbarous island, hit so very hard. The more refined French smother themselves with charcoal; or, as two of them did a few years ago, take a warm bath, put on a clean shirt, and blow their brains out simultaneously, leaving behind them what we barbarians would call a horribly blasphemous paper. But Austin's class was nearly safe, and so he read hard, and made it so.

This visit of his to Tyn-y-Rhaiadr was a very important one; for he not only fell in love with Miss Cecil, in itself an important affair, but he also made the acquaintance of Captain Hertford; and, moreover, had the dog Robin given to him as a present.

Austin Elliot

They had been at Bangor about a month, when one day Austin went out to Aber, in the afternoon, with Horton and Morton, for he was rather fagged with work, and left Lord Charles at home at Bangor over his Pindar. They went a-fishing for the smallest sample of trout I know of on the face of the whole globe, that evening, and caught a few of them; and in the evening stood under the highest waterfall in Wales, and saw the lace-like threads of water streaming over the black rocks from a height of one hundred and eighty feet, and after that turned merrily homewards.

Between the waterfall and the sea at Aber is one of the most extraordinary shoreless chasms I have ever seen. The stream runs through it, but, as we used to believe, no man has ever been through it since Creation. It is half a mile long, a succession of shoreless lyns and slippery rocks. And Austin, coming to the upper end of it, proposed to swim through. He never did, though some one else has actually done so since; for as he was beginning to undress himself, with that eagerness and haste with which young British and Irish men of three-and-twenty hail the opportunity of drowning themselves, or breaking their necks, Robin bounded joyously forward, and some one appeared coming rapidly towards them. They saw, in a few minutes, that it was Lord Charles Barty.

"Austin," he said, breathlessly, "the Lords have reversed the sentence of the lower courts, and acquitted O'-Connell. The only one of the four who went for him was Brougham."

"I told you so," said Austin. "What a noble way of smothering him. And old Brougham against him, eh? Lord! what a world it is;—old Brougham, eh? Conceive the slyness of the man, will you?"

"Don't you impute low motives," said Lord Charles; "it is the habit of a young and unformed mind."

"Go to Bath," said Austin. "I say, I am going to swim through this chasm."

" No, don't be an ass," said the other. " Come and walk with me; I have something to tell you."

" So you didn't come all this way to tell me about Dan, then ? " said Austin.

" No," said he. " I got tired of my work, and I thought of you and the other fellows having a jolly evening here, and I came out in a car. Besides, I have seen some one since you left."

" Who ? "

" Why, Lord and Lady Mewstone. They have come from Chester, and are going on to Tyn-y-Rhaiadr to-mor-row morning. He has called at your lodgings, and he is going to call again; and — and I thought I would come out and tell you, old fellow; that is all."

" By Jove, you are a good fellow," said Austin; " what the deuce should I do without you ? What had I better do ? "

" Let us stay here. You don't know what Hertford may have said, or what *she* has heard. As for *him*, his nose is far too high in the air for him to suppose that you had ever thought of her otherwise than as a goddess. Hertford would never have dared to let him hear anything. If he had, he would not be so affectionate."

" But do you think that she ever guessed ? "

" Lord knows ! I don't understand women. Hertford knows that you were deeply taken with her. How do you or I know whether he hasn't used that knowledge to keep his position with her ? How do you know, that in a gentle way, he has not let her know that he knows it, and so avoid the *congé* which he would most certainly get, the moment she came into power ? She is afraid of Mew-stone — everybody is afraid of him. I wouldn't go back to Bangor to-night. Stay here till they are clear off; it won't do you any good to see her again; and if she sees you, and if Hertford has been saying anything (may the deuce con-found him !) she might look confused, or something. So let's stay here at Lewis's and have a rubber."

And so they stayed and had a rubber, and poor Austin played very bad, trumped his partner's (of course, Lord Charles', for people generally pay dearly for actions of good nature in small things) knave, led out strong suits of trumps without any suit to follow, 'bottled' them when his partner led them first time round, drew two trumps for one — did, in fact, everything but revoke, from which he was kept by a mere brute instinct. Instead of thinking of his cards, he was thinking of Lady Mewstone, about whom he had as much business to think as of Noah's eldest daughter, about whose existence we have no information. But he had a patient, affectionate partner, who only laughed louder at each blunder. Lord Charles would do more for him than lose three-and-twenty shillings. Austin paid him for all his affectionate forethought one day. We shall see how.

The next morning, Lord and Lady Mewstone had disappeared in a cloud of dust towards Caernarvon. And Austin and his friend walked into Bangor, in time to take their hour with the good Professor.

The next night but one, Austin sat up very late over some work. He had hardly been in bed more than three hours, when he was awoke by being shaken, and, turning over, saw Lord Charles standing over him.

"Let me sleep," he said. " I am so tired. I have hardly got to bed."

" Get up, Austin," said the other. " We have been down to bathe. There is a screw steamer coming up the Straits. I am nearly sure it is the Pelican."

Austin was out of bed in a moment, and dressing quickly, ran down to the point. It was the dear old Pelican, lying about two hundred yards out from the point, with a little steam coming from her steam-pipe, every now and then giving a throb or two with her propeller, just enough to keep her beautiful sharp bows stationary against the green sea-water, for the tide was setting strongly down the Straits towards the bridge.

They have never improved on the model of the Pelican any more than they have on the model of the Great Britain. The lines of the Pelican, however, were more like those of the Himalaya than those of the Great Britain. If you put your two hands together before your face, expand them till they form a right angle with one another, and then bring them together until they form half a right angle, your two hands will have nearly represented the sides of the Pelican from bow to stern.

The Professor, and Horton, and Morton, were all there after their bathe, and, as Lord Charles and Austin came up, were admiring the beauty of the vessel. And, after a moment, Austin said —

"It *is* the Pelican, and there is my governor. Let's all come on board."

There never was such a reasonable proposition. They all bundled into a boat together at once. The Professor, when they were seated, reminded Horton that his hour came before breakfast, and that therefore they must not be more than ten minutes. Horton, finding himself on the high seas, grew insolent and mutinous, and broached the extraordinary theory, that the powers and jurisdiction of a coach or tutor, did not extend beyond low water-mark. The Professor fired up at this, and challenged him to produce his authority, and they were in full wrangle, and both beginning to get angry, when the boat swung to under the yacht's side, and they all had to tumble up on deck. It now appeared that the dog, Robin, had stowed himself away under a thwart, and, having discovered himself, was walking about in a dangerous way over the top of everything, proposing to do frightful things with himself, unless taken on board. When he was hoisted on deck, during which process he was as good as gold, he sent Aunt Maria's Pomeranian, head over heels, down the engine-room ladder.

At the gangway they were met by a handsome old gentleman — a genial, good-tempered-looking old gentleman

— whose eyes brightened up when they met Austin's, and there, somehow, they were all looking another way for a moment, as gentlemen will on certain occasions. But only for one moment ; in the next Austin was introducing them to his father, with an air of triumph in his handsome face, as if he was saying, " Come now, which of you has got such a governor as I ? "

" Mr. Elliot," said the Professor, " one of my pupils has mutinied in the boat, and has insulted me. He says that my authority does not extend beyond low water-mark."

" He is perfectly right, my dear sir," said Mr. Elliot. " I know, in the way of business, *a little* of that sort of thing, and you haven't a leg to stand on. If it were not so, your authority is merged into mine on my own deck. Ask Phillimore — ask any one. Gentlemen, I request that you will immediately come aft. Lord Charles Barty, a word with you."

He spoke to him for a moment, and then Lord Charles ran to the engine-room ladder, and roared out — " Go ahead full speed," and then ran to the side and called out — " Cast off the painter there." And cast off that painter was, and ahead at full speed that vessel went, with the Professor protesting against piracy and deforcement, threatening to take the matter into the Arches, protesting that Hayton was coming for his hour at ten, that he would be plucked, and that his widowed mother would sink into her grave broken-hearted ; but the cranks were gleaming, and the screw was spinning, and her head was for Holy Island, and they were all laughing at him, and so the Professor laughed himself.

" Father," said Austin, " you have stole Aunt Maria's dog, and my dog has tumbled it down into the engine-room."

Mr. Elliot had no time to explain, for, coming aft they saw that there were two ladies on board, sitting close to the wheel. The one, a large red-faced, ill-tempered looking lady, who was Aunt Maria, and a sweet, gentle, dark-looking little lady, almost like a Frenchwoman, who was Eleanor.

" By Jove," thought Austin, for an instant, " Eleanor is really very pretty. And how well she dresses ! "

Mr. Elliot presented the Professor and the pupils to Aunt Maria, and she received them graciously, though she was horribly cross (why you will guess soon). So Austin and Eleanor had just a few words together by themselves.

" Dear Eleanor."

" Dear Austin."

" How on earth did Aunt Maria and you come to go to sea with the governor ? If she offers to marry him, I'll ——"

" Don't be ridiculous, Austin dear. Suppose she was to hear you ? "

" She couldn't hate me worse than she does. I was only joking. I know the governor too well. But how was it ? "

" I had to have change of air, and Mr. Elliot asked us. We, neither of us, mind the sea, you know. So we came."

They had time to say thus much, and then it became necessary to introduce the Professor and Horton and Morton to Eleanor. Austin stood beside her while they were presented. There was one look in all the three faces, that of pleased admiration. He looked at her again.

" I never thought Eleanor pretty," said his most serene, illustrious, and imperial high mightiness to himself. " But these fellows seem to admire her. University men always admire every girl they come across," continued the *blasé* man-of-the-world, who had just been confessing to his friend that he knew nothing of that world. " And, besides, she *has* a sweet little face of her own," concluded the real Austin Elliot.

So she had. At breakfast, in the pretty decorated cabin, while the green water was seething past them, and through every open port-hole, the purple Caernarvonshire mountains were seen over the summer sea, as though set in a frame: at that pleasant breakfast, in the fresh morning air, it was evident that both Horton and Morton were quite of that opinion. Whether they talked to her, to Austin, to Lord Charles Barty, or to one another, they always looked at her, and watched to see what *she* thought of what they said. They were two clever young fellows, but they seemed more brilliant than usual this morning; they were two handsome young fellows, but they seemed handsomer than usual now; there was a grander air about them than usual. In ordinary times, among their fellows, they could be coarse and rude with the rest; but here, before this dark-eyed little girl, there was an air of high-bred chivalrous courtesy about them, not only towards her, but towards every one else. There was something about Eleanor which had changed them, had put them on their mettle. There *was* something in that girl after all. Austin was getting proud of Eleanor, in the same way as a Scotchman is proud of Glenlyon, as if he had helped to make it.

And Lord Charles Barty, good soul, sat and looked on, and laughed to himself — things were going on as he wished.

Aunt Maria was by way of being a clever woman; and, indeed, she was a clever woman in one way, though possibly if one had told her the grounds on which one considered her clever, she would have been very angry. She could talk about nearly everything, and had so much of the dexterity of a woman of the world, that her knowledge, by no means small, was made to go a very long way. She was very cross at Austin's getting Eleanor at the other end of the table, among his friends; but she knew it was no use being cross. The Professor had been handed over to her bodily, and she applied herself to her task with a will, and her task was twofold — to show off her own knowledge to him, and to pick his brains for future use.

Chapter XII

AFTER breakfast they all went on deck. Now, Mr. Elliot was an old-fashioned man, who hated smoking, and never for one instant tolerated it on his quarter-deck. But this did not prevent Austin wanting a cigar; and, besides, he wanted to think somewhat — wanted, in fact, to think about Eleanor, and the cause of her amazing success that morning. "The little brown thing," he thought, "how wonderfully pretty she is!"

The moment he came on the main deck, Robin loped up to him, and jumped on him; after that he dropped his tail and ears, and followed him.

The proper place to light your cigar is in the engine-room, particularly when the chief engine-man is your most particular friend and gossip. So Austin went down the engine-room ladder, while Robin stood atop, with his head on one side, one ear up and the other down, waiting to see whether or no his master would come up that way again, or whether he had to run round and meet him somewhere else. Aunt Maria's Pomeranian came and looked down too, but, not being able to understand the situation, sat on the deck and proceeded with his toilet.

"And how's a' wi' ye, Master Austin?" said the chief engineer. "How's a' wi' ye, my bonnie young gentleman?"

"So so, George. Well enough. I say, old man, you haven't got that meerschaum of yours? Let us have a quiet pull at it, with some of the Cavendish. When I do come to sea, I don't care a hang for cigars."

Austin had some other low tastes beside dog-fancying, you see. He preferred tobacco to cigars. He had his wicked will, and when he was in the first stage of complaining, he said —

"How is she, Geordie?"

" She's vera weel. She's going her sixty-twa."

" Those boxwood bearings didn't do, did they ? "

" They didna do so bad, but the hornbeam are better. Aye, none but a Scotchman would turn ye out such engines as they."

" Why they are Penn's, of Greenwich."

" Ayè ! aye ! aye ! they are Penn's, of Greenwich, De'il doubt it. There's his name on them. But wha made 'em ? A Scotchman, sir ; a Falkirk man."

" I don't believe you, Geordie. I have a good mind to take you by the hair of your head and bang your head against the companion-ladder, for that dreadful story."

" Oh, ye'll no do that to yer old Geordie. Hey, my bonnie bonnie boy, ye have got some Scot's blude in ye. Never such a bonnie boy as you came out of England. Where got ye yon dog ? "

" Miss Cecil gave him to me."

Geordie turned his noble Wilkie-like face round on him for one instant, and then turned it away again. He said —

" Mistress Cecil ! That's my Leddy Mewstone."

And Austin said " Yes." That was all they said ; but Austin knew that, somehow, his old friend George had heard something about him and Miss Cecil, so he held his peace.

" Yon's a bonnie dog," continued Geordie. " There is na such dogs in the world. No, my bonnie — my gude sir, I mean to say — no man kens what bonnie dogs are yon. That dog would follow you to death."

Austin peeped up the companion, and saw that they were all come out of the cuddy, and were on the quarter-deck (which, in this ship, was merely the roof of that house on deck which was called the cuddy). He had not finished his pipe yet, and determined to go forward ; so he passed by the machinery, and came up by the fore-companion, and found himself among the crew.

The watch were congregated round something — something with a sharp old voice belonging to it, which Austin thought was tolerably familiar to him, more particularly after he had heard it say —

" Believe that yarn ? In course I believe it. As a general rule, mind you, sailors is the very drattedest liars as walks. But this here ship's company, mind you, forms the remarkablest and astoundingest exception to that there rule, ever I hearn on. I should no more think of doubting anythink as any member of this ship's company took in his head to try and make me swaller on, than I should think of sitting on this here harness-cask, and a watching of cook's boy peeling of the taters with his nasty dirty little hands."

As the old man to whom the voice belonged was doing exactly what he described, his profession of faith in the veracity of the ship's company, was hailed with a roar of laughter by every one except the man who had " pitched the last yarn." Immediately after, they saw that Austin was among them, and drew off, smiling and touching their locks to him. He was a great favourite here, as elsewhere.

" Well, James ! " said he to Miss Hilton's old footman, for it was he.

" Well, Master Austin ! " said the old man, nursing one of his legs on the top of the harness-cask, " And so you're come to sea, eh ? and brought a hull biling on 'em with you. And a elderly cove, to walk up and down the quarter-deck along of Aunt Maria, while the young uns makes love to Miss Eleanor."

" Don't be an old fool, James," said Austin, laughing.

" You might as well say to a sailor," said the old man, raising his voice so that the ship's company might hear him, " you might as well say to a sailor, don't be a liar ! I might as well say to you, Master Austin, don't you be a *young* fool. Ah, well we can't help it, none on us ! We're all as God made us ; we was all born so, and as such we must remain."

" Were you born an old fool, then, you most disagreeable old porcupine ? " said Austin.

" No, I warnt," said old James, tartly ; " I was born a young 'un. My character has deweloped ; yours will dewelope in the same way as mine if you live long enough ; which Lord forbid ! "

" Come, old fellow ! you don't mean that ? "

" Yes I do, when I see some things. I don't want none that I loves to live too long, and see what I see. And I loves you, and you knows it."

" What's the matter now, old fellow ? "

" Drat the whole country of North Wales, say I ! " was the reply, " with its mountains, and its waterfalls, and its new lighthouse on the Lleyn, and its comings on board at Aberystwith, and its going ashore again at Caernarvon, accause you were at Bangor, and leaving she to stump up and down the quarter-deck, along of a tutor, in her aggravating old lilac jean boots ! Drat it all ! if it warn't for Miss Eleanor I'd go into an alms-house ! "

At the mention of the quarter-deck and jean boots, Austin looked there. Aunt Maria was walking up and down with the Professor. She *had* got on lilac jean boots ; and, what is more, those jean boots were the most important thing which took your eye. For being eight or nine feet over Austin's head, and her feet therefore more than a yard above his eyes, her whole figure was (to him) unnaturally foreshortened, as in early photographs.

Austin looked at Aunt Maria for one instant, and saw that James was alluding to her ; he turned round to mildly rebuke the old man, but the old man had been too clever for him. He had gone into the galley, and sat himself down alongside of the great fat jolly cook, in front of the coppers, with his heels under him like a tailor, watching the pots and pans on the stove. The cook caught Austin's eye, and gave a fat wink towards Austin, and a nod at the old man, as if he would say, " here he is." And lest you may think this a liberty on the part of the cook, I must tell you that Austin had been cook's very good friend, ever since he was six years old.

The engineer had let him know that Captain Hertford had been on board; and so when old James had talked in his grotesque and rambling way about some one having gone ashore at Caernarvon, Austin knew what he was alluding to. Captain Hertford! What could have made his father take him on board? And, moreover, now he came to think, why had his father brought Aunt Maria to sea with him? He wished he could get his father alone. At this moment, the Master came forward.

"Where is the governor, Mr. Jackson?" said Austin, suddenly; "he is not on the quarter-deck."

"Alone in his cabin, Master Austin," said the Master; "now's your time or never."

"Thanks!" said Austin, and bolted aft at once. He ran through the saloon, and opened the door of his father's cabin; his father was there, seated before a tableful of papers.

"My own boy!" said Mr. Elliot; "I thought you were never coming to me ——"

And we will go on to that part of the conversation which relates to the story which I have got to tell.

"Father," said Austin, "how come you to have Aunt Maria on board?"

"Dear little Eleanor was ordered a sea-voyage," said Mr. Elliot, drumming on the table with his fingers, "and so I offered her one, and she accepted it gratefully. Aunt Maria is her natural guardian, though she *is* of age."

"Who? Aunt Maria?"

"Don't be a puppy to me, on board my own yacht. You know who I mean."

"His own yacht! O Lord!" replied Austin. "Think of the pride and conceit of the man for an instant, will you have the goodness? O Lord!"

"Don't you be a puppy, sir, or I shall be very angry with you. Some one might hear you."

" Did it cut itself, shaving, in two places this morning, in consequence of the rolling of its own yacht ; and did it pull two tufts of nap off its best hat and stick them on its countenance ; and didn't everybody see what had happened the moment it appeared on the quarter-deck, and didn't they all grin and giggle most confoundedly ! "

" *Pax !* Austin, *pax !* " said Mr. Elliot, trying to look grave. " Come, don't waste time here in gibing at me, you have plenty of time for that ashore."

" Oh no, I haven't. If you were a civil person, you would come and live near me. There is not a soul in Bangor that I can chaff, as I dare to chaff you."

" Now you are going to be a monkey again."

" No I am not, only a puppy. Man, do you know how I will pay you out, for calling me those two names ? "

" Austin, my boy, be serious. Aunt Maria will be blundering down here presently, and spoiling our *tête-à-tête*, and you will find her deuced difficult to dislodge."

" Aren't you going to marry Aunt Maria, then ? " said Austin.

" I have not quite made up my mind about that," said Mr. Elliot. " I have very nearly done so, but I think there is something due to her feelings."

Austin was sufficiently sobered now. He sat down on a form, and watched his father eagerly, with a pale face.

" She has fifteen thousand pounds," continued Mr. Elliot. " A man at my time of life don't marry for love, Austin. Besides, *you* want some one to advise, strengthen, and lead you ; and who is there like Miss Hilton ? Yes, Austin, for your sake — for your sake only, my dear Austin, I have determined to ——"

Austin leapt up with something like an oath.

" Your gratitude is very natural, my dear boy," said Mr. Elliot ; " mind, it is for your sake alone that I marry. Say not another word. If my own inclinations were consulted, I should object to marry the most ill-tempered, unprincipled woman I ever met. But you are my first object, of course."

"Father, dear father, you are not in earnest?"

"No, but I told you to be, a quarter of an hour ago, and you wouldn't be. So I have taken this means to make you so, you butterfly. You see there are two sides to a joke."

"Yours was a cruel one," said Austin.

"Not so cruel as your coupling my name with that old woman's, my boy; don't do it again. Now listen to me soberly and seriously, will you?"

Austin did not reply. He was standing behind his father's chair, with his arm round his neck, and their faces so close together that they touched each time the vessel rolled.

Mr. Elliot went on. "Attend closely to what I say, Austin, my dear; and if anything happens to me, remember every word of it. Coming up the coast, I put in at Aberystwith."

"So I heard, dad," said Austin; "*I* am on your track."

"And there Captain Hertford came on board. You know Captain Hertford?"

"Yes; go on."

"I know him pretty well. He almost *asked* me for a passage, but I did not encourage him. But Aunt Maria, as we will call her, came to me and asked for him in set terms, and then, of course, I treated him with the greatest *empressement*, and had him on board."

"Good, father; speak low."

"Well, my boy," said Mr. Elliot, with his lips almost against Austin's ear, "there is a secret between Aunt Maria and that man, and I'll be hanged if I know what it is."

"Charles Barty, father," said Austin, "gives a very bad character of Captain Hertford. Mayn't he know something about Aunt Maria?"

"Go on," said Mr. Elliot. "Let us hear your say out."

" You know that Aunt Maria, when five-and-twenty, followed a certain captain to India, and came home again still Miss Hilton, without improving her condition in any way, except getting herself cured of sea-sickness, to which fact we are indebted for her presence here to-day. You know that."

" I know it, go on."

" Do you think that he knows anything to Aunt Maria's disadvantage, eh ! — anything of that sort ? "

" Perhaps ; not a bad guess for a very young man. Do you know who Captain Hertford is ? "

" I know something about him."

" I know very little. I know that he is unprincipled — that he is the man who helped poor Robert to his ruin."

" Robert Hilton ! "

" Aye ! Robert Hilton ; and that he has some secret with Aunt Maria, and that she is helping him to marry Eleanor Hilton, and her nine thousand a year ; that is all."

Austin brought his fist down on the table with a crash, and said something.

" Don't swear, sir — don't swear," said Mr. Elliot ; " it is not good *ton* to swear before your father, sir. The only time when a young man ought to swear, sir, is when he wakes up one fine morning, and finds that he has flown his kite a devilish deal too high, and that Miss Cecil had thought as much of him as she did of the groom that lifted her on her horse. Then a man *might* swear, sir, even before his father ; but not when he is leaving a sweet, amiable, beautiful — aye ! beautiful, in your teeth ! — young girl to be the prey of a rogue like Hertford. And — never mind ! you had no right to swear in my presence, sir ! *I* don't care about nine thousand a year, God knows ! You will have about fifteen hundred ; but you are a fool."

" But, father, I love Miss Cecil."

" No, you don't ! you love Lady Mewstone, and are therefore a knave as well as a fool. D—n it ! here's aunt

Maria herself. Sit down, and don't begin to grin again, you monkey."

" You had no business, sir, to swear in my presence," said Austin, as Aunt Maria opened the cuddy-door. " It is not good *ton* for the father to swear before his son, sir ! The only time when an old man ought to swear sir — "

" Hold your tongue, sir," said Mr. Elliot.

" Has your father been swearing, then ? " said Aunt Maria.

" Dreadfully ! " said Austin.

" Then I wish," said Aunt Maria, " that he would — I don't say swear, because I don't uphold that, even in a sainted man like your dear father ; but I wish he would say something strong about that dog of yours."

" What has he been at, Miss Hilton ? "

" At — nothing ! But he is such an ugly cur."

" Well, my dear Miss Hilton, he shall be out of your way in a few hours. By the bye, dad, you must set us ashore at Conway. Hayton is waiting for his hour with the professor. The loss of two hours might pluck him."

" All right," said Mr. Elliot; " her head will be that way presently — in fact, is so now. I am going on deck."

" Well, Austin," said Aunt Maria, when they were left alone, " and how are you, sirrah, eh ? "

" I am very bad," said Austin.

" Good heavens ! what's the matter — meagrims, hysterics, or what ? "

" I don't know."

" They say that you flew your kite at that girl of George Cecil's who has married that prig, Lord Mewstone. I denied it when they told me. I said you were not very wise, but that you weren't such a fool as that."

Austin looked at Aunt Maria. What a coarse, violent face it was. Old Hilton's sister. Well, *he* had a coarse, violent vein in him too, and she was something like him. He looked her in the face for a second, and then said, with a smile, " Give me your arm, and come on deck. Don't

be disagreeable, that's a good soul ; " which course of proceeding puzzled Aunt Maria, and made her do what he
told her.

And Mr. Elliot was as good as his word. He took them
for a cruise on that glowing Summer's day, and there was
not one of them who did not, ever after, connect the memory of the kind, good, and just old man, with one of the
most delightful days in their life.

They went to Holy Island, where the preventive men
had grown pale and flabby, from eating rabbits, and the
atmosphere was laden with the scent of onions, and where
the oldest of them looked, with his long grey hair in the
wind, not at all unlike an old rabbit, with a lot of onion
sauce emptied over his head : and where Mr. Elliot frightened the population out of their wits, by telling Lieutenant
Hodder, of the Coast Guard, that if Sir R. B. didn't repair
a certain wall, he should be forced to " look him up,"
which, being understood by a Welch bystander, as " lock
him up," and as such being translated into Welch, caused
a report that evening in the taverns at Beaumaris, that the
Queen had sent down an English lord in a frigate, to seize
the persons, not only of Sir R. B., but of the Hon. Col. D.
P., and Mr. A. S., and commit them all to the Tower, till
they had purged themselves of their contempt, which circumstance illustrates the advantage of a portion of her
Majesty's subjects talking Welch, while the rest talk English.

And re-embarking they went eastward, and at lunch
time were steaming merrily under the limestone slabs of
the Orm's Head, watching the brimming sea leap on to the
black ledges in fountains, and pour from them in cascades,
and Penmaenmawr hanging 1,500 feet aloft behind, a
wrinkled mass of purple stone. Then Conway castle, and
affectionate farewells in the pleasant Summer evening,
Eleanor, and Mr. Elliot, standing on the quarter-deck, arm-
in-arm, and waving their hands at them, to the very last. A
glorious day finished by a pleasant drive home, under the

over-hanging crags, with Robin leading the way, a hundred yards ahead, barking joyfully, as if he so approved of the whole proceedings that he could not hold his tongue.

" By Jove," said Horton, as they drove under Penmaen-mawr, " what a glorious creature it is ! "

" Ah ! " said Lord Charles, " is she not."

Austin looked suddenly and stealthily at him, and Lord Charles took the opportunity, suddenly and stealthily also, of making a face at Austin.

" Is she French, Elliot ? " said Horton.

" French ! oh dear, no," replied Austin. " She was built by White, of Cowes."

" Who was ? " said Horton, in amazement.

" The Yacht. The Pelican," said Austin.

" I was talking about Miss Hilton," said Horton.

" Ah ! I wasn't," said Austin.

" But is she French, you stupid ? " said Horton.

" No, she ain't," said Austin.

" She looks like it," said Horton.

" Does she ? " said Austin.

" The island of Anglesea, at which we are looking," said the Professor, suddenly, " is the Mona of the Agricola of Tacitus. The Mona Cæsaris is evidently the Isle of Man. In the latter case, a corruption of the Latin has been retained ; in the former—"

" Well, you needn't be sulky, Elliot," said Horton, rudely stopping the Professor's good-natured attempt at changing the subject, by saying the first thing he could think of.

" I ain't sulky, old fellow," said Austin, eagerly, " by Jove, no. I'll tell you all about it. Her mother was a French woman. It was a deuced good guess of yours. She is a noble little body, is she not ? I am so proud at all of you admiring her so, you can't think. She is, as it were, my sister you know."

The Professor, who was sitting next to Austin, quietly patted him on the back. They were all merry again directly. No one ever could withstand Austin's good humour, and it was quite useless to try. Even for Aunt Maria.

That day, Hayton had come for his hour's logic, and had met the Professor's mother in the hall. The kind old lady was in profound despair. Hayton was the only " shady " man of the lot ; the only " pass " man of the whole. The Professor never took mere pass men. He had made an exception with regard to Hayton, because he was one of the most popular men in the University. Every day was of importance. It would be so dreadful, thought old Mrs. Professor, to have one of their men plucked, and poor Hayton, too ! of all others, the general favourite. She was nearly in tears when she met him in the hall. She told him that the Professor had been carried to sea, and was at that present speaking hull down. What was it ? Was it Tacitus ? She would gladly lend him Bohn's translation for an hour. If it was Latin prose, she thought — she said it so kindly and hesitatingly, " she believed — nay, she felt sure, that she could detect — any — any grammatical error, if he wouldn't be offended. But what use was it," she said. " The Professor might be away for months. The Duke of Cheshire's yacht had come, and carried off Lord Charles Barty, and the rest of them. And who could tell when they would be back. This came of having noblemen in the party. She had always been against it."

" It's very kind of you," said honest Hayton, " but it's the logic. I am afraid you cannot help me."

At this moment, Dayton came flying round the corner. " I say, old fellow," he cried out, " Shall I give you an hour's coach ? "

Old Mrs. Professor shed tears of joy ; and the two patient young men sat up in the window, with their heads together, working at the logic, while the others took their holiday on the shining summer sea.

Chapter XIII

AUSTIN'S political education was going on famously. The ultra-Tory opinions, carefully instilled into him, ever since he could talk, by his father, were bearing fruit. Austin, at the age of one-and-twenty, was a very advanced Radical.

I suppose that the very best and cleverest men have a hobby of some sort, which the rules of society prevent their mounting out of the bosom of their families. I suppose that every man could bore you to death on some one subject, if you would only let him. Mr. Elliot had a hobby, and had ridden it continuously before Austin was old enough to rebel. He had bored him with his hobby, and that hobby was political talk.

By the time Austin was ten, he determined that, by hook or by crook, he would be bored no longer. Being too young to know that there were two sides to the question, he first began his rebellion by going to sleep, upsetting things, playing with the dog, and so on, while his father was talking. These efforts were utterly futile. Mr. Elliot not only wanted to instil Tory principles into his son, but he also wanted to hear himself talk. If he could not do the one thing, he was most fully determined to do the other.

However Mr. Elliot started in one of these political diatribes, he always arrived at the same result — that of praising Mr. Pitt and the Duke to the skies. Whenever Austin heard one of those two names mentioned, he used to get desperate. He began to hate them. And, on the other hand, hearing Fox and Sir Robert Peel so steadily and systematically abused, he began, out of mere obstinacy, to long to hear what they would have had to say for themselves. If he could only get hold of facts about these two men, he thought he could at all events have a wrangle with his father, which would be better fun than sitting mumchance, and hearing about that intolerable person, Pitt.

But there was no hope left for him whatever. His father had determined that he should be a Tory, and took care to form his opinions from his own facts. He, good man, so thoroughly succeeded in boring the boy, that, at twelve, Austin was mad to get hold of some facts on the other side, and fight his father. He did not care about the truth — how should a boy of twelve years old care much about political questions? He hated the name of politics, but he hated Toryism worse. He had, by his father's management, imbibed liberal opinions, before he had heard a single argument in favour of them.

The first weapon he got into his hands was this. Mr. Elliot, most temperate of men, let out one day, that Mr. Pitt used to drink a great deal of wine. Austin seized on this, and used it with amazing dexterity. It is surprising what a desperate man will do with a very inferior weapon. A Roman would show good fight with his stylus ; on occasion : I myself, have seen Mr. Dennis Moriarty junior, do the most magnificent battle with an old fire-shovel, till overborne by numbers. Yesterday only, I was shown a wooden dagger which had just been brought from Naples, a specimen of those which are made in prison by the Bourbonists, for purposes of assassination, after their knives are taken from them ; and a very ugly weapon it was. Austin used his lath dagger — Mr. Pitt's excess in wine — with the greater success, because his father had always impressed on him, that the great vice of Fox and his companions, was drunkenness.

But, after Austin's first half at Eton, he came home with a large quiver-full of barbed arrows, which he discharged at his father with enormous effect. He had got into bad company there.

The very first day he had been turned into the playground there, he, feeling lonely and somewhat scared, found himself beside another new boy, from the same house, in the same situation. They made friends that day, and their friendship only ended with death.

This was Lord Charles Barty : a noble boy of twelve, with some brains, and more ambition. He came of a great Whig house. Whiggery, as Mr. Elliot would have called it, had been his " life element " from his birth. When Austin, after a few days, told him his leading grievance, that young gentleman, aged only twelve, was enabled, by the help of his eldest brother, Lord Wargrave, to supply Austin with a few smooth pebbles from the brook, to sling at the Tory giant, and promised to bring some more soon.

When Austin began casting these pebbles at his father, in the holidays, Mr. Elliot was both amused and pleased ; at all events his boy was turning his attention that way. He would sooner see him a Radical than see him without opinions.

Half after half, the merry battle went on between father and son. The old Tory sub-secretaries, and such men, who formed Mr. Elliot's little society, grew greyer under the audacious speculations which Austin brought from Eton each half. " These opinions," said they, " were answered when we were boys." — " But never refuted," quoth Austin. At which his father would rub his knees and laugh, and the sub-secretaries would say to one another, that Elliot was getting into his dotage, and " that boy would go to the devil, sir, as sure as you are born."

Fired by Austin's speculative questions, Lord Charles Barty supplemented his usual holiday amusements, which were not generally very varied, by gaining a little political knowledge — by picking up stones for Austin to fling at his father. His usual holiday amusements were these — to interrupt his sister's lessons as much as possible, and in the absence of the governess, to (as he called it) make hay in the school-room. When she came back, boxed his ears, and turned him out, he would go to the stables and coax and wheedle the stud-groom into giving him a surreptitious mount. Lastly, he would take his blind brother, Edward, out for a ramble through the park, through the wood, over the broad turnip-fields, up to the top-most height of Kingsdown, where Lord Edward might lie on the short turf, staring to heaven with his sightless eyes, and listening to the music of the five tall firs that moaned in the summer air overhead.

The way he gained his political information was this. Whenever he dined at table, he used to stay until his father went into the drawing-room. And in his father's house he was pretty sure to find himself, after the ladies were gone, sitting next to a pretty strong Whig. And from this tolerably strong Whig he would get opinions; the ultimate destination of which was, that they were poured out on the head of Mr. Elliot senior, to his great amusement.

So by this process, by Lord Charles Barty getting arguments and giving them to Austin, and by Austin letting them against his father, both these young gentlemen found themselves, at twenty-one, in a state of very advanced Radicalism. And, as all young men at twenty-one, if they are worth anything, have their hero, so these two young gentlemen had theirs. I need not say that that hero was Sir Robert Peel. These furious young democrats had been ashamed to confess the fact to one another, the fact that their fetish was a so-called Tory, before the time when Lord Charles galloped over the goose on Putney Common. But so it was.

What was the reason that the wildest young Radicals of those times pinned their faith on Sir Robert Peel? I suppose because they knew, that should a pinch come, he would *act*. Would pitch party formulas to the winds. Horner's resolutions, and the Catholic question, had shown them that. Their instincts showed them that he was a true Radical. As he was in one sense.

When these two young gentlemen were elected Members of the Union, then the Thames got a-fire indeed.

They uttered the most dreadful opinions. They came down to that house, sir (that was little Pickles of Brasenose : he was President), and they held in their hands all sorts of dreadful documents ; and they had yet to learn : and they saw the honourable member opposite in his place, and played the deuce with him. They were the two most terrible Radicals at the Union, these two. There was no doubt of that.

But after all said and done, they were neither of them true blue Radicals. The metal never rang clean and clear. They both stopped short. Austin politically, and Lord Charles socially.

Austin thought Lord Charles went too far. Perhaps he did. His proposition was to pull down the old house, and then begin to think about building it up again, with such materials as heaven should think fit to send ; or should heaven send no materials, to let it build itself (which no house ever did yet, except the American house, which has tumbled down, and will have to be built all over again) : this displeased Austin. Lord Charles also seemed to think that no one should do anything as long as any one else existed who could do it better ; that we *must* have the exactly right man in the right place, or we were naught. At this Austin fired up, and said that in that case, Lord Charles and he might find themselves in the position, the one of a crossing-sweeper and the other of a shoeblack.

But in Lord Charles's model republic, there were to be no crossings, and no shoes. So Austin's illustration fell to the ground, and like many other silly people, he abandoned the argument, from shame of having made a clumsy illustration.

" Then what the deuce is to become of us ? " asked Austin.

" What does it matter ? What are a few worthless martyrs, like myself, in comparison to the great cause ? "

Austin submitted that it did matter, and that they had

better not be in too great a hurry. He would sometimes, indeed, laugh at the more wild of his friend's speculations. In theory Austin was a real Radical; but he did not wish his theories to be put into practice.

Lord Charles also stopped at a certain point. He had certain Radical theories concerning marriage, with which Austin one-half agreed. For instance, that the human race were all of the same species, and that no bar should be put to marriages between young people, if they fell in love. He was a high Tractarian, and made High-Church thought fit into his political theories with the most admirable dexterity; his reverence for marriage and women was of the highest kind; and he used to say that of all things ne would admire a nobleman who would marry his gardener's daughter. Austin agreed; but when he put the converse of the proposition about the gardener's son marrying—eh! Lord Charles got in a pet, and said that Austin never would be serious, and delighted in talking infernal nonsense out of pure aggravation.

" Don't be cross, Charles," said Austin.

" I ain't cross," said Lord Charles, angrily, blundering over Robin, and giving him a kick, at the same time using a word, which will never be used in the great republic.

He *was* cross. Austin had no right to say such horrible things. Amelia and the gardener's boy. Good God!

Austin did not laugh at him. He had tripped him up, and was content. The human-race theory would not hold water, it appeared.

Lord Charles was sulky for a time; but he called Robin to him, and put his cheek against the dog's face, in that way asking forgiveness for having kicked him. Robin begged him with his great eyes to say nothing about it, and laid his beautiful head on his knee.

" You have been a fool, Austin," said Lord Charles, sulkily. Englishmen are generally sulky when they have their own weapons turned against them; have got out of temper with their friends, and want to make it up.

"Ah! I know," said Austin, laughing. "You mean about Miss — Lady Mewstone, you Jacobin! Come, let us argue the converse of your proposition on this case. Come on. There is nothing offensive here. I am Lord Mewstone's equal in talent, and in manners. Why should I not have married Miss Cecil? I consider she has thrown herself away."

"I don't think that. I think that you are his superior in everything, and yet I think you made a fool of yourself."

"Why?"

"Because they two were in love with one another, and because you passed by a girl who is far superior to that highty-tighty, ambitious, politics-chattering daughter of old Cecil's.

"Well; I know that now."

"Oh, you do, do you? And confess yourself a fool?"

"Yes."

"Then what a sublime fool you will look if you allow Aunt Maria to bully her into marrying Captain Hertford."

"Charles, you are mad."

"Raving mad," said Lord Charles; "but that is what the dear old soul is after. She has got the whip-hand of Hertford about something, and he, I suspect, has got the whip-hand of her."

"How do you find all this out?" said Austin, aghast.

"I listen to the old women talking," said he; "they know a precious sight more about it than you do."

"Well, but I can't listen to the old women. Tell us what you know."

"There's Tom going," said Lord Charles; "hadn't we better get on with our Livy, if we are going to do so at all?"

"Come, no nonsense," said Austin; "tell me what the old women told you."

"The old women didn't tell me anything. But I want to ask you a question. Why should not Eleanor Hilton marry Captain Hertford?"

"Why! why!" said Austin. "Do you want to drive me mad! Because I would cut the infernal scoundrel's throat, if he dare to look at her. That's why."

"But it don't matter to you. You have got no interest in her."

"Charles, I love her."

"You always did, I know, in a sort of way; but, with the memory of that sad affair with the Right Honourable the Countess of Mewstone so fresh on your heart ——"

"Don't chaff. The thing is serious."

"I know it is," said Lord Charles; "but tell me one thing only. Do you really mean that you will ask Eleanor to be your wife?"

"I do."

"Hurrah! Now I'll tell you I know. I was in town last night."

"Well," said Austin.

"I heard a conversation between my mother and Lord Saltire. You know Lord Saltire?"

"He always speaks to me," said Austin.

"Now then," continued Lord Charles, "old Hilton made a *faux pas*, about some French business, in 1806; and every one cut him, except your father. At this time, Lord Saltire, who had only had a trifling acquaintance with him before, thought that he would follow his favourite amusement of flying in the world's face, by taking him up, saying, that he had a profound admiration for a man with so few prejudices, or some piece of cynicism of that kind; and although Hilton saw that Lord Saltire was only amusing himself by offending the world, yet friends were scarce, and Lord Saltire's humour suited his own, and they two knocked up some sort of a friendship."

"How did you find out all this?" asked Austin.

"By listening to the old women at their gossip. Don't interrupt."

"Just one moment. Have you heard Lord Saltire and her Grace speak of this before?"

"I have gathered what I have told you from another conversation. I will now give you the gist of the last.

"Lord Saltire began by saying, 'You don't know any eligible young gentleman who wants nine thousand a year, do you?' And she said, 'there is Charles listening to us, he is in want of exactly that sum,' and then there was some fun about it, and he went on. He said that Eleanor was, from some reason, completely under her aunt's thumb, and that Captain Hertford was eternally about the house."

"He is never there when I am," said Austin.

"Never mind that. He is there when you ain't there, which is much more important. He said, that he had been to call on her, after what he had heard, and that it did really appear to be true : that the poor girl appeared cowed and beaten, and that her aunt seemed a dragon. But he said, in conclusion, 'That is not all : the girl is left utterly friendless, and without society, with this enormous fortune, to the care of this old dragon of an aunt, and to a captain of dragoons, who is a great rascal. But what is uglier than all is this : old Hilton had a son who went to the dogs and died, and the last man who knew anything about him was this Captain Hertford, who has been a flame of the aunt's.' Now all this don't look over particularly nice."

"Now we had better get on with our work," said Austin.

"By Jove, we must!" said Lord Charles ; "but you will let me know what you are going to do."

"Of course ! How can I thank you enough ? Come on."

And on they went like young heroes. At half-past three, it was found that Lord Charles's handsome blue eyes could not keep open any longer, in spite of coffee and tobacco, and that the curly head kept tumbling down on the "Riddle and Arnold." Austin roused him up, and started him across Tomquad to his rooms in Peckwater. And

Lord Charles walked straight across the grass, which he had, we believe, no right to do; and while in that bland intoxicated state, into which men get at three or four in the morning, a week before examination, he was thinking that there must surely be more than 17,000 stars visible. He so nearly walked into the pool, or pond, called Mercury, that he felt it necessary to sit down, and congratulate himself on his narrow escape.

And there he found that Austin's dog, Robin, had followed him. He was glad of this, for he could talk to Robin; and Robin was most charmed by the whole proceeding, and sat complacently down by the stone rim of the pond, prepared for any amount of conversation!

"Robin," said this silly young gentlemen, "let us look into the pond, and see whether we can tell our fortune." So he leant over the pool, and saw, at first, nothing but the gold tassel on his cap. He took his cap off, and looked. Still not one hint of the future, only the outline of his handsome head reflected in the water. The stars were behind in the dark blue. Not one single black cloud between him and them. Oh! lying stars! oh! false, false water!

But the happy, heavy head fell down on something, and Robin nestled up against him, and dog and man fell fast asleep, there and then, in the middle of the quadrangle. One of the porters, who rose early to the let the scouts in, saw him lying there, and roused him up. In times long after, a tall gentleman, stone-blind, unknown to the porter, but whom you will know soon, came to the porter, and asked about the circumstance. And the porter took him to the place, and pointed it out. "His lordship lay here, sir, with his head on his dixenary, and Mr. Elliot's dog along with 'un; and I thought he'd a caught his death of cold, surely."

"But it never hurt him, you see," said the blind stranger.

"Ah! no, poor dear! it never hurt he. Talk about your tufts, he *were* a tuft."

Chapter XIV

THE very night on which Lord Charles slept by Mercury, Austin, dog-tired as he was, sat up and wrote this letter to his father : —

"MY DEAR CHILD, —

"If you don't take my advice about having your razors properly set by an 'expert,' the end of it will be that you will be carried off to Bow Street, and charged with attempting self-destruction. The last time I came into your dressing-room, you had an open razor in your hand, and had hacked your chin so, that you were all in a gore of blood. Besides, it does not look nice to go down to your office, with your face stuck all over with patches of hat nap. If you have no self-respect, think of me.

"Now attend to what I say, and don't argue, or fuss. Charles Barty and I go into the schools in five days. The responsibility I feel in leaving you to take care of yourself, will probably spoil my degree. Don't add to it, but obey me.

"Dear father, will you do this? Call on the Hiltons, and see what is going on there. Catch Lord Saltire, and make him tell you. It is an ugly business. I don't know what to do — I trust it all to you. Only go there and watch Captain Hertford and Aunt Maria.

"I will come up as soon as the examination is over. I shall not wait for the class list. I may get a fourth, and I may not. But I shall be equally dear to you either way, you self-willed conceited young person."

The answer was : —

"MY DEAR BOY,—

"You have made me so happy. I will see to what you mention. I thought you had given her up; and I have heard nothing new about Captain Hertford. It will be difficult for me to get anything out of Lord Saltire, for I hardly know him; *and I don't think he likes me:* however, I will try. I will watch for you like a terrier at a rat-hole.

" What care I what degree you take ? Suppose you are plucked, come home to me, my boy, and I will teach you to forget it. I had rather, in fact, that you did not take honours. I think that you would do in the world quite as well without. Why don't you slip in quietly for a pass ? — but, by the bye, it is too late, and I am sorry for it."

(Are there such things as white lies, after all ? This was either a black one or a white one, for the old man was in a feverish state of anxiety about his son's degree, if it were only a fourth.)

" Don't you be an impertinent young jackanapes about my cutting myself shaving ; it will be a long while before *you* do that, you monkey ! "

Lord Charles Barty and Austin went into the schools devoutly hoping that they might not be " gulfed " (left among the pass men). But diligence and pluck will do great things. Lord Charles and Austin, having compared notes, came to the conclusion that it was all over with them, and Austin posted off to his father with the cheering intelligence that they were both probably " gulfed." Austin had certainly got his testamur, and so had his friend, but they were both quite hopeless — so hopeless, that on the terrible day, Lord Charles actually went into the school's quadrangle, and up to that dreadful little door, and pushed into the crowd to hear the lists read. He thought one of them might be among the fourth. So he heard the first Class read through with indifference, but when Class II. was announced, and the first name in that Class was " Barty, Carolus, ex Æde Christi," his ears tingled in his head with joy ; and when, after reading through two C's and a D, the clerk of the schools came to " Elliot, Augustinus, ex Æde Christi," he sent his cap flying in the air, and went fairly mad : Austin and he, to their unutterable amazement, had got seconds.

Then an insane terror possessed him lest any one, flying on the wings of the wind, should carry the news to Austin before himself. So he posted home to his rooms, told his servant to pack up a carpet-bag, and away he went, after getting a most fearful " jobation " from the Dean for daring to appear in his presence without his cap and gown.

" What do you mean by this impertinence, my lord ? How dare you ? "

" I am very sorry, sir. I have got a second, and I am excited."

" Got a second ! — bah ! The University is going to the —"

" Deuce ? " suggested Lord Charles, who was afraid of something worse.

" Dogs, sir, dogs ! How dare you say deuce in my presence ! You can go down, my lord."

Chapter XV

" Now, father," said Austin, the first night of his arrival, " what have you observed ? "

" I have been a diligent and dutiful watchman, Austin ; I have been there every day for six days, but, unfortunately, I have observed nothing at all."

" Then you think that the letter I wrote to you is all nonsense ? "

" Far from it ; I think you are quite right. I know that woman, Maria Hilton, my dear lad ; I have known her almost all my life, and, unless she has much altered, she is just this — a selfish, unprincipled shrew."

" She always struck me as being something of that sort."

" I guess, I need not tell you why, that something of

this sort is the matter. You know that she is independent?"

"No; I never knew it."

"She had fifteen thousand pounds by her *father's* will."

"I did not know that; I always thought she lived on her brother. But what has that to do with it?"

"Silly! it makes her independent — it gives an impudence to her face, and a loud tone to her voice towards her little niece, which she would never have if she were dependent on her bounty."

"Good; you are wiser than I."

"That is very easy to be, goose! Well, she has sailed her boat in troubled waters, and so has Captain Hertford. I suspect that they have some sort of mutual confidence, and that both of them would like to have the whip-hand of Eleanor and of Eleanor's six thousand a year. She has no friends — her father took good care that she should have none, by his obstinate pride — and at this present moment I believe the case stands thus: — that Aunt Maria is trying to bully and wheedle poor little Eleanor into marrying Captain Hertford."

"Then," said Austin, "I'll tell you what we'll do — that is, you and I and Robin."

"And what is that?"

"Why, we'll go to Wilton Crescent, when both Aunt Maria and Captain Hertford are there, and I will take a thick walking-stick and beat him about the head with it, while Robin bites *her* heels, and you pull her nasty old cap and wig off, and chuck them out of window."

"I think that will be the best plan," said Mr. Elliot. "Then I will come with you at two to-morrow, if I can get away from the office. Don't bring too big a stick, or else you will kill the man, and get hung, and that is very disagreeable — there are always such a lot of people to stare at you."

"Then that plan of proceedings is settled," said Austin, who knew how his father loved a "dry joke."

" Yes, that is settled ; don't be later than two, and don't bring anything thicker than a malacca cane. Now let us change the subject. Do you know the Isle of Ronaldsay, by Jura ? "

" I have never been there," said Austin, knowing that, now his father had had his joke, his real plan was coming. " I know the song : —

> ' On Jura's heath how sweetly swell
> The murmurs of the mountain bee ;
> How sweetly mourns the writhed shell
> On Jura's shore, its parent sea.'

Is that any use to the present discussion ? "

" A great deal. I see you are in love with the island, and I shall probably want you to start there to-morrow night, if you can get ready."

" Hadn't I better start to-night ? " said Austin, very much amused, but knowing perfectly well that his father had a scheme in his head, and a good one too.

" No, not to-night. Before you start, I want to see whether Miss Elliot, senior, has any objection to come for a cruise in the Pelican. She has two strings to her bow, and I am the second one. She will probably come, and bring her niece. The Pelican is lying at Liverpool, waiting to take me through the Western Islands. If Miss Hilton dreams that you are to be one of the party, she either won't come, or won't bring her niece. Therefore, I order you, as soon as I have my answer to-morrow, to depart suddenly and secretly to Glasgow, and from thence to get the best way you can to Jura, from Jura to Donaldsay, from thence across the Kyle to Ronaldsay, and find out as much as you can about the set of the tide through the Sound of Islay before I arrive in the Pelican."

" By Jove," said Austin, " you are a jewel."

" So the plan of pulling off Aunt Maria's wig falls through for the present, then," said Mr. Elliot.

" For the present," said Austin.

" Oh, only for the present, of course," said Mr. Elliot. " Good night; mind your candle against the curtains."

The next evening Austin waited for Lord Charles at Paddington, for he knew that he would come with the news of the class-list. He heard the astounding intelligence of his friend's good fortune and his own ; and, just giving himself time to tell his friend the neat little plan about the island of Ronaldsay, he jumped into a Hansom cab, and told the man to go to Mortlake.

The man did not seem to know where it was, so Austin said, — " Go to Putney, then ! "

Now, in the year 1845, telling a man to go to Putney, was the same as telling a man to go to the deuce. And so the cabman took off his nose-bag (or rather, the horse's nose-bag), and said, " Bar sell ! "

" What's the matter with the man ? " said Austin. " Didn't you hear me tell you to go to Putney ? "

The man strapped the nose-bag under his seat, took up the strut, and mounted the box ; then he opened the trap-door above Austin's head, and looking down on him, said —

" I think you told me to go to Putney just now."

" Confound it ! What is the matter with the man ? "

" Well, now, look here," said the man. " A cabman has his feelings the same as any other man. You, and such as you, may think that he ain't, but he have. And when them feelings is lacerated, he naterally cuts up rough. I never said nothink to you, but without prover-cation you tells me to go to Putney. Now I tell you what it is, *I'm blessed if I don't go*, and you may take your change out of that ! " And go he did.

If it had not been for this little escapade on the cabman's part, he would have started an instant sooner, and would not have seen Lord Charles walk past him just before the horse got in motion, walking between Captain Hertford and a man whom Austin knew as Captain Jackson, a trifling circumstance, but well remembered after. " Charles has got among the Tories," he said to himself. And so Charles had.

We must pass over Mr. Elliot's sensations on hearing of Austin's good fortune. He was both astonished and delighted. " Good heavens ! " he said to himself, " if the dear boy has got a second with so little exertion, his talents must be of first-rate order. See how idle and giddy that lad has been, by Jove ! That lad can do anything after this. An idle, giddy young butterfly, and a second : by Jove it is amazing ; he will take the world by storm : for — with his manners, and temper, and talents, he'll take the world by storm. I am glad he *was* idle ; it is a great comfort to me that he was idle. It has shown what he is made of. A second, too ! "

Mr. Elliot either did not know, or did not choose to remember, how painfully Charles had worked, and he did *not* know the awful gulf there was between Austin's second, and a first. Austin would not have undeceived him for ten thousand pounds that night.

They dined together alone. If any young gentleman, reading these pages, makes the reflection that it must have been rather a bore for Austin to dine *tête-à-tête* with his father, let me assure him that on this occasion it was not the case. Neither of them bored the other. Once, just after dinner, Mr. Elliot, looking across, under the lamp, caught Austin's eyes gazing affectionately at him. He took no notice, but Austin looked so handsome, so good, so triumphant, that the good man went up to his dressing-room for a moment to look for his spectacles.

Perhaps that was the happiest night of all. I cannot say, for Austin had, from childhood, waded on breast high among summer flowers, and had hardly known sorrow. That merry face had, however, the capability of a different expression — an expression of sorrow and furious anger combined, such as one sees in the face of a child when it is what we call " *very* naughty ; " a look which at the same time pleads for pity and hurls defiance. No man but one had ever seen that expression on Austin's face, and that one man only on one occasion. The man was Captain Hertford, and the occasion was that of their drive together from Tyn y Rhaiadr to Bangor.

" And now, dad," said Austin, lolling on the sofa, " about — I beg pardon—anent Ronaldsay."

" You ought to have started to-night, monkey ; and you should have, if you had got a beggarly third, or anything of that sort. Of course, I am bitterly disappointed at your missing your first ; and I think that, after such a fiasco, you had better get out of the way till people have forgotten all about it."

" Child, child," said Austin, without moving, " you are out of your mind ! "

" I think it will be the best way. Start for Glasgow to-morrow morning, and after Glasgow you must go north by post."

" How many stamps shall I want ? "

" By post," said Mr. Elliot, scornfully, " and get across the Kyle of Ronaldsay in one of the fishing-boats."

" Very well," said Austin ; " now tell me this — What do *you* think of Eleanor ? "

" You mean really ? "

" Yes, I mean really."

" Well ! I think she has more determination and strength of character in her little close-set mouth than fifty Aunt Marias ; and that if — well, if there is what you young fellows coarsely call a row, that she might beat Aunt Maria. But she is an affectionate and sensitive little thing, and it will require something very much out of the way to make her show fight at all; and Aunt Maria is coarse and ill-tempered, though cowardly ; and she will bully that little thing, and frighten her into submission until — until — something or another happens to make little Eleanor show fight. There."

" A lame and impotent conclusion," said Austin. " Good night."

Chapter XVI

ALL the coast of Argyleshire, and the Mull of Cantire, and the mountains beyond, were wakening up under the same sun which decorated Ben More of Ronaldsay with ribs of gold. Those who stood on the rough little pier in front of the few fishing huts which make the village of Ronaldsay, and looked eastward, saw the fields on the mainland gleaming with the gold of spring, and behind them, a wilderness of purple mountain flecked and dotted with wreaths of silver mist, flying and dissolving before the morning sun. Those who turned and looked westward saw the sheets of heath rolling up into the great sharp mountain, embroidered with a curious fretwork of bright green grass from beside the rocky watercourses. But whether they looked east or west, there was a softness in the air, and a gladness in their hearts, which told them spring was come, and that the winter, so terrible to them, poor souls, had gone howling off to the northward.

The wind was south, and the tide pouring down the Kyle of Ronaldsay, knocked up a little sea. And through that sea, a boat with two sails came leaping, and springing, and plunging towards the shore ; and when she was near enough, three or four fine fellows jumped into the surf, and had her high and dry in no time.

And then from this boat there dismounted a young gentleman, and his portmanteau, and his dog : the like of which they had never seen before ; but the like of whose dog, they had seen very often indeed. It was Austin and Robin. Austin stood, splendidly attired, handsome, good-humoured, looking among the surrounding highlands ; and Robin was making friends with three or four collies exactly like himself, and half a hundred short-legged terriers.

And as he stood upon the beach, an old man — almost

the only one who could speak English, with that courteous independence which we admire so much in the Scotch, both Highland and Lowland, when it does not develop into impertinence, asked " what he could do for his honour ? "

" A very well-timed question, sir," said Austin. " I want to stay here for a week."

The old fisherman at once did what Scotchmen always seem to do in a difficulty — sent for the minister ; and the minister did what Scotch ministers always do when they are sent for — came.

" There is not a place in the island into which you can put your head, sir, except my house," said he the instant he caught sight of Austin, saying in Gaelic " Take that gentleman's portmanteau up to the manse instantly." At at all events, up to the manse it went ; shout the gentleman, " Hi ! " and " Hold hard ! " never so loudly.

" My dear sir," said Austin, " I never dreamt of invading you like this. But, to answer for my respectability, I have got a letter of introduction from — "

" Never mind, sir. Just think what an *enormous* windfall an educated gentleman is to me. A week only, said you, sir ? "

" Not more."

" I would it were a year. Are you in Parliament, sir ? "

" Not yet," said Austin, blushing.

" If you were I would ask you to say a word for us poor islanders, sir. The winters here are unco long, sir, and we are very, very poor. I will show you the wonders of our island, sir. I cannot show you a natural temple, like Staffa, or an artificial one, like Iona ; but I will show you how men can keep body and soul together under very adverse circumstances, and be patient, honest, and godly the while. And when you are in Parliament, you'll, may be, remember the Island of Ronaldsay, and speak a word for the Scottish poor."

" But what does your landlord do for you ? "

" The island is a loss to him ; and who could be foolish enough to pitch money into these bogs ? Our place is in Canada, I fear. The winter is very long, and we are very, very poor."

" I beg to call your attention to the fact, my dear sir, that you have not read my letter from the Mactavish."

" And I beg to observe, my dear sir, that I welcomed you to my house before I knew you had one," answered the minister. " Why, my dear sir, if you were deaf and dumb, the mere sight of your clothes would make you welcome. We see no dyed garments from Bozrah here. The Mactavish would pine and die in breeks, sir."

" He is a good fellow, though."

" He is, sir. He has the inexcusable fault of poverty ; but that is nigh his only one."

" How come the family to be so poor ? "

" An old story. In 1545, or thereabout, his grandfather went away to Edinburgh, with some long-legged, young Highland chiels ; and he wandered south, the loon, past Dunbar and Carlisle, to a place they call Derby, or some such name. The daft, rintherout callant. And the Government asked where he was going, and he said to London. And so they hanged him at Carlisle, and the present estates came into the family by his son's wife."

" And this happened so long ago as 1545 ? " said Austin, laughing.

" I am not sure," said the old gentleman, with a sly laugh. " It may have been 1545, 1645, or even 1745. I am only sure of one thing, that it was na 1845." And, by the time he had made his little joke, they had got to the manse.

" By the bye," said the minister, before going in, " you know that we had him here for two nights in this very house."

" What, the Pr — " ·

" The Prince, sir."

" Indeed ! "

"Yes, sir. Two nights after the Stornaway business, he landed here. The wind was strong from the west, and he was driven across to Ronaldsay."

"Yet I thought I could have accounted for every hour of his time between Lewis and Benbecula," said Austin.

"A mistake, my dear sir. I can show you the bedroom where he slept. — Is it true that Sir Robert is going to continue the income-tax in spite of the surplus (not that it matters to me, God knows) : and can you explain me why ? Only as a matter of curiosity : for we are too poor here to mind income-taxes ; but, God be praised, we are not so poor as the Donaldsay folk."

"Not so poor as the Donaldsay folk." Those words dwelt with Austin. He had never seen poverty before, and he told the good minister so frankly. He saw enough now. Chronic poverty and want of the most hideous kind. The row of cottages, or rather hovels by the harbour side, were miserable enough ; but it was up among the little cot farms in the hill that he saw, for the first time, what utter poverty meant ; up in these hovels on the hill-side, built with loose stone (there is no lime in Ronaldsay), through which every wind of heaven blew, summer and winter ; with their little patches of oats and potatoes. Here, indeed, was more than Irish misery.

"We depend," said the minister, "mostly on our potatoes here. Ronaldsay is a cold island, and oats are sweer to ripen. The potatoes here look nice."

Poor fellow ! He did not dream, that these same potatoes, their only hope, would have turned to stinking carrion before August.

As for Austin, he went in and out of these hovels with his friend the minister all the first morning ; and then began thinking for himself, perhaps for the first time in his life : with what degree of correctness the reader must judge. "All this silly windy turbulence in Ireland," he thought, "has origin in very great part from chronic poverty. And yet here are a race of men, as poor as the poorest Irish, superior to the Irish in physique and intelligence, by the most enormous interval; a race who in courage and endurance are notoriously not surpassed in the world ; a race attached to particular religious tenets as firmly as the Irish ; one might almost say a priest-ridden race ; and yet what does one find ? Patience instead of turbulence, manly independence instead of servility and an almost entire absence of crime, instead of continued horrible outrages." It was a puzzle.

" How do you account for it, Mr. Monroe," said he, addressing the clergyman.

" For what sir ? " said the old man, looking quietly up.

" For what I have been saying."

" You have been saying nothing."

And no more he had, but only thinking.

He apologized and stated his case.

" The Irish," said the minister, strongly, " are a priest-ridden people."

" So are the Scotch," said Austin.

" I wish ye were just a minister yersell, ye'd ken how much truth there was in *that* ; if ye had the handling o' em, ye'd find na a thrawner lot than ye are thinking," replied the old man laughing. " But, even if there were a grain of truth in your assertion of their being priest-ridden, you must still allow that your Scottish minister is a superior man altogether to your Irish priest."

" Why should I allow that ? " said Austin.

" For politeness' sake," said the minister. " But I will tell you a secret. Not only are the Scottish ministers a higher class of men than the Irish priests, but, what is of more importance, the Scottish population is as superior to the southern Irish population as a horse is superior to a donkey."

" That is a libel," said Austin.

" The greater the truth the greater the libel, Master Oxonian," said the minister.

"But I won't have it," said Austin; "I have seen very noble Irish people."

"Well then, we must put some of it down to education. There is the fact, account for it how you may."

"But look here, my dear sir," said Austin. "Can't one do anything among these folks? I mean, can I do nothing? I have money. If you were to point out proper cases to me, couldn't I leave money with them? You hesitate, because the lark is singing overhead. Think of the horrible long winter which will come on us so suddenly, and then say whether or no you dare refuse my offer."

"We are not beggars, Mr. Elliot. We have no claim on you."

"I tell you that you have. These are the first poor I have ever seen, God forgive me. I have no tenantry. I have no poor with more claim on me than these poor souls. Why, I gave nine pounds for this pin which is in my scarf, the other day. No claim quotha!"

The old man sat silent for a moment, and then spoke low and quiet. "I dare not decline to take any money that you may leave, Mr. Elliot; no, I dare not when I think of the winter which is coming. I may never account to you for that money, but I will account to Christ. He will be a more inexorable auditor than you, Mr. Elliot. You have guessed, sir, in some way, what we want. We want money. We have no circulation of money. We have here potatoes and oats, every bit of which we require, and fish, which we want also; but which, being our only staple of trade, must be sacrificed in Glasgow, to get cash for tobacco and groceries. We have no circulation of money. The Mactavish, who would give the coat off his back, has to educate his sons, and gets no rent from the island. He leaves us alone. We can ask no more, and have no right to ask so much. But he sins against his tenantry and himself."

"How?"

" His stomach is too high to let the shootings. It lies with you and him to make Ronaldsay almost a Paradise. You are rich. If you could persuade him to let you the shootings, and were only to live here three months in the year, it would make a wonderful difference in Ronaldsay. You have no idea what the circulation of another three hundred pounds a year in the island would be."

" Is there any game? " asked Austin.

" Not much," said the minister, " at present; but if *you* would take the island, *I* would take care there should be. I would use my influence, my dear sir. If —"

" Priestcraft," said Austin.

" You are a daft young gentleman, sir, and I am very angry with you. But listen to reason. You will want a moor some day; go round our island and examine its capabilities."

" I will. Now, here is an envelope, which you must pledge yourself not to open till I am gone."

This envelope contained an I O U from Austin to Mr. Monroe, for fifty pounds. The reader must form his own opinion on this piece of extravagance.

Austin was there for ten days, and before three days were passed, he had managed by a careless *bonhommie*, or possibly by some quality far, far higher than that; to make himself beloved by every one in the island whom he met. For there was about him a great-hearted geniality, which no one could resist. The Duchess of Cheshire had said that Charles's new friend seemed a very loveable person; and now old Elspie Macdonald, whose grandsons had been across to Ireland, hobbled up to the manse, with her dreadful wrinkled old face below her shoulders, and gave him a great shell, " a Chama cor," and refused the half-crown that Austin offered her. Austin knew as much about shells as about the Rosetta stone or the Fonetic Nuz; but he saw that the old crone meant him a high compliment, and let her see that he did.

A noble young kilted Highlander was told off, by reason

of his speaking English, to show him the round of the island.

"A remarkable laddie, sir," said the minister ; "a Frankenstein monster of my ain making. I was fearful at one time that I had lent my hand to the making of a poet ; but that sin has been spared me among others. He bolts knowledge in a brutal and gluttonous way, sir, without chewing, like a dog swallowing meat, a gobble and a swallow, and then ready for more. But he has a dog's digestion, sir, it doesna turn to wind wi' him, for which we must be thankful. If ye have lent your hand to pit seven devils of education into a man, ye would choose a man of smaller carcass. For if such a one as Gil Macdonald gangs awa among the tombs, it will be no safe for the passers-by."

So for eight days Austin brushed the heather, led by his long-legged friend, returning to the manse at nightfall, as happy as a king, and as tired as a dog. His eight happy days were gone before he could look round.

The two young men, starting early one morning, walked westward through the great bog, which fills up the centre of the Island of Ronaldsay, with the sharp crystalline peak of Ben More of Ronaldsay right before them, lying in a dark brown cone above the mists. And as they toiled across the bog, through the morning, they saw that mist dissolving, curling, brooding, in dark hollows, like piles of wool ; rising in fantastic wreaths, which were melted and swept away by the sea breeze ; and, as a last poor resource, hiding in clefts and glens, only to perish ignominiously before the steady blaze of the sun, as he towered stronger and stronger each moment over the distant hills of Argyleshire.

So on through the bog, until the heather began to roll and rise, and then leap up into scarps and terraces, and then run into long ribs, along which they walked, and saw mirror-like lakes, hundreds and hundreds of feet below. Some were perfectly calm, and some streaked with bands of frosted silver, as the wind, wandering into the sheltered corries, caught the surface here and there. Then there was no more heather, but a steep cone of yellow grass and grey stone. And last of all the summit — a breezy platform twelve feet square. Below, the ocean, with a hundred fantastically shaped islands : above, the vast blue sky : and around, silence, except the gentle whispering of the south wind among the grass stalks.

" Gil ! Gil ! " said Austin, after a pause. " This is a glorious country."

" Aye, it's a braw country," replied Gil, " in summer time. But we are unco poor, and the winters are very long."

" I shall think of you in the long winter nights, Gil," said Austin. " The winter nights are very long."

" Aye, indeed they are, both cold and long."

" If you feel them so, Colin," said Austin, " here in this free island, think what they must be to poor prisoners, alone in jail. Think of that. Suppose you or I had to spend the winter in jail, what should we do ? "

" *I* should ding out my brains against the wa', and dee like a man," said Colin, rapidly, snatching at the grass. " What gars ye think such things ? "

" I don't know," replied Austin, looking out over the sea ; " the rule of ' *contrairy*,' I fancy. Being so wild and free up here, half way between earth and heaven, makes one think of the other extreme, I suppose."

"' Aye," said Colin, " if the gentles are no miserable by visitation of God, it is forced upon the puir bodies to make themselves miserable. It would be a hard business for some of them if it were na for the de'il, who, like a true gentleman, is aye ready to assist a neighbour. Well, some amount of misery is necessary for the enjoyment of life, I suppose. I suppose you have no wish ungratified in life, that ye make yourself miserable with thinking of jails ? "

" I have one wish," said Austin.

" I may not speir what it is ? " said Colin, looking up eagerly.

" Aye, and get your answer, my boy. When will the swallows be here ? "

" In a few days."

" I am waiting for one of them. A little house-martin, that shall be on my bosom till one of us die. I tried to tame a peregrine once, but she has soared to her eyrie and left me."

Colin understood him so perfectly that he said not one word. And if you turn on me and tell me, that there are not here and there such Highlanders as Gil Macdonald, I turn on you, and tell you, that you have been staring at mountains, while you should have been studying men.

So Austin, Gil, and the dog Robin, sat for a while on the summit of Ben More of Ronaldsay, and heard nothing but the wind among the grass stalks.

" There is not one cloud in the sky," said Austin at last.

" There is one," said Gil. " I have been watching it this ten minutes. Look southward."

" By Jove ! " said Austin, " it is the smoke of a steamer."

" The Swallow is coming," said Gil.

" I think so, indeed, Gil," said Austin, peering eagerly to the southward. " That must surely be the Pelican. Let us hurry down."

And as they went, Gil said, " Listen to me, Mr. Elliot. We are going to lose you ? "

" Yes," said Austin ; " I am away with the Swallow."

" Will you take me with you ? I will follow you like a dog, for as long a time as you appoint, without wages. I——"

" Oh, stop," said Austin ; " don't say any more. It is quite impossible, Gil. I don't deserve this confidence. And I have a servant already. You cannot tell how you distress me."

" You should think twice before you refuse me," said Gil, eagerly. " You don't know the Highlanders ; we are so cunning, so brave, so devoted. Think twice."

" It is quite impossible. Don't think me unkind, but it is quite impossible."

" I'll think of you in the long winter's nights," said Gil. " Will ye no come back to us? "

" Aye, that I will," said Austin, eagerly.

Gil said no more. By the time they got to the town the population were all out on the beach, looking at the Pelican as she approached, stemming the surf's current of the Kyle of Ronaldsay with her beautiful sharp bows.

Austin had been prepared for this. His portmanteau was ready packed and in the boat. The good minister was ready in the stern sheets, and two sturdy Highlandmen were ready to stand to their oars.

" Ye'll come back to us again? " said an old man, as he jumped into the boat, acting as spokesman to the population.

" Aye, that I will," said Austin. And so he did.

" Are we to say good-bye for ever, Mr. Elliot? " said Mr. Monroe, after they were in the boat.

" For ever! ah, no! " said Austin. " I will come back again. Think of me in the winter-time."

" See here," said Mr. Monroe, " I have opened this envelope. You should take it back. Can you afford it? "

" Tush, my dear sir, perfectly. If I cannot, it is not for you to stand between me and the poor. Come on board, and let me introduce you to my father."

But the old man would not. He was shy of strangers, he said. He begged Austin would excuse him, and Austin did so.

As the boat neared the yacht, the steam was shut off. The swell in the Kyle was short and bubbling. Before Austin had had time to say good-bye, they were alongside. In the next minute, Robin was on board, and the portmanteau. In the next, he saw there was only Eleanor to receive him, and then looking over the side, he saw that the yacht was under way, and that the boat had sheered off for the shore, dropping astern every instant, as the sturdy rowers plied their oars in the short chopping sea, and the yacht slid on against the current.

Then he hurried Eleanor up on the empty quarter-deck, and drawing her arm through his, bade her wave her handkerchief, while he stood bare-headed. She did so, and there came a wild cheer from the shore. Soon after, the village was hid by a turn in the Kyle, and that was the last of Ronaldsay for a season.

Gil Macdonald had climbed up on a little cliff near the end of the village, and stood watching it all, with his hand shading his eyes ; and then and there he determined that if Austin did not come back in a year, that he, Gil, would go south, and seek him again. For the most extraordinary thing was, that our merry, gentle Austin had, after only one week's acquaintance, become a sort of necessity to this noble young Highland lion. Here had appeared to Gil Macdonald, fretting, after the manner of his nation, in his miserable little island prison, for the chance to go forth into the world, and do battle with his peers — here had appeared to him a noble young Englishman, a high-bred gentleman, from the crown of his head to the sole of his foot, in carriage and dress far beyond anything Gil had ever seen before ; and yet this apparition had treated Gil like a gentleman and an equal all the time he had been with him. The country where such as he came from must be the country for a Highland lad to win his way in. And as for Austin himself, he would follow such a man as that to the very world's end.

He felt something in his hand. It was the gold Austin had given him. He almost felt inclined to throw it away, but he put it hastily in his sporran and resumed his watch.

The yacht slid round the farthest black promontory of Ronaldsay, and the spring twilight came creeping over Argyleshire from the east, till only the summit of Ben More of Ronaldsay had a faint gleam of pink on the side towards the sun, who had now fairly northed from his equinox. But still Gil stood looking after the ship, with his hand over his eyes.

We shall see how he came south before Austin came north, and when and where he found him.

Chapter XVII

Do you care for the man at the wheel? I do not, one farthing! Elsewhere he may be a good man or a bad man, or may have eyes or ears; but when he is at the wheel, he becomes the man at the wheel, and is not supposed to have any more consciousness of passing events, than the spanker-boom.

As a rule, you will find that people do *not* mind the man at the wheel. They are very apt to take uncommon little notice of the officer of the watch, but of the man at the wheel they take actually none whatever. And Austin and Eleanor on this occasion never troubled their heads about there being such a person in existence; and as for Mr. Slapper, the sailing-master, he was in the forecastle telegraphing with his arms, like a madman, to the helmsman.

Eleanor, it appeared, had been taken by surprise. She had run up on deck without her bonnet; she had thrown a loose grey-hooded cloak (what was irreverently called in those days a fool's-cap and bells) over her shoulders, and she had her hand on her head, to prevent her hair blowing about. She looked positively beautiful; and when Robin leaped upon her, mad with joy, and her hair got loose, she looked more beautiful still.

Three times they walked up and down the deck in silence; but in all her Majesty's dominions — nay, in all the world — there were no two hearts so light as theirs.

Eleanor spoke first. "I thought," she said, "your dear father looked guilty. I felt sure we should pick you up somewhere."

" Did Aunt Maria guess ? "

" Foolish ! no, or we should not have been here. And
how did you like Ronaldsay, Austin ? "

" Very much."

" Have you fallen in love with any one there ? Remember, I insist on being told.   I always have been told."

" Yes," said Austin, " I have fallen in love at last."

" I should like to see her."

" You shall."

" You will tell me all about it."

" Yes," said Austin, " I will tell you all about it. And,
as he said so, he drew her towards him, and kissed her ;
and, as he did so, his eyes met hers, and she saw it all
now. And her heart was filled with a peaceful happy
content, and she laid her head upon his breast.

She had won him ; won him from all of them ; the
gentlest, handsomest, cleverest man in all England ; so
she thought in her pride. I should like to have seen the
flash of furious scorn which would have come over that
noble little face if any one had told her that she was
throwing herself away, and that with her vast fortune she
might have married an earl. She was proud of her money,
and knew the value of it. She was doubly proud of it
now. It would be Austin's.

" And so I caught you all alone," said Austin.

" Yes, all alone.   Mr. Elliot is in the cabin."

" He is most impertinent and disrespectful," said Austin.
" He should have been on deck to receive me.   How dare
he ?   Where is Aunt Maria ? "

" Oh, good gracious," said Eleanor, eagerly, " haven't
you heard ? "

" Of course I have heard," said Austin. " The seagulls and cormorants told me, while I was at Ronaldsay.
But I shouldn't mind hearing your story ; for they all
spoke at once, and quarrelled, and contradicted, and I
couldn't make out the truth of it."

" Why," said Eleanor, " the day before yesterday, she

was scolding old James on deck, and he answered her just as she was at the top of the companion, and she turned on him in her lofty, imperious way, and she caught her foot on the sill, and down the ladder she went, head over heels, and she has bumped and bruised herself all over."

" Has she hurt herself much ? "

" No ; but she is terribly cross. She sent for your father to her bedside, and requested him to put her on shore on a desert island, with a week's provisions, and some beads and tomahawks. For she said, that might possibly purchase the forbearance of savages, although she could not that of a pampered and ungrateful domestic."

" She is afraid of old James," said Austin.

" I know she is ; and I am afraid of her."

" You must not be," said Austin.

" But I *am*, and I shall be. You don't know what a terrible woman she is. Sometimes only, she is violent. But, at ordinary times, she has a continuous voluble way of scolding, which is more dreadful still. She does not raise her voice, but goes on for half an hour together, indignantly asserting her own case, from different points of view, until I am confused and frightened. Any statement of my case only makes her go over the old ground, a note higher, for another half-hour. She can fairly scold me into submission. And I warn you that I am completely and utterly in her power. When she takes to scolding me in that way I have neither temper nor courage to oppose her. Remember this."

Austin reflected for a moment. I am glad, he thought, that old James forms part of that household. " Eleanor," said he, " do you know who old James is ? "

" Very well. He was a shoeblack-boy, whom my father picked up out of the streets for charity. They were nearly the same age. He came to be his servant when they were both sixteen. He was at the taking of the Bastile with my father and Lord Liverpool."

"It might be considered only decently polite," said Austin, "if I were to go and see my father."

"And I ought to go to Aunt Maria."

"She will be in a pretty way when she hears of this," said Austin.

"Of what?" said Eleanor.

"Of my having proposed to you, and of your having accepted me," said Austin. At which Eleanor ran away, and Austin went down to see his father.

Mr. Elliot was sitting in the old place, at the head of the cuddy table, over his maps and plans, and Austin said, "Well, young fellow."

And Mr. Elliot said, "Aunt Maria has tumbled down the companion, and abraded herself."

"And I have proposed to her niece, and have been accepted," said Austin. "Come on deck, and let me see your dear old face by sunlight."

So the father and son went on deck, in the spring twilight, as the yacht sped out from the Kyle of Ronaldsay, into the more open sea beyond, towards South Uist and Benbecula. The man at the wheel may have smiled at the little passages he may have noticed between Austin and Eleanor ; but he did not smile when he saw Mr. Elliot's arm round Austin's neck, and the two heads, one so old and the other so young, bent down together in consultation.

And so, through the long spring evening, the steamer throbbed on her peaceful way, against the current, through the Kyle of Ronaldsay. Right and left, the rocky shores stooped down into the green sea water, and everywhere land and water were divided by a slender thread of silver surf. In one place the rocks came down grey, wrinkled, and bare, clothed for the last few feet only with a band of black sea-weed. In another the rock was less abrupt, and partly feathered with ivy and yew, and here and there a pleasant lawn of short green turf. In some places the rock fell away altogether, and a sheep-cropped, limestone down, came rolling and sweeping to the sea, which here was bounded by a half-moon of bright yellow sand. In one place there was a large fishing village, of white-washed stone cottages, where the women sat at the doors netting nets, and the old men were hobbling about tinkering old boats, and where the boys cheered them, and ran bare-legged along the shore. And, soon after, they met the able-bodied men of this village, in their fishing-boats, drifting homewards on the tide. In one place, along this beautiful strait, there was a flock of sheep, feeding high overhead, watched by a little Highland laddie, whose dog barked, and ran to and fro when he saw the ship, and whose bark was joyously echoed by happy Robin, from the deck. And, at another place, there was a wee bit kirk and a manse, on the hill-side, with the minister out in his garden, who took off his hat to them, and whose courteous salute they returned as the ship sped on.

" A happy land, Eleanor," said Austin ; " a land of settled faith, of intelligence, of truth, and of order ; a land not so over-populated but that the best men may be recognised and revered. Would you like to live here ? "

" I would live anywhere with you, Austin, even in Italy."

And at night, as the sun went down in the west, the ship began to plunge, and then to roll, and she plunged and rolled under the reeling stars, across the water which lay between the Kyle of Ronaldsay and Benbecula, for the south wind, blowing steadily, met the tides pouring southward through the sleat, and the sea was heavy.

Eleanor and Austin walked the deck until the stars came out, and the ship began to dive and leap, and send sheets of spray flying to leeward, and then she went below. The steward was superintending the laying of a cloth for supper. Mr. Elliot was in his own cabin ; so Eleanor, with an anxious look, feeling that her time was come, that there was no one to delay and gossip with, made towards Aunt Maria's cabin.

Aunt Maria was sitting up in her bed, with her maid beside her. She was in an ill temper, and her coarse violent face looked more coarse and violent than ever. There was something worse than coarseness or violence in those deep-sunk eyes and knotted eyebrows, but no one saw it as yet.

" Aunt, dear," said Eleanor, " what shall I bring you for supper ? "

" You wicked girl ! " said Aunt Maria ; " you miserable girl ! So your lover has come on board, has he ? So all this voyage was a settled plan between old Elliot and you to meet this profligate young idiot at Ronaldsay ! Oh, how I do hate meanness and ingratitude ! And look at the low meanness of this proceeding ! and then, when you have reflected, if you can reflect, on all that I have done for you, think of the ingratitude ! "

What Aunt Maria had done for Eleanor was — to live at her expense to save her own income, and to worry her life out. Eleanor *knew* this. But in the presence of this scolding woman, with her straight overhanging upper lip, her bushy eyebrows, and her deep-set eyes, she began to feel guilty ; she was, as she told Austin, a coward, and she said nothing.

" How long has he been on board ? " snarled Aunt Maria ; " and what has he said to you ? "

" He has been on board about four hours, Aunt," said Eleanor ; " as to what he has said to me, all I care for is this — he has proposed to me and I have accepted him."

" And you have dared ? " said Aunt Maria, furiously.

" Yes," said Eleanor, quietly. " I have dared ; I dare do anything when he is beside me. If you can get me away from him you may do anything with me. I am afraid of you, and you know it ; but *you* are afraid of *him* and of his father."

" Then you have accepted this boy, you wretched girl ! " said Aunt Maria.

" I have, Aunt."

"And Captain Hertford."

"Captain Hertford!" cried Eleanor, the warm French blood of her mother coming to her help, "that villain! that blackleg! How dare you couple my name with his?"

"How dare I, you silly girl?"

"Aye, how dare you! You would like him to get possession of me, and then, by his sheer brutality, to get the management of my nine thousand a year — you would like that!"

"I think you want guiding, child; but you are out of your mind to talk to me like that."

"I am not. You and I and Captain Hertford are bound together by a tie of deep disgrace; no one knows the truth but we three. Now, I am a coward, but I am no fool — if you press me with that man's attentions I will tell Austin everything."

"*You* tell him!" said Aunt Maria, scornfully; "suppose *I* were to tell him?"

"In that case," said Eleanor, "he and I should be married just the same; only, if I know the chivalrous soul of the man, more quickly than if you held your tongue. And in this case also, our secret would be worthless. You would be turned out of our house — you would have to live on your fifteen thousand pounds, and Captain Hertford would have to live on you!"

"Then," said Aunt Maria, scornfully, "if you have this hold over us, why not get rid of us at once? Why not tell him?"

"Because he is going into public life — because I should ruin him by hanging such a chain round his neck."

"You are a fool!" said Aunt Maria; "there is hardly a public man in the country without his skeleton. Tell him: I defy you! You know, if you told him, he would not marry you; that is the truth!"

"It is not the truth, Aunt Maria. You are like all entirely worldly people, one-half of you, a very foolish person;

you calculate only by the lowest motives, and never take higher motives into consideration. Austin is a pure, noble, high-minded man, utterly incapable of anything mean, and I also am acting, I believe, on the highest motives, in keeping this disgraceful secret from him. He would marry me to-morrow if he knew it. But he shall not know it, for he would never have the same fearless pride as he has now if he knew it."

" If he marries you he shall know it, and all the world besides ! "

" I think, Aunt," said Eleanor, quietly, " that it will be better for you not to break with me, and my devoted old Squire, James ; I think it will be better for you ! " and without waiting for Aunt Maria's reply she left the cabin.

Chapter XVIII

THIS was the last voyage of the good old Pelican under her present master ; what has become of her now I know not. I have not even heart to inquire whether or no she is still used as the yacht of the Secretary to the Shoals and Quicksands. Those who loved every timber, plank, and bolt in her, sail in other ships now. Our interest in them was the connecting link between us and the ship, and when they leave her, our interest in the ship must cease. She becomes, as far as this story is concerned, only a mass of wood and iron.

In life it is not so. Our affection for a ship one has once known well, is similar to our affection for a house one has once lived in, but intensified. Only last year, I went down to the East India Docks, and I came across the Or-well. It was like meeting an old friend. There was a board which said that I must not go on board, and a steward, who tried to prevent me, until I said I knew her, upon which he yielded at once, and let me go over the old deck, from stem to stern. It is hard when on board a ship in the docks, standing so unmoveably still, to realize that one has seen those steady tapering masts sweeping wildly across the blotched stars : or those sharp bows leaping madly up towards heaven in the agony of the storm : to recall the reeling, and rolling, and plunging, of the vast inert mass under one's feet, now resting so quietly from her labour.

Before the morning dawned the Pelican had threaded her way through the intricate channel between North Uist and Benbecula, and was steaming easily along under the cliffs of the latter island, and about nine, a preventive boat came off, and Mr. Elliot went on shore in her.

"The glass is dropping, sir," said the sailing-master, "and it is banking up to the west."

"Make haste, father," said Austin ; "don't be long. The glass is really falling very fast."

"Them as wants to know about dropping glasses," said a voice behind Austin, "should take my place (and Lord amighty knows they're welcome to it), and then they'd know what it meant. Them huzzies of ours is always at it. Why I dreamp last night as I see the hull bilin of 'em come down the kitching stairs, one atop of the other, with no less than six dozen of pipe-stemmed wines, and all the cut custards."

"The young women do break a great deal of glass, I suppose, Mr. James," said the good-natured sailing-master.

"Ah !" said James ; "I believe you there. They gets a tittling one another on the stairs, and down they goes. And out she comes in her dirty old flannel dressing-gown, and gives 'em all warning over the banisters. She's been a trying falling down stairs herself, now ; but I ain't hearn of anybody giving she warning."

This strong personal allusion to Aunt Maria forced Austin to stop a silent internal laughter, which, like Mr. Weller, he was trying to "come," and turn round.

"Well, James, how are you ?" said he.

"Breaking up rapidly, sir; and thank you kindly," said James.

"I am sorry to hear that," said Austin, with perfect gravity.

The old man was going to make some cynical reply; but he looked round and saw they were alone : his whole manner changed at once.

"Master Austin, my dear," he said; "I see you and she on deck last night. Is it all as we should wish it ? "

"Yes, James," said Austin.

"I thought so," said he. "Now you mind an old rogue, and you keep close to her. It would be a good thing for *she* (the old man so cordially hated Aunt Maria that he never named her if he could help it), if she could bully Miss Eleanor into marrying Captain Hertford, and then that the pair on 'em should have the bullying and bally-ragging of nine thousand a year. That would be a good thing, hey ! "

"It will never happen," said Austin.

"You mind it don't," said the old man, and walked forward, leaving Austin musing.

The glass was dropping very fast, and it was clouding rapidly up, from the south-west. Lunchtime passed, and Mr. Elliot was still on shore : they began to get impatient. They could see him through their glasses, walking about the lighthouse, looking into everything, directing here, consulting there, as if time were not of the slightest value.

"By Jove, sir," said the sailing-master to Austin, "I wish we had ten miles more sea room. Boatswain, run up second pennant and 3474."

It was done. Mr. Elliot was seen to notice it for an instant, and then turn away. He put up a cross staff in the middle of the lighthouse-keeper's potato garden, and then sent a preventive man, a quarter of a mile away, to the top of a hill, to get a line between the lighthouse and a sunk rock.

The sailing-master took a sharp turn on the deck, and muttered something. " Run out that gun and fire it."

Mr. Elliot did mind the gun. He came down to the beach with provoking deliberation, and at last got into the boat ; before he reached the ship, two sharp squalls had passed singing through the rigging, and a third, fiercer than either of the others, swept over her as he scrambled on deck. There was scarce time to cast the boat off, before the storm was upon them in all its fury. They were relieved by seeing the boat cast up on shore, with her crew safe ; then they had to think of themselves. The blast was so terrible and violent, that the yacht, although steaming ahead at full speed, was making no way at all, and the rocks of Benbecula not half a mile to leeward.

" I am afraid I have been very remiss," said Mr. Elliot, as he walked away aft, and the sailing-master followed him.

" Dare you run for the lee of Monach ? " said Mr. Elliot.

" We should be broadside on to Grimness in ten min- utes, sir," said the sailing-master.

" Then God forgive me," said Mr. Elliot, and went to his cabin.

He had certainly staid too long. Even now at four o'clock in the afternoon they were steaming for bare life, and it seemed losing ground ; the night was coming on, and the gale was increasing.

All that steam and iron could do, backed by a steady Scotch head to manage them, would be done ; but the storm was too strong for them, and the rocks were close to leeward ; their danger was very imminent. Mr. Elliot and the sailing-master knew it, and Austin guessed at it.

Eleanor, seeing Austin look so calm, was not frightened — or at least did not show it. She staid on deck with him through all the furious turmoil. They were wrapped in the same plaid ; and, in spite of the rush and boom of the seas, and the scream of the cordage, each could hear every word spoken by the other as plain as though they were walking together in a garden on a summer afternoon.

At last Eleanor went down, not long after dark. She looked into her aunt's cabin. That good lady was sleeping quietly, unconscious of all danger; and so Eleanor went to her own cabin and lay down.

She had looked into the main cabin, and seen Mr. Elliot busy with his papers and charts. She was quite reassured, and slept peacefully. But Mr. Elliot was not busy with his papers — far from it. He was quite enough of a sailor to know their extreme danger. When Eleanor passed into her cabin, he was leaning his head on his hands, and anxiously musing. Presently the sailing-master came into the cabin and spoke to him.

"She is actually making leeway at times, sir," said he. "As the sea gets up she will make more. The danger is very extreme, sir."

"And no anchorage?" said Mr. Elliot. "If we could only bite ground, we might, by steaming at anchor, weather it."

"We are in blue water, sir," said the sailing-master. "If there is no change it will be all over in an hour."

"And all my fault," said Mr. Elliot.

"Nonsense, sir. You were detained ashore by duty."

"Well, let us say so," the old man replied. "It will be all over in an hour?"

"Yes, sir, thereabouts," said the sailing-master.

When he was gone, the old man lay down his head and prayed. He prayed for his son Austin; that such a noble young life should not be cut off untimely, through his own carelessness. If he had seen a little further into the future, perhaps he might have prayed that it might all be over now, and that Austin and he might sleep together under the wild fretting waves of the Atlantic, and be spared the evil to come.

The brave little ship was leaping madly, and creaking in every timber; and underneath him where he sat the screw was spinning and clanking and buffeting the wild waters: sometimes coming half out of water, with an angry jerking hiss; and then throbbing bravely and diligently at its work ten feet below the surface. It was a mad fight between winds and waves on the one hand, and iron and steam on the other, and he, and all dear to him, were the prize.

The noise was so great that he could hear no one approach him. A hand was laid on his arm, and he started and looked up. Then he stood up altogether, and looked with astonishment at the figure by his side.

It was Aunt Maria. But she did not look as he had ever seen her look before. She wore the dirty flannel dressing-gown which that impudent old fellow James had mentioned, but on her head was a brilliantly gay cap, full of flowers, and in her hand she clutched an ivory fan, which she held upside down. But, startling as her dress was, it was her face that startled Mr. Elliot most. Her thick bushy eyebrows almost concealed her deep-sunk small eyes — and those eyes did not appear very steady; — and her complexion, usually such a deep red, was now a dull sickly yellow.

Mr. Elliot had been in many lunatic asylums in his life, but neither he, nor any other man, ever went into one yet without seeing a middle-aged lady there, who was uncommonly like Aunt Maria, as she stood before him this night in his cabin.

He rose, in his alarm, and looked keenly at her, trying to catch her eye. Hers would not meet his, but she broke silence first, in a hoarse unequal voice.

"I heard every word that your sailing-master said to you just now. I know that in an hour we shall all be — all be drowned."

"I hope not," said Mr. Elliot, politely. "The ship is in danger of going ashore, certainly, but there is every chance for us, Miss Hilton."

"Nonsense!" said she, catching his eyes, and dropping hers again at once. "I know that the end of us all is near. I curse the day when you deluded me into this voyage, that your scatterbrained son might make love to my niece, and have her money. Do you know what you have done ? "

" No," said Mr. Elliot, looking steadily at her.

" I will whisper to you." And she whispered to him, and his face grew a little graver as she spoke.

" Now what do you say ? If by any chance we were to be saved, would you break off the match ? "

" No," said Mr. Elliot. " In the first place, it don't affect the property. I am an executor, and I know that."

" I thought you had set your heart on your son's public career ? "

" So I have."

" It will be a noble one with that round his neck."

" He and I may have our own opinion about that. Why, if you believe that we are all to be drowned in an hour, do you tell me this ? "

" Because I hate you ; — because I always hated you ! "

" Always ? " said Mr. Elliot.

" No," she said, fiercely, " I loved you once. How dare you remind me of it ? I showed it, and that was my fault. I always hated you, and Jenkinson, since that day when I heard you laughing at me. How dare you ! I came to tell you this because I believe that you have not an hour to live, and that I thought it would annoy you."

" May God forgive you as I do, Maria," said the old man.

She turned to go.

" Won't you say ' good-bye,' Maria, for old times' sake ? " said Mr. Elliot.

Aunt Maria would not go so far as that, but she came half way. She burst into a wild wail ; she broke her fan into a hundred pieces, said that she was a miserable, ugly, mad old woman, who had never had justice done her by those she had loved, and so went weeping and wringing her hands, back to her cabin.

" Poor thing ! " said good old Mr. Elliot. " I wish I

could get her out of Hertford's clutches. Small chance of that! I must tell Austin all this some day, that is clear, but not yet. His love is a little too young to stand it yet; I shall wait till she has become a necessity to him. By-the-bye, I forgot we are all going to the bottom; we shall be ashore on Benbecula in half an hour."

But when Mr. Elliot said this it was nearly twelve o'clock at night, and the yacht, so far from toiling on to the coast of Benbecula, was driving (that is supposing her to go clear of the stage of Broad-harran, Lion's-head, and Eagle-island, which, as every school-boy knows, are the furthest projections of the county Mayo, in Ireland, to the west) — was driving, I say, straight towards that part of the Atlantic, where I am inclined to place the still undiscovered island of St. Borondon : in spite of the impudent lies of Marco Verde, before the worthy Pedro Ortez de Funez, inquisitor of the Grand Canary; who ought to have fried him in a frying-pan, for insulting the Holy Office with his cocks and bulls. And how it came that the good Pelican had turned her tail SW. by S., I will tell you in a few words, before we bid her good-bye for ever.

Austin, finding the deck untenable, for the driving spray, bethought him of the engine-room, and he went down there. Old Murray, the engineer, was standing steadfast before his gleaming cranks and leaping pistons ; and he saw that the engine was being worked at a speed he had never seen before.

The engineer shook his head without turning round. " If aught gives, Master Austin ! "

" Is there any danger ? "

" She'll just hold her own if naught gives."

" I suspect our lives are in good hands, old friend," said Austin, " and I know no one to whom I would sooner trust mine."

The old man looked lovingly on Austin, and Austin stood beside him some time. Suddenly the voice of the master was heard inquiring for Mr. Austin.

Some one said he was in the engine-room.

"Tell him to come quick. Say I have something to show him."

Austin dashed out of the engine-room, and up the only open companion-ladder. As he got on deck, the press of wind nearly suffocated him, but the ship was steady. There was very little sea, the wind had beaten it down. Above, all was black as ink, but the sea around them was a wild mist of white foam. The master shouted in his ear —

"Look a-head and aloft!"

He did so. A-head of the ship's bows, high aloft, there was a brighter patch in the inky sky, a patch of blue, in which were three or four stars, which seemed to reel, and dip, and rise again, as he staggered on the slippery deck; and across this patch, wreaths and wisps of storm-cloud were flying quick as lightning; but, awful as it seemed to Austin, these wreaths of cloud were not going *with* the wind, but from right to left, nearly dead against it.

"Good Lord!" he said, "why the clouds are flying against the wind!"

"It is a new trick they have got then," said the master; "wait and watch, Master Austin, you won't see the like again out of the China seas. This is what *I* call a ty-phoon. I reckon they have another name for it herea-bouts. Watch what happens, sir."

The patch of blue sky approached them, though not very fast, and as it approached them, grew larger. At last it was over head, and as they became aware of it, they became aware of these things also. That it was a great funnel into the sky, through a circular whirlwind of storm-cloud; and that the moment they were under it, the ship was becalmed amidst a heavy sea, which slopped about, here and there, in every direction.

They were actually becalmed, while all around they could hear the tempest howling and raving. The ship began to make splendid headway now, with her head S. W.

But in twenty minutes, the engines were ordered to go at half speed, and her head was put N. E. straight for the island which they had dreaded. Ten minutes after, the storm struck them from that very quarter, with increased fury, and the good Pelican, saved, with her engines going quarter speed, was drifting slowly and safely out into the Atlantic.

And in the morning, when the storm was past, she was leaping and bounding southward, over the bright blue waves, with a thousand happy sea-birds skimming and diving around her. And Austin and Eleanor were on deck together, already forgetful of the hideous night which had passed.

And now we must bid good-bye to the Pelican, and to Murray, the engineer, and the sailing-master, for our way lies in a different direction. Austin was about to part from these friends of his youth, these friends who had pampered and petted him, and to start in the world for himself. With what success, we shall see.

A month after his return to London he was on his way to make the tour of the East, with Lord Charles Barty. At Alexandria he picked up a letter, which told him that his father was dangerously ill. He turned homeward, and his faithful friend came with him. At Malta, he heard that his noble old father was dead. His burst of grief was wild and child-like, but his good friend, Lord Charles Barty, stayed him and comforted him, and took him home gently and kindly, and Austin rewarded him for it, one fine morning, as we shall see. He got home only to find the funeral sometime over, and to take possession of his property.

And now we must skip a few months, and pick up our story again at the end of them. These last events took place in the Spring of 1845. We shall take it up again in the beginning of 1846.

Chapter XIX

THE year 1846 had begun, Parliament had met, and the murder was out. Everybody had been perfectly certain of it, ever since Lord Stanley's refusal to join the new ministry ; but everybody now said, that they wouldn't have believed it. After Sir Robert had got up, immediately after the seconding of the address, and, in less than twenty minutes announced, that the failure of the potatoes had necessitated his resignation, and that his ideas on the subject of protection had undergone a considerable change ; some people, by far the larger number, were struck with profound admiration, some were violently angry, some were intensely amused, and all very much excited.

A new political star had arisen, though as yet it was very near the horizon, and its orbit was unascertained. Some time before Parliament met, the Daily Intelligencer, a paper which prides itself on the earliness of its political intelligence, announced that " they were informed," that the address would be moved, in the Commons, by the newly elected member for Granitebridge. But Sir Robert Peel knew better than that. The address was, on that occasion, committed to the older and wiser head of Lord Francis Egerton.

The newly elected member for Granitebridge was no other a person than Lord Charles Barty. A vacancy for that borough having occurred by the death of old Sir Pitchcroft Cockpole, the borough had been contested by Lord Charles and Captain Blockstrop. The gallant Captain was fearfully beaten, to his own great surprise.

The Captain had argued in this way. That Lord Charles, though coming of a Whig house, must, being a duke's son, be at heart a Tory. That was Captain Blockstrop's unalterable opinion. So he issued a rather liberal address, as *he* thought ; expecting to be opposed by the very faintest and mildest form of gentle Whiggery. When he read Lord Charles Barty's address, Austin says that his hair stood on end, and emitted electrical brushes, and his whiskers crackled like a cat's back.

Lord Charles's address was the most atrocious and revolutionary document which had appeared for many years. The Captain had said, " that, should it appear that the supply of food was likely to be seriously diminished by the failure of the potato crop, he for one would listen patiently to any arguments which might be adduced in favour of a temporary (mark him, a temporary) suspension of the duties," for many of the population of Granitebridge were bucolic and Protectionists. Lord Charles Barty had disposed of this question, and conciliated the Protectionists by saying, " that the Corn Laws were a festering ulcer on the body politic, and that every hour they were permitted to remain, was another hour of humiliation and disgrace to the country." The Captain thought that, at some future time, a slight enlargement and redistribution of the suffrage might possibly be advisable. Lord Charles Barty proposed manhood suffrage and the ballot, to be taken immediately, as *his* specific for the potato rot, and every other disease. The Captain, who seemed really to have taken some pains to inform himself of facts, thought that, in case of a suspension or abolition of the corn duties, some relief should be granted to the agricultural interest; say in a consolidation of highway districts, or in an alteration in the law of settlement. But Lord Charles either knew nothing (which is most probable) or cared nothing, about highway rates, or the return of worn-out paupers from rich manufacturing towns, to impoverished rural districts. He finished his address by telling the Protectionist constituency of Granitebridge, that, if the agricultural interest could not take care of itself, it was no one else's business to take care of them.

But he was elected by 258 against 164, for these reasons. In the first place, the good and gallant Captain, had made a most awful and Jack-a-shore sort of blunder. His strong point, the point on which he dwelt most, was that of Admiralty reform. Now it so happens, that Granite-bridge is not more (as the crow flies) than one hundred miles from the great arsenal of Plymouth ; and all the trim stone villas about the town, have been built out of the proceeds of filchings of copper, and nails, and rope's ends, from the dockyard there. The inhabitants of those cottages and villas, had each of them, at that very time, three or four relations down in Plymouth, in the dockyards there, filching away their hardest, at the copper and rope's ends, that they also might retire, and build villas like their relations. Now, you know, this was not the sort of constituency, to which to broach Admiralty reform. The Captain argued that, being so near Plymouth, they must be familiar with, and interested in, dockyard mismanagement. This was eminently true, but not in the sense the Captain meant.

Another point in Lord Charles Barty's favour was, that his name was Barty. The mighty sheets of deep red corn-land, which stretched west from the town, lying in pleasant slopes towards the south, were all his father's, as far as the eye could reach. The town itself, and the land about it, belonged to Sir Pitchcroft Cockpole. They always had a Cockpole, or a Barty for one of their members. They knew them, and could trust them : and these Bartys too ; they were all wild young hawks at first (except the blind Lord Edward), but they always turned out steady, devoted, useful public servants in the end. " I'm a Protectionist," said one old farmer on the hustings, " but I'd sooner have Lord Charles and Free-trade, than e'er a one else, with Protection. Though he is a owdacious young Turk, sure*ly* — drat 'un ! "

And a third reason for Lord Charles's return is this : when he and his friend Mr. Elliot came down canvassing, there was no resisting them. They were such a handsome, noble, merry pair of fellows, that they took the warm Devon hearts by storm. Lord Charles went about uttering the most atrocious revolutionary sentiments, in an airy, agreeable sort of way, and Austin went with him, and laughed at him.

One great event of the campaign, was the attack on old Mr. Pilgrim, the quaker, in the upper Croft. It will illustrate their very free and easy sort of tactics.

On the very first day of their arrival, as Charles Barty, Austin, and the attorney were sitting together after dinner : Brentmore pointed him out as an important and influential man — a man who, if the Captain ran them close, might make or mar the whole business.

" You must go to him to-morrow morning, my lord."

" I'll be hanged if I do. I shall say something terrible, and set him against me. I cannot converse with a quaker — I never tried."

" You will have to try," said the attorney.

" Wouldn't it be better fun," said Lord Charles, " seeing he is such an influential man ; for me to send a letter to him, saying that I consider him a broad-brimmed old idiot, and that I'll tweak his stupid nose for twopence. There would be some fun in winning the election after that."

" There would, indeed, my lord. You must go to him to-morrow. When the Tory man came down, before the breath was out of Sir Pitchcroft's body, to see how the land lay, he just called on Mr. Pilgrim, and from what he heard there, went away again."

" Who was the gentleman — who was the base Tory who dared to show his face at Granitebridge ? "

" A certain Captain Hertford," said the attorney.

Lord Charles and Austin became attentive.

" He has done a good deal of dirty electioneering work in his time, and now he is looking out for a seat for himself. He is engaged to be married to Miss Hilton, a great heiress, I believe."

" Will you be kind enough to tell him, the next time you

see him," said Austin, "that he is a confounded liar, and that I told you to say so."

"No, Mr. Elliot. A man of my figure, sir, as broad as he is long, and only ten stone, after all, can't do it, sir. It would be no use doing it, and putting it in the bill. No one is rich enough to pay me for the consequences of telling that gallant captain that he is a confounded liar. Suppose, sir, that *you* were to tell him so, and to say that *I* told you."

"You mark my words, I will," said Austin — "the abominable villain!"

"I understand," said the attorney, "that the young lady is quite under the influence of her aunt, and — by-the-bye, we must look over the lists, gentlemen," he added, quickly, for Lord Charles, after three or four attempts, had managed to give him a violent "drive" on the shins under the table.

Just outside the town at Granitebridge, there is a long lime avenue by the river side. Here, at ten o'clock that night, Lord Charles Barty and Austin walked up and down, smoking their cigars.

The winter's moon was overhead above the leafless trees; and far up to the north, in the moor, they could hear the river, here so calm, chafing among his granite boulders.

"Austin, old fellow," said Lord Charles, "when are you going to get married?"

"I wish I knew," said Austin.

"There is no cloud between you and Eleanor, is there?" said he.

"Not one vestige," said Austin. "There was a time, Charles, when I was not in love with that woman; but there never was a time when I did not love her."

"And your love for her grows stronger?" said he.

"Day by day, and hour by hour," said Austin. "But she — does she love me as I love her?"

"Ten thousand times better, Austin. I will go bail for that."

" Then why does she put me off ? "

" I do not know.   Because, I take it, she is in the hands
of her aunt.   You should make a bold push of some kind.
Look at her position, my dear old friend — just look at
her position.   God help her if anything happens to you ! "

" Her position is not good, certainly," said Austin, pen-
sively.

" It is simply horrible !   Here is a young lady — *a lady*
mind — with an enormous fortune, *very* handsome, in her
way ; clever and charming beyond conception, without a
soul to speak to in her own rank in life.   My blind brother,
and you and I, are the only friends she has in the world.
She is utterly debarred from all society."

" You see," said Austin, " her father did some queer
things in his time, and so no one takes her up."

" The world is very cruel, Austin, but it is not so cruel
as all that.   The reason that no one goes near her is, that
no one will have anything to do with her aunt."

" I suppose that is it," said Austin ; " and she is getting
worse and worse."

" Does she drink ? " said Lord Charles.

" I fancy so.   She is always terribly excited."

" Did you hear of her kicking up a row in church, last
Sunday ? "

" No," said Austin.   " Was Eleanor with her ? "

" Oh, no ; she and Edward were philandering at St.
Paul's, bless the two sweet Puseyites.   Austin, why are
you not jealous of Edward ? "

" And thereby deprive Eleanor of the only happy hours
of her life.   Why, if it were not for your brother, and his
sitting to play her piano, and his taking her about to the
churches and cathedrals on a week-day, she'd go mad.
Jealous of your brother !   I watched them one day last
week, creeping in under the shadow of the abbey wall.
She was leading him, for there was some anthem to be
sung, which they had heard of, and had gone posting off
across the park to hear.   It was Advent time, you know ;

and there are fine anthems sung then, about Christ's coming, and that sort of thing. And I followed them in, and, when the organ had done snarling and booming, and the voices began, I watched them, and there they sat, with their hands folded before them, like two stone angels. Your brother has a beautiful face of his own, blind as he is. Somewhat too much of this. One is talking nonsense, or near it. One always does, if one walks up and down at midnight, with the friend of one's heart."

" May the deuce have a man who don't," said Lord Charles. " That brother of mine has a noble face."

" Was Lord Edward always blind ? "

" Always. He began to sing when he was five years old."

" He never sings now."

" No, he lost his voice at fourteen. Before that, he used to go wandering about the house, singing some ballad, or hymn, which had taken his fancy, to some tune of his own choosing, in a strange, shivering, silvery voice. Once, I remember George and I were in the school-room, kicking up a row with our sisters, and plaguing Miss Myrtle : and we heard him come singing along the gallery, and we all grew silent and listened. And we heard him feel his way to the door, singing all the time. And he was singing " Lord Ullin's Daughter." And he drew the door open, while we all sat silent ; and you never saw a stranger sight. He thought no one was there (for we were all very silent), and went on singing ; and his blind face was flushed with passion :

> ' And still, as wilder grew the storm,
>   And, as the night grew drearer,
> Adown the glen rode armèd men,
>   Their footsteps sounded nearer.'

" Yes, he is a fine fellow. Let us, however, return to what we were talking about."

" That includes a great many things," said Austin.

" For instance : about Aunt Maria making a fracas in church."

" Oh, aye, she did. My people were at St. Peter's, and she came in, and the pew-opener had put some one in her pew. And she kicked up a row, by Jove, and spoke out loud. She was either mad or drunk."

" Was there any disturbance ? "

" Why, no. She recovered herself when every one looked round. But no one minded their prayers much. Well, I don't want to distress you, old fellow, but you had better know the truth. It was a *very* ugly business. She utterly lost command of herself. People were talking of it in London, and said she was drunk."

" What the deuce am I to do ? " said Austin impatiently.

" Make Eleanor appoint a day for marrying you. Don't be put off any longer."

" There's were it is," said Austin. " She *has* appointed a day. She has appointed a day in next April twelve-months."

" Next April twelvemonths ? "

" Aye," said Austin, " and stuck to it."

" That looks like reading the bill this day six months," said Lord Charles.

" No," said Austin, " she don't mean that. She is in her aunt's hands."

" She must be very weak," said Lord Charles.

" No ! " said Austin. " She loves me, as *you* know. There is some scandal in the house, most likely about her brother, who is dead, who robbed you at Eton. Aunt Maria knows something, and whips her in. What shall I do with that black-hearted villain, Hertford ? "

" Leave him alone. Give him rope enough to hang himself withal. If she allows her aunt to bully her into marrying him, you are well rid of her. By giving him rope, you may bowl out Aunt Maria."

" You are right. Meanwhile, your brother Edward is there continually ; and she, with her true toad-eating instinct, allows him to come unchallenged, when my appearance would only make a scene for poor Eleanor, after I was gone. Lord Edward is stone-blind; but not, as I have heard, deaf. On some occasions, Aunt Maria has behaved as though she considered that the loss of one sense involved the loss of all. I say, Barty!"

" Well, old fellow."

" About Hertford. I know that his scheme is to marry Eleanor if he can. The end will be, that he will try to get rid of me by forcing me to go out with him."

" Damn duelling!" said Lord Charles, suddenly.

" So say I," said Austin; "but that is his game."

Lord Charles chucked his cigar into the road and walked silent for a few minutes; at the end he said,

" Dear old fellow! will you pay attention to me? That *is* his game; I know it, Edward knows it. He will, in case of his finding himself outwitted, do that; he is a dead shot, he will force you out and kill you, if it becomes worth his while — you must be very careful and gentle with him."

" I have been, Charles," said Austin. " I know what you say is true, and I have been very careful."

" Aye, but it has not been worth his while yet. There is a strong talk about enforcing the law against duelling. *He* knows that. It will be his last resource. If he could get her, and her aunt safe abroad, he would shoot you tomorrow."

The interview with Mr. Pilgrim the quaker was eminently successful. It took place next morning at eleven, in this wise : —

Lord Charles was perfectly *snapping* to Austin as they walked towards the house; and Austin laughed at his woebegone look, till he assaulted him in a by-place where no one was looking. When they got to the quaker's house they were shown into a cool parlour, to await the great man. Austin took down books from the shelves, poked the fire, and dropped the poker, made jokes, laughed loudly at them, and generally misbehaved himself. At last he came round to the cellaret, and, seeing it was unlocked, prompted by a noble curiosity, he raised the lid. At this moment a heavy footfall was heard outside the door, and Austin dropped the lid with a terrible slam, just as the quaker entered the room.

He was a noble-looking old man, and he went straight up to Austin, with a sweet smile —

" Lord Charles Barty, I believe," said he.

Austin, as red as fire, pointed to the real man ; and the candidate, looking as red as Austin, said,

" I am Lord Charles Barty, Mr. Pilgrim."

" And this gentleman," said the quaker, sweetly, " who has done me the honour to look into my poor cellaret ? "

" That's Mr. Austin Elliot," said Lord Charles, " and confound him, he is always up to some of his fool's tricks in the wrong place. But he is mad, you know — as mad as a hatter. No one can manage him but me. I wouldn't have allowed him to take anything ; I don't think he meant to. He has a monomania for looking into people's cellarets. All his family had. His — his — his grandmother died of it ; and by Jove, sir, it's hurrying him to his grave ! "

" Indeed ! " said Mr. Pilgrim, with his mouth twitching at the corners.

" Oh, yes," said Lord Charles ; " but that don't matter. I say, Mr. Pilgrim, I wish you'd vote for me, and get the other people you can manage, to vote for me. I assure you that I will make a good, diligent member. All I care for is to get into the House and find my place in the world, It may seem a conceited thing to say, but I think I shall make you a better member than Captain Blockstrop, though he is a gentleman, and a good fellow. I was going to make you a speech, but that fellow Elliot has put it out of my head. Perhaps it is all for the best. If I remember right, there was a lie or two in the speech I was going to make you. Now I have blurted out the whole truth."

The quaker looked on him with a smile.

" I have two conditions, my lord."

Lord Charles recovered himself and looked keenly at him.

" Let me hear them," he said, " just to see if they tally with my own foregone conclusions. But mind, I don't change one iota of my programme, at your or any other man's bidding."

" There spoke a real obstinate Barty," said the quaker. " My conditions are these — You are pledged to sweep the corn-laws into the dust-bin of the past once and for ever. Do I understand that ? "

" You may certainly understand that."

" And you and Mr. Elliot are pledged to dine with me the day after to-morrow, and see what is in the cellaret ? "

" I am pledged to that also."

" Then all shall go well. My lord, I know you and your worth, and I know Mr. Elliot and his worth also, though he has peeped into my cellaret. I wish you a good morning, my lord. I have done one good service for you already. I sent that — that — military officer, Will Hertford out of the borough pretty quick. There is a great advantage in lending money at times ; you *can* get rid of a man. My old acquaintance George Hilton used to say that. Ah ! poor fellow. Sad for him to die and leave his poor little girl all alone in this wicked world. Good morning ! "

So Barty was returned by a noble majority, and Blockstrop once more went down into the sea in his ship, and put forth into the deep, taking his naval reforms with him ; and so the Admiralty was left in peace.

Chapter XX

ELEANOR lived at the house her father had occupied for many years, in Wilton Crescent. It was not a large house, and her household was small. She saw actually no society. Sometimes the monotony of her life was broken by the visit of an old schoolmate, but they never stayed long, nor did she press them. Hers was not a house for bright young girls to stay in. She felt it. She knew it. There was something so indefinably coarse, something so beyond and beside, all gentle domestic love, in her aunt, that she never pressed those girls to stay, and never of her own will, invited them.

She was a strange little being. She had to dree her weary weird, and she did so, with a depth of love, courage, self-sacrifice, and shrewdness, which you will appreciate when you know all. The fairy which had given her such boundless wealth, had given her counter-balancing gifts which made that wealth worse than worthless. She would gladly have given it all away, on certain conditions.

There was one reason why she clung to this wealth. There was one reason why she still rejoiced that, disgrace her as they might, that wealth was still her own. It would be Austin's. If he would only wait and trust her through everything, it would all be his. If he would only wait and trust her.

She was sitting at her piano. She was alone in her drawing-room, and the light of the level winter's sun was on her face. If there was, at ordinary times, a fault in that face, it was, that the under lip and chin were somewhat too short, and the mouth rather too closely set. That fault, if it were a fault, was not perceptible just now, for she was leaning over the keys, with her fingers upon them, studying the score of the music before her. Every now and then she would try it, and, each time she did so, the music grew towards perfection, until at last it rolled away triumphant and majestic. It was an old Huguenot hymn-tune, which she had found in her dead mother's portfolio.

The door opened. Her mouth grew close set again in an instant. She turned round and confronted her aunt.

Aunt Maria looked very flushed and odd. Eleanor said to herself, "she has been drinking." She sat down before the fire-place, and, after a pause, said, peevishly —

"Well, child."

"Well, aunt dear."

"Well, aunt dear!" she repeated sharply. "Eleanor, may God save you from the bitterness of having a sulky, obstinate niece, when you are got old like me! A niece who loves to lacerate a poor old woman's feelings, by making her ask and cross-question before she can get one word of information. There, God forgive you, after all I have done for you. Don't you know that to-day is the fifteenth, you wicked girl?"

"Alas, I know it well."

"Have you been out this morning?" said Aunt Maria.

"Of course I have," said Eleanor, in a low voice.

"Well."

"I have nothing to tell you. Captain Hertford went with me."

"Dear man!" said Aunt Maria. "Dear, blessed, sainted man! And, oh, he loves the very ground you walk on."

"I am sorry he should so far waste his love," said Eleanor. "I am, I am sorry to say, wicked enough to have the very strongest personal dislike for him. In this unhappy business, however, he seems to have behaved kindly and well. I do not judge his motives, I only judge his actions, aunt. He has behaved kindly and delicately towards me. and I will try to reward him."

"Ah!" said Aunt Maria, "if you would — "

"Now aunt, neither you nor he can possibly be silly enough to suppose that I shall marry him. When I talk of rewarding him, I mean this. He is gone to stand on the Tory interest at Glenport. Before he went, I told him that, if he would, as soon as he had ascertained the cost of his election, have an interview with my man of business, he would probably find those expenses provided for."

" Why, you fool," said Aunt Maria, " that is giving the man two or three thousand pounds without an equivalent."

" Well he has a heart somewhere, I suppose," said Eleanor, " or, supposing he hasn't, he is a gentleman ; and, having taken his price to leave me alone, will do so."

" I tell you he loves you, you fool. I tell you that he loves the ground you walk on. He is a man ; he is worth fifty coxcombs. You — "

" Don't scold, aunt. If he does love me so deeply, I must say he has taken the price of his election-expenses rather coolly. Don't begin to scold. I am not afraid of your scolding now. Austin will be with me to-day."

" I wish he was dead," said Aunt Maria. " I wish Charles Barty was dead; I wish Edward Barty was dead."

" When they are dead or when they have deserted me, aunt, you may take me and do what you will with me. God knows they are the only friends I have on this earth. All houses are shut to me, aunt. You know that. But I have a heaven that you don't know about. When Austin comes in and talks to me in his sweet gentle voice; or when Charles Barty comes branking in with his merry nonsense, I am in a different world to the one you know of, aunt ; and when blind noble Edward and I are at our music together — then, then, aunt, ah ! where are Captain Hertford and all the misery then ? — miles, miles below our feet, aunt ! "

" You go rambling about to church, with that blind fiddling idiot, in a way which in my time no girl would have dared to do. People will talk of it. Have you no sense of what is correct ? People will talk about you as sure as you are born."

"Very few people are likely to talk about you and I, aunt," said Eleanor. "We have learned that much, in spite of our wealth. If we keep quiet, we are at present insignificant."

Whereupon Aunt Maria began to scold, rambling on from misstatement to misstatement, until she had no new misstatement to make, and then beginning *da capo* with the original grievance. And that is the true art of scolding in all countries, I believe.

Chapter XXI

THERE is a place I know, which is unlike any other place I have ever been in. It is only the transept of a cathedral, and yet for some reason it is different to all other transepts. I cannot tell you why, but so it is. Possibly the reason is, because I have been more familiar with it than with any other, and because I love it far better than any other. The place I speak of is Poet's Corner.

On a certain day Austin Elliot was in Poet's Corner, sitting upon Chaucer's tomb. Those who walked up and down in the transept only noticed that a very handsome and well-dressed young man, with appearance of extreme youth, was sitting upon Chaucer's tomb. No one knew the profoundly deep schemes which were revolving within that youth's head, or under that youth's curls.

Austin had taken to heart what Lord Charles had said to him at Granitebridge, and, after a long pause, had acted on it. The mere fact that he had taken time to deliberate, instead of rushing off headlong and doing just what his friend had suggested, proved to him most satisfactorily that he was getting old, sagacious, knowing — nay, even sly. He had developed a scheme by which every possible obstacle to the happiness of all parties was to be removed. He had matured it, and now he was going to broach it.

It required the consent of four or five people, who were about as likely to agree as his Holiness the Pope and his Majesty the King of Italy ; but still his plan was a good one, and the idea of failure was not to be thought of.

Things were very unsatisfactory. Eleanor was engaged to him. He and she loved and trusted one another beyond the way of ordinary lovers. There had never been a shade of anger or jealousy between them for one second. He was his own master. She was of age. And yet things were most unsatisfactory.

The fact was that, as we have heard before, Eleanor refused to be married before the next spring — a whole twelvemonth. And meanwhile she was living, as it were, under the protection of her aunt — an awful woman, who looked red and wild — who had made a disturbance in church — who knew no one — whose very appearance was keeping people in mind of the scandals against Eleanor's father, which they would have laughed at, and forgotten, long ago, if they had not been reminded of them by the appearance of this terrible woman in the Park, in Eleanor's own carriage, every day.

And again, Captain Hertford was a man of very odd character, and he was continually in Aunt Maria's company. Captain Hertford was known to be a desperate, though successful, gambler, and a man of such courage and skill in the noble art of duelling, that he could still hold his head up among the very best in the land. Every one knew all sorts of things about him ; but any man who would have refused to go out with the gallant Captain would probably have had to withdraw his name from his Clubs. Captain Hertford was, in short, a notorious blackguard — a weed which can only grow under the infernal, devil-invented system of Duello ; and yet a man with whom it was necessary to be on good terms, and a Member of Parliament. He sat for a small port in D——shire. The people there had rather wanted a Tory Member.

They had very much wanted their railway. Captain

Hertford had undertaken their railway, and everything else they had asked, had spent a moiety of Eleanor's two thousand pounds, and got in handsomely.

Such were the two persons who seemed to use Eleanor's house as their own home. Austin's brilliant plan was, to marry Eleanor, and buy these two people off — to bribe them to leave her alone.

It was a good plan. Eleanor had behaved with the most consummate discretion. She had never appeared in public with her aunt; she had only a few old schoolfellows for her friends; and, as for going out to any sort of party, in any rank in life, she never dreamed of such a thing. Every one (for people were getting interested in her strange espiègle style of beauty, her immense wealth, her curious menage, and also her excessive modesty and good taste) — every one knew of her engagement to that young Elliot, and thought him lucky. Every one knew that she saw nobody except Austin and his two friends, Lord Edward and Lord Charles Barty; and after every one had seen the mother of these two young noblemen wait at the door of St. Paul's (Knightsbridge) until the curious little being came out, dressed in quiet grey silk, with a big diamond clasp to her cloak, and had seen the duchess introduce herself, and speak kindly to her; after this every one knew that she was a meritorious young lady; and they were right, for the duchess was never wrong. It was perfectly evident to every one after this that nothing stood between Eleanor and entire recognition, save the elimination of Aunt Maria and Captain Hertford.

A curious thing was, that Eleanor never appeared in public, except to go to church. On Sunday morning she was always at her place at St. Paul's (Knightsbridge); but in the afternoon, and every day through the week, she went anywhere and everywhere — the Abbey — Margaret Street — nay, between ourselves, Moorfields and Gordon Square. She always walked. If no one else was with her, she took old James; but this was seldom. Sometimes Austin would go with her; but generally her companion was blind Lord Edward Barty. They used to walk very fast, for they were a very strange-looking couple, and people used to stare at them. They never went anywhere where they had to make many crossings, for Eleanor was nervous about taking him over them. For this reason the Abbey was their favourite week-day resort, because the only difficult crossing is at the top of Grosvenor Place: after this you are in the Parks, and all is plain sailing.

Lord Edward knew every organist in London, and always knew what music there would be. He used to come to Eleanor's house, and they two would try to render it on the piano until it was time to start, and then they would go down to the Abbey and hear their crude attempt rendered for them by the master's hand, with every magnificent accompaniment which their hearts could desire.

On this day Austin had called at Eleanor's house, and had learned that she was gone to the Abbey, but alone. This determined him, instead of calling again, to follow her there and walk home with her; and so we find him sitting on Chaucer's tomb, and watching for her.

The place was very quiet, for very few people were sauntering about and looking at the monuments: but presently the organ snarled out its last magnificent dismissal, and two or three hundred feet came whispering across the pavement from the choir.

Eleanor was nearly the last. The little grey ghostly figure came stealing on from light to darkness so gently that her footfall could not be heard amongst the others, the little gloved hands were hanging at her side, her face was very calm and peaceful, and her eyes were set straight on Rare Ben Jonson, until she came opposite Chaucer's tomb, and she turned to glance on it as usual; and then her face lit up with joy, for Austin was sitting there, defiant of vergers, and laughing at her.

They were together in one instant, and her hand was on

his arm, for a minute they were both too happy to say one word.

" My darling bird," whispered Austin — for they were in a sacred edifice — " were you going to walk home alone in the dusk ? "

" Old James is with me, Austy dear," said she. " When Lord Edward is not with me, I always bring him."

" He is not here now," said Austin. " I wonder if he has gone to sleep. What a lark if he should be locked in."

At this moment a terrible disturbance was heard in the choir.

" Oh, Austin, whatever shall we do ? " said Eleanor.

" Stay here, my love," said Austin ; and he ran back.

A verger was just locking the gate in the screen, and seemed inclined to dispute passage ; but Austin pushed past him : and on entering saw a sight which turned him to stone. Old James had got hold of a verger by the hair, had dragged him down across a bench, and was beating him about the back of the head with Eleanor's best prayer-book. On benches around stood angelic, white-robed choristers in groups, who were saying, as loud as they dared, " Crikey ! " — " Brayvo, Rous ! " and " Evans, if you *please*, gentlemen ! " and making other low-lived remarks, which prevailed among the youth of our metropolis in the year of grace 1845—46.

Austin garotted and pinioned James, and turned him round. James, thinking Austin to be another verger, who had taken him in the rear, made savage bites at him over his shoulders, until Austin put him down in a safe place, upon which James remarked,—

" Well, you *are* a pretty sort of a friend ! If you had let me a gone on till he got stupid, I'd have shifted my hand and got the clasp-side of the book on the back of his head. Lord ! I'd have killed him in three minutes."

" It is better that he should be allowed to live, to complete the measure of his crimes," said Austin, pretty well knowing, from long experience, that old James had a very strong case — that, if not actually in the right, he was uncommonly near it. It appeared, from the choristers, and from the good master, who had fled for assistance, and from the other vergers, that old James was in the right after all. He had fallen asleep, until he was awakened by the departure of the last of the congregation ; he had then rapidly slid up to where Eleanor's gold-clasped prayer-book lay, to follow her with it as his duty was. The verger had got into the bench before him, and thinking he was stealing the best prayer-book he could see, had very properly caught hold of old James by his coat, and on his resisting, had struck him. As Austin and the master pointed out, it was only a case for mutual apologies, and a sovereign, given by Austin to the conscientious verger, made matters infinitely comfortable, and so he walked the old man off triumphant.

Old James had burst his braces in the *mêlée*, and insisted on stopping to mend them with a knife and some string, before he rejoined Eleanor.

Austin took this occasion to ask, " Why did you go to sleep in church, James ? Just think what it would have been for Miss Eleanor if I had not been here."

" Ah ! lucky you was. Uncommon seldom *you* comes to church a week-days, God forgive you ! Why don't you take her to church a week-days, like Lord Edward do, blind though he is ? I'm not one of they, as holds there's any harm in coming to church a week-days."

" Neither am I," said Austin.

" Then why don't 'ee ? " said the old man. " Lord Edward, he is a gentleman ; he'd be a gentleman if he were led down Piccadilly by a brown, curly-tailed mongrel dog, and a wicker basket in his mouth, for the boys to put bits of backer pipe and oyster-shells into it. Aye, he would, although, mind you, I'm not one of they as holds with blind folks in generally — they're mortal sly."

" But why did you go to sleep in church ? " said Austin.

" Because I had too much to drink in the morning,"
snapped the old man, who was undeniably sober now.
" You'd have done the same if you had had they wardens
to deal with all the morning. 'What's your name, and
what do you want?' says one, as has drunk with me fifty
times. 'Seggetary State's order,' I says, 'and none of
your nonsense ; Lamb and Flag at half-past one, old boy.
How is he?' And I seen him. And Lamb and Flag it
was at half-past one, and drat they warders and all belonging to 'em. Here's Miss!"

Austin and Eleanor dismissed old James, and walked
home together across the Park, through the gathering
darkness.

They hardly spoke one word, until wending through the
shrubberies they came on the lake, and then Austin spoke.

He gently and delicately laid the whole case before her,
as we have made it out for him above. He laid before
her the doubtfulness of her position in the world while
those two people, Aunt Maria and Captain Hertford, occupied the house ; and she agreed with him in both.

" My dearest!" she said, " do you not think that I must
feel all this more acutely than you? I am not a foolish
little body by any means ; I should get on well in society,
and I should be immensely fond of society. Do you
think that I willingly live with two such millstones round
my neck as those two people?"

" There is a remedy at hand," said Austin.

" I know it, but an impossible one."

" If you marry me at once, you will never be plagued
with them any more. I shall have authority, and will
banish them. My father's old friends would flock round
you, and you would take the place that your wealth and
talent entitle you to."

" All this, my dearest, is mere truism. But I cannot
marry you before next April twelvemonth, Austin."

" Now why not, my own?"

" Ah! there you must trust me, my Austin. There is

a skeleton in our cupboard. You are going into public life, and I am going with you; you will win a peerage, perhaps — at all events, be prominently before the world. We must have the road quite clear before we start our coach."

" And am I not to know what this skeleton is ? "

" Certainly not, until I tell you. It must not be said that we married while such and such was the case. If it be possible, I would rather that you never knew."

" But others know."

" We can buy them. You always knew that there were queer stories about the Hiltons. You have heard the stories about my father, you know all about my poor brother, you know about Aunt Maria. You love me, my Austin ; I have great wealth, which is all your own, and with which you must make your way in the world. There are scandals about our family which must be smothered. Until they are smothered and the road is clear, it would be fatal to your prospects for us to marry. I am at work day and night with you only in my thoughts, God knows, my darling ! to clear the way for you towards honour and fame. I am working for you, Austin, like a patient little mole, so diligently and slyly. If you claim my promise next spring, I will at all events lay all the facts before you, and you shall say whether you will have me or no."

" You will not tell me now ? "

" No. It may happen that you may never know. On that wild chance, I keep you in the dark. But still, if you demand, before you marry me, an account of everything, I shall have to give it you. At present, your happiness and mine is, as far as I see, bound up in your trusting implicitly to me. Will you trust me, Austin ? "

" I will trust you implicitly, my own Eleanor," he answered slowly, looking down into her eyes — who would not have trusted those patient, quiet eyes ? — " for I will trust you implicitly. I were a dog else, I think."

" Mind one thing, Austin ; keep near me, let me see

you continually. Never forget what I told you before.
She can scold me and frighten me into submission at
times."

" Cannot you get rid of her? "

" No. She would create a scandal when I want all
things quiet. You must do that — *you* must get rid of
her."

Chapter XXII

ALTHOUGH Austin resolved to trust Eleanor most fully
and entirely, yet, if we said that he was altogether satisfied
and pleased, we should be saying that he was something
more or less than human. He *was* a little, ever so little,
nettled, and it was a trial to him, that that great coarse-
faced brutal bully should be always in her house, and,
moreover, should know of things which he might not.
He hated Captain Hertford worse than ever; he hated
Aunt Maria worse than ever; but, nevertheless, he felt
sure that in a worldly point of view Eleanor was right.
The Hiltons *were* a queer family. If there was, as Eleanor said there was, something wrong, still it was better
that matters should be let down easy, and the road cleared
before they started. He determined to trust Eleanor implicitly.

It must not be supposed that Austin had come to this
resolution without assistance. After the conversation de-
tailed in the last chapter, he had sat in his room for an
hour or more, and had found himself getting peevish,
almost for the first time in his life; had begun to feel —
dreadful thought! that he was being fooled. Men like
him; men who have never been tried, and have looked
only at the surface of things; men who believe only in
the words which represent things, and have no actual
knowledge of the things they represent, are more apt to
be jealous and suspicious than those who have had their

noses actually to the grindstone; and know from experience what good faith and falsehood, trust and mistrust, really mean.

He was in a fair way to get jealous; when there was a bounding foot on the stairs — dog Robin leapt up and barked joyously, and the next minute Lord Charles burst into the room, crying —

"Come, come, laggard! to the House! Stafford O'Brien is on his legs, and there is all sorts of fun in the wind!"

Austin came at once. On their walk from Austin's lodgings in Pall Mall, he had told his friend everything; and under the influence of his friend's affectionate shrewdness, all the mists had cleared away; and by the time he had left his friend, and had squeezed into a tolerable place in the gallery, he was himself again prepared to enjoy the noble sport which was going on in the arena below.

Lord Brooke was speaking, but the people in the gallery were whispering to one another about Lord Granby's speech, which seemed to have been telling. Before Austin could hear anything of it, Lord Brooke sat down, and Lord Worsley rose. He made some terribly hard hitting. When Austin heard his quotations from old speeches of Sir Robert Peel's and Sir James Graham's, terribly telling as they were, he certainly, mad Peelite as he was, *did* wish that they had never been uttered; and he also wished, most piously, that the noble Baron was on board his yacht, or at Appuldercombe, or anywhere, save in that House, quoting those confounded old speeches.

Yet these attacks on his hero made him somewhat angry. Of course they were easily answered, but it was very provoking, to have to eat one's words in a laughing house. Austin began to grow warm with the rest of the world, and left Eleanor pretty much to herself for a week.

On the thirteenth he bethought him that he would have a joke with her, so he sportively sent her a valentine, and on Saturday morning, the fourteenth, he went to visit her, intent on hearing the fate of the valentine he had sent

her. The door was opened by old James, who said,
" Hush ! "

Austin asked what was the matter.

" Did you ever hear she when she was carrying on ? "
asked the old man ; "listen to her now ! "

Aunt Maria's voice was sadly audible indeed ; hoarse,
loud and irregular, coming from the drawing-room ; Austin
muttered something between his teeth, and went quickly
upstairs.

He opened the door, and she ceased when she saw him.
She looked very red and wild, and Eleanor sat opposite to
her, with her hands folded in her lap, perfectly patient, and
careless of what the old woman might say. The old
woman had evidently been scolding her hardest at her.
As Austin came in, Aunt Maria held her tongue, and
Eleanor looked up and smiled ; but Austin, being her
lover, could see what others perhaps could not. He had
previously once or twice, found her in a state of depression after one of Aunt Maria's scoldings, but on these
occasions she had always been herself again immediately :
on this occasion such was not the case. She looked up at
him and smiled, but Austin could see that she was not
herself ; that she looked wan, and pale, and anxious —
strange to say, Austin thought he had never seen her look
so handsome before.

He could not help wondering what Aunt Maria's in-
genuity had found to say, so very disagreeable as to
disturb Eleanor's equanimity : but in spite of thinking
about this, he could not also help thinking how very handsome Eleanor looked. She was sitting opposite her Aunt,
and was dressed for walking, with the exception of her
bonnet, which lay on the floor beside her. She wore the
long grey cloak which ladies wore just then, which covered
everything ; her chin, after her first look at him, had
dropped once more on her breast, and her hands were
folded in her lap before her, with quiet patience : and the
dull grey colour of her habit, and its almost foldless sim-

plicity, harmonised so amazingly well with the dull patience of her face, that she formed a picture, and a study of quiet endurance, which made Austin think he had never in his life seen any one so beautiful.

Aunt Maria was in a blind fury at something. She rose and left the room without looking at Austin.

" Has she been scolding you, my own ? " asked Austin, bending over Eleanor and kissing her.

" Yes, Austin. Where does she learn it all ? Where has she lived ? What has she done ? Austin, dear, take me to church."

" Let us come."

" Aye ! That is good of you," she said. " If it was not for the church I should die under it all. They should leave the churches open as they do abroad. Come on ; we shall be in time. Sometimes, Austin, when she is like that, I get away and go over to the church and find it shut, and then — ah ! then — you don't know what it is, my own."

" I don't know," said Austin ; " but if it distresses you, my love, I can be sorry. I don't like going to church. You must teach me to like it."

" I will. Austin, should you be very angry if I were to join the Romish Church ? "

" I ! Angry ! No. I should not be angry. You would find it a mistake, though. It won't hold water."

" Will the English Church hold water ? " said Eleanor.

" Why, yes, distinctly so. But what on earth do you want to subscribe to the whole business for ? Surely you get as much or more at St. Paul's as you do in Cadogan Street. Have you ever been there ? "

" Yes."

" I wouldn't go again. I don't think you have thought much about it. You don't know how much you subscribe to. Have you been there often ? "

" Yes."

" Don't go again. I don't like your going there. Did Edward Barty take you there ? "

"No; I went there by myself. I tried to get him to go, but he got angry."

"He was quite right. Why did you go?"

"Because it always stands open. And if you were a woman, and had Aunt Maria to live with you, and a bitter trouble, which you can't tell to the love of your heart; you, Austin, would be glad to slip away sometimes and get into the quiet church, and kneel, and forget it all."

"It may be so," said Austin. "Meanwhile, you must pray for me. Here we are at the church-door. I wish we might sit together.'"

"We may pray together," said she. "Austin, will you come to the Abbey with me to-morrow morning?"

"Surely I will," said he. And they went into church, he to one place and she to another, as is the custom in some churches. When he met her again at the church-door she was still anxious and silent, and seemed to have a different expression on her face, to any Austin had seen before.

On the pleasant Sunday morning he came to take her to the Abbey. The look of yesterday had deepened. She looked very worn and anxious, and he was much distressed. The morning was a bright, slightly frosty one, and the sun streamed into the old Abbey through the south-eastern windows and fell upon the beautiful young pair of lovers as they sat together. Eleanor was absorbed in her prayers, but Austin was vacantly watching the lines of light in the thick atmosphere — how they shifted and crossed one another as the sun went westward — was wondering how the deuce those old monks got it into their heads to build such a beautiful place, and why the fellows of the present day could not, in that respect, hold a candle to the men of the thirteenth, fourteenth, and fifteenth centuries. He thought of these things in a vague, ruminant, ox-like frame of mind, instead of attending to his prayers; with about as much earnestness as a fly in the sunshine; and very nearly determined to ask some one about it. Possibly he might have asked some one, some day; but they had to stand up at this point of his cogitations, and the mere act of standing up, set him thinking about the Bill, and what an awful sell it would be for Lord Lincoln, if Hilyard were to beat him for South Notts. He went on thinking about the chances at Newark long after they sat down again. He was actually smiling at the thought of the Duke's anger against the renegade, and thinking how much better it would be, if the Duke would keep his god-like rage penned in his own bosom, when he felt Eleanor's hand on his arm.

He had been very inattentive, and he blushed and looked down on the Prayer-book which lay open between them. Her finger was on the very passage in the Litany which the priest was intoning at that instant — we humbly venture to think, one of the most sublime pieces of uninspired prayer, put up by man to his God! —

" That it may please thee to preserve all that travel by land or by water; all women labouring of child; all sick persons and young children; and to show thy pity upon all prisoners and captives."

Those who do not appreciate fully that passage in the Litany, had better hear it read out by the captain in latitude sixty south, when the sea is thundering and booming, and the ship is reeling and rolling, and the wind is screaming, and the cruel icebergs are gleaming, half-seen, in the snow-fog, and the horrid long night is settling down over the raging ocean. They will find out what " travelling by land or water" means then, I'll warrant them. The time came when Austin realized one part of this glorious prayer; and not the part by any means that he ever dreamt of realizing; and when he did so he remembered, that, as soon as this one paragraph in the Litany was finished, Eleanor removed her hand from his arm once more, and went on with her devotions; and that he began to think how quietly Lord Henry Lennox had got in for Chichester; and of the meeting of the labourers in Wiltshire, and what a strange business that was; and of Lucy Simkins' speech and Mary Ferris' speech.

And of Lord Charles Barty's furious blind rage when he read those speeches aloud; and how, when he had come to the passage, " I biled they challucks for my children, and the neighbours said they was poison; and I says, then, they'd better die with a full belly than a empty one; " that young nobleman had rushed up and down the room crying out for free-trade or revolution. And so, feeding his soul on his own indignation against the protectionists, Austin, not regarding the service, went on until he was nearly as furious as Lord Charles himself. And, all the time, quiet, patient Eleanor was sitting at his side, leaning ever so slightly against him. She, too, had within her causes, deep enough, of anger and indignation, deeper possibly than Austin's indignation on account of the Wiltshire labourers, and his anger against the Duke of Richmond and Mr. Miles. But the mere feeling of her lover's shoulder against her own made her quiet and contented; and although the cloud on her face grew darker and darker, as time went on, yet still, though her face was pinched and anxious, she was happy. She would have sat there, leaning against his shoulder, and have died as she sat, with perfect contentment. When the sermon was over, and they rose up, she took up her burden once more, and carried it.

" My Eleanor," said Austin, as they walked home, " you are looking worn and anxious."

" I am, Austin. To-morrow afternoon I shall be myself again."

" Shall I come to you to-morrow morning ? "

" No. To-morrow is penance day. You have often laughed at me as a Tractarian, dear Austin. I do penance once a month."

" What kind of penance ? " said he, trying a harmless joke.

" A pilgrimage, Austin."

" Whither ? "

" You must not know.   You must not follow."

" I will not follow, if you give the order," said he.

" Then I give it," said Eleanor.

Austin was quite contented.   In the first place he had
thorough confidence in Eleanor, and had a shrewd suspicion that it was best not to know too much about the Hilton family history ; in the next, there were affairs to the
fore, which engaged his attention more than the easy con-
fidential courtship to which he had committed himself.
This was the spring of 1846.   All England had gone
politically mad, and Austin among the rest.   His father
had always placed political success before him, as the great
object on this side of the grave, while he had spoken with
truly ministerial reserve about success on the other.   Old
Mr. Elliot had been very anxious to make Austin ambitious,
and Austin had refused to be made ambitious ; but had
gone about, with his hands in his breeches pockets, laughing at the whole business, until —

Well, until this year, 1846.   Ever since he was a child,
he had read about great political struggles, just as we used
to read about the old European wars, until the Crimean
campaign came upon us, and turned all the familiar
printed words about the deeds of our fathers, into letters
of blood ; which we eagerly compared with those which
told of the deeds of our brothers ; and the history of war
became once more a terrible reality.

Austin had thought that great political earthquakes had
come to an end in 1831 ; that politics were certainly the
occupation of a gentleman, but were not likely to be very
interesting, because there was no question, nor was there
likely to be one.   Sir Robert Peel's statement in January
undeceived him.   The change of opinion of three of the
first men in the country, showed him that there was sport
a-field ; and, after the first leonine roar of the Duke of
Richmond, he began to go mad with the rest.

And in this manner the leaven of political ambition,

which his father had so carefully worked into him, had begun to act with a vengeance. And so, just at the time we speak of, his courtship of Eleanor, his attention to her affairs, his jealousy of Hertford, and his distrust of Aunt Maria, were quite secondary objects : had his jealousy been excited before, so much as to make him extort an explanation from Eleanor, it would have been better for them both.

Chapter XXIII

Austin sat the long debate of Monday out ; and left the House at half-past two. There was news from India, which was announced by Lord Jocelyn ; and then the weary Corn-law debate began, and Sir Robert Peel, getting on his legs, spoke calmly and deliberately for four hours, explaining what had taken place in the autumn, and other matters, while Austin sat and listened as patiently as a reporter. So the next morning, instead of riding out before breakfast, he lay in bed, in a happy sleep, till eleven, dreaming, among other trifles, that Sir Robert Peel had sent Aunt Maria with a hostile message to Sir John Tyrrell, and that Colonel Evans was escorted to the hustings opposite Northumberland House by a troop of Sikh cavalry, headed by old James. He slept so long, that his servant would not stand it any longer, and woke him ; and as soon as he had breakfasted he went off westward to see Eleanor.

She was quite herself again, though she looked very pale. He had a happy morning with her. He gave her, from recollection, the heads of Sir Robert Peel's explanation. She sat sewing at her needlework all the time, and every now and then asked a question. She not only appeared interested, but she was so. When he had done, she put her needle into her canvas, and deliberately expressed her opinion that it was unsatisfactory ; that the one hitch in it was, that he ought to have gone to the country, and had not done so. And Austin argued with her, and tangled her wool, and said she was obstinate and disagreeable; but she stuck to her opinion about the dissolution, and would not be talked out of it. And so they passed a long happy morning together, and were both of them sorry when old James announced luncheon, and they had to go down to the dining-room, where was Aunt Maria, boisterously good-humoured, and very red in the face, who amused herself by continuous railing abuse against Sir Robert Peel.

And a most exciting and delightful month it was. The four friends — the brothers Barty, Eleanor, and Austin, were more together this month than ever they were afterwards. Lord Charles Barty spoke once, and spoke very well indeed: and Austin and blind Lord Edward, who had sat patiently in the gallery to hear him, brought him home in triumphant delight to Eleanor, and made her give them supper in honour of the great event; and a right pleasant supper those four noble souls had. Then all sorts of things happened, and kept them alive. Sir De Lacy Evans got in for Westminster, at which Lord Charles and Eleanor were glad, though Austin would have preferred Captain Rous, as he liked a snack of Toryism in his politics. Then Lord Lincoln was rejected for Notts, which made them all sorry, and made Lord Charles say what *he* would have done if *his* father had *dared* to influence his election for Granitebridge. Then there was a Polish insurrection, which caused quiet little Eleanor to utter the most ferocious and revolutionary sentiments, about the Emperors of Russia and Austria, and which incited Lord Edward to compose a piece of music expressive of the woes of Poland and their triumphant redressal; which was played by hammering away at the black keys until they were all out of tune, and then beginning on the white; and, when they were finished, putting on the pedals and working both together in one magnificent crash. But, in spite of all this, the Polish revolt ended as all other Polish revolts will, until the cows come home; and the Poles got lovingly corrected by their father, Nicholas.

Then came the news of Moodkee and Ferozeshah; and Eleanor cried about Sir Robert Sale; and Lord Edward got into the organ-loft at St. Paul's, and induced the organist to let him play the people out; and he played such a triumphant symphony, that the people all came back again, under the impression that, this being Lent, the organist had incautiously refreshed himself with strong liquors on a fasting stomach; and the organist had to go secretly to the back part of the organ and let off the wind. It was a happy month for these four innocent souls, and before their golden happy laughter Aunt Maria retired into her dressing-room, and had her meals and scolded her maid there, to every one's great content.

And Captain Hertford came but seldom that month — whether he was busy, or because for a time he felt himself beaten by the young people, we cannot say. It was the happiest month that these four had had, since they had known one another.

Did either of the three others know of the weary grief that was at Eleanor's heart; of the dark cloud which settled down on her face each night, as soon as they were gone, and had left her alone to the long night-watches? Not one of them, or they would surely have said that she was the most valiant and noble little martyr on earth. Many things had to happen before Austin found it out; and one of that group never found it out at all.

Patiently she would sit at her window, looking southward across the crescent, at one light in some sick person's room opposite, and wondering whether their burden was so heavy as her own, until the last footfall died away in the deserted street. Sometimes Aunt Maria would send for her after they were gone, and say such terrible things to her, as only one woman can say to another — nay, as only a woman well practised in scolding like Aunt Maria can say. But Eleanor would only sit and listen, with folded hands. She had a grief deeper than Aunt Maria, a grief which made Aunt Maria's furious scolding sound like the singing of a mosquito outside the net — a sound which makes your sleep uneasy, but which does not wake you.

That happy month drew to a close. On the 14th they were all together. The cloud which had settled on Eleanor's face every night after they had left her, grew visible by day. On the 14th of March, when they were all together again, Austin noticed that she looked anxious and pale. Lord Charles's wildest Radical sallies only brought a faint smile into the close-set mouth, and a feeble flash into the great gray eyes. Austin knew that the time of her monthly pilgrimage was approaching, and did not wonder; the others thought she was ill. Lord Edward formed a theory of her having caught cold at church, and she encouraged it.

It was Sunday evening. Lord Edward had gone with her to the Abbey, and the two sinners, Lord Charles and Austin, had not gone with them. They were spending the evening at her house, and laying out plans for the next week. There would be no important debate the next night, and Lord Charles said that if Eleanor would promise to give a supper afterwards, that he would go down to the House and speak on the Silk question; but she said :

" You must not come here to-morrow or the next day. Austin knows that I cannot receive to-morrow. I have to meet my man of business to-morrow, and that always agitates me so that I am fit for nothing the next day. If any of you are going to be kind, you may call on Tuesday and ask how I am, but I cannot receive you. I have passed a very happy month. If we four young people should never pass such another together, let us always look back on this one. Good night."

The next month was not such a pleasant one by any

means. Politics were becoming embroiled. Mr. Disraeli was saying the most terrible things, and Sir Robert's temper was not always equal to bearing them. Every one was getting hot and angry, and saying things they did not mean. And Austin, having less to do with the matter than most others, was rather hotter and angrier than anybody else. They saw but little of Eleanor, and she for her part wished that the Corn bill was done with for ever, either one way or another.

Chapter XXIV

So little did Austin think about the matter which had troubled him before, that the day of Eleanor's monthly pilgrimage would have passed by altogether without his having noticed it, had it not been for a mere accident, the history of which is this.

Austin had a very good habit of riding out early in the morning before the streets were full, and the smoke had settled down; and on the 15th of April he woke early, and said that he would ride out.

He rang the bell, and when his servant came he ordered his horse to be saddled while he dressed, and called "Robin."

The servant called "Robin" too, but Robin was not in his usual place at the foot of the bed, and on further search it became evident that Robin was not in the house, nor in the street either.

"I brought him in last night," said Austin. "Run round to Miss Hilton's, and see if he is there."

By the time Austin had done dressing, and was standing on the doorstep, in a pair of yellow riding trousers, and a blue neckcloth, his man came back. The dog was not there. It became evident that the dog was stolen.

Austin was vexed and irresolute. At last a foolish

scullion-wench, in the lower regions, incautiously volunteered information. Austin's servants immediately claimed that she should be haled before him, and interrogated.

She came upstairs in pattens, with a mop in her hand, her hair all tumbled and tangled, in a dreadful fright. Austin's valet offered to hold her mop for her : she refused. He tried to take it from her ; she fought him and beat him, and was ushered into Austin's presence, red, triumphant, with her mop in her hand.

Her mysterious communication about the dog amounted to very little indeed. She had found the dog scratching at the door, and had let him out for a run, " Which the Milk had seen her."

" Find the policeman, and tell him," said Austin ; " as I come home I will ride round by James's."

Riding about the west end of London before nine o'clock on an April morning is a very pleasant pastime. The streets are nearly empty, and you can dawdle as much as you like, while in Piccadilly and such places ; the air — should the wind have anything of west in it — is as fresh as it is in the country.

Everybody's horses are out exercising, too : and you can see their legs, eyes, tails, and noses showing out of their clothes, and may, if you like, drive yourself mad, by calculating, on the " ex pede Herculem " plan — by an effort of comparative anatomy far beyond Owen — what sort of horses they are, and how much they are worth apiece. You can also see the British cabman free from the cares of office, and many other strange sights, not to be met with later in the day.

It was a very pleasant ride that Austin had on this spring morning. He rode slowly over the piece of wood pavement between Sackville Street and Bond Street, and then trotted till he came to the small patch opposite Devonshire House (both these are laid down in good granite now), where there was a horse down as usual. Then he walked slowly down the hill, and, turning into the newly-opened park, had a gallop along Rotten Row, and, passing out by Kensington Gate, began to feel his way slowly eastward once more.

Through fresh squares, where the lilac was already budding, through squares and streets which grew grander and grander, till they culminated in Belgrave Square itself, and then into the lower part of the town which lies south-east of it.

It is astonishing how rapidly the town degenerates to the south-east of Belgrave Square towards Vauxhall Bridge; or, to be more correct, did degenerate, in those days. From great mansions you suddenly find yourself among ten-roomed houses. So you rapidly deteriorate to six rooms, to four, to old bankrupt show vans taken off their wheels, and moved on the waste ground, like old worn-out hulks; and, after them, dust and ashes, and old paper-hangings, and piles of lath and plaster, and pots and kettles, and swarms of wild children; to whom this waste of ash-heaps are mountains, and the stagnant fever-pools, lakes — who build here for themselves the fairy castles of childhood, with pot-sherds and oyster-shells, and who seem to enjoy more shrill wild happiness, than the children of any other class in the community.

Austin paused before he came to this range of dust Alps. At the junction of two low streets, between Vauxhall Bridge and Millbank, there stood a house by itself, with a garden in front, and a leafless arbour. This was James's, and James himself, in his shirt sleeves, was in the front garden, drowning some puppies in a bucket.

As Austin reined up, and paused before this house, the population turned out to see the splendid apparition. Such a handsome young gentleman, so nobly dressed, on such a beautiful horse, before half-past ten, was really something to look at. Was there never a lady of Shalott among those busy worn needlewomen, stitching behind the dirty blinds, who looked out and fell in love with this noble young Camelot? Who knows?

" She left the web, she left the loom,
    She made three paces through the room,
    She saw the helmet and the plume,
    And she looked down to Camelot."

Poor things! Sitting there feeding on their own fancies, month by month, it is a wonder how respectable, as a class, these poor folks are. If it were not for the cheap novels, what would become of them?

Austin drew up. Mr. James was so busy drowning the puppies that he did not hear him. So Austin cried out, "Hallo!"

Immediately he heard an unknown number (he says nine hundred, but that is an exaggeration) of dogs, dash out of barrels in the back yard, and choke themselves with their collars. Before they had got wind to bark, a sound was heard as of a strong man swearing. At which these dogs (number unknown, Austin saw afterwards thirty-five bull-dogs, and a cloud of black-and-tan terriers, which, to use his own vigorous expression, darkened the air) all rattled their chains, and went silently back among the straw.

All except an invisible small dog, who, from the volume of his voice, seemed to be the very dog in the "Arabian Nights," which came out of the walnut-shell. He continuing to bark, was audibly kicked by the strong man, and Mr. James, having drowned the last puppy, came towards Austin, hat in hand.

Mr. James, a great, handsome giant, was, and is, one of the most remarkable men in the country. He was the greatest and most successful cynoclept, or dog-dealer, in England, and consequently in the world. If a Chinese Mandarin had sent an order to Mr. James for a dozen fat, blue, hairless dogs, to be cooked for a *fête champêtre* at Pekin, Mr. James would have executed the order by the next mail, without winking his eye. Mr. James was the greatest dog-fancier in England, and, I am exceedingly sorry to say, that Austin was one of his best customers.

I have hinted at Austin's low taste for dogs before this.

With all his high political ambition, this low taste was one black spot in his character. He had an ambition to possess the smallest black-and-tan terrier in England, apparently for the delectation of his groom, for they were always kept at the Mews with his horses. The groom became, to a certain extent, debauched through these dogs. Prizefighters, and far worse, used to make court to that young man, and take him to public-houses, free of expense, for the mere privilege of handling these wonderful dogs, the largest of which did not weigh more than four pounds. Austin had sometimes given at the rate of four guineas a pound for them. Robin had never considered them to be dogs at all, and had treated them accordingly.

The enormous sums paid for these dogs, and the fact of their being regularly stole once a week, and recovered and sent home by Mr. James, had ended in Mr. James, great man as he was, being a creature of Austin's. He considered Austin to be a type of the real English gentleman, the last hope of a degenerate age. Consequently, when he had done drowning his puppies and saw Austin at his gate, he advanced towards him with a very low bow.

" James," said Austin, " I have lost Robin."

" What o'clock, sir ? "

" About seven."

" Then I can't let you have him before to-morrow morning, sir. My cads were all out before that. Will half-past eight to-morrow morning do, sir ? "

" It must, I suppose," said Austin, " unless he comes home by himself."

Mr. James was much amused by this supposition. He said that Mr. Elliot would have his joke ; and requested that Austin would dismount.

Austin did so, and Mr. James called for Sam. Sam came. The invisible strong man before mentioned — a young man, in his shirt and trousers, who had not washed himself, and who looked like a prize-fighter under a cloud — which indeed he was. With him came Mr. James's own favourite dog — a white bull-terrier, who smelt Austin's legs and gave him a creeping up his back. After which he went into James's yard and bought the dog which came out of the walnut-shell for seven guineas.

Mr. James had not done with Austin. It appeared that in the next street, towards the river, there was a dog, belonging to a master sweep, which Mr. Elliot *must* see, if he wanted to know what a dog was. Austin, having given a shilling to the obscured prize-fighter, who was waiting for an opportunity to wash, mounted his horse and accompanied Mr. James and Mr. James's bull-terrier.

The master sweep was in his gateway, and between his legs was a white bull-terrier, exactly like Mr. James's. Mr. James took his dog by the neck, the sweep did the same. Austin called out, " James, I won't have it ! " but it was too late, the dogs were at one another's throats, and the douce respectable Mr. James was transformed into a shouting blackguard ; while Austin found himself, in spite of his feelings of shame, looking on at the most brutal sport in the world. Every man who sets two dogs to fight, ought to be beaten with a good thick stick.

Whether it was that the residence of such a great cynoclept as Mr. James had debauched the neighbourhood and given to it a tendency to keep surreptitious dogs : or whether the fact of its being what Mr. Dickens calls a " shy " neighbourhood, with infinite facilities of sending all dogs to play with the children on the dust-heaps, in the rear, on the appearance of the taxgatherer, induced every householder in these parts to keep a dog, I know not. But there was a dog in every house ; and the moment the sound of the fight began, they rushed forth to see the fun. Some leaped out of the windows of garrets, where they had been confined for their sins ; others walked staggeringly along the tops of walls, bristling with glass bottles ; some squeezed themselves, panting, through impossible places ; and one fell into a water-butt, where he paddled and sneezed, until his mistress took him out by his tail, and banged him about the head with her shoe; but the result was, that Austin, standing there on horseback, with the hope of stopping the cruel work at the first opportunity, found that his horse's legs were in, as it were, a bath of dogs, who yelped and snapped and snarled round the two rearing combatants in the midst.

And then suddenly he became aware that his own dog Robin was in the midst of them. Whether he had dropped from the skies, or risen out of the earth he knew not, but there was Robin — his own Robin — going round and round the dogs, and through and through the dogs, asking this one, how it came about, and that one, who was getting the best of it, and another one what they had better do? Robin — gay, handsome, rollicking Robin — was there, making himself agreeable to the ladies, giving the best advice to the gentlemen, under the very nose of his own master's horse, not having recognised either horse or master in his excitement.

Austin heard some one call the dog by name behind him. He turned round, and he felt sick and faint, as well he might.

For there, in the midst of all this squalid black-guardism, was Eleanor — Eleanor herself. She was dressed in common, almost shabby, clothes. Her veil was up, and her eyes were red with weeping; and on her face was the very expression which he had expected to see there on this very day of the month — worn anxiety, grief, and shuddering terror.

She was standing on the pavement feebly crying, " Robin ! Robin ! " but when she saw his face she cried out, " Austin, Austin ! come to me ! "

Chapter XXV

AUSTIN caught Mr. James's assistant, and got him to lead his horse home. And in the next moment he was by Eleanor's side, and Robin was bounding gladly around them. She took his arm, and they walked homewards together.

Poor Eleanor was very much distressed, and agitated. She had her veil down, and was crying, and Austin gently comforted her. When she had partly recovered from her tears, she said, " It was so naughty of Robin to run away from me after those dogs." Austin would have liked to ask an explanation of her appearance there, but he did not like to. Eleanor was very much distressed and hysterical, and he wisely held his tongue.

Nevertheless, he was very much inclined to be angry with her. She had been going to church a great deal lately, — going on week days too, — and always to what he would have called ' Tractarian ' churches. Once she had asked him if he would be angry, if she were to turn Papist. Now Austin's sole religious creed at this time, was a political hatred, derived from his father, of the ' Catholics,' and never having risen so high in religious thought as Tractarianism, he felt a nearly equal jealousy of them. He got it now into his head, that Eleanor had some spiritual adviser, either very High Church, or Papist, who had persuaded her to take these monthly journeys in this garb, to this neighbourhood, on the grounds of religious mortification. It was by no means an unnatural conclusion. He was inclined to be angry with her, and determined to argue with her on the folly of it.

He was very much inclined to be angry. He had very nearly succeeded in making himself so, when she pressed his arm, and said,

" Are you angry, Austin ? "

"No," he said, — "I mean yes. I am furiously angry, my darling. How do you think that you can please God, by appearing in such a place as that where I found you, in such a dress? Don't you suffer penance enough at home, every day of your life, without allowing a priest to bind a grievous burden on your back, which he, himself, would not touch with one of his fingers?"

Ah! if she had told him the truth! She saw his error. She saw that he thought she was making some kind of religious pilgrimage, and she encouraged his error. In her deep love for him, in her anxiety for his honour and fame, she encouraged it. It was not so very long after this, that sitting at her dressing-table, she noticed that her hair was slightly grey. She put down her brushes, and thought of her foolish, foolish falsehood.

"Austin," she said, "let me get to heaven my own way. Don't talk of this again. If you were sick, or in prison, would I not visit you?"

He comforted her, and said no more about it, and indeed, after a few days, did not think very much; for there was much to think about elsewhere, of a far different sort.

The tiresome iteration of the Corn-law debate began, as time went on, to be relieved by fiercer and fiercer personalities. Honourable members were saying things to one another, such as they had not said since 1831, and have not said since. In the House it was bad enough, but in the clubs it was worse, by all accounts. Honourable and gallant Members at the Carlton, were threatening to pitch Right Honourable Members and future Chancellors of Exchequer out of window, in the direction of the Reform Club. "Or did so, in at least one instance," as Mr. C— might say, in hedging a general statement of this kind, and might also continue, "future Exchequer Chancellor *not* pitched out of window after all. Honourable major, threatening that same, hereafter apologising with a certain leonine simplicity and honesty, not without grandeur. On which occasion, also, we find that leonine major savagely, and with feline snarl (yar-r-r! To thy Cairn, Vermin, lest a worse thing befal thee) turning on a certain too eager jackal of his, a Captain Hertford. Jackal apparently (judging from infinite annual register, and newspaper-file crudities) without even the jackal-merit of cunning. Only merit, apparently, having teeth, and biting nobler than he. But a poor thing in jackals, now happily passed away into limbo, for evermore let us hope."

To add to the confusion, in this same pleasant month of May, an opinion began to obtain, among those who were in the same position, of knowing but little about the matter, but of talking a great deal : that although the bill was safe enough in the Commons, it was not safe in the Lords. This caused a great deal of fidgety irritation, and Lord Charles Barty went about (to use a trope) with a pan of burning charcoal on his head, threatening utter annihilation to his order, should they impudently dare to follow their own convictions.

In the midst of it all, Mr. Smith O'Brien, driven to the verge of madness at not making a sensation equal to his merits (O'Connell extinguished a year since in a blaze of high-handed justice, and no successor of sufficient mendacity and talent appearing), conceived the noble idea of refusing to sit on Saxon railway-committees, and got himself shut up, in more ways than one, if the reader will forgive a piece of harmless slang. He was rewarded for his heroism, by appearing the next week in perhaps the best caricature in *Punch* — " The Naughty Boy who didn't care."

Altogether, in this month of May, people were getting unwisely excited about this Corn-bill, and non-electors began to stand about at street-corners and discuss it in a loud voice : which is an ugly symptom, in a close-packed city of two millions, the most open part of it, a mere Saint Antoine, *not* cut up east, west, north, and south by the boulevards of a paternal Government, anxious to remain a

Government. People were getting very much excited in the House and out of the House; and what would have happened in 1848 if the Lords had thrown out the Bill, we are almost afraid to think.

In the middle of all this, Lord George Bentinck got up and made, what we must all, I think, confess, a most terribly telling speech against Sir Robert Peel. He unluckily tried his hand on a proposition about the admission of oats, showing a degree of ignorance or carelessness almost incredible in a man aspiring to lead a party. Mr. Goulburn went about with him amidst the laughter of the House. In the discussion which ensued, Captain Hertford spoke for a few minutes, and succeeded in making Lord George's case worse than before. The instant he sat down Lord Charles Barty was on his legs.

It is possible that the House was relieved to find the quarrel transferred to two such insignificant members as Captain Hertford and Lord Charles Barty. At all events, they appeared so. Lord Charles did not speak well; he did not speak like himself. His heart was so full of furious animosity against this man Hertford, that he said things he ought not to have said. He insulted Captain Hertford, and there were cries of order. He had gone too far, when he sat down again beside Mr. Huddersfield the lawyer, radical member for a city in the West ; that gentleman said to him, " You have gone too far, Barty. That man will have you out."

But Captain Hertford took no notice of it. People were saying all sorts of things about one another just then. Lord Charles had not said anything about Captain Hertford, *much* worse than what Mr. Disraeli had said of Sir Robert.

Austin had that evening led Lord Edward Barty up into the gallery, and they two had heard it all. When the debate was over, and they were waiting for Lord Charles in the old place under the end of Henry VII.'s chapel, Lord Edward said —

" Austin, Charles has insulted that man. He will have a message to-morrow morning."

Austin said he hoped not. No message came. And then poor blind Lord Edward got an idea into his darkened head, which he acted on, the full effect of which we shall see.

We are obliged, however, to follow Captain Hertford on his way home this evening. We wish we could take the reader home in better company.

If any one had been able to see in the moonlight the vindictive scowl that was on his coarse face, they would have augured ill for any one who should venture to thrust his company on the Captain in an obtrusive manner that night. A handsome young Frenchman, either not knowing or not caring what his state of mind might be ; came up, took him by the arm, and burst into the most exaggerated form of French laughter.

" Ha ! ha ! but Milor used you sadly, my dear friend. By the prophet, but he laughed at the most sacred beard of my own Hertford. Come, let us shoot him. How say you, is Milor to be kill ? "

Captain Hertford showed no outward irritation at this man's presence or manner. He answered quietly enough.

" Milor may go hang, rot, anything he likes, for the present, my friend. Commilfaut, where have you sprung from ? "

" From the gallery of the imperial Parliament of Great Britain, where I have been listening to the burning, furious, and yet lucid eloquence of my friend Hertford on ze oat. 'Twas a droll subject, but ' nihil tetigit quod non ornavit,' like Doctor Goldsmiss in the *triste* old Abbey."

" Don't be a fool, Commilfaut."

" I will not when I am dead and buried, perhaps. Till then fool I shall always be, dear Captain. Come and play the billiard — one game — by dam ! Only one game."

After a few moments' consideration, Captain Hertford said yes, and they went towards a billiard-room near the bridge, which was still open, at all events to the Captain.

The billiard-marker was a rather gentlemanly-looking young man, though with a decidedly dissipated air about him. Some day, some wise man will write the lives of eminent billiard-markers. It ought to be a very interesting book, for the lives of most of them have been singularly erratic and tragical.

They began playing, and talked about indifferent matters in English; but after a time Monsieur De Commilfaut having made a hit, turned to the marker and said in French: "That was a good stroke, was it not?"

The marker looked stupidly at him and said, "I beg your pardon, sir?" M. De Commilfaut repeated the question, and the marker turned with a puzzled air to Captain Hertford for explanation.

"The man don't understand French, don't you see," growled the captain; "go on."

"I perceive that the pig-headed brigand does not, as you remark, understand the language of Europe; which is a charming discovery, as we can now discuss a few little matters, which I would be glad to have discussed." This was said in French, and from this time the conversation was carried on in French, a language which Captain Hertford spoke like his mother tongue.

"And how is my sweet cousin?" said De Commilfaut.

"She is a fool," said Captain Hertford sulkily.

"She is. She don't appreciate me. Has, in fact, refused me an absurdly small loan of nine thousand francs. Eleanor Hilton is a young lady of incorrigibly bad taste. She prefers, for instance, you to me. Can anything be worse taste, my Captain?"

"Nothing, I suppose," said the Captain, wincing. "Women are strange creatures; they will sometimes like a man better than a monkey."

The Frenchman was so delighted with this elegant sally of the Captain, that he went into the wildest fit of laughter. He gave his cue to the stupid marker, sat on a bench, and laughed till he cried. After a time he took his cue again in a feeble manner, but before he could strike the ball the fit came on again, and he laughed till he cried again ; by degrees he became quieter, and went on with his game.

"But I am glad to hear, my little pig — if, as you say in your Parliament, you will allow me to call you so — that you are at the best with this infinitely rich, espiègle, but very obstinate little cousin of mine, Eleanor Hilton ; and for this reason among others, that since she has refused me (by the mouth of an aged mountebank, whose ears should be served up *au gratin* at the devil's next dinner party) this trifling loan, I am at this moment ' *in nubibus*,' which means under ze cloud, unclassical cabbage ! "

At this moment the marker broke out into a short laugh, and they both quickly turned on him. The marker explained.

"The French gentleman has played your ball, sir. I always notice that too much talk don't do at billiards any more than at whist."

The mistake was rectified, and they resumed the game and the conversation still in French.

"I suppose," said Captain Hertford, "that you are going to mention my little debt to you ? "

"His little debt ! Holy grey ! the wealth of these islanders ! Forty thousand francs a little debt ! "

" *I* don't call it a little debt ! It is a mode of speech," said Captain Hertford. "You cannot get blood out of a stone, though, my friend."

"Alas, no ! I know it. For this reason I am overwhelmed with joy to hear that you are at best with our determined little cousin ; that you are about marrying her, and about paying me my poor forty thousand francs."

"You will have your money if you wait," said Captain Hertford, sulkily. "I shall certainly marry her, and you will be paid in good time."

"I am sure, dear Captain. She has, then, thrown overboard this handsome young scoundrel — this Elliot ? "

"No, she has not."

" I shall watch your play, then, with the greater anxiety. I have seen him — he is amazingly handsome — and I have seen them together. I followed her when she was leading a blind Milor, a Sir Edward, and she met him — this Elliot — and I watched her ; and I have had my good fortunes like another, and I can see. And she loves him."

" I am quite aware of it," said Captain Hertford.

" And what are you going to do ? "

" You asked me to-night," replied the Captain, " why I did not take a shot at Lord Charles Barty, for his cursed insolence in the House. I'll tell you why. If I had out Lord Charles Barty, and even hit him, it would necessitate a slight seclusion abroad, and the leaving the field in the hands of the enemy. I am waiting for an opportunity of insulting this fellow Elliot, and killing him."

" Recommending yourself to my little cousin's good graces by killing her lover," said the Frenchman. " Well, I have heard of that succeeding. But that course also, my friend, will involve a temporary seclusion in the centre of European thought and intellect, Paris ; and our cousin will be left to lead about the blind Milor, and will, as I hear, probably take the veil, which will be the devil itself."

" Not at all," said Captain Hertford. " If she was got away from Elliot and his confederate, Lord Charles Barty (who would, too, were he his second, have to retire also), her aunt could bring her abroad, and we might do anything with her. Marker, go and fetch me some soda-water and brandy."

The marker departed.

" Do you suspect he understands French, then ? " said Commilfaut.

" No ; but one can't be too cautious. If that girl refuses to marry me, I have a secret of hers which is worth three thousand a-year to me."

" And what is that ? "

" Dear friend," said Captain Hertford, " would it be a secret if I told it you ? "

" Why no," said the good-natured rascal of a French-man, laughing, "only remember my forty thousand francs, or I will force you to challenge me, and choose swords, old cabbage."

And so these worthies departed, infinitely satisfied. But their interview compels me to call attention to a little story which I have to tell. And which I will tell as dramatically as I can, so that it may not be dull.

This billiard-room, where these two worthies had just held their villanous conversation, was at that time the nearest billiard-room to the House of Commons.

Austin Elliot was exceedingly fond of two things. The one of hearing debates in the houses, the other of playing billiards. When waiting for a debate to come on, what more natural than that he should beguile the time with a game of billiards? Still more natural that he should play his billiards at the house nearest handy, so as to run off at any time. More natural yet, that he should, with his hearty manner and open hand, get well known there, say *very* well known to the proprietor Perkins.

At this point in our narrative, we must go back to a period ten years antecedent, and begin all over again.

When Austin and Lord Charles were at Eton, there had been an agreeable plucky boy there, whom they both knew, by name Mapleton. This boy had gone to Brasenose, Oxford, and from thence to the dogs : horribly in debt, disappearing into outer darkness ; having, in fact, in his wanderings, rambled into that land in which policemen and low persons of that kind have power. It was a sad business — the only thing to do was to forget that such a lad ever lived.

But, about six months before this time, Austin had received a letter from this lad Mapleton, out of the Queen's Bench, praying for help for the sake of old acquaintance ; and Austin had gone away to him at once, with his good heart full of old school recollections, steadily ignoring all later passages in this lad's life. Only reflecting that he might be saved yet.

He heard the young man, Mapleton's story, he paid the debt for which he was in prison, and both he and Lord Charles promised that if he should deserve it they would help him up the ladder again.

At this time it happened that the then billiard-marker at Perkins' forged Perkins' name for 96*l*. 10*s*., and got the money. He found this so pleasant, it being vacation time, and billiards slack, that he begun to steal the billiard balls by twos and threes, and sell them in Greek Street, Soho. This thriving also, and the 96*l*. being capital untouched, he stole Perkins' cashbox, and absconded. But remembering that there was one more set of new balls left, he, so to speak, *un*-absconded again, and came back to fetch them. But the measure of his sins being full, it fell out that Perkins met him on the stairs and essayed to arrest him. They fell downstairs together, Perkins cut his head open against the umbrella-stand, and the marker would have escaped, had not Mrs. Perkins rushed out of the parlour, stunned him with the hearth-broom, and got in the police. After this there was no marker at Perkins' but Perkins himself; who pathetically told Austin and Lord Charles, that his tobacco business was going to the very deuce for want of a billiard-marker, and they both cried out, " Mapleton," and Mapleton came, and stole no cash-boxes ; but passed on into higher walks in life after a time.

And this was the young marker who marked for Captain Hertford and M. De Commilfaut, the night they had their important conversation. Add to this that, in consequence of five years' Continental experience, more or less disreputable, he understood French better than Captain Hertford, and from old Eton recollections, knew a little more Latin than M. De Commilfaut ; which made him nearly betray himself, at the Frenchman's new construction of *in nubibus*.

No wonder, then, that he, only now the poor ghost of what he might have been, or what he might be yet, but with his poor weak heart full of gratitude, took his post in front of Cheshire House, very early next morning.

By and by the Duke came out, rosy and fresh, eager to get some pure air before the smoke came down ; to take his two turns round the square, and his look in at his stables, and wish to goodness he was back at Esham, among his beasts. Next came Lord Edward, blindly staring, with his hand on his valet's shoulder, away to the north-east for prayers at Margaret Street. Lastly, Lord Charles, in white trousers, tall, handsome, and gay, going one knows not whither ; ready in his happy, youthful vitality, to go anywhere where a gentleman might. Him the poor billiard-marker stopped, and into his attentive ear poured all he could remember of the last nights' conversation.

Chapter XXVI

ALL he could remember. It amounted to this — as far as Lord Charles could understand it — that this billiard-marker had heard Captain Hertford say that he intended to provoke Austin and shoot him : and that he (the Captain) was assured that Eleanor would marry him, as soon as that was accomplished. With all the poor fellow's eager honesty, he made a game of " Russian scandal " of his information after all.

The marker and Lord Charles Barty played at Russian scandal with a vengeance. Lord Charles thought that if he were to tell Austin of it first hand, there would be a furious outbreak on Austin's part, and that there would be a duel, in which, as a matter of course, Austin would be shot stone dead by Captain Hertford. So he went up and waited outside of the chapel till his blind brother came out, and told him (with Russian scandal variations), and they both agreed that Lord Edward should tell the story to Austin, softening it in every way ; just to put him on his guard against quarrelling with Captain Hertford, until there had been a grand consultation as to what the three friends were to do.

Blind Lord Edward performed his commission (in the Russian scandal way) ; he contrived to make Austin understand, that Captain Hertford had in a public billiard-room, in the presence of witnesses, asserted that he was engaged to Eleanor, and also, that he was only waiting for an opportunity to pick a quarrel with Austin, and shoot him.

About the first part of this communication Austin laughed heartily ; about the second he looked very grave.

" Edward Barty," he said, " surely *you* do not distrust Eleanor ? "

" I would answer for her with my life," said the blind man.

" And I," said Austin. " This Hertford is a creature of hers. She paid his election bills. He knows something which she wishes to have hidden from me. That is the reason of their familiarity. I will challenge her about it, and have it explained. But I know her well enough to know that the idea of her marrying him is preposterous, mad, not to be entertained by a sane man. She hates him. She knows and despises him as well as we do. I am surprised that you should have even repeated such a report to me."

" Dear Austin," said Lord Edward, " we are all agreed about that part of the matter ; no one is anxious about that ; it is about you that we are anxious. *I* have no doubt but that Captain Hertford believes that if he could get you out of the way, and get Aunt Maria to take her abroad, that he would have his way. He believes that we know Eleanor too well. But, old boy," continued Lord Edward, feeling out into his eternal darkness for Austin's well-loved face, " If the dog shot you, in pursuing his villanous plan, what would there be left for the rest of us but misery and remorse, and impatient waiting for death, that we might feel your dear hands again ? "

There was no one to see the expression on Austin's face now — an expression seen by Captain Hertford two years ago on that face at Tyn-y-Rhaiadr, and to be seen by the worthy Captain once more — an expression of mingled fury and fear. He burst out with a snarl —

" Damn him ! Is he the only man who can shoot with a pistol ? What sort of country is this we live in, that a dog like that, by possessing a certain dexterity — a dexterity which a Sikh Soubadhar, or a French chevalier d'industrie, could communicate to my own groom — should hold the happiness of us all in his hand like this ? By God, Edward, it is shameful ! Nothing to be said, nothing to be done, but by the grace of this low blackleg, who has the one accomplishment of hitting a man at twelve paces with a pistol ball ! "

" It is an inevitable evil, Austin."

" It is not inevitable. The land is groaning under the system of the duel, and the land will be rid of it. Curse on the fool who invented it, and a curse on all fools who follow it. Therefore, Edward, a curse on myself ; for let him beware, I will play Best to his Camelford — mark me, I will ! "

" I only know this," said Lord Edward, " that I will not have it ; you shall not go out with that man. I will take measures —"

" Your measures, my poor Eddy," said Austin, " would only necessitate my blowing my own brains out instead of his. Remember, that any step taken to prevent a meeting between this man and me, after what has passed, can only end in utter irretrievable ruin to me."

" I know ! I know ! alas how well ! But you will be careful, Austin."

" I will not go within a hundred yards of the man," said Austin, " my anger is over in that last burst. If you could see my face, you would know it."

At this time they were walking arm-in-arm round the garden in Grosvenor Square.

" See your face ! " said Lord Edward, " aye, I wish I could see your face. Does it seem strange to you, to know a man who does not know what seeing means ? I was born blind, you know, and ever since I could think I have tried to compare the things I love. They have told me that you were beautiful, and I have tried to realize your face. Sometimes I have thought that it was like the scent of violets, sometimes like the noise I hear on the terrace at Esham on a summer evening, when the children are playing on the village green down below ; and sometimes when you and Charles get wild over your politics, that it is like the mad scream of Ernst's fiddle, when he makes all the muscles of your back tingle, and the nerves about your face quiver again. What a fool you would be, if you were blind, Austin."

So Captain Hertford, by such talk as this, was removed millions of miles from Austin's consideration. But when his clothes were off and he was horizontal in bed, the inexorable Captain reappeared. And Robin, the dog, who slept with Austin, got impressions, whether of thieves or fire I know not, which made him sit up till morn, and pant ; for which he got his reward from the boot-rack at various times in the night ; but still, after divers more or less dexterous retreats from flying boots, he sat up and panted conscientiously until morning dawned.

Chapter XXVII

WHAT was to be done ? Lord Charles, his brother, and Austin all consulted, and the answer was, " Nothing as yet." What *could* be done ? The very slightest motion on their part would bring on the very meeting they dreaded ; unless they resorted to civil protection, in which case there would be absolutely nothing to be done, according to their code, but for Austin to blow his brains out.

Poor Lord Edward, sitting in eternal darkness, not being able to know men's faces and what expression accompanied such and such words, formed a project which no one but a blind man or a madman would have formed. His project was this, to speak to Captain Hertford himself. He had been in Captain Hertford's company three or four times, and always when Eleanor was present. He had never seen his cruel, gluttonous face, and he had only heard his voice; and the Captain's voice, in the presence of Eleanor, his benefactress, was not so unpleasant. It was subdued to a sulky, respectful sort of growl. And judging from his voice alone, and, pluming himself on his shrewdness, Lord Edward came to the conclusion that he was not quite so bad as the others wanted to make him out; that, at all events, he would try what could be done with him. I must tell you how he fared.

Captain Hertford's plan of operations just at this time was most certainly nearly the same as that which he unfolded to the Frenchman at the billiard-table. But we must remember that he was a *stupid* man, whose cunning was of a very low order. He had, as he most truly said, a secret of Eleanor's by which he might extort money from her; but when that secret was known to Austin, as he felt sure it would be on the very day of their marriage, he had cunning enough to know, that it would be worth much less in Austin's hands than in hers. Moreover, were Austin out of the way, and he safe abroad, he felt sure that Aunt Maria had still power enough to scold Eleanor into going abroad, in which case he hoped to get her to consent to marry him.

Here is where the man's low cunning failed him utterly. Eleanor had always been so gentle and so kind to him, for the sake of what he had done for her and for the power that he still held in his hands; that the fool never dreamed that she loathed his presence, and that she hated the day when she first saw him.

Eleanor, in addition to her own terrible domestic troubles

— tangible every-day troubles — which she and her faith-ful old footman bore patiently together ; had got, from her native shrewdness, a terror lest Captain Hertford should conceive the plan of doing exactly what he was thinking of doing now — involving Austin in a quarrel, killing him, and getting her abroad, under the sole pro-tection of her aunt, whose madness was developing day by day.

That is what was the matter with Aunt Maria. She was getting mad. Her fierce fits of scolding were becom-ing fiercer, and sometimes her maid would come up ter-rified into Eleanor's room in the dead of night, and they two would listen to the dreadful old woman scolding away to herself below, as if her maid was present.

Poor Eleanor did not know which way to turn among all these terrible apprehensions. But she made a solemn vow to herself, — that if Austin were killed and she forced abroad, that she would embrace the Popish faith, and claim the protection of the good Archbishop of Paris, whom she knew.

So that as Captain Hertford's scheme stood at present, she would have utterly wrecked it. But Lord Edward Barty changed the Captain's scheme, and it was never put in execution. Captain Hertford formed another one, and we shall see how that succeeded.

One pleasant morning in this May month, date I should say about the 12th, Eleanor and the worthy Captain sat together in Eleanor's drawing-room in Wilton Crescent. They were quite silent. Some commonplaces had passed, Hertford had brought her some Cape jessamine, and she had thanked him, and relapsed into silence, wondering whether he had anything to say; rather wishing he would go, but on the whole taking rather more notice of Robin, who had come to her on a furtive visit, than of the honour-able and gallant gentleman.

Her regular, rather small features, had become some-what pinched and worn lately, and her air was a little languid. Her eyes were as brilliant as ever, but her mouth was more closely set ; and altogether her face was more marked, and she looked older. She had had not very much of artificial education, but she had inherited a certain grace of posture from her mother, and I know not how many grandmothers and great-grandmothers. Every attitude which she put herself into was graceful. Her present one was very much so, it was the one in which one most commonly saw her : sitting in perfect repose, with her hands folded on her lap, without one fold in her drapery awry or out of place. She had the art of sitting absolutely still for any length of time with the most perfect grace ; and that is a most difficult and rare art, and also a most useful one.

It puzzled Hertford on this occasion. He had something to say to her, but he was a very stupid man, and he never could start a subject of conversation without assistance. On this occasion he got none ; judging from appearances, and knowing her as well as he did, there did not appear the slightest reason why Eleanor should not sit in that posture, with her hands folded in her lap, in that exasperating manner, for the next two hours. The Captain got angry, and at last he said, — " I beg your pardon, Miss Hilton."

Eleanor merely turned her head, and looked at him with an expression of languid curiosity. She changed her attitude, but it was only more graceful than before. Hertford had to go on —

" There is a knock at the door. I am glad of it, for it will cut me short. I have to thank you for your extraordinary generosity about my election business. I am grateful, I assure you."

" My dear Captain Hertford," she said quietly, " no one could have deserved my assistance more than yourself. I will always be your friend, as long as you deserve it."

The door was opened, and James snarled out, —

" Lord Eddard and Lord Chawls. That gal Susan have

dropped my best cut water-jug and broke it. She were a washing on it at the scullery sink, and she let go on it, and down it come. Says she's all of a tremble 'cause she dreamt last night, as the carpenter she keeps company with in the country, cut her throat with a bevilling-plane, and buried her body in a old saw-pit. Drat her, I wish he had." And having said this, he departed, and banged the door behind him, while Eleanor's face was lit up with a smile.

On seeing Hertford, Lord Charles paused for an instant, and consequently Lord Edward, who had his hand on his brother's neck, and was being led by him, paused too. A singular pair. Both very handsome, singularly alike in feature, dressed similarly from top to toe; and yet with such a strange difference between them. Charles had a pair of bright, honest blue eyes — Edward was stone-blind. Looking at Lord Charles first, and then at his brother, had the same effect as if you looked at the well-known face of a dear friend, and immediately after at a sightless, staring, marble bust of him.

" Miss Hilton," said Lord Charles, " I have piloted Eddy here ; he says you will take him to church. Do, that's a dear soul, for I must go. Good-bye."

Hertford had risen too, and when Lord Charles was gone, looked towards the door ; Eleanor said, — " Captain Hertford, would you mind stopping — I have something to say to you ? " And on this the Captain sat down again.

The bell was even now ringing for church, and Eleanor must hurry away, and put on her bonnet ; and so Lord Edward was left alone with Captain Hertford, and Hertford sat and stared at the blind man, who groped his way to the piano, and began softly playing snatches of sacred music. He had never been introduced to Captain Hertford. There was no reason why Captain Hertford should speak to the brother of the confounded puppy who had insulted him, and so he sat and stared at those sightless eyes.

Those sightless eyes! The darkened windows of a house in which sight lies dead, shrouded in grave-clothes of strange misconceptions, until the dawn of the Resurrection shall begin to gleam in the East, and the dead shall rise upon their feet. The eyes of the blind are more awful to look at than the eyes of the dead.

Yes, more awful. The eyes of the dead have looked, (at one time), upon the earth in which their time of probation has been passed, and their eyes have carried the outward semblance of their fellow men, into their soul. But the blank staring eyes of those who have been born blind, have looked on nought but darkness from the beginning: and the soul imprisoned behind them, has only groped about in the night of its living tomb; and has learnt to love only by the sense of hearing and touch.

What a strange riddle the earth must be to a man born blind. We all know of the blind man, who thought that red was like the sound of a trumpet; and we remember it, because it was, in some sort, a good guess. But think what a puzzle the whole world must be to a man in this state. Try to remember if you have ever awaked at night, in pitch darkness; and how the nibbling of a mouse was to you the stealthy working of the burglar's centre-bit; and the rustle of a few withered leaves in the night wind, became the fierce crackle of burning beams.

Try to think of a man in a chronic state of misconception, and do not blame Lord Edward Barty for what he did.

Living in a very small circle, under his terrible affliction, with few hopes, few amusements; his source of information, the being read to by his valet — he, labouring under the consciousness of a want of information, avoided conversation and society. By this means he had not got the great lesson which society teaches, — knowledge of the value of words; and so —

And so — after playing at the piano for a time, he stood up. Captain Hertford sat at the other end of the room, and silently watched him.

"What a devilish curious thing," thought Captain Hertford, "to be always in the dark, like that fellow."

Lord Edward began to feel over the nearest table to him, with his fingers, as though looking for something. Captain Hertford was right. There was something very strange and weird in watching the long fingers wandering about among the china and bijouterie, or what not, which lay on the various tables ; something very strange in that beautiful darkened face ; which, with an instinct, the depth of which no man can fathom, was always turned towards those white hands, which its eyes had never seen ; and never would see.

"It is uncommon curious to think of," thought the Captain, "but that fellow has never seen any other fellow in his whole life. There is something very horrid about it."

There was. Lord Edward was feeling his way softly round the table, towards Captain Hertford, in sightless silence, getting nearer and nearer every instant with his long thin fingers ; it *was* very horrid. Hertford held his breath, and felt a strange creeping come over him. One of his big hands was on the table, and Lord Edward's long hands were coming slowly towards it, feeling their way through the books, and press-papers, and paper-knives, — and yet Captain Hertford kept his hand still on the table ; there was a kind of fascination about the blind man's eyes.

At last, Lord Edward touched his hand, he took it up in his, and Hertford did not resist. Lord Edward spoke, and Captain Hertford listened, listened to strange words, words which at first made him sit dumb with terror, brave man as he was.

"Feeling about in the everlasting darkness which surrounds me," said Lord Edward, "I have come across the hand of a man. It is a hand which has held a sword, and used that sword at the gates of death. It is the hand of a brave man. And yet that hand will soon be slippery with innocent blood. It will be the hand of a murderer soon ! "

Before Captain Hertford had made up his mind whether

or no the man who was talking was a madman, as well as blind, the other went on.

" Captain Hertford ! I cannot prevent you killing Austin Elliot. It were almost better that he should be dead, than that he, with his feelings of honour, should live on, if I were to interfere and prevent you fighting him. I do not speak of him. I speak of yourself. I know that you have laid a plot to assassinate him. Every detail of your plot is known to me. That rascally gambling cousin of Eleanor's, that Commilfaut, might be brought into court to-morrow to convict you of a conspiracy. You are quite in my hands if anything should happen to Austin ; but I am held down from taking steps to save him, for the reasons I have mentioned. I only tell you this, that if anything does happen to him, nothing shall save you. If you were ever on any provocation to fight him after this, nothing could save you. I am in possession of your whole scheme, Hertford ; now what will you do ? "

It seemed, from the expression of the Captain's face, had any one seen it, that what he would do, would be to take Lord Edward by the throat, and beat his brains out against the wall. All he said was, " Wait, my lord — wait, will you ? You are presuming very considerably on your infirmity."

" Not I. I am quite without fear, I assure you. If my life would save Austin's I would gladly give it. I will wait. Think for a little, Captain Hertford, and tell me what you mean to do."

Captain Hertford saw quickly that he was in a scrape. That if they had got hold of his conversation with Commilfaut, it would be impossible for him to fight Austin, without incurring far more serious penalties than those consequent on an ordinary duel. He felt, in one instant, that his plan of having Austin out and shooting him, was gone to the winds. He gave it up. Austin was safe from that moment, *if he had sense to stay in England*.

But Lord Edward's words, coming as they did upon the

strange fit of superstitious terror, arising from the fact of his creeping towards him in that strange, silent way, had raised a very mad devil in him. It is a mere silly truism, a thing hardly worth repeating to an intelligent person, that bad people are never so cruelly vindictive, as when they are recovering from a fit of terror. He would have liked to revenge himself on Lord Edward, but that was impossible. But ——

But there was Lord Edward's brother. He could hit him hard there. They talked of enforcing the laws against duelling, but was not P—— acquitted? They would not dare to do more than they ordinarily did on such occasions, if he had out Lord Charles Barty. The young prig who had insulted him in the House, till even the Whigs called order. Now he rapidly began to reflect, now that his rage was turned that way, that his reputation would be a ragged one if he did not. It would be a political duel. He had precedent here. Canning and Londonderry; Wellington and Winchelsea. Yes, that handsome young dandy should be scapegoat. He had brought it on himself.

And also Austin would have to go abroad, if anything happened. And Messieurs the French Officers were dexterous, and, yes, on the first blush of it, it would do. So he spoke.

" Lord Edward."

" I listen."

" I will take an oath to you. Austin Elliot shall, if he be so minded, spit in my face, and I will not go out with him, unless he comes abroad. Will that content you ? "

" I always said," said Lord Edward, " that you were not a bad man. I thank God I am right. Let me call you my friend, Captain."

" No, I will not do that. You have insulted me, and in a cowardly way, because you knew I could not resent it. I will not meddle with you. You have a shrewd tongue, Lord Edward."

And before they had time to say anything more, uncon-

scious Eleanor came in ready for church, and led off Lord
Edward. They went to church, and sat like two stone
angels through it all, until some one, who had come up
from Oxford, played out, in a triumphant hurling storm of
sound; and, when the last echo had done humming in the
roof, they waited together at the bottom of the organ-loft
stairs, till they heard the well-known sound of his wooden
leg stumping down; and, after an affectionate greeting,
carried him off to lunch at Eleanor's.

And this was the result of Lord Edward's interview
with Captain Hertford.

Chapter XXVIII

IT was a wild week this which followed. The "non-
electors," who had begun by merely sneering at Peel's ter-
giversation, and rather laughing at the Bill; now had got
earnest about it, in one way or another, and were showing
a slight tendency to congregate. The more intelligent
among them had found out, or had thought they had
found out, what the intention of the Bill was. The great
fact that the duty was to be reduced at once from sixteen
to four shillings, was enough to excite them somewhat,
for bread was dear. Their excitement was over pretty
much on Saturday morning when the Bill was passed,
though, as far as this story is concerned, the Corn-bill was
never passed at all. It *was* read a third time at four on
Saturday morning, but, before we come to that period, we
shall not be thinking much about corn bills.

Austin was in a very vexed and excited state that week,
and he said it was the Bill; nay, more, he actually believed
it was the Bill, with which he had nothing whatever to do,
not even having a vote for Westminster. He was excited
and angry about Captain Hertford.

There was no doubt about one thing, according to the

code of honour of those times. Austin had heard of threats uttered against him by a bully and an enemy, *and had taken no notice of them.*

This consideration was driving him mad all that week. He felt like a guilty man. What would the world say if they knew all? If they knew that he was in possession of Captain Hertford's language about him, and knew that he had not noticed it. It was terrible.

" What would the world say if it knew all? " Unluckily the world knew a little too much; and, as to what it would say, Austin found *that* out on Thursday.

Lord Charles was in his rooms with him in the afternoon, and making or trying to make Robin sit up in a corner and hold a pipe in his mouth. His father had given his sister Minny a dog on her birthday, a spaniel dog, with long drooping ears on each side, like the speaker's wig, which would sit up and smoke a pencil-case; and so, why should not Austin's dog? Which circumstance shows that this desperate young Jacobin thought of something else beside the salvation of his country.

Austin was very silent and anxious. Whatever he thought about, the question always came back. What would they think if they knew?

Presently a man came in; an old friend; a very tall, awkward man; a man who at Eton had been a long shambling lad, whose shoes were always coming off, and who never could be taught to swim, or to row, or to do anything in that line, except get in the way. A fellow who was always getting his eye blacked at cricket, and his ankle sprained at football. A fellow who was always top of his form, and was always up half the night doing other lads' impositions (or whatever they call those inflictions at Eton). A fellow who was always getting into trouble for some one else; who would have died sooner than betray another boy. Who, as a boy, had been beloved, reverenced, and bullied by every one who knew him; a maker-up of quarrels; a pleader at school with masters, at the University with dons; a high-hearted, noble creature, whose shoes were never tied, whose hair was always tangled, whose coat was never brushed, who went on till he developed into one of the shrewdest and most clear-headed lawyers of the day. Early in his career he had been christened "Daddy," which name always stuck to him, and will stick to him, even if he gets on the bench.

He had been to the United University Club, and had heard conversation there which made him go and seek Lord Charles. He had found Lord Edward, and having told him what was the matter, had heard from him of his last conversation with Captain Hertford. He had at once determined to speak to Austin himself. Also, hearing of what passed on that occasion, he thought that Austin was perfectly safe, or he would have cut his tongue out sooner than say what he did.

"Austin, I have been at the Club. Charles Barty, attend to me, and leave that dog alone. They have been talking of you there."

"Aye!" said Austin.

"Yes; a certain blackleg bully has been taking your name in vain; and they were wondering why you have not noticed it. I, as a man of peace; a man who, if need were, would make no more of falling on this man Hertford, and beating him myself, sooner than that anything should happen to you; I, even I, think that you ought to notice it. Go about with this fellow, in some public place, and bring him to account. If I did not *know* that he will not take it up, but will put his tail between his legs, for uncommonly good reasons, I would not give this advice; you know I would not. Go about with him, and force him to deny what he has said. I will go bail that nothing follows."

So sadly right, so sadly wrong.

"What has he been saying?" said Austin, quietly.

"Well, go down to the Club and ask the men there. I will not tell you. Well, he has been coupling his own name and Miss Hilton's."

" Indeed ! " said Austin.

" Yes, old boy, and you should contradict him, if only for her sake. Don't go too far. Send him quietly to his kennel, and he will go. If he don't, *send him to me.* I will not have you talked of by a fellow like that. Now, good-bye, go to the Club."

And so he went. Lord Charles rose, and began walking up and down the room, looking very grave, as soon as they were alone.

And Austin said " Well ! "

Lord Charles said, " Well, Austin."

" There is no doubt about it now, I think you will allow."

" I am afraid not. I am afraid you *must* do it. God help us. All this that Daddy says about his not having you out, may be true, or may be moonshine. Whichever it is, you must tax him with what he has said. You may have to go out with him. However ; it will be time enough to think of that, when he asks you : which Daddy says he won't."

" I don't care which way it goes now. I am perfectly happy again," said Austin. " Charles, for the last day I have felt like a thief ; now, that I am committed to the adventure, I am myself again. I ought to have been committed to it two days ago. It is not too late to remedy that. Let us go down to the Club, and talk as loud of Hertford as he has talked of me. My reputation will be right again in ten minutes. Wait for me till I brush my hair."

When Lord Charles was left alone, he sat for a few minutes with his hand on Robin's neck. And then he bent down his head on the table, and prayed.

What strange kind of prayer was that ? Was it a prayer for guidance ? No. It must have been a prayer for mercy and forgiveness. For he had made the resolution to watch Austin and Captain Hertford, lest they should come together ; to insult Captain Hertford himself, and go out with him; and to save Austin at the sacrifice of his own life.

Why? Ah! that is hard to answer. Some natures, however darkened with regard to a higher system of morality, have in them a kind of dull, blind chivalry, which will lead them to all lengths; and, at five-and-twenty, if we can remember so long ago, friendships are very warm. Why is Bill led out of the dock to ten years' penal servitude, because he won't turn evidence against Tom? Explain me the one thing, and I will explain you the other. I take it that Bill and Lord Charles Barty act from much the same motives, only that Bill would not have wilfully compassed the death of a fellow-creature. Lord Charles Barty's life is a more graceful one to write about than Bill's, with his beer and his skittles, and his vague notion that the policeman, protector of society, is also the enemy of mankind. But, ah! what a poor fellow would he be who would not acknowledge that both are capable of most chivalrous devotion.

Perhaps the advantage lies with Lord Charles in this; that he would actually go to death for his friend; whereas poor Bill, were it a capital matter, would, after standing all day in the hot court, staring with eager eyes, hot lips, and lowering face at the counsel for the prosecution; and with the same hot lips, but with more eager eyes at his own counsel, — after all this, I say, would, in the end, not being held up by a certain something which some call chivalry; give way and tell the truth for the sake of dear life: and would afterwards go away a free man and take to drinking, and drown himself ultimately in the Regent's Canal, as the only solution: which we can only hope he will not find to be an eminently unsatisfactory one.

Lord Charles's resolution was taken, and when Austin had brushed his hair and had come back, Austin only saw that he looked grave, and wished that he had looked gayer.

" Come, cheer up, Charles," said Austin, " I am not dead yet Faithless friend, you ought to keep up my spirits."

Lord Charles smiled, but did not laugh.

"I know why you can't laugh, old fellow," said Austin. "Do you think I could laugh if I was going out with you? Come on, let us go to the Club and kick up the preliminary row."

So they went. At the club, among the old University set, such few of them who happened to be there, Austin expressed his intention of morally or physically pulling Captain Hertford's nose to-morrow, which was quite satisfactory. Lord Charles slipped away and went to Captain Hertford's lodgings in Pall Mall.

An obtuse maid, being inquired of, represented that the Captain was not at home, that he had gone out of town that afternoon, that he had gone to Malta on business, by the two o'clock train, but would be back to dinner the next day at five. This being, on the face of it, an impossibility, in the present imperfect state of our international communication; it became necessary to call in the Captain's landlord Runciman. The King of Bootmakers deposed that the Captain had been down to Malsam, the town he represented, to see if the other member, Mr. Nogo (C), would be well enough to come up and vote; and that, also, the Captain would most certainly be back late the same night, and that the maid's story about his coming back the next day at five, was a fiction.

The next morning Lord Charles, never for one instant flinching from his purpose, rose somewhat earlier than usual, and having dressed himself with great care, and after taking a few turns in a certain passage, knocked at the nursery-door, and at once passed in.

He was greeted with a wild cry of welcome. His little brothers and sisters were in the position of " being got up," and were strewed about like rosy apples. Two of them, still in their night-gowns, were dramatizing a scene in real life, which was at the same moment enacting in another part of the room — that is to say, they had stripped a doll stark naked, and were washing it in a washhand basin —

a process which, (her bust being of wax, and the rest of her being of calico and sawdust) rendered her unavailable in her capacity of doll, for evermore. Another was sitting up in his crib, and was driving four-in-hand to the "Star" at Richmond, with a pair of list garters, lent by the youngest nursemaid; and another was being tubbed. This fellow leaped from the hands of nurse to embrace his brother; but seeing the door open and the way clear, some sort of devil entered into him, and caused him to run, stark naked as he was, violently down stairs. He reached the hall with great success, but was captured by a solemn young footman, and led back again in a proud and vainglorious state of mind. Half-way up the stairs he bit the footman, who hoped that his lordship was not going to be naughty; which speech, being addressed by a very tall man to a naked child of three, struck Lord Charles as wonderfully funny. Meanwhile, above stairs, while all the nurses were out on the landing looking for the fugitive, Lady Florence held a regatta in the hip-bath with her brothers' and sisters' shoes, three of which were unfortunately swamped and sunk.

Lord Charles kissed them all. His brother George was at Eton, and his eldest brother, Lord Wargrave, in Italy; so nothing remained but to see his father and mother.

His father was in high feather. Lord (somebody or another) had accepted his offer for a certain mare. She had been sent home, and he invited Lord Charles to come down to Esham on a secret journey with him, and see her. Lord Charles pleaded the debate, and his father wondered whether poor Edward would like to come. At all events, he might get some flowers from the gardener, and give them to that quiet little girl that his friend Elliot was going to marry. That girl seemed very kind to Edward; his mother said she was a good little body, and so on.

His mother was in her dressing-room. He did not trust himself much here. He said he had come to wish her "good morning." He kissed her and left her.

He asked the servants where was his brother Edward. His Lordship had gone to Church. It was as well. He left his father's house — a house of order, domestic love, of old renown and of chivalrous honour — to pursue his adventure with a worthless bully. When he thought of what that house might be by this time to-morrow, he grew sick, but he never flinched.

Was it ridiculous and out of place, that even now he should go round to the stables, to have a look at the horses, and to speak a word with the men? It was not very absurd in him. In his father's house the servants took rank after the children. The servants were all from the estates. Forgiveness was extended till seventy times seven, and discharges for misconduct were very rare: generally attended with utter despair on the part of the culprit, and with tears, and a temporary seclusion on the part of the Duchess. No; on the whole there was nothing ridiculous in his visiting the stables.

He went into every stall, and he spoke to every man and boy there. He was the favourite of the family. He never rebuked but gently, and he always stood in the breach between the culprit and his father's anger, to the very last. People who know about these things say, that in some large old-fashioned establishments of this kind, there is a certain devoted affection which arises between master and servant, quite apart from interest. One would fancy that such a thing was quite possible. One has known of convict servants risking their lives for a good master; is such a thing impossible among footmen and grooms? Or is Jenkins, selfish, cowardly, and effeminate, to go down to posterity as the type, instead of the exception — merely because his master dresses him like a Tom-fool?

We know not. We only know that these servants were glad to see Lord Charles, and that he was, in his way, wishing them "Good-bye;" for at this time he believed that he would never see them again. He ordered the man who was supposed to have the care of his person, to bring his cab to Mr. Elliot's lodgings at four, and then he went back to Captain Hertford's.

The captain had come back late last night, but was gone out early that morning. There was nothing to do but to go on to Austin's, and keep him in sight all day. But Austin was gone out too: his servant did not know where.

So Lord Charles got breakfast at his club, and waited impatiently. These two men might meet. Austin might have gone in search of Captain Hertford. Men came and talked to him. There was very little doubt that the Corn-bill would pass that night; there would be a long fractious debate, an iteration of every argument on both sides, but it would be read. Not that Lord Charles cared much about it now.

And where was Austin? He had come home, and going to bed, had asked for Robin his dog. Miss Hilton's servant, old James, had called and fetched Robin away that evening. Miss Hilton's footman had reported, in the course of conversation, that one of Miss Hilton's maids had lit a bit of fire in old Miss Hilton's room, with the register down, and finding the room full of smoke, had run through the streets bareheaded, raising the town, till she fell down in a dead faint at the engine-house door.

Austin knew that the next day was the day of Eleanor's monthly pilgrimage; if any one had told him that he meant to watch her, he would probably have struck him. And yet in his feverish state of mind, he went down early next morning, and looked at Mr. James's dogs.

He was in that worthy's front garden, listening to that worthy's platitudes with a deaf ear, when he saw his own dog, Robin, come bounding out of a by-street, from the direction of Millbank, and hunt a hen who was taking her breakfast in the middle of the road. He watched the street out of which he had come.

He saw Eleanor come out of that street. She was leaning on Captain Hertford's arm, and was talking eagerly to him—she who was his, by every tie and vow that could be made, was leaning on the arm of the man who was seeking his life — she who could keep a secret from him, could be in confidence with that bully, that assassin! There was no doubt about his purpose now. Either that man or he should die. The time came soon when he got his lesson; the time came when he would sooner have blown out his own brains, than fire a pistol at the most worthless man alive, but the time had not come yet.

It was no use following them then; Hertford would be down for the debate that night. He went home, and soon after Lord Charles came to him.

Austin poured out his furious indignation to him, not only, alas, against Captain Hertford, but against Eleanor. Lord Charles only continued to assure him quietly, that the time would come when he would be sorry for what he was saying; that he, Lord Charles, would go bail for Eleanor with his life.

The weary day wore on. The day which both of them had looked forward to with such hope. There was no doubt that the Bill would be read a third time that night, and the Lords dare not —— Alas, how little either of them cared for the Bill now, or for the Lords either!

At half-past five they both, by tacit consent, went down to the House; Lord Charles to his place, while Austin fought his way into the gallery. At this time affairs might have arranged themselves anyhow; the way they did arrange themselves was this.

Captain Hertford and Lord Charles were both eagerly anxious to meet, as we know. But at about ten o'clock Lord Charles remembered that his father would be soon leaving the House of Lords, as he knew that he was going to Lady Something's party, or ball, or drum, or what not, for he had heard him say so. He had a desire to see his father again. He saw Austin, as he thought hopelessly wedged in the gallery; he saw Captain Hertford sitting sulkily opposite; he thought that he might safely slip out for five minutes and see his father once more.

Austin saw him rise and go ; he saw Captain Hertford rise and follow him. Then he turned on the crowd behind him in the gallery, and fought his way out like a madman.

When he felt the cold night wind on his face he found himself among a crowd, a crowd of all sorts of people, fidgeting and talking about what was going on inside the House.* He felt puzzled and confused among so many fresh faces, until he saw a policeman whose face he knew, and asked him whether he had seen Captain Hertford.

The policeman, touching his hat, said, yes ; that Captain Hertford had followed Lord Charles Barty in the direction of the Peers' entrance. Austin hurried that way as fast as he could go.

At that time the passage to the Peers' entrance was a squalid sort of alley. With high slab palings on the right, and on the left a strange wooden building, beyond all again an archway. On the left, also, was a high wooden screen, perforated with square holes, which represented, unless we forget, Dr. Reid's ventilating apparatus. (" I tell you," said Lord Brougham once, " that I don't want explanation, I want air.") Altogether it was an odd sort of transition place, rendered more untidy by a low railing which ran along one side of it, nearly half-way across.

Up this passage Austin hurried. He was too late. He heard voices in dispute, raised above the common tone of conversation. When he came up there were three people in a group. One a peer ; Lord Charles Barty, who leant with his back against the railings ; and Captain Hertford who was opposite him. These were the three.

" You have heard what passed, my lord," were the first words that Austin heard. " I have told Lord Charles Barty that he is a liar."

" And you also heard, Lord Sayton," said Lord Charles,

---

* The author left that crowd at a quarter past eight or so.

"that I, walking up here with you, and seeing Captain Hertford following me, turned on him, and without the least provocation, told him that he was a bully and a scoundrel, and that I also repeat my assertion now. I suppose there is nothing more to be said, unless we intend to scold and fight like two costermongers."

"Well, I should say not," said Lord Sayton. "The affair seems plain, though I am devilish sorry for it!"

"This quarrel is mine!" said Austin, breathless.

"It should have been, by all accounts," said Lord Sayton; "but you are rather late, ain't you? Do you want me?" he added, turning round towards the two others.

"No, thank you, Sayton," said Lord Charles.

"I shall be glad of your assistance, Lord Sayton," said Captain Hertford.

"I spoke to Lord Charles Barty, not to you," said Lord Sayton. "You can notice that if you like: you will not find me packed in the Strangers' Gallery of the Commons, when you want me!"

"You shall answer for that speech, Lord Sayton," said Austin.

"Very well," drawled that most stupid of men.

They separated, and Lord Charles and Austin went away together. After a few steps Lord Charles ran back and overtook Captain Hertford.

"Shall you send your man to-night?"

"It will be better."

"Send him to Elliot's lodgings; I shall not go home. We shall never speak again. If anything happens to either of us don't bear any malice. I shall see you in the morning."

Chapter XXIX

LORD CHARLES went home at once to Austin's lodgings, which were very close to Captain Hertford's. Austin persuaded Lord Charles to go to bed, which he did without much persuasion. Austin waited up for Captain Hertford's friend.

He was not long in coming. He was a Captain Jackson, whom Austin had seen before — the man whom he had seen before walking with Captain Hertford and Lord Charles Barty just before he had started for Ronaldsay. He had been to India since, and had come home wounded from one of the Sikh battles, almost with the news of Feroseshah; a man of the Indian army, a good-natured gossiping man, a great Shickaree by his own account. Austin had listened to his tiger-stories often, and wished it had been some one else who had come with the message now — some one possibly, with whom he could have picked a quarrel.

Captain Jackson began: " Is there no way out of this miserable business ? "

" Do you see any, Jackson ? " said Austin, eagerly.

" Well, I am sorry to say that we are determined (utterly against my wishes, mind you) to go through with it. And I am sorry to say that we (utterly against my wish), having been insulted in the house, when we passed it over, and being again grossly insulted to-night, are determined to have a public apology."

" That is impossible," said Austin. " But I'll tell you what I will do."

" I don't think you have anything much to do with it, have you, Elliot ? You should say what *we* will do."

" What *I* will do is this," said Austin. " Barty is in bed and asleep. I will myself meet Hertford, and exchange shots to-morrow morning, before Barty awakes."

" I am sorry to say," said Captain Jackson, " that we, knowing your nobleness of character, have anticipated that course of action, and that we won't have it at all. Lord Charles Barty must apologize, come out, or ———"

" God help us," said Austin.

" Amen ! " said Captain Jackson sincerely. " You have never been at this sort of thing before. You will have to leave a good deal to me. If you will trust me, before God, to whom we both must give an account of to-morrow morning's work, I will see everything fair. You have no pistols."

" No ! "

" Will you let me bring mine ? They are smooth-bored and devilish bad. We may get out of it in that way. Got passports ? "

" No, never thought of it."

" Then you must come with us. Hertford warned me that something was in the wind yesterday, and made me get a family passport, in which our worthy captain figures as Mr. Jones *père*, and Lord Charles, you and I, as his promising sons. If one of us is taken ill we can account for it. Hertford, of course, having the character of a man rather too ready for this sort of thing, wishes to stand with the world as the soul of chivalry. So he made me get the passport. God grant it may not be needed."

" God grant it," said Austin.

" Once more, Amen. With regard to time and place ? "

" What do you propose ? "

" I am sorry to say," said Captain Jackson, " that we, having provided the aforesaid family passport, are more in a position to insist than to propose. We, unless you can bring strong reasons against it, propose the firs at Hampstead, at half-past seven to-morrow morning. It must be so, my dear Elliot, or we shall be stopped. The quarrel has been heard of, and the affair will be stopped else. If you oppose an early meeting, your man's reputation won't be worth an old shoe."

It was undeniable. Austin agreed, and the captain departed.

Austin went round to the stables, where his own horses were kept, and to his terror found that all was dark and shut up. He did not know exactly where his own servant slept, or he would have tried to arouse him. What between his terror for his friend's reputation and his terror at his friend's danger, he was nearly mad. He was at this moment very nearly going to the police-office and putting the matter before them, but he dared not. If he had done such a thing as that, his friend would for ever after have been socially and politically dead. The difficulty now was to rouse a sleeping groom without awakening the others. Lord Charles's groom must be sleeping with one of his. It was a ridiculous difficulty, but it made him stamp, and curse the day he was born.

Luck assisted him. A man came into the mews, and as he walked aside to let him pass he saw it was Charles Barty's servant. He ordered him to bring the cab to his lodgings at five.

" Are you going out, sir ? " asked the man.

" Yes," said Austin. " You must be secret and quiet. I will reward you well."

" I am sorry for it, sir. You was always a kind gentleman. I will be there, sir, punctual."

Then Austin went back, and going up to his room, where Lord Charles lay asleep in his bed, he sat in a chair all night, listening to the long-drawn breath of the sleeper.

He sat and thought all night. Ah Lord ! it had all come to this. His own reputation tarnished, and the friend of his heart going out next morning in a quarrel which by rights was his. He knew that, however this business turned out, his own reputation was gone. He had had two hints to that effect these last few days, and both of those had come from men eminently friendly to himself.

His reputation tarnished ! Ah, it was maddening. How

lucky that his father was dead, and that his death did not lie at his son's door, for that would have killed him outright. This man Hertford had been taking his name in vain. Austin had heard of it. His own friends at the United University Club had talked about it. Austin himself had gone down to the Club and talked threateningly of Hertford. The little world he lived in was expectant ; how would that expectation be satisfied ? By finding that he, Austin Elliot, had allowed the friend of his bosom to fight his battle for him ; by allowing Lord Charles to go out with one of the deadliest shots in England.

It was unendurable, but there was no remedy in his code of morality. Therefore, although it was unendurable, it was endured, like most other unendurable things in this world.

But his own disgrace was not one quarter of the mischief. Suppose anything were to happen to Lord Charles ? Suppose he were to be wounded? Suppose he were to be lamed for life, for that was possible — how would Austin feel then ? The cloud he himself was under now might be cleared away. He might force Captain Hertford to go out with him — nay ! he was already determined to do so. It would be necessary. But if his friend was maimed in this encounter, he felt as though he could never hold up his head again. He determined that if any one proposed more than one shot, that the shots should pass through his own body.

So the short night wore on, and he sat in his chair without sleeping, trying, from time to time, to make out the outline of his friend's face in the dark. As the East began to grow bright, and the sparrows began to twitter outside the window, he dozed ; but he must have wakened again within half-an-hour. The room was quite light now, and he could see his friend.

He was sleeping as peacefully as a child. The beautiful face was turned, in its expressionless repose, towards Austin. One bare arm was thrown half out of bed, with the palm of the hand uppermost, and the fingers relaxed ; the other was laid under the sleeping man's head, among his close brown curls. It seemed a happy sleep, for he smiled, and babbled inarticulately in his dreams — a happy schoolboy sleep ! Austin had awakened him from such a sleep at Eton, in old times, more than once, to come bathing, or boating, or birdnesting. He remembered how that face had changed, from the half-unconscious expression fixed on it by some happy dream, into consciousness, into loving recognition of the friend who had awakened him. He remembered all that, and knew that he had to awaken him once more — to what ? What expression would the face take now ? What kind of curse would shine out of those eyes, as soon as the lids of them were raised, and the soul behind them awoke to the appreciation of the lamentable truth ?

So there grew on poor Austin a horror and a dread of the sleeper's awaking ; and as he slept on, a new dread — the dread of having to awaken him himself. But it must be done, and be done soon. Now there came into his head a something long forgotten, as long-forgotten trifles will come into men's minds, at times of awful anxiety like this. It would have made him smile at another time, but he remembered it now. He had read in some blackguard book about prizefighting, that the men who trained the prizefighters never awoke them in the morning, but that they put the window open, and that, after a short time, as soon as the fresh morning air reached the poor fellows' faces, they quietly awoke. He remembered this now, and opened the window. In a short time, Charles Barty turned in his bed and awoke. His eyes met Austin's, and he smiled affectionately ; but as consciousness came to him, that smile faded into an expression of anxiety, and almost of horror. If he had sat up in bed, and heaped curses on Austin's head, Austin could have borne it better than that look.

But it was late — they must hurry : that was something.

They would have breakfast when they came back. The other people were to bring a doctor with them, so there was nothing to do but to drive fast. They spoke very little, and on indifferent subjects; Austin drove. Once Lord Charles turned round, and talked to the groom standing at the back of the cab, and gave orders about his hack being brought somewhere that afternoon. The groom said that his father's cob was lame, and perhaps his Grace might like to borrow his Lordship's hack. Whereupon Lord Charles confounded his father's cob (to Austin), and wished to God that his father would find himself in horses, and not be everlastingly borrowing his.

They were late. When they got on to the heath, they saw a dog-cart standing, with a groom at the horse's head, and further on, they saw three men waiting for them — Captain Hertford, Captain Jackson, and the doctor.

They hurried forward. Captain Jackson and Austin went apart, and matters were soon arranged. " We must be quick, Elliot," said Captain Jackson.

They were very quick. The men were placed twelve paces apart, back to back, and their seconds gave them their pistols. Captain Jackson was to give the word. Austin and he retired, and Captain Jackson said, " Gentlemen, are you ready ? Fire ! "

They both faced one another at the same instant. Charles Barty raised his hand high over his head, and fired in the air. Captain Hertford took deliberate aim, and fired two seconds afterwards. The instant he had done so, Lord Charles leapt a foot off the ground, and then bringing his heels sharply down upon the turf, toppled over headlong on his left shoulder, and lay perfectly still.

Austin was beside him in an instant, but he was quite dead. Austin turned the heavy head over, and saw the last sign of life which appeared in that beautiful face. Two nerves in the hollows beneath his eyes quivered and throbbed for half a second, and then stopped for ever.

If I were to pile Pelion upon Ossa with grand words, I

could give you no idea of the catastrophe more terrible than this. Lord Charles Barty was shot through the heart, and was lying, stone-dead, at the feet of Austin Elliot.

Chapter XXX

AUSTIN had never seen death before. This was his first introduction to it. He was holding the face of the dead man between his two hands, and looking down with a strange incredulous terror into the sightless eyes.

And the dead man was his friend, a man he loved as David loved Jonathan. He had never done anything or thought anything, for he knew not how long, without this man coming into his mind. " What will *he* think about it ? " " What will *he* say about it ? " had always been his first thought after he had done anything. Now, now —

The two others were with him in a moment. Captain Hertford said, " This has all been fair. I am off for France." Jackson broke out into tears. " By God," he said, " this is a most horrible business ! I wish he had struck me dead before I came out on this accursed errand ! " But Austin said nothing. He was kneeling on one knee, with the dead man's face between his hands, and a claw like that of an eagle, griping at his heart.

" We must get away," said Captain Hertford. " We had best be quick. Elliot, you will have to come with us."

" I shall stay where I am."

" You are mazed," said Captain Hertford, impatiently. " We shall be in trouble for this. Time is precious. You must cross with my passport."

" I tell you I shall stay where I am," said Austin, looking up at Hertford with that painful look of mingled terror and anger which Captain Hertford had seen before, and which he now remembered.

"Then I have done my duty and must go," said Captain Hertford. "Jackson, we must make haste."

They left him kneeling at the dead man's head. In a few moments Jackson ran back, while Captain Hertford waited for him.

"Elliot, don't be a madman. Come away. There will be the devil to pay for this, God forgive us! You must come with us. You shall!"

"I shall stay here."

"You are mad! Think better of it and come with us. Your mind is gone!"

"I know it is. Good-bye."

So Captain Jackson went reluctantly away, and left Austin with the dead man.

Lord Charles's groom came next. He touched Austin on the shoulder. "Mr. Elliot," he said, "is my lord wounded?"

Austin looked up in his face and said, "Your lord is dead!" He saw the man turn pale and sick. Then he saw him kneel down beside what had been Lord Charles, and untie the dead man's neckcloth. Then he opened his shirt and felt his heart. And lastly, by some strange instinct, he closed the dull staring eyes, which were never to open again. Then the two stood silent for a time.

"What is to be done now, sir?" said the groom at last.

"What is to be done?" said Austin. "Done! says he? Why, bring him to life again, and let me lie there dead and cold in his place. We have been hardly used, Tom. There is no mercy in Heaven, Tom; or, if there is, it is all kept for those who whine and cringe, and I have never done that, nor has this dead man. What have he and I done that this has happened? Answer me that. What have he and I done that things should come to this?"

Tom was only a poor groom — a man not worth your notice in any way; but even he had a dull feeling that Mr. Elliot, dear gentleman! was beside himself, and was blaspheming in his grief. If you had given Tom a week to answer, he would have answered, "You have both of you done many things to deserve this; and the mere fact of your being here this morning proves it." But Tom did not get a week to think of his answer. He was thinking of how his dear dead lord's body was to be decently moved, before people came about and gathered into a crowd.

The problem was solved for him. Two policemen came up, and the elder of them said, "Is this gentleman dead, sir?"

"He is quite dead," said Austin, quietly.

"A duel, sir?" said the policeman.

"Yes, a duel," said Austin. "This dead man is or was Lord Charles Barty, the Duke of Cheshire's son; I am Mr. Austin Elliot, of the United University Club. I was his second, and I give myself into custody. Now, do be quick, or the people will be about."

He had not made many turns up and down before an inspector appeared, and Austin told him everything. "You will not take that groom into custody, will you, inspector?" said Austin.

"I ought to, sir," said the inspector.

"But don't do it," said Austin. "If it lay in the sphere of your duty to burn down Somerset House, you would not like to be taken into custody and leave the business to some one else. Now, see what that groom has to do. He was bred on the estate, and will do it quietly. He has got to go to Cheshire House and burn it down over their heads. He will go into the servants'-hall and ask to see the old nurse who nursed them all. And he will tell her; and she will tell the Duke; and the Duke will tell the Duchess, and they will curse my name, and the day I was born, and shut up the house close and dark. Lamentation, and mourning, and woe! I beg pardon. My head is going over this. If you knew all the circumstances, you could not wonder at it."

" God help you, sir ! "

" Amen. But you will let this poor groom go ? You were less than a man if you did not."

That was easily arranged. And then came the terrible business of removing the corpse : and I will go no further, only hoping that I have not gone too far already. But if I thought that I could do more than I have done, to give honest men the contempt and the loathing, that I feel myself for the system of duelling — for the principle of making the devil arbiter of differences instead of God, I would go further. I would go all the length to which Jules Janin, or the younger Dumas, have gone in a very different cause.

Austin walked away with the inspector of police like a man in a dream. It seemed to him as if all the universe had sunk round him, and left him standing on a pinnacle far above the reach of human sympathy. It was so *horrible*. It was not so much that he was sorry or grieved, or that he could have wept wild tears for the fate of his friend ; that state of mind was not come yet, and was not to come for a long while. At present, the whole business was ghastly, horrible, unbelievable. It *must* be untrue. Charles Barty, merry, handsome, clever, the most loveable of human beings, so gentle, so good, such a thorough gentleman — Charles Barty, the man whose life had hitherto been a sort of beautiful, merry joke, yet who had shown promise of great things, should occasion arise, this man could not be dead ! It was impossible that Death could have dared ! But Austin had seen his body put into a baker's cart, and had seen the legs fall.

Alas ! Austin, he was dead enough ; and you, my poor butterfly, having lived three-and-twenty years in a fool's paradise, your religious faith absolutely *nothing*, your political creed only built up out of the formulas used by your forefathers, in discussing questions which have been extinct many a long year agone ; your social creed being, that it was a good thing to get asked to such and such a party, and that you ought to get up pedigrees and know all about everybody — you, poor Austin, when you saw Lord Charles put into the baker's cart and driven slowly away ; were at the edge of a very black hell indeed. No wonder that you clung to the police inspector as a reality, at all events — as the link which connected you with the world which seemed to have sunk away under your feet.

It was well that Mr. Elliot was dead, or this would have killed him with a broken heart. That he who had brought up his son on formulas, social and political — which meant something in his time, but which now meant little or nothing — should be out of the way and not see that painful look of puzzled horror on his son's face, that was well. Poor Austin was the Louis Sixteenth of duelling — the last, the kindest, the best of those who stuck to the old rule — the one most severely punished.

When they got to the police-office, the magistrate was trying the people who had got drunk the night before. Austin sent several special messengers, at the inspector's advice, to old friends of his father's, and sat wearily at one side of the court, listening to the other cases.

A chimney-sweep, for nearly murdering his wife. He had been remanded and remanded again, until the house-surgeon had pronounced his wife sufficiently recovered to go and give evidence. There she was, a drunken drab, with her head all plastered up with bandages. The house-surgeon had thought her dying at one time, and had sent for the magistrate to take her evidence : then, under fear of death, she had told the truth, but now, when in the dock, looking at the miserable, degraded, brutal hound she loved so well, she lied and lied in his favour, till the magistrate threatened to commit her for perjury ; and at every fresh lie (God help us !) her face seemed to grow grander and nobler, till she looked almost beautiful. " She," thought Austin, " would die for that wretched cur, and I —"

Two boys, brothers, ages seventeen and eighteen. They

had got the trick of going to Cremorne and such places, and spending too much money. They had put their silly heads together and committed a clumsy forgery — a forgery than which nothing more idiotic ever entered into the mind of man. They had torn a cheque out of their master's book, filled it up for ten pounds, and with the most clumsy imitation of their master's signature, had gone together to the bank and presented it. They were given into custody at once, and there they were in the dock, huddling together like two frightened sheep. The evidence was conclusive, and the magistrate asked them what they had to say. Whereupon Tom, the elder brother, moistening his dry lips with his tongue, confessed his guilt, and said that Bob, his younger brother, knew nothing about it. But Bob wouldn't have this by any means ; he asserted shrilly that he had stolen the cheque, forged it, and had took Tom to the bank with him when he presented it, because they knew Tom and didn't know he, and also that Tom was a devil to lie, and always had been, which ask their mother. The chivalry of these two poor fools towards one another was one more stab in Austin's heart. Now that the horrible catastrophe had come, he could see that by rising to the level of a higher law he might have saved his friend.

Then they shoved into the dock a boy who scuffled, and lost one shoe, and had it handed to him by the policeman ; and after he had put it on, stood up again. A boy, gentlemen, of the sort worth attending to because his clay has not been burnt to brick, but is still plastic. A boy who may yet be made a man if you can get hold of him. The very boy, gentlemen, of all persuasions, from Roman Catholic to Unitarian, that you *are*, thank you, getting hold of — all honour to you. A boy with a shock head, his hair down over his forehead, who when spoken to puts his fists into his eyes and lifts his elbows up above his ears, expecting a blow. *You* know him, messieurs the Scripture-readers, brothers of the holy order of St. Francis, district visitors of the Swedenborgian, or whatever you call yourselves, you know the young dog; and, in spite of all your attempted proselytizing and your squabbling, you all mean him well! Have we not seen your good works?

This shock-headed boy being put into the dock, and accused of being concerned, with his elder brother, still at large, in the tripping up of an old gentleman and the stealing his watch, "didn't know nothink about it!" and in spite of the truculent cross-examination of Mr. Barney Moses (from the office of Ikey Moses and Son), and the hints of the magistrate, that in consequence of his youth he would be held innocent, he still aggravatingly and perversely persisted in "knowing nothink about it," without orders from his elder brother.

Then was this thieves' honour higher than gentlemen's honour? Was it the same article, or a spurious one? There was no time for Austin to think out the question, or he would probably as a reasonable man have settled it this way: — That up to this year 1846, the best and highest men in the land had never had moral courage to decline the test of the duel; that he was one of the first victims of a new state of things; that, acting on the old rules of honour, he had done nothing with regard to this miserable business, but what was inexorably right and necessary. That, through mere ill-luck, his own reputation was tarnished, and his friend killed. That was the truth; but Austin could not see it just now. He placed the honour of these thieves and prostitutes above his own, and wished for death.

The charge against him was made. The magistrate required two sureties of 500l. each. They were instantly forthcoming, from two, or if need were, from a dozen of his father's friends; and Austin, after thanking them, went rapidly away and took a passport for France, and then went to his lawyer.

He and his lawyer sat late. He gave him orders to prepare deeds, conveying all his property to Eleanor in case of a conviction (which was inevitable),* and told him that he would appear and sign them in good time. He then made a short will, leaving all his property to Eleanor, in case of his death before his conviction. Then he wrote to her a short note, requesting *her* to make good, out of his effects, the loss of his father's old friends, with regard to his bail. And then he went home.

His servant was waiting for him. He paid the man's wages, and gave him a paper, which authorized him to sell his three horses, his cab, and his dog-cart, at Tattersall's, and to pay the money into his banker's. This paper was not worth very much in a legal point of view, but he knew his man, and knew that he could trust him. He told him also to take care of his dog Robin ; and should anything happen, to take him to Miss Hilton. Then he had his landlady, Mrs. Macpherson, up, and settled with her, while his man packed his portmanteau.

It was four o'clock in the afternoon before all this was done, and then he sent his man for a cab. His fool of a servant cried, and prayed him that he would let him go with him, but Austin was pale and resolute, and went alone.

A strange journey. One of the maddest, silliest journeys ever undertaken. First he went to Calais, and very soon found that Captain Hertford was not there, and had not been there. Then he posted to Boulogne, and spent three days there making inquiries. Captain Hertford had evidently not been there either. The Police Bureau knew nothing of him at all. Monsieur must have been fright-

* It seems doubtful whether or no this document or documents would have been worth the paper they were written on. The law about duelling may be found in Mr. Samuel Warren's article in " Blackwood," on the duel between Lord Cardigan and Captain Tuckett. Our legal knowledge is insufficient to decide whether or no the conveyance of the property of a man under bail, to a friend, will hold good. Our own ignorance on this point is not very surprising. But it *is* surprising that the question, so very important, seems not to be decided yet.

fully deceived by interested persons ; no such person had been there. Monsieur, weary of life, feeling hot about the head, thought he would go bathe, and did so. The bathers sat on the shore, and ate hot *gauffres*, and read " Le Juif Errant," not yet grown stale, and " Monte-Christo," which will never grow stale. But no one knew anything of Captain Hertford, or any such man. Had not Prince Louis Buonaparte shaved off his moustaches, put two planks on his shoulders, and walked out of Ham, what did Monsieur think of that, as an instance of French courage? Hey then ! Monsieur was forced to confess that the prince had shown courage of the very highest order. But finding no intelligence of Captain Hertford, he crossed again to Dover.

There seemed only one port left now to which Captain Hertford would be likely to have gone — he must have taken passage from Brighton to Dieppe. *He might* have gone to Havre; that was still possible. Austin remembered that he had said, " I am off for France," and felt sure that he would get on his track. He was more likely to have gone to Dieppe than to Havre. Austin went down to Brighton, and crossed in the steamer Venezuela, which steamer, I sincerely hope, is gone to the bottom long ago ; for having endured a gale of wind in her through one night, about two years before the time I speak of ; and having endured many gales of wind, in many ships, in all sorts of strange seas since, I have come to the conclusion, that the steamer Venezuela is (or I hope was) the worst, wettest, and most abominably dangerous sea-boat ever built.

Mrs. Taylor, of the " Hotel d'Angleterre," dead, I fear, many years agone, the best and cheeriest landlady that ever roared out of an upper window, — " Alphonse (you stupid lout, may God forgive me !) Venez-ici toutedesweet, pour brusser les souliers de jeune Mossoo ! Drat the man, he's a iling of his hair ; cochon ! — entendez-vous ? " Mrs. Taylor, I say, knew nothing of Captain Hertford ; but Austin, going into the public room at the Hotel Angleterre, met a man whom he knew, who gave him the information required. A university man, in ill-health, come over for change of air and scene.

" This is a bad business," he said. " But, Elliot, mind me, I don't believe one word of what they say against you. I know you too well, to think it possible that you thrust forward that poor fool of a nobleman to fight your quarrel. It is a lie ! "

" It is, indeed," said Austin.

" I know it is. I think that this Captain Hertford is sorry for what has happened. We must be just to all men, Elliot. My cousin went in the same boat with him to Antwerp last week, and he says that he looked as pale as death, and as wild as a hawk."

There was still time. The Dart was getting up steam outside the hotel windows. Austin was not very long in getting on board of her. Next morning he was at Brighton, the same day in London. The same night with a *pour voyager* passport, on board the Antwerpen ! In twenty-four hours at Antwerp.

At the Bureau of police, he got on Captain Hertford's trail at last, and he followed it like a bloodhound. Captains Hertford and Jackson, it appeared, had arrived suspiciously, with very little luggage, and had taken tickets for Aix-la-Chapelle. He followed on. At Aix-la-Chapelle he was puzzled again. He was in Prussian territory, and the police were not so communicative. But he luckily remembered, that Herr Nielsen Keilleter, the greatest man in Aix-la-Chapelle, was an old friend of his father's. He called on him, and the good old man, little dreaming what he was doing, gave him his assistance. Captain Hertford and Captain Jackson had gone on to Cologne, further than which, in those days, the railway did not go.

Here, at Cologne, he was once more left to his mother wit. He got hold of a *lacquey de place*, who desired to shew him the cathedral, the eleven thousand virgins, the skulls of Gaspar, Melchior, and Baltasar, and, as old James would have said, "the hull biling," for one thaler. Being interrogated, the commissionaire deponed that Captain Hertford was, at that same speaking, staying in the hotel at Deutz. Austin having paid his thaler, repaired there, and found only a gentle old Indian colonel, by name Hanford, whom he disturbed at his dinner. He was quite at fault again, and had to leave the old man's presence abashed.

Ah! it was a weary journey. Hope quite dead, and life quite worthless. He went out and sat upon the wharf at Deutz, and looked at the river, sweeping, hissing, boiling on, under the young May moon.

A great river. The first he had ever seen. It came, they said, spouting in a thousand cataracts out of the ever-lasting snow, and then went gleaming and sparkling on through such wildly beautiful scenery of feathering wood-land and hanging rock, as no one could realize without seeing. There was a grand catastrophe at Schaffhausen. After that, it was a mere dull sweeping waste of waters, and at last, down there below Düsseldorf, the mighty river, born in the eternal snow crystals, begins to creep ignominiously towards the sea, through fifty sluggish canals.

So poor Austin sat there for a time, trying to compare his life to that of the Rhine; quite forgetting that the river only became useful and beautiful after its catastrophe at Schaffhausen, and that its real usefulness and its real beauty, increased with every mile, till it reached the sea, and was lost in the eternity of the ocean. And after a time he held his way across the bridge of boats, towards the great cathedral, which heaved up its mighty ribs above the sleeping town.

He gained no further intelligence of Captain Hertford. But in his eagerness of purpose his wit was sharp. He knew that Captain Hertford gamed, and would be very likely to be found near gaming tables. His ignorance of the world generally, and the continent in particular, were so very great, that he did not know which were the places hereabout, where men came to lose their money. So, with an Englishman's instinct, he sent for the landlord.

The landlord's son came: a handsome young fellow, who had had his nose slit in some childish Burschen duel. At Austin's question he seemed puzzled. Answered that there were tables at Aix-la-Chapelle, at which Monsieur (they spoke in French) could have played (being a foreigner) to his heart's content.

Austin told him that he did not want to play. That he wanted to find a man, whom he was most likely to find in the neighbourhood of a gaming-table.

" An affair of honour, then," said the young man.

" Well," said Austin, " it is something of that sort. I feel sure you would not betray me."

The young man at once grew heroic and mysterious. He, too, had had his affairs, but what imported it to speak of them. He laid his finger on his wounded nose, and Austin did not laugh; though when he compared in his mind the childish fencing-match, in which the young man had been engaged, and the affair in which he would find himself in a few days, he felt very much inclined to do so.

This young man informed him, that the next place on the general route of tourists where one played was a place called Ems, in the Duchy of Nassau. That one went from hence by steamer to Coblence, and by *diligence* or *voiture*, as one pleased, to Ems. That there were two companies of vapour vessels on that river, both of which professed to take one to Coblence. The one, the Cologne company, possessing a magnificent fleet, swift as the wind, officered by gentlemen, supplied with every luxury; the other, the Düsseldorf company, composed of miserable and rotten boats, slow, dirty, officered by abusive villains, who too often succeeded in the dearest wish of their hearts, that of *abimer* in the depths of their noble river, not only their rotten boat, but also their deluded passengers.

Austin having been previously recommended by a friend to go by the Düsseldorf company, as being the best of the two, felt very much inclined, after this exhibition of spite, to do so. He decided to go on by the first boat, and did so. It was a Cologne boat.

He remembers that after they got beyond Bonn there was some fine scenery, or he thinks there was, because a noble young American, with whom he made immediate acquaintance on board, kept calling his attention to it. But he was too anxious to care whether the hills were ten feet high or ten thousand. His time was getting short. His bail would be forfeited in little more than a fortnight, and Captain Hertford as far from being found as ever.

He slept that night at the " Giant," at Coblence, and the next morning rumbled quietly away towards Ems, up the pleasant Lahn valley, before the mists had fully rolled away from the summits of the sheets of feathering woodland, which rose overhead on all sides.

He put up at the Hotel de Russie, and, after breakfast, went down to the Kursal, which round the Kesselbrunn, and the Kränchen, was thronged with all sorts of people drinking the waters ; and here he loitered for something like half-an-hour, until some one pushed against him accidentally in the crowd, and apologized to him. It was a magnificent Tyrolese, the first that Austin had ever seen. The man's enormous stature, the honest repose of his face, his grand dress, and his elegant easy carriage, attracted Austin. It was a new animal, and a very remarkable one. He smiled and returned the man's courtesy in French. Following him with his eyes, he saw that, grand as he was, he was only the keeper of a stall for the sale of Tyrolese nick-nacks, but he determined to have some talk with him. He went up and bought some trifle or another, and engaged him in conversation for a little time. At last he asked, " Had he a chamois head ? " The man had not, " But if Monsieur would accompany him to his brother's stall, he should have his choice of several."

Monsieur did so, and as Monsieur approached our younger brother's stall, he became aware that Captain Hertford was standing in front of it, bargaining for a pair of gloves.

Austin turned to the Tyrolese, and raised his finger. The man, with instinctive high-bred courtesy, bowed, and turned back to his own stall, and Austin stood, not quite certain how to proceed.

Captain Hertford bought his gloves, and turning into the main room of the Kursal, approached the counter in front of the spring. It was evident that he was going to drink his waters.

He had the red Bohemian glass raised to his lips, when Austin came behind him, and said, quietly, "Captain Hertford!"

Captain Hertford was no coward; but he knew the voice, and when he turned he was as pale as death. When he saw Austin's wild face, the glass he held fell from his hand, and flew, splintered, in a hundred ruby crystals, about the stone pavement at his feet.

"I suppose you know what I want of you," said Austin.

"Do you want satisfaction?" said Captain Hertford, in a low voice.

"Yes."

"It is a mistake. That last business was devilish horrid. Do you repeat that you want satisfaction?"

"Yes."

"Very well, your blood is on your own head. Shall you send to-day?"

"Yes. Who am I to send to?"

"Jackson and I are at the Hotel d'Angleterre, over the river. Good morning."

He did not know a soul there; he had to go and find Captain Jackson to get an introduction to some one. Captain Jackson found him a Frenchman, who was much pleased with the business, and who proceeded to make all arrangements. He returned soon to Austin, and told him that they were to walk out that very evening to a place called Dausenau.

They, at the time appointed, sauntered up along the road, to the quaint old village, and turned up to the left, into a romantic, deeply-wooded glen; through the bright green meadows of which a bright trout-stream came flashing and pausing, and babbling pleasantly of peace, and spring-tide, and hope. Austin for one instant, mad, ruined, and desperate as he was, felt the influence of the June evening tide, and longed to be at rest — in his grave if need were — to be anywhere but where he was. Feeling no fear, but a mixture of grief, remorse, and horror difficult to bear, preserving reason at the same time.

While in this frame of mind, he passed near a mill and out into a meadow, and there was the author of all this misery and woe before him. In less than ten minutes he was standing cool and calm, face to face with him, with a loaded pistol in his hand. Surely Hertford's day of reckoning was come. Not yet.

Austin had no more intention of firing his pistol at Captaid Hertford, than he had of blowing out his own brains. The last affair had been, as Captain Hertford said, so horrid, that Austin was determined that he would never again have any hand in a repetition of such a thing, unless he himself were the victim. So when Captain Hertford had fired, and he heard the ball whistle close by his head, he turned coolly away and fired at a piece of rock among the copse on the right of the meadow.

But Captain Hertford insisted upon another shot; and this brought on a general wrangle, during which it became painfully evident that the gallant captain had been drinking. There was nothing to be done but to place the men again, it seemed. This time Austin again fired away to the right, and, luckily for himself, was very slightly grazed on the leg. The affair was, of course, instantly stopped. Austin had fought his first and last duel. He had satisfied every requirement that the most punctilious bully could make. He had hunted Captain Hertford over the Continent till he had found him, had had him out, and had been unluckily wounded by him. He appealed to the three others ; they confirmed him. Jackson said that he would take care that everything should be known in London on his return, and Austin limped off back to Ems, somewhat lighter in heart than before. He had faced one of his troubles successfully ; his reputation was secure again ; he could look a man in the face ; he had made due pilgrimage to the outraged idol, honour, and had done sacrifice. The god was slightly in his debt — or, at all events, things were about square between them. This was, so far, satisfactory. He knew (who better ?) that this fetish he had been taught to worship, was a cruel and vindictive demon ; but, like a true idolater, he believed that, by overloading his idol with sacrifices, he might lay it under obligations, and, so to speak, have a case against it, a case which, under some sort of law, would hold good, and must be attended to.

"Was it for this," says the old nigger in that most beautiful book, "The Cruise of the Midge," after he had pitched his idol into the lee scuppers in his wrath, "was it for this that I gave you chicken, and stick fedder in your tail — eh ? " He, like Austin, had a strong case against his fetish.

Chapter XXXI

AUSTIN made his appearance in due time at his attorney's office in Lincoln's Inn. The clerks looked very grave, and one of them showed him into the presence of the old man. Austin saw him rise hurriedly and turn pale when he appeared ; Austin shook him warmly by the hand.

"So you have come back," said the attorney. "Ah, foolish, foolish boy. How I have hoped and prayed that you might be too late. But stay; there is time. My dear Austin, let me beg you on my knees, for the sake of your good name and your father's memory, to go back to France this night. Think that in three days it will be too late for ever."

"I cannot, old friend, in honour. The wrong I have done to the law shall be punished by the law. Say no more about it."

The old man said no more. He did not hide from Austin that he feared a conviction ; that he hardly knew how it was to be avoided.

"God's will be done. You feel sure of a conviction ? "

"Almost."

"The jury acquitted P —— last March," suggested Austin.*

"In direct opposition to Erle's summing up," said the old man, eagerly. "And why ? Because they believed that it was Liston's operation which killed S ——, and not H ——'s bullet. That is why. They gave him the benefit of that doubt because — because — well, because their sympathies went *with* P ——. They considered him blameless — only a young fellow who had done what fifty others had done before him ; gone out with his friend."

"And their sympathies will not be with me, then ? " said Austin.

"No," said the old man steadily. "If it kills me to say so to your father's son, I will say it. This duel has been talked about a great deal. Lord Charles Barty was a young man of great promise, and the newspapers have written leading articles about it. It has made a great stir in London. But all ranks and all parties agree in condemning you. Everybody knows, or think they do, that you and Captain Hertford were rivals for the hand of this Miss Hilton. Everybody has heard that you went to the United University Club, and spoke threateningly about Captain Hertford. Everybody (except myself and those

* Referring to the Gosport duel.

who know you) believe that you let Lord Charles fight this duel for you. Among others who believe this are the jury. The judge will tell them, in summing up, to banish from their minds all that they have previously heard about the case ; but they won't, not if I know 'em ; they never do, confound 'em. Look at P ——'s acquittal, Austin, my poor boy, and there read the story of your own conviction."

" I see what you mean very well," said Austin ; "that in P ——'s case they knew, from what they had heard elsewhere, that he was, as near as possible in such a case, blameless ; that in mine, from what they have heard elsewhere, they believe me more morally guilty than the principals themselves ; and, therefore, that they will convict. Is it not so ? "

" That is the state of the case. But there is time to get out of the way. You can make everything good, and so on. It is nothing. You ought to be off now. Come, let us go."

" No," said Austin, " I think not. I think, old friend, that we will see this matter out to the very end. I am so careless of life now, that I would rather be punished in this world somewhat. It would, at all events, give me the feeling, to the end of my wretched life, that if I had sinned, so also had I suffered. It may not, you say, abate one jot of my eternal punishment hereafter ; but, speaking in a selfish point of view, I would sooner let this matter take its course. I will not have the whole of the retribution, which must come on me sooner or later, left for the next world."

" I do not know what more to say, Austin Elliot," said the attorney. " Must we go on ? "

" Certainly, I have broke God's laws, as well as man's. I have been mad. Do you know what I have been doing abroad ? "

" No."

" Committing another crime. I hunted that man, Hertford, till I found him, and then had him out. I need hardly tell you that I would have died sooner than fire at him. But in doing this I have committed another crime, I fired away from him, but still I gave him the chance of adding to his guilt in murdering me. I will take my punishment for both, and try to bear it. But I shall die. Let us speak of business. About those papers which you were to get ready ? "

" This plan of yours," said the attorney, after a long pause, " of conveying your property won't do. I have had the best opinion about it. Lord Cardigan tried it six years ago, and it is the opinion of the best men that you had better trust to the mercy of the Crown. In Lord Cardigan's case, it was a flagrant attempt to defeat justice. It would not be allowed again. It must not be even mentioned. Your chance is submission. If you choose to sign your will, do so. You will go and see Miss Hilton to-morrow ? "

" No ; Eleanor has made her bed, and must lie on it. I love her, old friend, but she could keep a secret from me which she could tell to that cut-throat bully, Hertford."

" I wish I was in possession of facts," said the attorney. " If I was, I should find that you were utterly wrong. I know that as surely as I know that the sun shines. Come, go to her."

" I ought not, I dare not, I will not. Have it which way you will. She, by her absurd affectation of mystery, helped to make me mad and jealous. If she cares for me, let her come to me in prison, and make it up there. In prison, I say. They won't *hang* me, will they ? By Gad ! they won't *dare* to do that."

" Erle," said the attorney, looking steadily .at Austin, " when summing up in P ——'s case, laid down that every one present at a duel, either as principal or second, was guilty of murder. They *could* hang you, you know. Perhaps they won't. Indeed, I don't believe they will. Transportation for life is generally the next sentence, after that twenty-one years, then fourteen. Fourteen years is a devilish long time, and you might be at Boulogne to-morrow morning."

This was the hardest assault that Austin had had. He stood firm under it, and the attorney, seeing nothing was to be made of him, told him that, if convicted, he would probably be imprisoned for a month, possibly for six. And after this they parted.

*　　*　　*　　*　　*

Let her come to him in prison, if she really loved him. Let her explain her deceit there. And there let him tell her that he had forgiven her — that he was a ruined man — that it did not consort with his honour that their engagement should go on — that his pride would not allow him to link an heiress of such brilliant prospects, with his own desperate fortunes. Then let them part for ever.

Austin went to prison in due time, and dreed his weird there as we shall see. But she never came near him there. And yet have I done my work so very poorly that you distrust her? I hope not.

Chapter XXXII

IT was a most interesting case, and the court was crowded. The newspapers had been clamouring for a conviction. P —, they said, had been acquitted through false sentimentality on the part of the jury. The news-papers did not complain of this. P —— was as innocent as a man might be under such circumstances. A noble young fellow, who could not have acted in any other way; a man who bore the highest character in every way. But still a conviction was wanted, and this was the very case in which to convict. This young man, Elliot, had noto-riously thrust his friend Lord Charles Barty into a quarrel, which should have been his own, and had sneaked out of it himself. By every law, human and divine, by civil law, and by the laws of honour, this Elliot was the man to make an example of.

The question was, " Would he put in an appearance ? " The more long-headed and shrewd people said, " O Lord, no ! there was not a chance of it. That you might make your mind quite easy on that score, my good fellow. That they believed they knew something of the world, and that they put it to you, as a judge of human nature, and a reasonable being, whether it was likely that he would put in an appearance after three weeks' law." The men, who knew Austin best, thought quite differently, and had to endure what the deep dogs before mentioned said of him, which, accompanied as it was with that peculiar contemptuous smile, which the deep dogs aforesaid generally assume, when they are being deeper than usual, was very hard to bear, but which had to be endured (as we said before of unendurable things) nevertheless.

" It was against Austin Elliot's interest to appear. Therefore, he would not appear." Conclusion not all right, by any means, in consequence of the omission of a rather important middle term. It is astonishing how some shallow men, merely from the fact of denying the possibility of a man acting on high and disinterested motives, get to think themselves worldly wise ; and it is still more astonishing, how wiser and better men than themselves shake their heads, and give them credit for worldly wisdom and knowledge of human nature. Why, the pickpockets and thieves in any police-court, will show them what nonsense they talk, when they place self-interest as the only source of human action. But if you bray a fool in a mortar, he will only turn round on you, and offer to prove that he was right from the beginning.

So, when Austin's name was called, and he stepped quietly into the dock, and stood there pale and anxious, but perfectly calm ; the wise men were slightly puzzled, but made out in a few minutes, the theory, that Austin's game was to submit, throw himself on the mercy of the court, and save his property. Oh! deep-dyed idiots! So utterly unable to appreciate the grief, the despair, the horror in that wild young heart; and the strange, half-heathenish feeling, which was there too, that he might, by suffering in his own person, atone for his sin; and that by faithfully and unflinchingly going through this adventure to the end, by enduring courageously all the consequences of it, that he might perhaps raise himself to the level of his dead friend. So the mainspring of all human action is self-interest, gentlemen! So you have never had a friend, and never want one! Let us grant you, that the Samaritan was going to stand for Jericho, and was glad of the opportunity of striking a blow at the Levite interest, and let us have done with it. He only gave the landlord two pence, and we never hear of his having come back and paid the rest of the score. Is that the way you would argue? Very well; he did the thing very cheap. He was a long-headed man. You will probably, however, not find him in the same circle of the Paradise of Fools with yourselves.

It all turned out as Austin's attorney had predicted. Every member of the jury had been talking about the duel this three weeks past.

The escape of Prince Louis Buonaparte from Ham, and the Barty-Hertford duel, had been the main subjects of conversation among them for that time. When they sat in that box, they were requested to dismiss from their minds all that they had heard outside that court. A modest request this, to ask twelve men to forget what they had been talking about for the last fortnight. It was not complied with; it was childish to suppose that it could be; no one ever did think that it would be; Austin was condemned before he came into court. Counsel spoke on each side. The counsel for the prosecution were very moderate, the counsel for the defence did their best, which was nothing. The judge summed up almost in the very words of Mr. Justice Erle two months before, in a similar case, but every one of the jury had formed their own opinion ; and that opinion was identical in all the twelve of them, to wit, that Austin had not acted " honourable," and so they found him guilty of manslaughter. A perfectly just finding ; but on perfectly unjust grounds.

The judge gave a glance at the jury, in which, said some who watched him, there was a slight gleam of contempt. He paused before he passed sentence, and when he began to speak, he spoke rather low. " It had pleased Almighty God," he said, " for some inscrutable reason, to strike down the prisoner at the bar, in the very beginning of what some had thought would have been a very noble and glorious career. He, as an old man, earnestly prayed the prisoner at the bar, that in the solitude and seclusion, to which he was now to be condemned, that he would take this lesson to heart, and remember that God only chastened in his infinite love."

A pause, and a profound silence. The jury felt uneasy, and began to wish they had done like P—'s jury, and let the young gentleman off.

The judge went on, though his voice was a little husky. " I would not add one iota to the terrible remorse which I know you feel. Nay, I would lighten it. Remember my words in prison. If this chastisement is taken to heart, the time will come, Austin Elliot, when you may bless the day in which you stood in that dock. I am condemning you to social and political death. At this moment a cloud passes over your life, hitherto so bright and happy, the shadow of which will remain, and will never wholly pass away from you again, on this side the grave. The jury have done their duty. It remains for me to do mine.

" One year's imprisonment."

The turnkey tapped him on the shoulder, and he followed the turnkey out, and was given over to a policeman. He brushed the shoulder of the next prisoner, a young man, a burglar, who looked at him curiously, and laughed, and said that it was a good thing that the swells got it sometimes, though if he had the giving on it to 'em — . Austin didn't hear any more than that, and did not appreciate or care about what he had heard. He was confused, and felt as if he was going to be ill. He asked for some water, and they gave it to him, and then he sat down and began thinking.

A year. This was 1846. Then it would be 1847. What was the day of the month? He could not remember, and asked the policeman.

The eleventh of June. The policeman repeated it twice, and then Austin thanked him, but his mind was elsewhere. A woman who sat opposite to him, a weary witness, had got on odd boots. They were both black jean boots, and were both for the right foot. One was trodden on one side, and the other was gone at the toes, but Austin was wide awake enough to see that they were both right-foot boots. You couldn't take *him* in. What a fool the woman must be ; perhaps she was drunk when she put them on. She looked a drunken sort of a drab. But there was something funny in it. Austin, God help him, had a quiet laugh over it ; and soon they told him it was time to go.

And so he went, patient and contented enough, for happily he was just now past feeling anything acutely. As he was going down the corridor, something struck him. When he had started from home that morning, his dog Robin had followed him, and would not be driven back. He remembered that now. He asked a policeman, who was standing by, to see after the dog for him, and take him to Miss Hilton's, in Wilton Crescent, and said she would give him five shillings. The man said, " Yes, he would," and Austin thanked him, and as he stepped through the crowd into the prison van, he looked round for his dog, but could not see him.

Robin had seen him, though, and was quite contented. His master, thought he, was busy to-day, and was now going for a drive. Robin had waited for Austin in all sorts of places, for all sorts of times, and had seen Austin get into all sorts of carriages and drive away without thinking about him. His custom, on these occasions, was to tear along the street, in front of the vehicle into which Austin had got — be it cab, carriage, or omnibus — with joyous bark, ready to take his part in the next pleasant adventure which should befall. So now he dashed through the crowded Old Bailey at the hazard of his life, racing and leaping in front of the prison-van which held his ruined and desperate master, as if this were the best fun of all.

The van took Austin to the great bald prison by the river-side, and he was hurried in. The cruel iron door clanged behind him, and sent its echoes booming through the long dismal whitewashed corridors. And the clang of that door fell like a deathknell on his ear. "I am condemning you," said the judge, "to social and political death." He knew it now. The door jarred, and clanged; and the world knew Austin Elliot no more.

Outside that great prison-door all was glorious June sunshine; the river flashing on, covered with busy craft, towards the tall blue dome which rose into the air above the drifting smoke, far away eastward. The June sun smote fiercely on the long prison-wall, on the quiet road which passed it, on the great iron door which had shut in Austin Elliot and all his high-built hopes and fancies. There is not a duller place in all London than that river-terrace beneath the prison-wall. There is never anything to see there. People who have cause to go that way generally hurry past; there is nothing to see there in general.

But for many days after this, people who had passed in a hurry came dawdling back again: for there was something to attract them, though they would have been troubled to tell you what. There sat, all this time, a dog against the prison-door, in the burning sunshine — a dog who sat patient and spoke to no other dogs, but who propped himself up against the nails and bars, and panted in the heat, and snapped sometimes at the flies. Those who turned and came back again knew, by their mother wit, that the dog had seen some one go into that prison, and had set himself to wait till he came out again ; and they spoke in low tones the one to the other, and tried to get the dog away, but he would not come. And one slip-shod drunken woman, whose husband was also behind that door, urged by some feeling of sickly sentimentality, which we will charitably attribute to gin, if you please, lest we should be accused of sentimentality ourselves ; brought the dog what we strongly suspect to have been her own dinner, and stood by while he ate it. Robin, poor dog ! made many friends during his solitary watch under the burning prison-wall ; for the people who pass by Mill-bank are mostly of the class whose highest idea of virtue is a certain blind self-sacrificing devotion — (reasons of such devotion, or merit of object, not to be inquired into by respectable folks, if you please).

So Robin kept watch in the burning sun, and got himself precariously fed by thieves and thieves' wives. Some-times the great door behind him would be opened, and then he would lope out into the middle of the street, and, with his head on one side, peer eagerly up the dim vista of whitewashed passages beyond. The blue-coated warders would whistle to him, and say, " Here, poor fellow ! " but he would only shake his long drooping tail for an instant, almost imperceptibly, and stand where he was. If there was a stranger present, the blue-coated warders would tell him, that that was the dog of a young swell, they had got inside for duelling, and that that dog had been there for above a week. Then the door would be shut again, and Robin would take his old post in the sun, and catch the flies.

For more than ten days he stayed there. At the end of that time he went away. The great door was open one day, and three or four warders were standing about. Robin had gone into the middle of the street, when a very tall, handsome young man came walking by with his eyes fixed on the prison.

He nearly stumbled over Robin. When Robin saw him, he leaped upon him, and the young man caught him in his bosom. And the young man was of the Scotch nation, for he said —

" It's his ain dog, if it's no his ain self. What, Robin, boy, do you mind Gil Macdonald, and the bonny hill-sides of Ronaldsay ! "

Chapter XXXIII

So went matters outside the prison-door, in the bright summer sunshine. Inside that door a generous, noble-minded, unselfish young man ; a young man who had, in his time, according to the light which had been shown him, his lofty aspirations towards the only good he knew of, political and social success ; was left without a friend or a hope, beating himself to desperation and death against his prison-bars. Dare you come in ?

But, in going, we may take this comfort with us : Austin would have required very long drilling to have made a high place in public life. Of that I feel quite sure. He was far too impulsive and thoughtless ; far too prone to believe the last thing which was told him, to accept the last theory put before him, and to say that it must be the best ; to have succeeded. Practice would have given him the power of closing his ears to argument, and acting only on foregone conclusions. Practice might have given him the trick of listening to his opponent, and ignoring all his sound arguments, catching him when he tripped : would have, in time, formed him into a shallow and untruthful debater, of the third class, like — (Heaven help us, where are we getting to now ?) He was born for nobler things than to be a little dog, doing the barking for big dogs with thick skins and strong nerves, who meant biting. He would, I fear, have dropped into a low place. His habit of seeing the best side of all opinions, and of having none of his own, his terror of adverse criticism, and his almost childish anger against opponents, would have made him but a poor man for public life. He would have successively believed all creeds, till he had none of his own.

That June morning we know of, they shut the gate behind him, and he knew that it was all over and done. He felt that he had died his first death, and that the clang of that door was as the rattling of the earth on his coffin. At that moment, he saw, so great is Divine mercy, among the burnt ashes of his past life, one gleaming spark of hope; he had, at all events, seen the worst, short of death; he was young and the world was large; his imprisonment would be over soon, only a year. The world was very large. There were other worlds besides this cruel, inexorable English one.

But that spark of hope disappeared for a time, when the sordid unbeautiful realities of his prison life began to be felt. His idea was, that he would be locked up beween four walls, and left to eat his heart, until his time was out. Lucky for him it was not so. There were rules in that prison, so degrading, that his mere loathing of them kept him from going mad. Little acts of discipline and punctuality, which, in his sane mind, he would have acknowledged as necessary, but which now irritated him. He had to go to chapel in the morning; he had to come out to the door of his cell, and touch his cap to the governor; and to do other things worse than this, little things, which he would not so much have cared to do when free; little things which, had he been travelling, in the desert or the bush, he would have laughed over, yet which now, when he was forced to do them, degraded him. He did not know, till afterwards, that, by powerful interest, all prison rules possible to be relaxed, had been relaxed in his favour. He did not know that the honest martinet of a governor was in a state of indignation about the relaxation of those rules ; and held, very properly, that there was no such thing as rank and influence in *his* republic. Austin did not know this. He did not notice, until he came out among the other convicts, that he, of all there, was the only one whose hair was uncut, and who wore his own clothes. Then he began to have a faint inkling that he was being treated leniently, and to think that they had done kindly by him, in not yielding to his wish. For he had asked them the first morning, when they made him go to chapel, why they would not let him lie on his bed, and die quietly.

It was a long while before he mixed with the other convicts there. The first night he was brought in he did not sleep at all. There was a booming in his ears all through the short summer night, and the power of connected thought was gone.

At seven he had dropped into a short uneasy slumber ; then a great bell had rung, and the warder had waked him for chapel. He asked him why he could not let him die in peace ? But he must come to chapel.

So he slouched in with a hot heavy head, and slouched out again. At the door he saw a warder, and looking on him with eyes, which though dull and lustreless, had a momentary spark of ferocity in them, asked him where the —— he was to go next ?

" To his cell," the man said quietly, and not unkindly.

Poor Austin blundered on, he knew not whither, he knew not for how long. He knew not where his cell was. He went on for, what seemed to his fading intellect, hours. Through one long whitewashed corridor after another ; at last there were stairs, and he went down, down, holding on by the balustrade.

At the end was an open court where many convicts were washing themselves ; when they saw Austin they began whistling, and jeering at him. He did not mind it, but stood blinking in the sunshine, peering about him, till they all stopped whistling and talking, and remained quite silent — quite silent, poor wretches; for Austin, as he stood there in the sunshine, was a strange sight to look on. His personal beauty, always great, was rather enhanced by the fever-flush on his cheek, and the great passionate grey eyes were now, with the pupils enormously dilated, staring with the fixed look of incipient delirium.

Unimaginative fellows, these convicts. After a moment's silence, one of them, as spokesman, said, "that cove's ill!" and this so well expressed the feelings of the community, that they went on washing themselves, and comparing notes about the Past and the Future; about what had been done, and what, please Heaven, would yet be done (in their line of business), leaving Austin to the care of the warder.

Austin petulantly appealed to him. "They told me to go to my cell, but I can't find it. They have taken all my money away, or I would give you five pounds to take me back, and put me on my bed; and I can't promise you anything for certain, because the Crown has a claim on my property; but if you will take me back to my bed, I pledge you my honour as a gentleman, that Miss Hilton will give you five pounds. It is all broken off between us now, you understand — and, perhaps, she has not used me well, but she will give you that. I want to lie down and die. Come, now, I would do it for you. We are all the same flesh and blood, convicts and warders, and Whigs and Tories. If I had taken care, and not broken God's laws, I might have been a warder, in time you know, when I was fit for it; and if you had gone out with the friend of your heart on one accursed May morning, and seen him tumble dead at your feet, you might have been a convict. If I had been warder, and you convict, and you had come to me with your head whirling round, and ten thousand remorseless devils tearing at your heart, and asked me to lead you to your cell, to die in peace, I would have done it; by God I would! Come, now!"

Austin Elliot

Poor Austin! He was near getting release from all his troubles for a time; he was in the first stage of a brain-fever. The warder quietly and kindly took him back to his cell, comforting him with such comfort as a prison-warder has to give. He never claimed five pounds from Miss Hilton or from Austin; he never thought about what Austin had said any more. But his kindness to poor delirious Austin was the best day's work he ever did in his life. Austin was partly delirious, and never remembered one word of what passed. The man never told his own story; therefore, how came it, that after all this miserable business was over, in happier times than these; this warder found his private affairs inquired into; found that the inquirers had discovered that he, the warder, had started in life as a farmer, and had incontinently failed in consequence of trying some of Mechi's experiments without Mechi's money, and had been bankrupt, and glad to be made a warder at Millbank? How was it that this warder found himself asked, as a personal favour, to come, with a salary of £250 a year, and superintend a certain model farm on a certain island? Which splendid rise in life was the consequence of his kindness to Austin on this morning.

Austin was delirious, and remembered nothing of it. He never told his story. There were none but convicts by. One of them must have told his story for him. Yes, there was one convict, a very young man, with a foolish, weak face, who had come towards Austin the moment he saw him come into the yard, and had watched him with a look of eager curiosity, who had heard it all. This young convict was the maker of that warder's fortunes.

Chapter XXXIV

AUSTIN got back to his cell, and somewhat regained his head in solitude. He lay on his bed all day, and a little after dark the warder before mentioned came in, and got him to go to bed.

He slept for a time, not, luckily, for very long. Then he woke with a feeling of horror upon him, a feeling that something terrible was coming. He got out of bed, and felt for the bell.

Round and round the room, from end to end ; how damp and cold and strange the walls felt ! — and where the devil was the bell-rope ? His servant, he knew, slept in the room overhead. He was ill ; it would be better to call for him. He called out, — " Edward ! Edward ! " many times, and waited to hear the door above open : but it did not. Confound the lad ! — why should he choose this night, of all others, to be out ! He had better feel his way into bed again, and wait till he heard Edward go upstairs. He began feeling his way towards his bed again, but he did not get to it. In a moment the whole ghastly truth came before him. For one instant he remembered all that had happened, and he knew where he was. Then he gave a wild cry, and fell down on the cold stone floor insensible.

The warder heard him, and came in. He got him on to his bed again, which was a lucky thing for Austin, for if he had lain long insensible on the cold stone floor, in his fever, he would have died.

His fever was violent and obstinate ; he was often delirious for a day at a time. He knew the doctor and the warder now and then. At the end of ten days he was still delirious, but he recognised some one who came to see him then.

Gil Macdonald, pondering about many things, after the last terrible famine winter, during which the Ronaldsay folk had lived on rotten potatoes, seaweed, and limpets; had gotten it into his head, that he must, as soon as he could see things a bit right, and save money enough, go south. South — from his barren, mountain highland home, where mighty men, such as he, were eating their hearts in starvation and idleness — down to the rich country of England, where there was a career and fair play for all; where a "long-leggit hieland chiel" might find his place among these broad-shouldered, grey-eyed, thoughtful English, and be welcomed as a friend, not as a rival. Gil had heard the Mactavish call these men "Cockneys," by which he, Gil, understood, a set of effeminate fellows, enervated by living in a warmer climate. But Gil was far too true a Scotchman to set his watch by the Mactavish's clock, or by Christopher North's clock, or by Professor Blackie's clock; and so he had come to the conclusion, having heard Englishmen, who had come north, talking of England and the English, that they were a very manly and noble set of fellows; and argued, that if the English *were* fools, as some tried to make out, so much the better for him, who had a strong notion that he was not a fool. If they were the fellows he thought, why then it would be all the better to live among them.

Besides, Austin Elliot was an Englishman, and lived in England, and Austin Elliot was the one person around whom most of Gil's hopes for the future grouped themselves. Austin was the most heroic and amiable person he had ever seen, and the memory of him was, perhaps, brighter in the Scotchman's mind, than the reality. But he must first get south, and see Austin. If Austin could help him he would; if he could not, at all events Gil would see him again — that would be something. So strange was the admiration of this young man for Austin, he being in many points — not unimportant ones — somewhat Austin's superior.

One brilliant June morning he landed from the Leith steamboat, and strode wondering along the streets, looking at the names over the shop-doors to see for a Highland one. Having "speired" of one MacAlister, who was taking down his shutters, and whose personal appearance gave Gil the highest hopes, he did as he was told; he walked "aye west" for eight miles or more toward Mortlake, where Mr. Elliot had lived. He found Stanhope House, and rang, waiting for an answer with a beating heart.

Old Mr. Elliot, the servant told him, had been dead above a year; young Mr. Elliot lived at such a number in Pall Mall.

So Gil, resting a little, and taking a frugal meal at a public-house, strode eastward again, carefully asking his way at Scotch shops only — not that he was distrustful by nature, but only cautious; and it was an unco muckle city, and a stranger didna ken. So he asked his way at the Scotch shops only.

Feeling his way, with many mistakes, he came at last to Pall Mall. Here he made his only non-Scotch inquiry that day. Seeing a handsome, goodnatured-looking young dandy, very like Austin, standing at a corner, he took courage to ask him whether or no that was Paul Maul? The young gentleman answered civilly that it was Pell Mell. This made poor Gil fancy that he had gone wrong again; he determined to trust none but his fellow-countrymen for directions. He walked on till he saw a Highland name over a shop, and went in and asked. He was right this time. The house at which he determined to ask was the very house where Austin lived: he saw that by the number. He asked the landlord, who was in his shop, unscrewing the breech from a rifle, whether or no Mr. Elliot lived there?

The landlord, hearing the dear old music of his native accent, took off his spectacles, and said at a venture, in Gaelic —

"He did live here, God forgive us; but he is fretting out his brave heart in prison now, my son."

Poor Gil sat down. In prison. He remembered almost the last words they had spoken together at Ronaldsay, and he felt as if the hand of God had smote him.

" In prison ! "

" Aye, the weary day."

" I have followed him all down from Ronaldsay, all the weary ! weary way, and I find him in prison at the end. Do you mean the same man as I ? Do you mean Mr. Austin Elliot, the young Saxon lord, with the laughing eyes, that were blue like Loch Oil, and Loch na Craig, when the wind sweeps down on them from Ben More on a June morning ? Have they dared to tie up the stag in the byre ? Have they dared to put the salmon in the goose-dub ? Had they dared to chain the scolding pere-grine on the popinjay perch ? "

Thus, in his anger, in furious Gaelic, Ossianically spoke poor Gil. Alas ! it appeared they had dared to do all this, and that there was no undoing of it at any rate what-ever. His fellow-countryman had him into his parlour, and told him all about what had happened. And when Gil had grown calmer, they had together a regular good Gaelic palaver, towards the end of which this astounding fact was discovered — that Gil's great-uncle's second wife was sister to the Reverend David Macpherson, a placed minister, who had served Glen Ramshorn for forty years ; and that the Reverend David's third sister had married the gunmaker's own uncle's third cousin, an Aberdeen stonemason, whereby it was as clear as day that Gil was the gunmaker's nephew. So Gil was good for a bed in Pall Mall, and, if need were, ten pound or so, for the rest of his life.

That afternoon Gil walked down to the prison, by the river, to see what he could do with regard to getting at Austin. And there he found Robin, as we saw. And when he had spoken to one or two of the warders, he came back again to Pall Mall, and brought Robin with him ; and then, taking off his coat and baring his great arms, he set to work and cleaned guns, while Robin lay beside him, with his nose between his paws, and watched him contentedly. Long into the night he worked, a patient, intelligent giant; holding the creed, that a man was born to do the work he found to his hand, and that when the work was done it would get paid for in some form. And, next morning, when the sleepy apprentices came lumbering downstairs, there was Gil again, hard at it, having had a few hours' sleep on the sofa, in the parlour, with Robin. A true Scotchman — going on their old good plan, of showing what they were worth before they bargained for their wages.

This appearance of Gil Macdonald was very important for Austin, or I would not have dwelt on it. For, the fact is this, that Gil Macdonald was the only person who ever went near Austin during his imprisonment. Some cast him off, and some were prevented from going near him; we shall know who were in the former, and who in the latter category soon. Meanwhile Gil Macdonald was the one link between Austin and the world he had left.

The gunmaker, Austin's landlord, Gil's kinsman! was a west-end tradesman, and knew intimately some very great people. So, next morning, when Gil, after doing the work of ten men, proposed, at breakfast, the utterly untradesman-like scheme of adopting the plan of the creature Donald, in "Rob Roy" — to wit, getting himself made warder, letting Austin out, pitching the keys into the Thames, and then — and then — (that part of the plan not developed yet); at this time, I say, the gunmaker seeing that his kinsman's notion of morality would not do in such a southern latitude, rebuked him severely; but, at the same time, bethought himself of a certain great man, a customer; and coolly waited on that great man, in his dressing-room, for the purpose of showing his lordship the most beautiful pair of barrels ever forged.

When he got into the great man's presence, on these credentials, he but the barrels on the ground, and coolly told him, that he had merely used them as an artifice to gain an audience with his lordship. He then told, shortly and quickly; knowing that time was precious here, Gil's story; and made Gil's request, that he might be allowed access to Austin.

His lordship was very much interested and pleased. " By Gad, Macpherson," he said, " this is a wicked world. They are all leaving that poor fellow there to die in his desperation. I don't say anything about Edward Barty; but conceive that wicked little thing — that Miss Hilton — having had the indecency to bolt abroad, and follow that black-leg bully Hertford. It is utterly atrocious. Your request is granted to the full. Let this young fellow have access to this poor boy. You are a good fellow, Macpherson, and this young Highlander must be another. I will write to Captain Somes at once. Good morning."

So Gil Macdonald had the *entrée* to Austin, and he went to see him that afternoon.

How did he find his hero, his gallant young gentleman, the man to whom he had meant to come, asking humbly that he might follow his glorious fortunes! He had found him at last.

Here he was, on the narrow prison-bed, in the half-lighted cell, in a close, dead atmosphere, which made poor Gil breathe hard, as though he had been running. Here he was, deserted by every one, all his beauty gone, with his great blue eyes staring in the madness of his fever; here he was, delirious and alone, crying continually for help night and day, to those who never answered, and who never came.

But he knew Gil, and Gil said, " Thank God for that ! He knew him even in his madness, and stretched out his fevered hands towards him, and said, how long he had been coming; but that now he was come, they would get away together, to the glens of Ronaldsay, and wander by the cool streams, among the green shadows of the wood by the waterfalls. And they would go together, up into the dark, cool caves, and watch the blue sea out beyond, in the burning sun ; and he would bathe in the linn, and his head would get cold again, and then his reason would come back. But he would never come near the wicked town any more. His head, he told Gil, had got heated with sitting-up in the gallery of the Commons so long, and hearing the weary debates. But that was all past and gone for ever. Charles Barty was dead, and they were all dead but he and Gil ; and they, too, must get away to Ronaldsay, and leave the hot streets, and the cruel lying crowds, that haunted clubs and such places, and lied about men, until they went mad. They must get away from these into the mountains, and end their days in peace."

Gil told all this to the gunmaker and his wife that night, over a frugal supper. It was not told or heard without tears. Those three leal and trusty Scotch bodies made a compact, that though all the world had deserted poor Austin, yet they would stay by him to the death. Then the gunmaker and his wife went to bed, and Gil and Robin went into the shop.

Gil cleaned guns till there were no more to clean. Gil cleaned guns, making himself grimy beyond conception. Then he remembered that one of the apprentices had been ordered to clean a certain gun-lock, the first thing to-morrow morning. And he got possession of this lock, and a certain book, and pored over them both ; while Robin lay with his nose on his paws, and watched him with bright clear eyes. After half an hour with lock and book before him, Gil began to understand the difference between main-spring, sear-spring, sear, and the rest of it, as well as he would have done after a wet morning, in the class-room at Hythe. Then he asked himself what was the matter with this particular lock ? Then he compared it with a newly-cleaned one, and came to the conclusion, that the sear-spring was clogged with oil. And then at twelve o'clock he took the work to pieces. This was a bold and remarkable action, but what is more remarkable, before half-past one he had cleaned that lock, and put it together again (which is not so easy a matter, particularly when you have no one to show you the difference between the Bridle pin and the other pins). When he had done this, he felt proud, and almost happy, in spite of his poor hero, who was raving there in his prison cell.

Almost happy; nay, possibly quite, for this reason. Gil had the great want of his heart, the great craving of his whole life, satisfied at last. He hardly knew it. He knew only this, that in Ronaldsay, he had always felt, that he was a man lost, and thrown away, a man capable of he knew not what, and without means of finding out. Now he found that this gunsmith's work, little as he knew of it, little as he had done of it, was in some way filling up a void in his heart. The fact was, that Gil, for the first time in his life, had got to WORK, and he was as satisfied over it as is a dog when he gnaws a bone. The feeling of an Englishman, a Scotchman, and one kind of Irishman, over his work, is similar to that of a Turk over his pipe. It is a sedative. But in the one case, the results contribute more towards human well-being than in the other.

In spite of his late night over the work, Gil was tinkering in the shop before the two apprentices came sleepily squabbling down stairs. He went to Austin again that day, but Austin was as bad as ever, and was as bad as ever for many days. Still Gil was always with him. Gil grew grimier and smelt stronger of train-oil as time went on, until the brave young kilted Highlander had grown into a smudgy gunsmith in a leather apron; all the romantic beauty of his personal appearance gone clean away to the free winds of heaven. Sad degradation indeed! That he, the untamed stag of the mountain, should condescend to this! That Gil, the idle Highlander, should develop into Gil the sage shrewd diligent young smith! Worse still, that our taste should be so depraved, as to make us admire him the more, the more eager, diligent, and grimier he grew.

There came a morning, when the warders reported to Gil, on his visiting the prison, that Austin was better, and had gone to sleep. He waited till he woke, and then Austin's reason had returned, and he knew Gil in reality; not as he had in his fever, as only one of the figures in the perpetual shadow-dance which went on before his eyes, in which Gil's figure was only a little more real than the others. In a week from this time he was convalescent, and then they began to consult.

The first thing done was this: — Austin wrote to his attorney, Mr. Compton, asking him whether or no the Crown had made any claim on his property. He wrote a very cold, stiff note, for he was indignant. The old man had never come near him in his illness. His note was answered by the old man's junior partner, Mr. Brogden. It appeared that the anxiety and worry caused by Austin's trial and conviction, had ended by Mr. Compton's being laid up by a very serious attack of illness. Mr. Brogden proceeded to tell Austin that the Crown had made no claim on his property, and would *certainly*, he believed, make none, provided Mr. Elliot *remained perfectly quiet*, and let the whole matter slip by. It would be better for Mr. Elliot not to communicate with their office any more till better times. Clerks would talk. Some of the newspapers had been troublesome over his case. The new secretary was very well disposed to Mr. Elliot, but they must be quiet. Mr. Elliot might trust them, and —

"The new secretary!" bounced out Austin. "Is Peel out then? Good heavens! Surely the Lords have not *dared!* But what does it matter to me?"

Gil felt horribly guilty. The fact was, that he had been so busy with his guns, that he did not actually know whether Peel was in or out. He felt very foolish, and spoke of other things. But that night, when he went home, he made his kinsman prime him with the details of the great Corn-law storm, which had passed so high over his head, without moving his hair; and next day was en-

abled to tell Austin that the Lords had not dared; that
the Bill was law; and that Sir Robert had come to grief
over the Irish Arms Bill. He was so busy over his gun-
cleaning business, that he had not time to ask what Irish
arms were. If he had been made to say what his notion
of the Irish Arms Bill was, he would probably have
thought that it was the account rendered to Parliament,
for certain casualties at Donnybrook Fair. After this he
informed himself about politics, but on this occasion he
was relieved, when Austin said to him —

" Gil, never let you and I speak of these things again.
My imprisonment here renders me politically dead. I cannot tell you, because I have no strength to tell you, how
hideous my silly boy's dream, of succeeding in politics,
without one single qualification, seems to me now. The
Corn-bill has passed, and has crushed me under its wheels
in passing. Let us talk no more of these things. I have
to begin life again; I will, God help me, begin it in another spirit."

It was all very well for Austin to talk like this to Gil,
but it had not very much effect on him. Austin's sad example was no use to Gil. His kinsman was a politician;
and after his first inquiries into politics for Austin's sake,
he began making more for his own. He began to take a
strong interest in the matter, and in a month could give
his opinion, and defend it. His frame of mind at the end
of a month was Radical.

Gil's next enterprise, on Austin's behalf, was to go secretly to Wilton Crescent, and to find out where Miss Hilton was, and what she was doing. This was to be a very
secret expedition indeed. Gil performed it with all his
Scotch caution. But his caution was unnecessary. He,
knowing nothing, bluntly brought back this intelligence —
that Miss Hilton, with her aunt, her butler, and the rest of
her household, had started for the Continent, the day after
the duel. There was no one in the house but a char-
woman.

Then Austin turned his face to the wall. This was the hardest of all. She had deserted him then ! He could forgive Lord Edward Barty — nay, he would dread to see him. He could forgive his father's old friends ; they had never liked him since he had turned Radical. But for her to have deserted him, and thrown herself into the arms of that dog Hertford ! Ah ! this was very, very bitter !

That she, who could make those religious pilgrimages, to such strange places in such strange company, could not have come to see him or to ask after him in his misery ! If she had only sent old James ! *Could* she have known that he distrusted her after that morning — that miserable morning before the last debate, when he had seen her in company with Hertford ? *Could* she have known of the cruel words he spoke of her to Lord Charles Barty ? If she knew these things, it might account for her neglect. She might be angry with him ; she might have gone abroad in a pique.

No, no ! she *could* not have known it. She must be false, false ! She must be falser than it is possible to conceive. And he, poor fool ! loved her more than ever — loved, that is to say, the quiet, calm little woman who used to sit with folded hands in church — loved her, in fact, as she used to be — the old, quiet, patient Eleanor, who existed no longer.

He did not love her as she was now, then. Ah, yes ! that was the bitterest part of it. Fallen, base as she was, he loved her more than ever. It was well that he should turn his face to the wall.

I have shown you, with most inexorable justice, all the worst points in his character. Most of them — such as his flippancy, his want of earnestness, and other faults of this class, which he shared with many young men — were faults of education. These died a natural death, the moment the prison-gate slammed behind him, and he was brought face to face with reality. But his worst fault — a certain jealous pride, showing itself outwardly in almost hysterical anger — remained there yet. And now, before he rose from his narrow prison-bed, he saw that it was there, and set to work to conquer it.

He thought over his life, and he saw that fault staring out on two or three occasions, in a very ugly manner. He remembered Miss Cecil, and his furious anger at everything in heaven and earth, when he found out that she was to marry Lord Mewstone. He blushed at this, and tried to forget it, but could not.

Then he began thinking of the poor fellow who was dead, of poor Lord Charles. How often had he half quarrelled with him at school, when he had been jealous, because the dead man had been friendly with some other boy, and Austin had fancied himself neglected. How often, later than this, had he been fractious and rude with him, merely because their social positions were so different, and because he, Austin, was afraid of being called a tuft-hunter. He remembered now five hundred things which he had said to his friend who was gone, which he would have given the world to recall, but which could never be recalled.

Again: had he done his duty by that poor, dead brother of Eleanor's, at Eton? No, he had not. He had been too much ashamed of him. He had been angry and indignant at that boy's very existence. That he and Lord Charles, with their sublime, high and mighty boy-aspirations, should have a boy given to thieving forced on their company: it had been intolerable. Now that he was in prison himself, he thought that, perhaps, a little more genial kindness, a little less high-handed patronage, might have saved that boy. But it was too late.

Lastly, he began thinking about Eleanor herself. The old Adam was a little too strong for him here, yet. For he *had* trusted her, as woman was never trusted before. He had let her go those mysterious pilgrimages of hers, down into this very Millbank quarter, dressed in her maid's clothes, and asked no questions. And at last he had found her walking arm in arm, in the lowest part of the town, with the accursed Hertford. He could not accuse himself here. Not yet.

And now she had deserted him in his trouble, and gone abroad after that man —

Still he recognised the fact that, all through his life, there had been a tendency to jealousy and suspicion, and he determined, even now, that if Eleanor could ever clear herself to him, that he would forgive her, would tell her so, and part with her for ever. But still, could she clear herself ten times over, *his* duty was evident. He would never link his ruined fortunes to hers. If she had been penniless, it would have been a different matter. But as it was, it was perfectly clear it would be dishonourable, after what had happened, to renew his intercourse with her. The world would never hold him blameless if he did.

The end of poor Austin's illness was also the culminating point of his misfortunes; after this, his affairs began to mend — very, very slowly, but still to mend. When he rose from his sick-bed, and began to walk about his prison, there were still nine months of confinement before him. They were weary months to look forward to, but he felt he could get through them without maddening himself, now that Gil Macdonald was coming to see him almost daily. In his present state of weakness and depression, he tried to think, tried to hope, that, by mere patience, he might live on till things came right again. One thing only now was unendurable. Poor Eleanor was abroad, alone and unprotected, in the power of Captain Hertford and her aunt. That was maddening to think of. Badly as she had treated him, something must be done there. He thought the matter over as well as he was able. There seemed only one hope. He got leave from the governor, and wrote the following letter to Lord Edward Barty.

"MY LORD,

"I know that we can never meet again as friends on this side of the grave. I know the horror and detestation in which you must hold my name, after the late catastrophe. But I beg you, in God's name, to listen to what I have to say.

" You used to love Eleanor Hilton. She is gone abroad unprotected. Her aunt has taken her away into a foreign country, where she will be in the power of the man who has caused all this misery, and his disreputable companions.

" Now I ask you, who have so often knelt and prayed by her side, whether you will stand by and let this go on. If you have a grain of chivalry in your composition, Edward, you cannot, you dare not. I swear to you, Edward, deeply as I love you, if you, knowing what you know, stand by and do nothing, that I will cast you off with the same loathing and contempt, which you now feel for me. Eddy! Eddy! for the sake of the love we once bore to one another, you will save her.

" I remain, my Lord,
" Your Lordship's obedient servant,
" AUSTIN ELLIOT."

Gil had instructions to take this letter to Cheshire House, and to put it into Lord Edward's own hands, and get an answer. Admiral Villeneuve had instruction to form a junction with the fleet of Admiral Gravina, and to pound and blast the British fleet from off the face of the waters. Neither Gil Macdonald nor Admiral Villeneuve were successful, and they both had strong doubts of their success before they began to execute their orders.

When Gil (having got off as much of his grimness as was possible) reconnoitred Cheshire House, his heart sank within him. The house stood a long way back from the street, and was fronted by a high wall, in which were two carriage-gates. In one of these gates was a wicket ; and Gil, after a quarter-of-an-hour's watching, became aware, that this wall and gate were the outworks of the place, and must be carried, either by stratagem or force, before he could hope to do his errand.

He saw a great many people come and ring the bell. Most of the people who brought letters had them taken by the porter, and had the door shut in their faces. This would not do. Austin had told him to put his letter into Lord Edward's hand, and get an answer.

At last he opened his first parallel. He rang the bell, and asked to see Lord Edward. The porter answered civilly, but shortly, " Out of town ; " and Gil retired and leaned against a lamp-post.

The thing had to be done, and must be done somehow. Gil only knew this much : that this was the house of poor Lord Charles's father ; that the mention of Austin's name might not be a good passport there, and that he must be cautious. He was very much puzzled. If Austin had sent any one but a very cunning Scot, his mission might have failed altogether. But Gil, with his patient vulpine cunning, succeeded better probably than an Englishman or Irishman would have done. He had waited some time, and was thinking of doing all sorts of things, when the wicket was opened, and a fine boy of about sixteen, in deep mourning, came out, and walked away slowly along the street. Gil had heard the porter call him, " My Lord."

Gil instantly gave chase, and overtook this lad.

" I beg your pardon, young sir, ye're no Lord Edward Barty, I'm thinking ? "

" No ; my name is George Barty. My brother Edward is abroad. Can I do anything for you ? "

Gil paused an instant ; but when he looked again into the honest face of the lad he took his resolution.

" Yes, young sir — I mean my lord — ye're a lord, are ye no ? Open this letter, and gie me the answer to take back wie me ; for he loves you and yours, dearer than his heart's bluid, after all done."

The boy opened the letter, and read it. He gave no answer at first ; he bit his lips hard, and tried not, but the tears would come. Gil walked a little way off, and looked at the sparrows upon the house-top.

At last the boy came after him, and touched his arm, and said :

" Do you see Mr. Elliot ever ? "

" Nigh every day."

" Are you in his confidence ? "

" I should be. I am only a poor highland lad. But when ye, all of ye, left him to rot in his prison, I was the only one faithful to him."

" You are wrong," said the boy eagerly. " Others are faithful to him. I am faithful to him. Edward is as true as steel to him. We know how blameless he was in the matter. We know that he followed this man abroad and got wounded. Take this letter back to him, and tell him to burn it. Tell him that Edward followed Miss Hilton abroad instantly, and has been with her ever since. They are at Ems now. She is in trouble about her aunt; but don't tell him this. How is he ? How does he bear it ? "

" He has been at death's door, and no one nigh him."

" Poor fellow ! Give him my love — George Barty's love; and say, we have not forgotten him."

Gil came back and reported all this. Austin was glad that Lord Edward was with her. That was very good news. So Lord Edward was as true as steel to him, was he ? Perhaps. But he might have written a line to say so. As true as steel, hey ?

" God forgive him ! " he said, the next moment. " When did Lord Edward ever write letters, blind as he was from infancy. He *could* write in a way, so Austin had heard ; but since Austin had known him, he had always dictated his letters to his valet. He would cast this miserable jealousy out of his heart once and for all. Edward Barty *was* true to him ; his delicacy had only prevented his writing. It was easy to find excuses for a blind man ; but who could find excuses for Eleanor ? Why had she not written ? Not one line ; not one short word to say that she had thrown him off. His anger against her increased day by day ; but, alas, his love for her grew none the less. He loved an *eidolon* — an Eleanor who never had been, except in his own fancy — a true, faithful, patient little being, who always sat with folded hands, whose face never grew animated, save when he was present. He had loved such an one, but she had never existed. Eleanor Hilton who lived, was false and cruel. Not one line all these three weary months. How wicked these women could be at times!

Poor Austin's resolution to uproot from his heart his fatal error of causeless jealousy, seemed to hold well enough, until he began to think about Eleanor; about the very person whom he loved best in the world, and whom, if he had only known it, he had best cause to trust — the one who had suffered more on his behalf than any one else who cared for him. It was natural possibly, that he should be most jealous about the one he loved best, but it was very hard upon Eleanor.

She *had* written to him again and again, letters full of wild love, tenderness, and comfort. Lord Edward Barty had dictated several notes to him also, and inclosed them in hers. They had left them to go to post with the other letters.

But Aunt Maria's maid, acting under orders, had brought them all to her mistress, who had read them, and then put them all into the fire.

Eleanor's troubles began to get more heavy to bear than Austin's; Austin's silence aggravated them very much, she did not know what to think. Was he desperate, under his terrible misfortune, or did he know of her secret? He was in Millbank prison himself; could he know? She told Lord Edward everything. He advised her to say nothing; he was getting angry; Austin ought to have written.

At this time Lord Edward received the following letter : —

"DEAR BROTHER,

"I met a big fellow, an awful big fellow, as big as old

Hoskins, but not *so fat*, in the square yesterday. He spoke like an Irishman, and said that Austin was anxious for you to take care of Miss Hilton. I said you were doing so. He said that Austin had been dying, but was well again, and that every one had deserted him.

"Florence has shoved the mignonet-box out of the school-room window, and broke the geraniums in the drawing-room balcony, and has caught it. Jim was sitting on the edge of his tub, kicking nurse, and the tub turned over him, and the water has gone down and spoilt the library ceiling. He caught it too, but not so bad as Florence. The houses are up, and we leave town to-morrow.

> "Your affectionate brother,
>> "GEORGE BARTY."

On the receipt of this they wrote to Austin again, but again Aunt Maria's maid was terrified into stealing the letter, and again Aunt Maria put it into the fire. What old James was doing at this time we shall see directly. But the effect of this wicked old woman's plot was this, that Austin thought they had both utterly deserted him; that he thought that Eleanor, at least, should have written to him; and that he was very angry, and very jealous.

Chapter XXXV

AUSTIN had never been moved into the hospital; the doctor preferred dealing with him where he was. After a time he began to get better, and was able to walk about.

At first he always waited for Gil Macdonald, and took his arm for a turn up and down the long corridor, and then lay down again; but after a time he felt the want of more exercise, and used to rise and walk out by himself. At first, when he began to do this he would wait till the long corridor was empty, and then come out, and begin his solitary walk. To show how villanously penal sentences are carried out in certain cases, I may mention, that when Austin began to recover, the governor called on him every day (under protest); and that if Austin, in his solitary walk, wanted the support of a warder's arm, it was his own fault if he did not have it. He was their Picciola — their "poor little thing" — their prison-flower! — the only innocent man among nine hundred. What wonder that they (officially) petted him? Poor, handsome, patient, innocent young gentleman! Yes! they grew very fond of Austin — they were just like every one else.

But after a time Austin began to feel the want of new faces, although those faces were those of convicts. One night, when he was getting strong, he lay on his bed and thought, and a strange thought came into his head. This thought put itself into many forms before it came to this. — Could not he, Austin, do some good, infinitesimal it might be, if he mixed with the other convicts? In the eye of the law he was no better than the worst of them, but he was still higher than the highest of them. Surely he might do *some* good.

" By merely mixing with them, and talking to them, we might raise their moral tone," thought he. Speaking to them of higher things would — must — do them some good. One does not like to say that he was wrong; but still it becomes apparent that he had not acquired what we may call the Australian instinct — that is to say, did not know a convict or jail bird when he saw him; did not recognise the class of man as a distinct one; did not perceive the extraordinary difference in appearance, between an honest man under a cloud, and a rogue. In fact, I am sorry to say, he came to the conclusion that he might raise the moral tone of the convicts around him by talking to them on an empty stomach.

He determined to go out into the yard and talk to them;

but he was still weak, and a little nervous; and so, putting it off from day to day, he contented himself by walking up and down the corridor in front of his cell.

One day there was a fracas there; it was only a few days after he was able to walk up and down alone. It was not a very great riot; it was a loud dispute between a warder, and a tall young man in a convict dress. Austin, weak as he was, walked down to see if he could assist the warder. He found him in high dispute with the convict, and in the convict, he recognised the young man who had looked at him so eagerly, the morning after he had been brought to prison.

And as Austin looked on the young man, he had sense to see that he was not quite recovered from his fever; that his brain had not quite got the better of the delirium yet. However, he was far too sensible a fellow to be deluded by any mad fancies. "If a lunatic," he said to himself, "only *knows* that he is mad, and can keep that faith in his head sufficiently long, he may defy all the Masters in Lunacy put together." Austin knew that, probably, his brain was not quite right, and so he banished a certain idiotic fancy from his mind indignantly. He banished his first mad fancy, and took a practical view of things. Here was a young convict in high dispute with a warder. He would intercede for this young convict; would get hold of this young convict, and talk to him about Shakespeare and the musical glasses, until all the other convicts should come and listen with this one. And so Austin would elevate the moral tone of all of them, until they should become penetrated with an abstract love of virtue (for Austin, in his political creed, ignored the religious element), and so they should all become reformed; which meant, although he did not know it, that all their foreheads should become broader and higher; their eyes should look straight at another man's; and they should give over fiddling with their buttons, when they spoke to an honest man.

It appeared that the dispute with this convict and the

warder was rather a strange one. The young man had been coming up to speak to Austin, when the warder, too zealous in Austin's cause, had turned him back. Austin thanked the warder for his kindness, and allowed the young convict to speak to him.

The young man spoke first. " Your name is Elliot? " he said.

Austin said " Yes."

" I knew that the first moment I saw you — that morning when you came out in the yard among the rest of us. I had not seen you for a long while, but I felt sure it was you."

" Then you have seen me before ? " said Austin.

" Ah yes, often."

" What is your name now," said Austin, " and where have you seen me ? "

" Then you do not remember me ? "

" No," said Austin. " I had a silly fancy about you just now ; but I don't remember you. If you have known me, tell me where ? "

" I knew you when you were at Eton. Do you remember Tolliday's boy, Jim Charlton ? "

" Yes."

" I am that boy."

" Indeed you are nothing of the kind," said Austin. " Jim was a light-headed boy, your hair is black. What is the good of lying ? "

" I don't know ; no one speaks the truth here. I remember you, though. You were always kind enough to me ; you used always to be with a young swell there, Lord Charles Barty. How I hated that boy. What has become of him ? "

" D——n you," said Austin, " you had better take care."

As he turned fiercely on the man, he saw nothing but a look of puzzled curiosity ; his wrath was stayed at once ; and when he had looked at the young man's face for an instant, he considered whether or no he was going mad again.

"Don't get in a rage, Austin Elliot," said Charlton. "What has become of that cursed young prig?"

"Dead — shot in a duel. I was his second, and am here for it. *Will* you hold your tongue?"

"Yes, directly. One question more. What has become of that other fellow who was always with you and Lord Charles — Robert Hilton?"

"He is dead; he died three years ago at Namur," said Austin.

"May the devil take him," said Charlton. "I shall be out of this in six months, and I was depending on him. I know enough about him to bring me in a tidy income. So he is dead. Well, no loss, except to me. He was a worthless young scoundrel."

"He was nothing of the kind," said Austin. "He was half-witted, but he was neither worthless nor a scoundrel. How dare you speak so of Miss Hilton's brother? He stole things. He was half-witted, I tell you. What have you done that you are here? I'll tell you what, little Bob Hilton, poor little devil, was in some respects immeasurably your superior. Come now."

This was, do you perceive, the way in which Austin carried out his plan of elevating the moral tone of the convicts around him, by talking about Shakespeare and the musical glasses.

Chapter XXXVI

AUSTIN grew to like this young convict. He had, it appears, behaved pretty well, and was a somewhat privileged person. When Gil was not with him, Austin used to walk a great deal with this young fellow, Charlton. Gil was glad at Austin's having found some one in the prison of whom he could make some sort of a companion; he wondered at Austin's choice, but respectfully acquiesced. He did not like Charlton, but that was his fault, of course,

for Austin *must* be right.   Austin's heroic nature, thought
Gil, though in other words, could not err : so he accepted
Charlton.

The fact was that Austin, so far from having become
less heroic in Gil's eyes, since his misfortune, had become
infinitely more so.   When he had found his hero in misfortune and disgrace, his hero worship only grew the stronger
for those circumstances.   Pity was in his thoroughly chivalrous mind, superadded to his old admiration, and made
his love for Austin only stronger.   But when Austin grew
well enough to tell him the whole story, his admiration
grew into a sort of barbarous reverence, combined with
self-congratulation, at his having been shrewd enough to
have picked out Austin, as the very man to follow to the
death.

The fact of Lord Charles Barty having succeeded in
thrusting himself forward into the quarrel before Austin,
was certainly a distressing accident — but Austin's hunt
after Captain Hertford, his wandering hither and thither
after him, with the dread of his trial hanging over him all
the time, his patient search after him, the cunning he displayed in it, his calm behaviour when he brought the wolf
to bay, and his noble generosity in refusing to fire at him
after all — formed, in Gil's Highland imagination, the most
beautiful and glorious tale he had ever heard.   I suppose
that it is true, that heroic natures are apt to worship an
idol which they suppose to possess the qualities they most
admire themselves.   Faithful, high-souled valour, were the
qualities for which Austin was getting worshipped, and
his worshipper was showing those qualities, to a higher degree than ever had Austin.

Gil had made friends with the apprentices.   They were
two good-hearted, ordinary, English lads, who were not so
much learning their trade, as having the details of their
trade knocked, so to speak, into their heads.   Gil Macdonald was a fellow of genius and energy.   A Quentin
Durward of a fellow ; a man who would not consent to

be starved at any price, and so had come South. The apprentices had asked "*Scotchy*" to have some beer with them, but Scotchy would not, because he wern't sure whether or no he could treat them in return. They wanted Scotchy to go to Highbury Barn with them; but Scotchy wouldn't. They couldn't make friends with him : Scotchy didn't want them to ; *he* wanted to make friends with *them*. He did so ; he appealed to their generosity ; and it is a queer sort of English apprentice, who can stand *that* appeal. Gil got first one of them, and then another, to show him little tricks in gun-making which he did not know, and they had gladly done so ; after this Gil would sit up half the night easing them of their work. Yes, Scotchy was a good fellow, though he would not go to Highbury Barn. So Gil and the apprentices got fond of one another, as English and Scotch lads always will, if there is no fool by to make mischief between them.

So much for Gil ; and he deserves so much at least. We must return to Austin.

This young convict which he had taken up, or to be more correct, had taken up with him, persisted for a long while in calling himself Charlton. He was a fellow of very few words, but when he did speak he showed some knowledge of educated society. He was, to a certain extent, a companion to Austin. He was evidently, thought Austin, not a gentleman, but he had seen a great deal of gentlemen. One day Austin fancied that he might have been a billiard-marker, and asked him the question.

"Yes," said Charlton, " I was a billiard-marker once. God bless you ! I have been all sorts of things. I drove a Hansom cab once."

" Did you ? "

" Yes. I drove one of the cleverest horses ever you saw. The horse had been in Astley's, and was almost like a Christian, by Jove ! And one day, when I was in the public-house, a fellow hails my cab, and the waterman runs away after me. And the fellow gets in, by George !

without noticing that there was no one to drive, and roars
out ' Treasury ! ' and away goes the old horse like a steam-
engine, by himself, and when he gets to Downing Street
he comes up short, and sends the fellow forward with the
crown of his hat against the splash-board : and when the
fellow gets out to slang the cabman, by gad ! he finds
there's no cabman there. Yes, that was a devilish clever
horse, I say ! "

" You can't expect me to believe that," said Austin.

" Why not ? "

" Why not ? I'll tell you. Because you are always
lying. Why do you ? "

" I don't know. If you tease and plague me about my
lying and thieving, I will not come and walk with you any
more."

" But you must tell me one thing," said Austin. " Your
name is not Charlton."

" No," said the other sulkily. " My name is Goatley."

" What, are you little Bob Goatley, at Tolliday's ? I
thought I knew you."

The other, whom we must now call Goatley, walked
sulkily away.

By the end of August, Austin had recovered his health
completely. Goatley and he were still together a great
deal. Goatley always grew sulky, the very instant Austin
tried to learn anything about his former life, and at last he
desisted from asking questions. As these few weeks went
on, Austin talked a great deal with him. He so continually attacked, by scorn and ridicule, his habit of lying,
that the poor fellow made some improvement. Before
the end of September a great event occurred, no less a one
than this.

It happened suddenly. It came on Austin and Goatley
like an earthquake, or a whirlwind. They were both
dazed by it, like two bats in the sunshine.

Goatley had told Austin, on the 26th, that there was a
disturbance in the prison. He had taken not much notice

of it. One of the warders, the last thing at night had confirmed it, and had stayed a moment and told Austin the cause of it, but he had nearly forgotten all about it next morning.

At eleven he was let out to walk in the corridor, and Goatley was there waiting for him. He told him, that in two of the corridors, the riot had been most serious. That the prisoners were all confined to their cells, except he, and a few others who could be trusted, and that one of the officers had been nearly murdered.

Everything was quite quiet for two days. At the end of that time the cells were unlocked, and the convicts were let loose again to their exercise.

Austin was shrewd enough to see that there would be another riot. The instant that the men were let out of their cells, they began to gather in knots, and to talk and gesticulate. The efforts of the warders to keep them apart, and make them move on, were quite unavailing. The confusion grew worse every instant; the warders were being pressed on, and mobbed. They tried to get the men back to their cells, but they would not go; they were encouraging one another to violence, but as yet no blow had been struck. The warders were as one man to twenty. Affairs looked very terrible indeed.

Austin whispered to Goatley, "keep with me," and pushed his way through the crowd, towards the governor's lodgings. They met him running, five steps at a time, up the long stone staircase which led from the lodge.

"Stop, for God's sake, sir!" said Austin. "The slightest spark will fire the powder, now. Your appearance might be ruin."

He had paused for an instant, but he said, "I must go on, I tell you. My poor officers will be murdered. I must be with them. I have a company of the Guards in the yard. It is a matter of a moment. Stick by me, Mr. Elliot, as you are a gentleman."

At this moment there was a shout and a yell from one

distant part of the prison, and immediately, in every long-drawn corridor, it was repeated ten-fold. Eight hundred convicts had suddenly burst out into aimless furious madness ; and there were forty poor unprotected warders among them.

The governor ran madly on towards the riot. Austin and Goatley ran with him. As Austin, who had met the governor, turned to follow him, he saw that the great gate was opened, and that a company of the Grenadier Guards was coming on, out of the sunshine into the semi-darkness of the prison, swinging steadily forward, with sloped arms and fixed bayonets. Order tramping on inexorably, to sweep away disorder, by the mere sight of it. He heard Sir Robert Ferrers give the word, "double," and then he was after the governor, with Goatley close behind him.

The whole of the corridor was filled with a crowded mass of angry, desperate men. Those nearest them had made some preparations for an attack on this side. So the instant the poor governor ran towards them, Austin saw him felled to the earth like an ox, with the leg of an iron bedstead.

But before the man who did that had time to strike another blow, Austin was upon him. He saw, with the eye of a general, that this man was the only one there who was armed, and that the possession of this weapon might save the governor's life. He caught the man's arm in his, and, bending down his head, bit his wrist until he let go his hold ; and then, with a rapid, dexterous blow, sent him tottering and reeling, and spinning round and round, till he came headlong down upon the pavement like a dead man.

He glared defiantly about him, but he was the only man there who was armed. The governor was sitting up, looking wild and mazed ; before him were two men, both in the convict dress, fighting on the ground, rolling over and over. The convicts were crowding round these two men, and kicking one of them whenever he came uppermost ;

their attention to those two men saved the governor's life.

Austin had just time to notice these two men fighting, when the convicts began whistling in a sharp shrill way, and whooping, and yelling. In one instant were all gone. No one was left but the man he had knocked down, who was snoring heavily, the governor himself, and the two still-fighting convicts——

And Sir Robert Ferrers. The mere sight of that kindest and gentlest of men, in uniform, with a drawn sword, had been quite enough for the convicts. Profound tranquillity was restored, even before they had seen a single man of his company.

All this took exactly as long to happen as it took Sir Robert Ferrers to double across the hall, up some sixty stone steps, and through the corridor. He rapidly ordered his lieutenant to see everything quiet instantly ; and, putting up his sword, ran to separate the two convicts.

One had got the other down, and the one underneath was getting black in the face. When they got them apart, it was found that the winner was our friend Goatley, and that the other was one of the most desperate characters in the prison. Goatley had saved the governor's life ; there was no doubt of it. The governor, weak and stunned as he was, called Sir Robert's attention to the fact ; but Goatley was found to be in a state of wild feline excitement, breathing short and hard, thrusting every one aside who got between him and the object of his vengeance, showing the strongest inclination to go in, and, as Sir Robert said, "finish" his man. As they were leading the other off, Goatley made a rush at him, and Sir Robert, interposing, he and Goatley came down together on the floor, and Sir Robert's sword got broke in two ; but he stuck to Goatley long enough to prevent mischief, and Goatley was marched off to his cell in a furious, mad, cat-like frame of mind, ready for any amount of assault and battery.

That evening Sir Robert waited on a certain great personage, with a note from the governor, and gave an account of the whole business. The great man told Sir Robert something which made him stare.

" By Gad," said he, " that is the sort of thing men put into novels. How very extraordinary ! "

" Is it not ? " said the great man. " But mind, it is all in confidence. It is best to say nothing."

The next morning an order came down to the prison, for the immediate release of Austin Elliot and William Browning. William Browning, it is necessary to say, was the young man, whom we have known by the aliases of Charlton and Goatley.

Austin slept late, and they would not wake him. Was it that they had a disinclination to lose him ? I think so. When he woke at last, the warder who had led him back to his cell on the first miserable morning of his imprisonment, stood beside his bed, and told him that the gate was open, and that he might walk out into the world a free man.

After several repetitions, he realized it at last. He tried to thank the man ; he tried to pray. He succeeded in neither. He laid his forehead between his knees, and did the best thing he could do — he sobbed like a child.

He saw the governor in his bed, and in bidding him good-bye, earnestly thanked him for his kindness. He went into the lodge. They were all waiting to say good-bye to him. He must think of them sometimes, they said. They did not like to say that they were sorry to lose him, but such was the case ; there was not one honest face left behind in that gloomy prison now. Austin did not know till after, that sooner than sadden his dismissal, they had kept from him the fact that two warders, whom he knew, were killed the day before. " They were on duty," they said. " They would give Austin's love to them, and tell them how sorry he was not to have wished them good-bye." He did not know till afterwards, that he had sent his love to two poor cold corpses, which lay under sheets, in the dead-house. No! they closed the great iron door behind him without telling him that. And he stood blinking and trembling without, in the blazing autumn sunshine.

*　　*　　*　　*　　*　　*

A well-dressed young man was standing in the sun under the prison wall, and he came to meet him. Austin saw that it was Goatley.

" I did not know you at first," he said. " I have only seen you in your prison dress. You got your discharge, too."

" Yes. I thought you were going to cut me. I was only waiting here to say good-bye."

" Why good-bye? "

" We can never see anything more of one another. I am far too disreputable a person for you to know. Say good-bye, and let us part for ever, Austin Elliot."

" I shall say no such thing," said Austin. " You are coming with me to Canada, and there you and I, and Gil Macdonald, will die respectable old men. Come along. It were strange, indeed, if I deserted you now, my boy."

" If you had," said Goatley, " I would have been back *there* in a very few days."

So patient Gil, filing grimly over his guns, looked up from the vice, wiped his eyes with his big black hands, and said, " Gude guide us ! " for Austin Elliot was standing in front of him, and bidding him good-morrow. And that same night, Gil took the two apprentices to a Scotch store he knew of ; and, at his own expense, made them and himself also, so very drunk on whiskey and water, that the outraged majesty of the law, required that they should be all three locked up at Bow Street, until they had purged themselves of their contempt. They were not back before eleven the next morning. But Mr. Macpherson was not angry ; he only winked. And Mrs. Macpherson said, " He's no awake yet. It does my heart good,

Gil Macdonald, ye daft devil, to think that he is back in his ain house again after a'. If all the world were like you and he and our gude man, Gil, why it would be no muckle the waur, hey ? "

Chapter XXXVII

WE must leave Austin here for a short time ; and this is almost the first time in this tale, in which we have left him. But we must leave him, and see how matters were going on at Ems. If sternest fate did not say " no," we would have preferred to make Ems the place in which some pleasant genial story got itself wound up ; in which every angle in one's tale was rounded off ; in whose mountain meadows happy lovers met, and parted no more. But that cannot be. With all its wonderful beauty, it is a wicked little place. Under the auspices of the Duke of Nassau, the play runs higher than at most places on the continent ; there are many men who curse the day on which they first saw its lovely winding valleys, and hanging sheets of woodland.

The morning of the duel, old James went off into town on some errand or another. Towards two o'clock he heard the terrible news and brought it home. He looked so wild and scared, that his old enemies, the maids, grew frightened too. They forbore to tease him, or to laugh at him ; but besought him, in eager whispers, to tell them what was the matter. At last he did so, and then they stood all silent and terrified. " Who is to break it to her ? " asked one at last.

No one knew ; it was a business no one would undertake. Even the very housekeeper, who had nursed Eleanor when a baby, shrank from the task. Lord Charles killed, and Mr. Austin in prison. God spare her from telling such news. At last, the youngest and most heedless of the servant girls, suggested that they should send for Lord Edward.

It was a good idea, but James would not agree to act on it. He said she must be told at once, lest the news should come to her any other way; and, after a long pause, he undertook to go and tell her himself.

He went up to the drawing-room, and found Eleanor alone there. She saw that disaster was written in his face; and she prayed him, for old love's sake, to be quick, and strike his blow. He did so; he told her all, as quietly as he could; and then she fell back in her chair speechless. She never said one word, good or bad. She tried to undo the handkerchief round her throat, but could not; then she feebly clutched her hair with her hands, until one long loop of it fell down across her face; and then she clasped her hands in her lap in her old patient attitude, and sat pale and still.

Old James was kneeling at her feet, and praying her to speak to him; when he heard the door locked behind him. He started up, and Aunt Maria was standing between him and the door. Old James, valiant old soul as he was, grew frightened. She had got on her dressing-gown only, her hair was all tumbled and wild, her great coarse throat was bare, and her big black eyebrows were nearly hiding her cruel little eyes; she looked redder, angrier, madder, than ever. He saw that she had heard every word; he saw that she had locked the door behind her, and was standing silently scowling at them; and for one moment he trembled.

But only for one instant. His darling Miss Eleanor was there, and his courage returned; he faced her, furiously.

"Give me that key, you old Atrophy!" he said, (meaning, possibly, Atropos; Lord knows what he meant!) "Give it up to me, I tell you!"

"Come and take it, you old dog! You old thief! you beggarly, old, barefooted shoeblack boy! that my fool of

284

a brother picked out of the gutter, fifty years ago, because you had a face like a monkey, and made him laugh! Come and take it! Do you hear?"

James was politic. Aunt Maria was decidedly the strongest of the two. He fell back on his tongue, which was nearly as good a one as Aunt Maria's.

"*Your* brother!" he said; "*your* brother! O Lord!"

"Put it in Chancery," she said. "Put it in Chancery, you penniless old rogue! Aha!"

James gave a glance at Eleanor, and saw that she was quite unconscious of what was passing. With infinite shrewdness he remained perfectly quiet, and let Aunt Maria begin at her.

She came towards her, pointing at her with the key.

"You little snake! — You little devil! — You little sly, smooth-faced, pianoforte playing minx! So you set on your two gallant bully lovers to murder Will Hertford, did you? He has given a gallant account of them! He *is* a man! why his little finger is worth ten of your Bartys and Elliots! One dead and the other in prison! Oh, brave Will Hertford! Get up, do you hear, get up! you little devil!"

"Leave her alone," said old James; "or by the Lord, I'll — "

"Assault your mistress's Aunt, and be walked off to the police-station, is that it? I am going to use you, Master James, and when I have done with you, pitch you on one side, like an old shoe. I have won the game! Take this key, open the door, and send her maid to her. I have won the game, old snake!"

It would have puzzled Aunt Maria to say what game she *had* won. Originally she certainly was very fond of Captain Hertford, and was so still. She had had a plan of marrying him to Eleanor, and gaining some sort of power over her wealth: this had given her her intense hatred of Austin; but what with drink and incipient insanity, all power of keeping one plan before her, had gone long ago.

Passion had supplanted reason. She loved Will Hertford still, in a way, and she hated Austin and the Bartys; she had nothing left to guide her now but a mad woman's cunning.

She displayed a considerable amount of it this day. She went out, and ordered the maids to pack up everything for a long journey, and shortly afterwards made her appearance, dressed in the height of fashion, looking quite sane and collected. She ordered the carriage, went to the bankers and got money, went to the passport-office and got passports; she went to Mivart's, got a courier recommended to her; went to the Hotel Sablonière, in Leicester Square, and fetched the gentleman home. Then she gave directions to the housekeeper about shutting up the house, and discharging the servants, and lastly, she sent the courier to secure berths on board the Soho, for Antwerp.

Then she went up to Eleanor. She was sitting near the window, weeping bitterly. Aunt Maria was in good temper now, and was very gentle with her.

" My love," she said, " I am glad you are better. In my grief this morning I used harsh words to you. Are they forgiven ? "

" I know nothing of them, aunt ; yet, if you used them, they are forgiven."

" Are you better, dear ? "

" I am quite well, aunt ; only my heart is broken."

" Nonsense, everything will come right. See here. Austin will be liberated on bail, and will go abroad. We ought to go abroad instantly. Can you travel ? "

" You can do as you will with me, aunt. Only, dear aunt, I have been so patient and loving to you, I have never returned you one angry word. Aunt, for God's sake don't scold me ! "

" Tut, tut, silly one. Who is scolding ? Come, we start to-night, bid your maid get ready."

The next night they were at Brussels, and old James made one of the party. It was his first expedition into

foreign parts, since the taking of the Bastile, and his prejudices against foreigners were as strong as they were in
1792. But there he was, and there were three strong reasons for his being there. First, Eleanor had asked him to
go ; second, he was most fully determined that happen
what might, he would never lose sight of Eleanor ; and
thirdly, that Aunt Maria was most fully determined that
she would keep this dangerous old fellow under her own
eye.

What could the old fellow do ? His dread of what
might be the end of Eleanor's being carried abroad, was
boundless. But old Mr. Hilton had managed his affairs
in life so well, that he had died, leaving not one single
personal friend behind him, but Mr. Elliot, and now *he*
was dead. There was actually no one left to appeal to for
help, but blind Lord Edward Barty. James scrawled a letter to him, and Lord Edward started on the trail at once,
and overtook them at Brussels. Aunt Maria showed no
disgust at his appearance ; she was very gracious and genial, and kept her temper for her maid, whom she kept in
the most terrible subjection, partly by her tongue, and
partly by wielding against the unfortunate woman, a certain supposed clause in her will, susceptible of instant
alteration ; on suspicion of the poor wretch's having ex-
changed a single word, in confidence, with old James.

Aunt Maria found walking exercise necessary, and so
she used to walk out every day, to take and fetch the letters from the post office, near the Place de la Revolution.
Meanwhile, Eleanor had a piano in her room, and Lord
Edward used to come and play it, and wonder why on
earth Austin had not answered their letters.

Old James, both here and elsewhere, was far too much
engaged in a vast, chronic, ceaseless squabble, with the
whole Belgian nation, to be at all available for any reasonable business : his life was one great wrangle about the
food. And moreover, he had a most vivid remembrance of
holding Mr. Jenkinson's coat tails tight in one hand, and

Mr. Hilton's in the other; of looking cautiously between the shoulders of those gentlemen, and of seeing all St. Antoine, seething, and howling, and leaping, and raging over the bridge, into the Bastile. He fully believed that people in foreign parts did that sort of thing once a month or so, and that the Place de la Revolution, where they lived, was the spot set aside by the Government for the performance, at stated periods, of the same sort of Devil's dance, which he had witnessed in Paris fifty years before, for a week or so. He had always been very particular about his money too, and now was worrying himself to death, from having to change good money, into coins, with whose value he was totally unacquainted. In short, the poor old fellow was in a totally unavailable state for all reasonable business.

When they had been there a short time, Aunt Maria expressed her intention of breaking up the camp, and going to Ems. She was the only person in the house who read Galignani. She read one morning a short account of the duel at Ems, between Austin and Captain Hertford; she determined to follow him to that place.

Nobody opposed her, and they went. When their carriage drove up the street, Captain Hertford was standing by the arch, which crosses the street by the Kursal. When he saw her face, he cursed and swore so awfully, that Captain Jackson, who was standing by, said,

" I say, Hertford, don't use such language; it isn't good taste."

" I can't help it," said he, "when I see that cursed old woman's face. It makes me mad to think what she has brought me to; I can't go to England, I don't care so much about that; I must resign my seat in Parliament, that is the very deuce, but it isn't that. It is that young dandy Charles Barty — I can't get him out of my head. I wasn't sorry at the time — I don't know that I am sorry now — but he came down so sudden; it was so devilish horrid. — Did you ever see anything more horrid! I've killed my man before, but not such a lad as he ; it is always coming back to me — the brandy is no good against it. I tried that, and it made it worse, so I dropped it."

" I wish to God, you *would* drop it," said Jackson fiercely. " Why the devil do you go on harping on this wretched business ?   What do you think *I* must feel about it ? "

Captain Hertford remained silent.

" I beg your pardon, Hertford," continued the other; " don't let us mention that duel again. I should be very glad, if you would tell me the truth about your connexion with Miss Hilton."

" I will do so, Jackson — I think you are a good fellow. — Don't pitch me overboard. — I shall blow my brains out, if you do. Old Maria Hilton had always a great admiration for me, which was not reciprocated. But I always kept in with her, and kept friendly with her. Well! Hang it, sir, she bought my company for me. There ! "

Captain Hertford paused. They walked together down the terrace, which hangs over the river ; but Captain Hertford had come to a dead stop.

" You were going to tell me," — said Jackson.

" About little Miss Hilton ; well, Jackson, if you had been brought up such a neglected Arab as I, you would have been as bad as I."

" I might be worse."

" Well, you *might ;* however," resumed he slowly, " through Miss Hilton, I of course grew to be acquainted with her nephew Robert. He had been expelled from the army, for stealing everything he could lay his hands on. She asked me to see him at Brussels ; I did so. I took him up rather, because I thought she was fond of him. — Never mind why I took him up. He robbed me of some letters belonging to Lord Mewstone, and got the signature copied, by a clever rogue, on to a cheque. Finding himself discovered, he bolted to Namur, where he committed suicide."

" A tender-conscienced thief."

" Yet he was well brought up : he was Miss Hilton's brother ; I brought the news back to England. There old Miss Hilton pointed out to me, that Eleanor Hilton would be a great heiress, and, that I ought to marry her ; and so the scheme was begun ; I went down to Wales ; and found Elliot, the fool, falling in love with my worthy half-brother's future Countess — I encouraged him."

" But, how went your scheme with Miss Hilton ? "

" Hot and cold, hot at first, and afterwards, when she paid my election expenses, very cold indeed. Still, I always had hopes ; and the old woman kept them going. What led to this miserable affair was this : I got cleaned out on the City and Suburban, and some tradesmen were troublesome, and then, I went about and said that I was to marry her. I was very familiar with her. Well, I had a secret. — I did not exactly *trade* on it ; but I used it. I was a great deal with her ; I am a needy man, and I talked about marrying her ; and Elliot heard it."

" People say, that you had a plan to shoot Elliot ; and to get the girl abroad, and that that plan got blown upon, and that you had out Lord Charles Barty instead. Is there any truth in that ? "

" Yes, a great deal. That was the plan proposed to me by the old woman."

" It seems to have been attended with the most brilliant success."

" The most brilliant," replied Hertford bitterly. " I have lost my seat in Parliament : I cannot go to England ; and if it were not for my wonderful luck at the tables, I should be very poor."

" Well, you have not told your story altogether consistently, Hertford. I could not expect you to do so. But at the same time you seem to have succeeded. You have shot one man, got the other locked up in prison (that is no fault of yours), and now the girl has followed you here."

" That is true," said Hertford. " The scheme has succeeded wonderfully. I wish to God I had never heard of.

it. I *am not* rascal enough to go on any further with it, Jackson."

" I don't think you could, could you?" said Captain Jackson.

" Why not?"

" She would hardly see you after what you have done. This lord was her friend, and they say she was fond of Elliot."

" I tell you," he said, " that if I were rogue enough I could make her aunt bully her into marrying me in a month. You don't know the old woman."

Lord Edward Barty and Eleanor had a very peaceful and quiet time at Ems. I believe that Captain Hertford was in earnest about not prosecuting the villanous scheme, which had ended in the death of Lord Charles Barty, and the imprisonment of Austin. But if he had ever so much intended to take advantage of Eleanor's situation, the presence of the trusty Lord Edward Barty rendered it impossible.

He was continually with her. He could not be happy without her. She, with her patient ways, had become a necessity to him. As for his falling in love with her, he simply never knew what it meant. He had loved his brother Charles much better than he was likely to love her ; he at present loved his brother George much better than her ; he liked her better than Lord Wargrave, and not so well as Lord George, that was all. She was kind to him, and he liked her — nay, he loved her ; but he thought that it would be much pleasanter when all this trouble was over, and Austin came and married her. Then there would be glorious times indeed.

Of course the little world of Ems — not an entirely respectable little world — talked about them, but I don't think any one was the worse for their talking. The two people whom they talked about never heard it, and so it does not much matter. Eleanor and Lord Edward were left in peace all that summer without much to disturb them, except their anxiety at not hearing from Austin.

Aunt Maria was never troublesome now; they hardly noticed what she did with herself. Old James called their attention to her first, after they had been there nearly a month.

Eleanor was sitting at the piano alone, in her great high bare room, trying some music. James opened the door very quietly and came in. She heard him, and turned round on the music-stool.

She looked ten years older than she had looked before all this had happened. She had shown her sorrow to no one. She had been eating her heart in secret; keeping her griefs for the long dark hours of night, and showing a brave front in the daytime. She had been doing this months and months before this unhappy duel. Her hair had grey streaks in it before things came round again.

" James," she said, " where have you been so late ? "

" I've been to Marksburg, to see they sojers a marching. They're a marching from St. Goar to Coblentz ; pretty nigh two regiments on 'em. And I goes over in a boat to see 'em, and there they was, with kitching candle-sticks on their elmets. Fine men to look at — ah. And then I went in over the way, and seen 'em playing. Lord, worn't she taking the money in ! "

" Who ? "

" *She.* Have she made her will ? "

" Do you mean Aunt Maria ? "

" In course I do. Do you know that she have won a thousand pound in eight days ? "

" My aunt ! Is she playing ? "

" Ah ! and winning, too. And so is Captain Hertford. He and she have had a tussle ; acause he haint been to see her often enough."

This was Aunt Maria's employment. She was gambling desperately. One day in September the end came.

She had at first won, as James had told Eleanor, above

a thousand pounds. Then her luck turned. She lost. She nearly recovered herself again ; lost once more — began to lose terribly. She was more than five hundred pounds " to the bad " one evening when she went to play for the last time.

She had had a quarrel with Captain Hertford. His luck had been terribly good this season ; he had been winning, and winning. She took her place opposite to him that evening, and for the first time cut him dead.

He won beyond all precedent. As he won, she seemed to lose in proportion ; she wrote cheque after cheque. At last, when she had lost eight hundred pounds, she got up, and made a scene which no one there ever forgot.

She rose up, and in a sharp snarling voice denounced Captain Hertford. She called him an ungrateful hound, unfit to live ; she screamed out before them, all the plot against Austin and Lord Charles Barty, and then said that he, Captain Hertford, had known all along that she was only an illegitimate half-sister of old Mr. Hilton's. She said fifty other frantic things, which, of course, no one attended to. The end of it was, that the gamblers huddled away out of the room like a herd of frightened sheep, and left the terrible old woman standing there in the middle, perfectly insane, trying to bite at the hands of the two croupiers who held her.

After a time they were able to move her. They had a terrible journey with her to England. Her reason never returned. Eleanor got her safe home at last. Their old house at Esher had, as I prophesied, been taken as a madhouse. Aunt Maria, poor soul, was taken there, and there she staid till she died ; always under the impression that it was their own house still, and that the other patients were only so many visitors.

Chapter XXXVIII

AUSTIN slept long the night after his release. He slept late into the day, like a tired child, and at last when he woke he lay still, waiting for the dreadful bell, which in prison had summoned him and the other convicts to rise from sleep, to quit the paradise of dreams, and come back to earth ; to the cold, hard, reality of the dull, squalid, hideous prison life.

At first, when he had wakened to consciousness in gaol, he had always, for a moment or so, fancied that he was back safe in his old room at home ; and that the past was merely a series of bad dreams : and he would sit up in his bed to shake them off — sit up and look round, to find his worst dream only too terribly true.

After a time, he grew to be cunning in his sleep ; to know that he only awoke to misery, and so to hold on, with obstinate tenacity, to the fag end of a dream, as long as possible, in order that he might keep it going until he was roused by that dreadful bell ; for he found in practice, that the poorest dream, underlain as it might be with the sickening dread of waking from it, was preferable to the waking itself, and to seeing the four whitewashed walls. The very stupidest old dream, a dream that he detected and laughed at while he dreamt it, was better than waking and seeing the prison walls around him.

On this morning he dreamt that he was hunted through Hyde Park by something or another, which was called 974, until he came to Apsley House, at which place he managed to rise into the air, and triumphantly flew nearly over the Green Park, leaving 974 to come round by Constitution Hill. He wished to keep in the air until the bell rang, but he could not. He came down in front of Buckingham Palace and woke.

He waited for the bell. That bell never rung any more

for him — it rings still for eight hundred miserable souls, but not for him. After a few minutes, he began to see that he was in his old room again; he sat up, and found that it was true. For a minute, he thought that the whole past had been dreamt, but the next he knew that it was real; that he had been in prison and was free. He fell back again and tried to pray, but the utterance of his prayer was swept in a whirlwind of passion.

He rose and dressed himself. His resolution had been made long ago in prison; he rose from his bed calmly determined to act upon it at once. It was the result of long, calm thought, when his head was cool, and his intellect perfectly clear and unbiassed. He had said to himself in prison, " What is the right thing to do ? When I get free I shall be excited, my judgment will not be so clear as it is now. The resolution made now must be inexorably carried out, without reason or argument, when I am free."

What was his resolution ? Possibly the most foolish one ever made — at all events, very foolish, as are all resolutions made in the same spirit; that is to say, resolutions made without the saving clause, " that they may be altered by circumstances and after thoughts : " these are indeed, if persisted in, not resolutions, but obstinacies. Austin had make himself a *non possum*, and he was going to act on it at once; lest the *non* should be swept away and high-souled martyrdom should become a more difficult matter. His grand resolution was this — to see Eleanor safe under the protection of the Duchess of Cheshire (who was very willing to be kind to her), and then himself go to — where ? Why Canada ! and see her no more : and he carried out his resolution most inexorably. He knew that she loved him, as he loved her, and he would not be so base as to follow her with his ruined fortunes : that was one argument, and the great one. Besides, she had shown her good sense and propriety by deserting him, which was another.

"Gil," said he, sitting by the forge that evening, "I have been to see my attorney."

"May the deil d—n a' attorneys, barristers, and writers to the signet, and him first of all," was Gil's reply.

"Why?" asked Austin.

"Why!" said Gil, "why! After lee'ing till the deil dinna like to hae him, could he no lee loud eneuch to keep ye out of prison? Being paid for his work in hard guineas and everlasting perdition, and then no doing it after all. Why? quoth he."

"Don't you be an old fool, Gil. Mr. Compton is as noble and good an old man as any in the kingdom. You will know it soon; you shall meet him."

"Meet him soon! I'm no saying contrary. Life is short, and no man's salvation is sure. But I'll no speak to him."

"I hope you will, Gil."

"I'm obleeged to you; but there, as here, I'll choose my own acquaintances."

"Don't be cross with me, Gil."

"Cross wi' you. God forgive me! Cross wi' my ain master (ye'll no get a highlandman to say that every day of the week,) cross with ye!"

"I thought you were. Look here; that Mr. Compton has watched my interests very carefully; he has been a very faithful friend. The Crown has not claimed my property, and he has taken good care of it."

"The Crown no claimed your property?"

"No."

"Have you got your own wealth back again? Has the Queen gi'en ye back your siller?"

"She never took it, God bless her!"

"So ye'll no want to learn the gun trade — so we'll no have to sit pontering here together, over the dommed old gunstocks — so all the happy days I had pictured to myself, are all blasted awa to the winds. 'Tis a weary ungrateful world."

" It is nothing of the kind, Gil. Listen to me."

" I'll listen to ye. But I did hope to see your lang white fingers grimed with the rust and the oil, and to hear ye say, ' we've done well to-day, Gil.' Born an aristocrat, die an aristocrat. Are ye never to know the weariness of thirsting for work, and the peace and happiness of getting work to do at last, master ? "

" Don't call me master, Gil ; call me friend."

" The tane involves the tither, I'm thinking, or should, if I understand it right. Now, I'm listening."

" Then I will speak, Gil, faithful old friend. There are better trades than gun-making."

" I'm no denying it. The trades of Prime Minister, newspaper editor, or keeper of a disorderly house, are a muckle deal more remunerative ; but all three more precarious."

" Now don't be a fool," said Austin, laughing, " or I won't speak to you."

" A fool ! quoth he," replied Gil, smiling, and hammering away. " I thought we were Radical. If my master is going to turn Tory, and object to an honest bit of Radicalism from a puir working man, why I must turn too, and sing my last song, like a hooper in the death thraws :

'   The Deil was aince a Tory,
            Tory oh !   Tory oh !
    But he heard another story,
            Story oh ! story oh !
      " Every gentleman now is a whig," says he,
      " And each devil must dance the new jig," says he ;
         " And Russell and Grey
           Are the men of the day——" '

" Where did you get that infernal doggrel ? " said Austin, interrupting him.

" My father's uncle's first cousin singed it at the Deuk of N—'s door, not long agone. They would no have fleered at the puir Deuk, had they kenned that his ain flesh and blude would turn against him. Say yer say, master."

" If you will let me.   Let us be serious, Gil.   Will you come with me to Canada ? "

" Hey ? "

" To Canada."

" Aye, to the world's end.   But there before all places."

" There is a most brilliant career before us both there. I must not stay in England.   If, after what has happened (I speak to you as the only friend I have in the world, Gil, and the best, save one, I ever had) : if, after what has happened, I should stay in England, I must get thrown against some one, and that would end in dishonour.   Let us come to Canada : are you willing ? "

He looked at Gil's face, and saw that he need not have asked the question.   Gil's face was radiant.   He murmured —

" Sawmon, and park deer, and muckle red deer, called wapiti, whilk they misname Elk ; and real elk, whilk they misname Moose ; and a rink at the curling in winter time ; and corn land five shilling the acre.   And he asks me, will I go ? "

" I see you are willing.   Let us go.   Let us take that poor convict Goatley with us.   Let us try to do something for him.   Who knows what his opportunities have been, Gil ?   Do you agree about that ? "

" God's wrath should light on us if we left him behind. Poor creature !   There is good in him somewhere, or he'd no have stuck by you and the governor the day before yesterday.   Canada, quoth he.   And you with your wealth there.   Think of the poor starving Ronaldsay folk, master : think how leal, and trusty, and quiet they have been through this horrible winter.   It is no business of yours," continued Gil, laying his hands on Austin's shoulders, " but, for my sake, and it's the only favour I'll ever ask ; help some of them over.   I'll go bail that, in mere money, they will pay every farthing of which you advance ; but that is only insulting you.   *You* know what a grand work is before you.   I see you know that."

" I do, Gil; and, please God, I will do it. Is there no nobler work than griming•my hands with rust and oil, hey? Is mechanical work the highest or the lowest kind of work, hey? Would you have me cast aside all my education, and set to work cleaning gun-barrels, hey? How now, old man?"

" I was wrong; and wealth, in a good man's hands, is one of God's greatest blessings. I had a fancy, that you and I might have gone through the world together, as equals. And the fancy was dear to me, I'm no denying. But it is gone; you have nobler work in hand than gun-cleaning."

So he had. Austin had a grand life's work before him, and he did that work gloriously well. But neither he nor Gil knew where his life's work lay, at this time. It did not lie in Canada, but in a far different place.

" Gil," said Austin, " we will go through the world as friends and equals, though you may choose to call me master. We will go to Canada, and Mr. Monroe shall send us over the Ronaldsay folks, and we will call the estate Ronaldsay. But I have something to do first. I shall have to go abroad. I must start to-morrow; I cannot leave England before I have done something. I must see Lord Edward Barty, and also, if it be possible, the Duchess of Cheshire. By the bye, where is Robin?"

Gil pursed up his mouth as if he was going to whistle, and said —

" It was no my fault."

" Is he dead?" said Austin, in a low voice.

" No, he's no deid."

" Is he lost?"

" No, he's no lost either. It was no my fault; a dog who will to Cupar, maun to Cupar. I whistled till my een danced in my heid, and I cried, ' Here! lad, here! The cow's in the potatoes!' But he'd no listen. He kept leaping up on her braw grey silk gown, and she kept bending down to him, and saying — ' Robin! Robin! my own darling Robin!' till it would have garred ye greet, sir, to hear her. And he caught sight of Lord John Russell's grey cat (it was in Chesham Place, ye ken) and hunted it into his lordship's ain area, and ran between his lordship's legs, as he was approaching his ain door, and misbehaved like any Tory; and so he went with her, round the end of the railings, and into her house with her, and the door was shut."

" With her! — with whom ? "

" With Miss Hilton."

" Is she in London ? "

" I dinna ken. She was twa days ago. But with these here-to-day and gone-to-morrow railways, a body must be cautious in speaking."

Chapter XXXIX

So she was safe in London; that was something off his mind. He gave Gil long instructions to try and get hold of old James, and to cross-question him (a hopeful plan), but Gil was not required to act. A note came from Eleanor the very next morning : —

" DEAR AUSTIN,

"I sent James to the prison yesterday, and he brought back the news that you were free. Is this to continue ? Are we never to see one another again ? "

He replied promptly, and at once : —

" DEAREST ELEANOR,

"It is impossible, considering everything, that I should ever meet you, or Edward Barty, again. Our eternal and final parting must come soon ; it is better that we should not make it more bitter by another meeting."

This letter was despatched, and, of course, there was no answer to it.

Eleanor wept bitterly and wildly over it, but she saw no remedy. She said that misfortune had soured Austin's noble nature; that he was not himself. She must get speech with him; there must be something unexplained. In an evil moment she read the two letters to Lord Edward Barty.

He was furiously angry; he made her a scene about the matter. He said that Austin's wrong-headed, obstinate pride was below contempt. He, after all, had suffered no more than the rest of them; and here was he, in his insane vanity, refusing to answer their most affectionate letters, until he was out of prison, and then sending such an answer as that! " I tell you, Eleanor," he said, " that if we want to get our own dear Austin back to us, we must let him go at present. He will come to us in the end, my dear creature, but we must show him that we are angry now. We have sacrificed everything to him, and he treats us like this. It is monstrous."

" Lord Edward," said Eleanor, " Austin has been deceived."

" By whom ? "

" By me. I have deceived him. He has found it out, and he distrusts me."

" Deceived him ! — about what ? "

" Never mind. I did it, as I thought, for the best. I fear he has great cause of complaint against me."

" Fiddlededee ! I won't ask any questions, because I know something about your family history; but take a blind fool's advice — don't run after him. Let him come to you. He *will* come, Eleanor. Let *him* come, and make his explanation. Wait until *he* is thrown against *you*, as he must be in a week or so. Come now; trust me you will find yourself the more hereafter."

" But, if I were never to see him again."

" Pish ! The very fact of your having his dog with you,

will bring on some sort of communication. Leave things to time, Eleanor; he will come back to us, when he is tired of isolation."

This would have been most excellent advice, had it not been for this: that Austin was just now making every preparation for the start to Canada, and that the getting no answer to his last note hurried his movements.

" It is all for the best," he said, " she is right not to answer. She is wise; it is my fault. She deceived me shamefully; and she knows it; she does not know that I love her, better than ever; my honour, as a man, would be tarnished, if I made her any further advances. I wish to God that her nine thousand a-year was gone to the devil. I wish she was penniless; in that case I would go to her to-morrow. But she deceived me, and she has nine thousand a-year; and the whole thing is impossible."

So the Canadian preparations went on, and Austin and Goatley took a lodging in the Commercial Road, to be near the docks, and to see after the shipping of their " notions."

Gil deserted the gun trade, and came with them, after a week. They were very busy. Austin was making great preparations; he was going to buy a great tract of land in Canada, and to introduce a new system of husbandry. He was not in the least aware that all kinds of agricultural implements might be bought in Massachusetts and Connecticut, cheaper than in London. So he bought away; bought implements from Deane and Dray, to the tune of hundreds; which implements were the best in the world: for English use: bought, for instance, two or three broad-wheeled carts with Crosskill's axles, eminently adapted for macadamised roads, but hardly for the backwoods; and so on. But he was very busy, which was something.

One night, sitting gloomily in his lodging, in the Commercial Road, after having been on board the ship all day, he thought of his dog Robin; and a desire arose in him, to have that dog back again. The dog was with Eleanor, and he determined to go after it the next day. He did go after it, and he got it ; and in this adventure, he, as nearly as possible, met Eleanor herself face to face.

He did not meet her; but if he had, they would have explained everything to one another ; even that dreadful circumstance, which rankled in Austin's heart deeper than all : — his finding her walking with Captain Hertford, in Millbank. This was the fact, which made him so obstinate with her. He could have forgiven her desertion of him, he could have forgiven every thing but her deceit, and his discovery of it.

So he went for his dog. He watched at the end of the railings in Wilton Crescent, and he saw her come out. The dog was not with her. She was going to church. He waited patiently till she came back, and still he waited on.

By-and-by, after more than an hour, the little grey figure came out again. Ah, Lord ! How Austin loved her. Why did he not go up to her, and speak ? Because the jealous devil, which he had made believe to banish, was holding high court in his heart.

Robin was with her now ; he came out of the door like a thunderbolt. There were five sparrows in the middle of the road, at dinner. Robin would have nothing of that sort ; he sent them flying up into the lilac trees and chimney pots, for their bare lives, and then he danced, barking, round Eleanor.

Eleanor was walking towards St. Paul's Church, probably going to Westerton's. Austin was standing behind the corner of the railings, at the south-west corner of the Crescent. He saw that the dog was going with her the other way, and he whistled shrill and sharp. " I wonder if she will know my whistle," said Austin.

She did not, but the dog did. He paused, with one ear up, and the other down ; and his head on one side. Austin whistled once more. This time, Robin came rushing towards him, like a race-horse ; and left Eleanor calling

"Robin! Robin! you naughty dog, Robin, come here, sir!"

When Austin saw that the dog was on his trail, and that Eleanor had not recognised him, he ran round into Motcomb Street. An instant after, Robin came tearing round, on the grand circle-sailing principle; (that is to say, that a circle is a circle: and that the nearest way from one place to another, is a straight line drawn between them;) combined with that of circular storms, which is, that you go one-fifth per cent. to leeward for every revolution. He, Robin, sailed on these principles, but violated both. The first, because he assumed himself to be sailing on a convex surface, instead of (as was the case) practically a plane. The second, because he did not allow sufficient latitude for his progressive momentum. The combination of these two errors, acting together, caused him to make too wide a circle in coming round the corner, and to bring himself against what we may be allowed to call, the leeward area railings of Motcomb Street, and to give a short howl, at having bruised himself against them; which last fact, would be better theorized on by Dr. Brown, than by either Maury or Reid.

By the time that Robin had picked himself up, Austin was at the end of the street. He whistled again, and Robin came tearing on once more. Austin stepped round the corner, into Lowndes-street, and waited; he was safe here. Robin found him by Gunter's shop, and leaped up, frantically yelping in the madness of his joy; and Austin, then and there, the street being empty or nearly so, took Robin to his bosom, and hugged him.

"You never see such a queer start in your life," said one of the young men at Gunter's, to one of the young ladies at Miller's (to whom he was engaged) that evening. "*I* know him, and all the whole business; how he was in prison, and all that. And I see him come cutting round the corner like a lunatic, and I says, 'He's broke out, and the police is after him!' And I run out to see if I could get him through the shop, or upstairs, or anythink. And then I seen him hugging of his dog to his bosom. And well I knew the dog. He used to come into our place with the whole lot on 'em ; Lord Charles, poor fellow, and Mr. Austin, and the blind one, and Miss Hilton, from number fifteen ; and he used to chivy the cat into the window among the bon bons, and play the deuce and all. And one day he upset the table with Lady Dumbledore's wedding-cake on it, and then there was the dickens to pay. *I* never see such a dog."

" And so poor Mr. Elliot was glad to get his dog back again," said the young lady from Miller's.

" He was *so*, poor gentleman ; you never see anything like it. Here he stood, as it might be me, and there was the dog, as it might be you, and he catches the dog to his bosom — "

And the young man from Gunter's immediately received two sound boxes on the ear, as a caution that prose narrative must not be assisted by dramatic action.

The Canadian preparations went briskly on. Gil worked like fifty Gils ; and Austin, partly in the novelty of feeling free again, and partly to extinguish thought, worked as hard as he.

He would not think : he would not pause. His resolution had been taken when his head was cool, and must be acted on now : so he was intensely busy.

Goatley, the convict, worked as well as he could, but that was not very well. He had a careless, sleepy way of doing things, which provoked Gil very much. He never let Goatley see that he was provoked ; for Goatley was a kind of sacred person to Gil. He was an unaccountable being, and he had played the man at the right time. Gil was kind to him.

Austin kept him near him continually ; for he was afraid of his meeting some old companion, and getting into trouble ; but Austin hoped to keep him straight till they got to Canada. He was an odd, wayward, unaccountable creature. He never gave Austin much account of himself, that Austin could rely on. If Austin pressed him too much, he became vacant and irritable ; if further, a kind of dumb sulky devil would take possession of him, and he would hardly answer at all, or only in the most transparent lies, which he could see irritated Austin.

He at ordinary times spoke but little. Sometimes he would, after a long silence, break out with an abrupt question. After sitting a long while one day, he broke out,

" If I was in your place I should take out a large quantity of potatoes. May-be, they haven't got the same sorts there."

There was nothing more in this than the mere silliness of an utterly ignorant person. But there was a great deal more in the way in which, after he had once started this notion, he ran it to the death. He got it into his head that there was something in it; and walking about the Commercial-road with Austin, he was continually stopping him at every potato shop, and making inquiries about ash-leafed kidneys, and regents, and so on. He was fully persuaded that he would make his fortune in Canada, by taking over new sorts of potatoes. Austin told Gil that the poor fellow seemed mad on the subject. Gil replied,

" A good thing, too. He had better go mad on one single subject. Mad he is, and will be. He had better gang mad on ane point, than on a dizzen."

" Do you think he will go mad, Gil ? " said Austin.

" Deil doubt it ! A' this leeing, and this talking so and so, shows that his brain is softening. It will end in general paralysis ; a slight dropping of the lower jaw, combined with occasional violence."

" Who told you that ? "

" Naebody. I just, thinking about the young man, ran my eye over Dr. Tuke's book the ither night. I'm no agreeing with the doctor in all things, but he has muckle experience."

Since Austin had taken his degree, he had confined his reading to the newspapers. He changed the subject.

One day, when all things were nearly ready, and Austin had come to be as well known on board the good ship Amphion as the skipper himself; he took Goatley with him, to help him in stowing some packages. They worked together all the morning. When, at noon, they came out on the wharf again, Goatley said suddenly, —

" I am going away from you to-morrow."

" Whither ? " said Austin.

" To a public-house. To the ' Black Bull,' in the Commercial-road. I have business there."

" You will come to me in the evening," said Austin, " for you will not sleep away from your lodgings. I am so fearful of your getting among your old companions, my poor fellow."

" Is that why you watch me so ? " said Goatley.

" Yes, that is the reason," said Austin ; " you are so weak and foolish, my poor lad. I think how much I owe you, and think how anxious I am to give you a new start in life, without temptation. I do watch you, and I will."

" Very well," said Goatley, " you are quite right. But you need not watch me to-morrow, I am going to see a relation, the only relation I have, who is coming to wish me good-bye."

" You never told me that you had any relations," said Austin.

" I daresay not," said Goatley, sulkily, " but I have. And one of them is coming to bid me good-bye to-morrow."

" One of them ? " said Austin. " You said there was only one just now."

" Never you mind what I said ; you've often called me a liar. Don't you ask any questions, may-be I won't tell you any lies."

Austin knew enough of his man to let the subject drop. At noon the next day, Goatley left the ship, and Austin.

going the same way, saw him walking rapidly up the Commercial-road.

"It would be mere charity to follow him," thought he; "I think I had better follow him. I do not like to trust him. Robin! Robin!"

It was time to call "Robin! Robin!" A marine-store-keeper's cat had been over to visit a puffing grocer's cat opposite, and was picking her way homewards, across the muddy street. Robin ran after her. She, like an idiot, ran away, and Robin, by the law of gravity, or some similar law, bolted after her. The cat, not being able to make her own port on the present tack, in consequence of the enemy being to windward of her, put her helm down, altered her course four points, and made all sail for the nearest harbour to leeward, which was the pigeon-fancier's; and Robin, disregarding the law of nations, made a perfect Wilkes of himself, and chased her right into the neutral harbour, overturning a cage containing five-and-twenty "blue rocks" in his career, and at last succeeded in forcing an engagement in the pigeon-fancier's back-parlour, under his table.

Here he found himself under the guns of several neutral batteries, which opened fire on him and the cat, with perfect impartiality. The cat bolted up the chimney; but Robin, as in duty bound, returned the fire of the neutral batteries — that is to say, setting our figure aside, that the pigeon-fancier and his wife (who were at dinner) tried to kick him out, and that he showed fight, and snapped at their legs.

At this moment, when war seemed inevitable, diplomacy stepped in, in the person of Austin. Robin was rebuked. The affair was gone calmly into. Apologies were given on the one side, and frankly received on the other; and the whole thing was comfortably settled. Then Austin walked away up the Commercial-road with Robin, laughing, with no more notion of what was going to happen to him than has the reader, perhaps not so much.

He went into the "Black Bull." He asked the landlord whether a young man had come in just now. The land-lord said what sort of a young man, and Austin described Goatley.

"What, Browning?" said the landlord. Austin had never heard of him by that name, but felt sure of his man, because the landlord had recognized him from his de-scription. The reader will most probably not remember, that this was the name given by the Secretary of State to the convict Goatley.

Austin said "Yes," feeling sure of his man. The land-lord said that he was there; that he was going to Canada, and that one of his relations had come to bid him good-bye; they were in an inner parlour now.

Austin was glad to find that Goatley had not deceived him. He told the landlord that he would go inside, and take a glass of ale and a biscuit, and wait for the young man.

So mine host showed him into a rambling old room on one side of a passage, with some fifty angles in it. There was a bagatelle-board there, and Austin ate his biscuit and sipped his ale, and knocked the balls about. Robin had some biscuit, and lay down on the hearthrug.

Austin began to be aware that there were voices talking low in another room — in the room on the other side of the passage. Robin became aware of it too, and began to be naughty.

At first he only put his nose against the door and whined. Austin went on knocking the bagatelle-balls about, and making the most wonderful strokes. He got petulant with Robin, and ordered him to lie down; but Robin would not: he reared himself up against the door and scratched at it.

Austin made a beautiful stroke: there never was such a stroke. Some of these bagatelle-boards were very good. He was placing the balls to see if he could do it again, when Robin reared up against the door, and began barking.

Austin hit him a tap with the cue. But it was no use : the dog was mad. He did not mind the blow. He began barking furiously, and tearing at the door with his teeth.

Austin d —— d him, and opened the door for him. The dog dashed across the passage, and threw himself against a door on the other side, which burst open. Austin followed to apologise.

Only two steps. There he stood like a stone image in the squalid passage, with the billiard-cue in his hand.

He saw a public-house parlour before him, and a dirty table, and a picture of the Queen, and a horse-hair sofa. And on that sofa sat Eleanor Hilton, and beside her the convict Goatley. The convict had his arm round Eleanor's waist, and Eleanor was tenderly smoothing his close-cropped hair with her hand.

He was amazed for one instant — only for one. When Goatley turned his head towards him, attracted by the sudden entrance of Robin, Austin saw it all. Now he understood Eleanor's mysterious pilgrimages ; now he knew her secret ; now he knew why he had found her walking with Captain Hertford on the 15th of May ; now he knew why he had thought himself mad when he had first seen this man in prison. All the truth came to him suddenly like a blaze of lightning on a dark night ; when Goatley turned his face towards him, and he saw it beside Eleanor's, he understood everything. This Goatley, this convict, was Robert Hilton — the thief at school, the swindler in the army, the forger of Lord Mewstone's name. It was Robert Hilton, Eleanor's own brother. And he dropped the billiard-cue, and cried out like a strong man in pain, " Eleanor ! Eleanor ! I see it all. Can you forgive me ? can you ever forgive me ? "

Chapter XL

THERE was no great need of explanations after this; for there was but little to be explained. In the happy peace which he felt in having her beside him once more, he never thought of asking her, why she had deserted him. That had been the thing which had angered him more than any; but it was nothing now. She had run into his arms with a low glad cry when she had seen him; and he was sitting with her, with her hand in his. He was listening to her dear, dear, voice again. Explanation! — one half of her conduct had been explained; if she could not explain the other — why then — what mattered it. He had got her back again, what cared he for explanations.

She opened the question. "Why did you never answer my letters, dear Austin?"

"Your letters, faithless woman! why did you never write to me?"

"Edward Barty and I wrote to you, until hope was dead, Austin. Did they all arrive during your fever? The governor has not dared to suppress them."

"The governor dare do a great many things, Eleanor. He dared to run unarmed among eight hundred outcasts for instance. I don't know whether he dare suppress my letters; but I know that he would not, if he dare."

They were much too happy to think about the mystery. They found it all out afterwards. Aunt Maria's maid confessed everything when taxed with it, and threw herself on the ground and prayed for forgiveness, let her hair down, kicked her shoes off, made them a lady's maid scene about it; and being forgiven, was carried off whooping and plunging, and holding on tight by everything she could get hold of. And after her departure, when old James came back into the room to pick up her shoes and her hair pins, and so on; he looked very much ashamed of himself, and confessed that *she*, meaning poor Aunt Maria, had been " too many for him."

Robert's statement was this, as far as they could trust it. He said that when he ran off to Namur (he would not go into particulars), Captain Hertford followed him. That he told a friend of his (Robert Hilton's) to spread a report of his suicide. That his friend met Captain Hertford and told him. That Captain Hertford had without making any further inquiries returned to Brussels. And also that Captain Hertford was uncommon glad not to see him (Robert Hilton) in the dock.

This was all Austin ever got out of him : from this he formed the theory, that there was something " queer," some gambling transaction, or something of that sort, between Robert Hilton and Captain Hertford. He never proved it, and poor Hilton getting more stupid every day, now never told him ; but he thought that it was the case. Another thing which puzzled Austin was this, did Captain Hertford ever really *believe* that Robert Hilton was dead ? That puzzle was never solved either.

Eleanor's statement was this : Captain Hertford had returned from abroad and brought the news of her brother's death at Namur. Aunt Maria introduced him as an old friend. She had seen him a good deal from that time (summer of 1844) until October, 1845. Then one day he came and told them not only that her brother was alive, but that he was in Millbank for swindling. That Lord Mewstone was a most vindictive man, and that the secret of Robert Hilton's existence should be kept from him. He was very vindictive about that forgery for instance.

Eleanor and Austin, when they came to think about it, were of opinion that Captain Hertford was very anxious that Robert Hilton should not appear in the dock in the matter of the Mewstone forgery. They may have done him an injustice, they never made out anything clearly against him here.

Eleanor, hearing this terrible news, determined that her

brother should be free and out of the way, before she consented to marry Austin. It would have been such a death-blow to all his high hopes, to marry a convict's sister. She kept the secret from him out of mere love and consideration for him. No one knew the secret but Aunt Maria, Eleanor, old James, and Captain Hertford. She used to go and visit the poor fellow once a month, on the fifteenth of each month; and Hertford, who seems to have pitied her at one time, sometimes went; it was on returning from one of these expeditions that Austin met her, holding Captain Hertford's arm.

Yes, everything was explained. The black cloud had passed suddenly, and beyond lay the prospect of the future, glorious and golden; peaceful beneath the calm summer sun.

Chapter XLI

WHEN Austin left Ronaldsay in May, 1845, the potatoes were just coming out of the ground, and the women and children, in the lengthening spring evenings, were weeding them, and opening the earth between the rows, and regarding them complacently. The rich dark green leaves were showing handsomely above the dark ground. It made one's heart swell with thankfulness, to see the noble promise of a harvest. The old wives no longer knitted, looking towards the sea, where the good man and brave young sons and husbands were toiling at their weary fishing, but they took their knitting into the potato yard, and watched here how the plants came on. And little Ronald, and little Donald, and little Elsie, and little May, gave over paddling at the pier-end, and came home and weeded the potatoes, and made believe that they were sorting the lilies and roses in the MacTavish's grand garden, at Glen Stora Castle, away yonder in Argyleshire.

Sweet summer settled down upon the island. The old

folks had ease from their chronic rheumatism; the young men stayed late on the quay, and the young women stayed with them. Elspeth, the beauty of the island, did not bring the cows home by herself now; when she came down the glen there was always some one with her:

> "A voice talked with her 'neath the shadows cool
> More sweet to her than song."

The potatoes throve bravely. Before you were prepared for it, the plants were a foot high, covered with purple and white blossom. And the children gathered them; the purple ones were my Leddy MacTavish's roses, and the white ones were the lilies which the Saints in heaven carried in their hands before the Throne, ye ken.

It was a pleasant summer, and the potato harvest promised bravely. For years the island had not been so merry; there was but one anxious face on it, and that was Mr. Monroe's. He had been warned of something, which the others knew not of. Night after night, he wrestled with God in prayer; not for himself, ah, no! but for those, whom God had given him. He prayed, that if it were possible the cup might pass away; and it did pass away after they had drank of it. Through the darkest hour of it all the good man's faith in God never wavered for one instant, and he lived to know how much wiser God was than he.

The minister had a trouble on his mind; they could all see that. The older Christians would have had him unburden his mind to them, but he would not: they were content. He was a sainted man; he was one of God's elect; they were content, though they would have liked to share his secret sorrow with him.

One day in July, he went to see one of the oldest of his flock; a very old woman, with a very quiet beautiful face: a woman who was so calmly assured of her salvation, that Heaven had began with her in this world. I talked with such a woman in the West, last year, and very awful and beautiful that talk was; although the doctrines which she held, were as far apart from my own, as the poles.

Mr. Monroe found the old woman sitting in the sun, knitting, and looking at the potatoes. The children were busy weeding them, all except baby, who desired to weed with the rest of them, but who was too confused in his mind, as to which were the potatoes, and which were the weeds, to be trusted. He had been accommodated with a horn spoon, and a crab's-shell with a string let into it, which served for a cart; and left to the care of the colley bitch.

"God save you, minister!" said the old woman, in Gaelic. "Will this brave weather not serve to raise the cloud from your brow? Am not I worthy to share the secret trouble which makes wrinkles on the forehead of one whom I shall wait to welcome in Heaven?"

"Why should you share it?" said Mr. Monroe, in the same language; "why should I darken the glorious evening of such a life as yours, before the sunset comes? I will not. For sixty years you have known nothing but poverty and hard work; your husband, your son, and two of your grandsons, have sailed away, and the sea has devoured them. Shall I throw a shadow over the few days which remain between you and your rest? No."

"There is a cloud in the heaven somewhere," said the old woman; "your eyes are younger than mine, and you see it, though I do not. It will burst over Ronaldsay, I know that by your face. Minister, I would be sorry to take my reward before my labour was done. Let me share your sorrow. The tide flows up and down the Kyle, as of old, and the full moon floods the creeks and caves under the cape; Benmore stands firm in the West. What is your sorrow, minister?"

"I cannot tell you."

"See the brave potatoes. Raise the cloud from your brow, minister, and look at them. The bravest crop for years. Raise the cloud from your brow, and thank the Lord with me. See, they are harvesting * already."

" Harvesting ! "

" Go and see."

He went in among the potatoes. The children had done weeding, and were making nosegays of the potato flowers.

"Here's minister! See here, sir, these ones are the French roses from my lady's garden at Glenstora, and these white ones are the lilies of heaven. 'Tis a braw game, minister, is it no ? "

Mr. Monroe looked at the potato halm. The potatoes were harvesting with a vengeance : the leaves were getting yellow and curling up black at the edges. He clasped his hands together and said " Thy will be done, O Lord ! "

Mr. Monroe had been warned of this. He had hoped and hoped, and even now he continued to hope. They dug their potatoes up. One half of them were rotten, the rest rotted in the places where they were stored ; " graves," as we call them in England. At first they hoped that they might pull through the winter and have seed for next year. That hope soon left them ; in the first week in November potatoes were cheaper in Ronaldsay than any one could recollect. They were all in their little market at once. But at the end of the month, when the leading Protectionist was trying to deny the whole business, there were no potatoes whatever. The potato crop had failed.

I should like to meet with a poet who would make *that* a line in one of his poems. " The potato crop had failed." How we should laugh at him ! A potato is ridiculous enough, but a rotten potato—bah !

All through November the south wind poured steadily up through the Kyle, and filled Ronaldsay with mist and gloom. But in the first week in December, when the days were getting towards their shortest, the North wind came

* Harvesting. This is the expression we use in Hampshire when the halm of the potato turns yellow, and it is ripe. I do not know the Scotch term ; certainly not the Gaelic.

down, drove the mists away, and invested the island with a cold, cruel, merciless beauty. Under an inexorable brazen sky, every crag came out clear and sharp as crystal, every cataract was turned into a glacier, every little spouting burn on the hillside, into a beautiful ice palace. The lochs were frozen three feet thick ; but the curling-stones lay neglected under the bed-place, and the faded ribands upon the handles only served to remind the young men of the merry rinks last year, before the potatoes rotted, and left them all starving.

The old folks died first. That was as it should be. One could not complain at that ; one might envy them, but one could not complain. They had had sixty years of this sort of thing, and it was hard if they were not to enter into their rest, before the misery grew to its full head. The loss of the dear old faces at the fireside was very sad, and the hearts of those who were left behind starving ached sorely ; but God had taken them from the misery, which grew more terrible as the winter went on, and He knew best.

Then the children began to die, and this was very bitter —very, very hard to bear. The bonny bare-legged little things, who had done no wrong ; who paddled in the surf, that made wreaths of those infernal potato-flowers, and called them the lilies of heaven. This would not do to think of. To be locked up here in an island in the Atlantic, without one chance of making one's voice heard till it was too late, and to see one's own bonny darlings dying before one's face ! Hush ! It was well for the MacTavish that these men were Scotchmen, not Irishmen ! It was well for the peace of the kingdom that these things happened in Ronaldsay and Lewis, and not in Manchester and Birmingham.

'Twas a weary Halloween for the poor souls. The men who dug the graves noticed that day by day the frost got deeper into the earth. The fishing-lines froze like wires, the blocks refused to run, the sails were stiff as boards, and the women who wearily, with blue fingers, knocked the limpets off the rocks, to save themselves from starvation, began to notice that even the salt water in the little pools among the rocks was beginning to freeze. And they came home and told the men, and the men lost heart, and went no more a-fishing. How could they? Did *you* ever sit hour after hour fishing, with fourteen degrees of frost, and in a state of starvation? The men stayed at home, and lay in the bed-places.

And then *they* began to die. Yes! The oldest of the able-bodied men, began to lie down, and to fall asleep, in a strange quiet way. Perfectly happy, perfectly calm. They would lie for a day or two, and at last give over speaking. In the morning they would be found quietly dead, without the sign of a spasm on their faces. This is no novelist's fancy; the author has seen what he is describing.

All this time, the island lay in the bright brazen sunshine, more beautiful than ever. The ducks and the snipes had fled southward; the curlew and the peewit had followed them, and the moor was silent. But for the shadows of the crags and corries, which sloped so long towards the north; and for the fantastic glaciers on the hill side, which in summer time were wimpling burns; one might have fancied, if one only used the sense of sight, that it was spring-time; the island had never looked more beautiful. After Christmas, it got a new and more awful beauty. The wind was still steady, and quiet from the north; but one day, Gil Macdonald pointed out to Mr. Monroe and the MacTavish, a long low light brown line of cloud, which was backing the lower summits of the Argyleshire hills, to the south-east.

For two days, the dun vapour had grown and spread until it had obscured the sun. When it had fairly disappeared, a broad red orb, into the snow cloud; Gil Macdonald, said, "I'm wishing you good day, old friend, belike I'll never see ye again."

In the morning, the wind, which was in front of the dull cloud, begun to blow. The thermometer rose to six degrees of frost, and there stayed, and would come no higher, in spite of the south-east wind. Then the edge of the cloud reached them, and the dust at the corner of the little street in the village begun to grow white; and soon after, the air was filled with straying crystals of snow, which rose and fell, and whirled about, and was driven into every cranny and corner. And those who looked towards Ben More, saw that the towering peak was rapidly growing from brown to grey, and from grey to silver.

For two days, the snow came down; and then the north wind came down once more, and laid his deadly icy hand on the island. The sky was clear again; blue over head, but a gleaming yellow towards the horizon. Ben More towered up over the vast sheets of snow, which covered the island; a tall peak of ghastly white, barred with lines of purple crag.

The moment the snow cloud cleared, Mr. Monroe started Gil Macdonald over the hill, through the snow, with provisions to an outlying family at Loch na Craig, on the other side of the mountain. The wind which had come up with the snow had been strong, and the south-east side of the mountain was pretty bare. Gil, the lion-hearted, made brave weather of it till he came to the shoulder of the mountain, which overlooks Loch na Craig. But his feet went the swifter, in consequence of an anxiety which had taken possession of him.

He reached the shoulder of the hill, and looked over into the corrie of Loch na Craig. Then, he sat down on a rock. He saw the whole horrible disaster.

The snow, which they, looking from the south-east, from the windward side of the mountain, had seen eddying, and curling, and fuming before the wind; which they had seen blown from the steep side of the mountain nearest to them; had all settled down here, in this corner of Loch na Craig. All that Gil saw before him, was a vast amphitheatre of smooth white snow ; and in the centre, a patch of green ice, about an acre in extent. The sloping sides of snow represented the noble corrie ; and the acre of ice, showing in the middle, was all that was to be seen of the five hundred acres of the beautiful Loch na Craig.

He saw that a terrible disaster had befallen. One little farm, near the head of a little glen, he thought, he would force his way to ; the chimney was yet showing above the snow. Alone, fearless of the deadly snow sleep, bare-legged in the freezing snow ; he forced himself to the door of that little farm house, and getting no answer, he broke it in.

They were all dead. The old folks and the children had died before, and now the younger men and women had followed them. All dead. This same accident had happened before. Corrie na Craig had been filled with snow ; but then, the huts had been full with oatcake and whiskey, and the people had lived to make a joke of it. But now, the peat was still smouldering on the hearth, and Gil found six of them dead. These people had died more from starvation than from cold ; and there were three other families down by the loch, buried fifty feet deep.

Gil called out, " was any one alive ? " first in a low tone, and afterwards, when not so scared at the sound of his own voice, in a louder. He got no answer. He sped away to the village, and told Mr. Monroe, and the Mac-Tavish, that there were forty less souls on the island, to starve.

Austin's fifty pounds had done good service at the be-ginning of the famine. It was as nothing among a popu-lation of two thousand, in a state of absolute destitution, but still it was a great godsend. Mr. Monroe hoped for all sort of things, for a mild winter, for Government assist-ance, nay, " God forgie him," for the death of the dow-ager, Mrs. MacTavish, who had retired to Clapham, near London, and whose death would put another £800 a year at the MacTavish's disposal. But it was no use hoping.

Austin's fifty pounds was gone, and things got worse and worse, and he wrote to the MacTavish to come to him at once.

MacTavish came instantly. He looked round with Mr. Monroe, and saw what a disaster was impending. He went back to Argyleshire at once. He ordered his two sons home from Cambridge, and told Mrs. MacTavish to do her duty, and keep the creditors at bay: to scrimp, save, and borrow every farthing she could, and send it to him in Ronaldsay. He was horribly poor, and desperately in debt. He had taken no rents from Ronaldsay for years; but the Ronaldsay people were flesh of his flesh, and bone of his bone; and so the great coarse bare-legged, highland giant, came back to them in their trouble; to live with them, and, if need were, to die with them.

"Our own people, Monroe. Our own flesh and blood, Monroe."

As for Mr. Monroe, he well earned his crown of glory in this terrible winter, even if by long continuance in well doing, he had not earned it before. I know that what I have just written will be called by some people heretical, but it shall stand, and shall be repeated. He earned his crown; with his hair growing greyer week by week; with the people that he had loved so well dying round him; with the souls which he, in his way of speaking, would have said that he had brought to Christ: passing away from him too quickly for one word of farewell; that noble man worked on. I feel that I am unworthy to write about such a man. But there are such men. If I did not know one or two of them, I would not have dared to say so much about Mr. Monroe.

Let the glorious fellow be. Let his works speak for him. *He* is no fictitious character, though I have altered his name, and changed his locality. There was another hero developed in this miserable winter, by name Gil Macdonald.

His restless soul, craving eagerly for work, of which

there was none to be got ; settled down, concentrated itself, in the work which Mr. Monroe and the MacTavish
put before him. By night and by day, through frost and
through snow, he, the best hill walker in the island, sped
swiftly on messages of help and charity. But all the Gil
Macdonalds, all the Mr. Monroes, all the MacTavishes in
the world, could not send the thermometer up above freezing, and so the people died on, and despair began to settle down on all of them.

Then MacTavish's money failed. There had been little
enough of it at first, for he had contracted heavy debts, to
send his sons to Cambridge. First, he heard that the
bailiffs were in his castle. Then his wife wrote, to warn
him that writs were out against him, and that he might be
taken. Gil Macdonald heard this, and merely mentioned
it about among the young men in conversation. They
were dull, heartless, and desperate enough, these young
men, but it would have been a bad business for any bailiff,
who had tried to follow MacTavish to Ronaldsay.

"Our own flesh and blood, Gil. Our own flesh and
blood."

Things went on from bad to worse. Wearily each
night the MacTavish and Mr. Monroe met, only to tell
each other of some new disaster. One night MacTavish
refused even the miserable supper which he and Mr. Monroe allowed themselves, and walked sulkily up and down
the room. At last he broke out. He threw up his arms,
and clutched his hair wildly in his hands.

"I will not bear it, Monroe ; I will not bear it."

"Be quiet, MacTavish ; dinna rebel."

"I tell you that I will rebel," he answered furiously ; doing exactly as Austin did on one occasion. "I tell you
that I will not bear it. I tell you that God is unrighteous,
unjust, vindictive. I have done enough to deserve His
anger, but these poor sheep, what have they done ? "

"Colin, Colin ! " said the old man, throwing himself
down before him, and clasping his bare knees, " dinna

blaspheme in your wrath. Trust God, and think that every wild word uttered now, will be a worm to eat your heart till you meet him."

" I will not ! There is no mercy in heaven ! My own people dying like dogs, and no help. I tell you that I will curse God and die ! "

" Ye may curse God, but ye'll not die, my ain boy. He will punish you for this. He will let you live, MacTavish, till every wild word you have uttered just now will be a scorn and a loathing to you, till you see your folly and wickedness, and beg for forgiveness."

" Words ! words ! What is the use of cramming one's ear with them ? I am hopeless and desperate, I tell you. What are words to me ? Feed my people."

" Perhaps, Colin, by a little patience and humiliation they might be fed. Will you listen to me ? "

The MacTavish sat down and listened, and as he did so, his face grew calmer. At last he said, " Say no more, Monroe. I were worse than a dog if I did not."

He wrote the following curious letter : —

" Grandmother, — I am humbled. I am humbled by famine. My people are dying here like sheep. I ask for nothing for myself — I only beg for them.

" I ask your forgiveness, certainly. I was in the wrong, let us say. My pride is so broken, that I will allow anything. You will gain your suit about the farms at Inverhadden. I'm a ruined man, and have no more money to spend on law.

" Send me a thousand pounds worth of food here instantly. If you don't, we are all undone ; for it is useless asking my mother. Forgive me or not, grandmother, but, in God's name save the Ronaldsay folk !

" MACTAVISH.

" *To the dowager Lady Tullygoram, Barrock Lodge, Argyleshire.*"

To which Lady Tullygoram replied —

" Ablins, my ain Colin, we may both have been too tena-
cious of our rights. A body does na like to see herself
wronged out of her own dower rights. The three Inverhadden farms have gone with the dower-lands of Tullygoram, for sax centuries, and I was no justified, in the interest of future dowagers, in giving up my rights. God
kens, my bonny boy, I bear ye no ill-will.

" I send you twa hundred pounds. With the help of
God, I will keep the Ronaldsay folk for you till better
times. I have cleared the execution out of your castle, and
sent the two lads back to their studies. Though what the
deil garred ye send them to a cockney university, I dinna
ken.

" ELSPETH TULLYGORAM."

So poor MacTavish was humbled, and prayed to be forgiven for the wild words he had used in his madness : let
us hope he was forgiven. Better times began to dawn on
them after this ; but things are not mended all at once.
When the tide is receding, and shipwrecked men, who
have clung all night to the rock, begin to hope that the
worst is over, and that their way to the shore is safe ; often
there comes some angry receding wave, and once more
washes high above their heads, and makes them despair
again.

So it was with the Ronaldsay famine. The MacTavish
departed at the end of January, leaving things in a much
better state. In February the frost broke, and then the
new enemy appeared — typhus, bred by starvation and
hardship. At first the people began dying nearly as fast
as in the famine ; then it got better, and then it got worse.
Lady Tullygoram and the MacTavish did all they could —
tried to keep a population of two thousand, for a year ;
with indifferent success, as you may imagine. When the
men got to their fishing again, the island got more cheer-

ful. But there were no seed-potatoes. The last money that Lady Tullygoram could scrape together, was spent in buying seed-potatoes. She paid, noble old body! two hundred and seventy pounds for them in Glasgow, and sent them off as fast as they could be bought. The Ronaldsay folk got them all into the ground by the first week in April.

Gil Macdonald waited and saw the potatoes put in. He saw them come up ; they looked bravely. He waited still longer ; everything seemed mending. Then he started away, and came south to London to find Austin.

They began to dig in September : they were all rotten again — worse than last year. The sun began to south towards another winter worse than the last. Lady Tullygoram had spent every farthing she had. The MacTavish was as good as ruined : there was nothing but blank despair before them.

A Highland Society agent came over, and talked to them of fair lands sixteen thousand miles away. Some prepared to go, but for those who stayed (for only a few could go) what a prospect! MacTavish had applied for the Government loan, but, as he said, there was not the wildest probability of his being able to set one man to work on the money before next spring. Things looked blacker than ever.

Mr. Monroe preached patience. On a Sabbath-day in November he preached earnestly and almost fiercely to them. " I tell you," he said, " not to rebel. I tell myself not to despair. I tell (say you) the surf not to moan on the reef ; the wind not to whistle through the heather ; the burn not to roar in the linn. Still I tell you to be patient — you, whose children have died before your eyes. I tell you to trust in God. You and I will meet at his throne, and then let none of you look me in the face, and say that I did not tell you this, that you must trust in God, for He cannot be unjust.

" Unjust ! Is there one man or woman in this church to-day who does not envy those who have gone before us, and are waiting to welcome us — when we have dreed our weird — when we have done our day's work — when this tyranny is overpast? My ain people, for whom I have wrestled night and day in prayer, do not rebel. The riddle may whiles be hard to read, but trust God. Do I pray for rest? No. I only pray that I may be spared to see the end. The wild winter is coming down on us once more. Let us pray that we may win through it, or, if not, that we may die trusting in God."

So he pleaded to them on the November Sabbath ; and in the evening, in solitude, he prayed for them — prayed as he had done the year before — that the cup might pass away.

On the Monday morning, the answer to his prayer came. Over the morning sea, across the Kyle, from the mainland, a boat came plunging and leaping across the short, chopping swell, caused by the meeting of the tide and the south wind. The boat came over with a mail-bag, and in that mail-bag there was only one letter, and that letter was from the MacTavish to Mr. Monroe.

" DEAR OLD FRIEND,

" May God forgive me, if I have done wrong. What *could* I do ? It is like tearing my heart out by the roots. It is a bitter, bitter dispensation.

" I have sold the island of Ronaldsay to an Englishman. It was the only chance of saving my own people — my own no longer — from starvation.

" They say he is noble and generous. He is, I know, very wealthy. He will, with his wealth, if he keeps half his promises, make the island a prosperous and a happy one. I have no heart left to say more.

" Yet I must go on. You must be gentle with him. You must tell the people to be gentle and polite to him. You know how proud and captious these English are. Give way to his every whim. If he is properly flattered, he may be induced to settle and build a house on the island; to do by the island what I, God forgive me! have never been able to do.

" He will be with you directly, Monroe. Be prepared. Get him to settle there. The pampered Cockney has got some whim about the island. Flatter it. Oh God, Monroe, that it should have come to this ! "

Mr. Monroe turned to the few old peasants who were standing round him, and said —

" Here is bitter news. The MacTavish has sold the island."

" And us with it," said the eldest of them. " Aweel, things could be no waur. But hech, sirs ! For a MacTavish to sell his ain flesh and blude to the Duke of Argyle ! "

" It is not the Duke of Argyle. It is an Englishman."

" It does na much matter," said the old man, " that we, who beat the dust out of their coats so brawly at Dunbar, should be bought up by them, body and banes, like kye."

" Which battle of Dunbar do you mean ? " said Mr. Monroe, sharply. " You seem to have forgotten either the first one, or the one which we call Preston Pans. There were twa battles by Dunbar, old man. Don't be a fool. Come home with me ; I see hope in this."

So he did. This Englishman had money. Englishmen were noble and generous, in spite of their airs and graces. So Mr. Monroe, after laying his head on the table and weeping, because the MacTavish was no longer master of the island; raised his head and smiled, because the island had been sold to an Englishman; who was very likely an insolent and exacting person, but who, at all events, would take care that his tenantry did not starve during the next winter.

Scotch pride is harder to humble than even English pride ; but such a winter as 1845 —46 will humble even a Scotchman's pride.

God forgive Mr. Monroe ! The dear man went as near

— well — fiction, as any man should. He did not know even the name of this abominable Englishman, but he represented him as a model of high-hearted generosity. As for his wealth — there — Mr. Monroe felt justified by representing it as enormous, but unluckily he launched into figures, which he should not have done; and these figures grew under his hand, and got beyond his control in the most terrible way. Sometimes he "harked back," and tried to make them smaller by ten thousand a year or so; but the Ronaldsay people did not like that; and so at last he expressed the income of the London Shopkeeper by waving his two hands abroad; as much as to say, that your figures failed to express the immense amount of income, of this Cockney shopkeeper.

At this same time Mr. Monroe committed himself to the statement, that the new owner of Ronaldsay was a cheesemonger — and what was more awful still, a cheesemonger in Piccadilly. Mr. Monroe denies having ever said such a thing; but one morning he was taxed with it, and instead of boldly denying the matter on the spot, he weakly gave in to it, and prevaricated. From this time it was an accepted fact, that the island had been bought by a cheesemonger in Piccadilly, which was a street in London. Mr. Monroe never knew how this happened, but the folks were in a state of excitement, and he did not dare to contradict them. He went about like a guilty man — hoping, for his soul's sake, that some one *might* have told him, that it was a cheesemonger in Piccadilly, and that he *might* have forgotten it. He knew nothing of the new owner of Ronaldsay — not even his name : nothing, save that he might be expected any day; therefore this astounding canard about the cheesemonger was annoying. His object was to prepossess the people in favour of the new owner, and to get that new owner to stay on the island. At this time the good man was overheard to wish, that that feckless billie, Gil Macdonald, had stayed at hame, and not gone daundering down South.

But at last the cheesemonger from Piccadilly came, and took possession of his property after this manner : —

One morning, in the end of November, five or six days after the receipt of the MacTavish's letter, it was reported to him that a steamer had rounded the south point of Donaldsay, and was bearing up for Ronaldsay. She carried no pennant. It was not the Shoals and Quicksands Lords coming their rounds. This was your cheesemonger coming to take possession.

So it was. A small screw steamer came up, and eased off the pier of Ronaldsay. Mr. Monroe tumbled into a boat, went on board, and clambered into the waist.

Some one came forward to receive him — Gil Macdonald. No other. Mr. Monroe started back ; but the cheesemonger fiction had been so burnt into his brain by repetition, that he said —

"Why, Gil, ye told me in your letter that ye were in the gun-making trade — guns and cheeses ! Is your master a general dealer, then ? "

He passed on towards the cheesemonger and his wife, who stood on the quarter-deck. But there was no cheesemonger there: Austin Elliot and his wife Eleanor stood before him. Austin said, " Dear Mr. Monroe, I am your new landlord, and I am come to live and to die with you." And the minister cast his hat on the deck and said, " God has been very good to us, Mr. Elliot — God has been very good to us."

And so just when a story gets to be worth telling it has to come to an end. I have told you how Austin Elliot, generous, and ambitious, got fed on wind — would have gone, Lord knows where, if it had not been for his dog. Now that he has developed into a useful man, we must leave him. The story of the work which he and Eleanor did in Ronaldsay would be but dull reading.

*　　　*　　　*　　　*　　　*　　　*

Once more the morning sun rises behind the hills of Argyleshire ; once more the summer's morning raises the peat-smoke from a thousand cottages, in ten thousand purple valleys; once more the dawn smites the peak of Benmore of Ronaldsay, and creeps down; until the island awakens, and the men of Ronaldsay come abroad to their labour.

But it shines on a new Ronaldsay now. On vast tracts of young larch plantations, emerald green, among the dark heather; on broad yellow patches of soil, turned up on the lower hill-sides, where they are trenching the land for agriculture; better still, on sheets of rye and clover, giving good promise of a noble harvest. No more famine, no more dull, heart-gnawing sorrow, in Ronaldsay now. "He may do *anything* with Eleanor's money," said old Mr. Hilton, on his death-bed, little dreaming what he *would* do with it; little dreaming that his ill-earned money would be spent in making the desert of Ronaldsay to blossom like a rose.

See the morning comes lower yet, and lower, until it shines strong and full on a new castle, built on the rise behind the village; on a broad stone terrace; on a little dark lady who walks abroad in the dew to look at her flowers, and leads a brave little lad, of three years old, by the hand.

A peaceful, calm little lady, dressed all in gray. She says to the toddling boy, "Come on, Charles; let us be ready to meet father as he comes from the hill!" and presently Austin comes brushing through the heather towards her, and takes his boy in his arms; so he and Eleanor walk slowly home along the terrace.

Who are these aloft here, on the windy mountain, in the morning air? A strange pair. One is a gigantic man, a kilted Highlander, with a square thoughtful face, who is leaning, in repose, against a rock; the other is also a tall man, but stone-blind, who turns and feels in the dark for his companion, though the level sun is blazing on his face.

"And so ye're no going to leave us, my lord," says the

Highlander. " Dinna leave us, my lord ; you have made yourself a necessity to us. I never flattered any man born of woman ; but I must say this much, you would be sair missed in Ronaldsay. Why the bairns would greet, and the dogs would howl, if they missed your kind dark face, at the quay end, when the boats come hame. Dinna gang South, my Lord, into that weary hurly-burly, with a' its Whiggeries, and Toryisms, and Papistries. Stay with them that love you, and play on your bonny new harp."

" I think I will live and die in Ronaldsay, Gil," said the blind man. " It is kind of you to lead me up here. I am looking towards the sun, now, for there is something in my eyes, which I think must be light ; I must be looking towards those purple mountains on the mainland, you tell me of. I love to look towards the east, Gil ; for the light which will open my eyes, and show me the faces of those I have loved so well, will come from thence, on the morning of the Resurrection."

So Lord Edward Barty and Gil Macdonald stood on the shoulder of Benmore, and looked eastward ; while Robin the dog sat like a statue among the heather at their feet, and looked eastward also. And so the whole story comes to an end.

THE END.